Dating in DECAY

DATING IN DECAY

THE OUTBREAK RESPONSES
BOOK 1

LINDSEY MONTGOMERY

Dating in Decay

© Copyright 2025 Expressive Press, LLC

All rights reserved.

Paperback ISBN: 979-8-9927094-0-7

No part of this book may be reproduced, distributed or transmitted in any form or by any means, including photocopying, recording or other electronic or mechanical methods, without the prior written permission of the author except in the case of brief quotations in a book review.

This is a work of fiction. Names, characters, places and incidents are the product of the author's imagination or are used fictitiously. Any resemblance to actual events, locales or persons, living or dead, is coincidental.

Editing & Proofreading: Elizabeth Nover, Razor Sharp Editing

Cover and Internal Graphics: Lindsey Montgomery © Copyright 2025 Expressive Press, LLC (Created using Canva and InDesign)

 Formatted with Vellum

CONTENT & TRIGGER WARNINGS

Hello, (potential) reader! This story has a happily ever after, that includes romance, humor, and zombie chaos. However, some content may be triggering for individuals. In order to protect your mental health, the following is a list of what could be the most triggering elements. This book includes:

- Profanity
- Kidnapping/Captivity
- Violence
- Blood and Gore
- Killing/Death
- Detailed Sex Scenes (for those who prefer fade to black, spice happens in chapters 22, 25, and 28)
- Parental Loss (implied)
- Loss of a Friend
- Pedophilia (implied)
- Torture
- Intended Sexual Assault and Rape (implied)
- Dismemberment

If you have questions, please feel free to email me at info@
lindseymontgomery.com.

PLAYLIST

Scan QR Code to Listen on Spotify

The Man Comes Around - *Johnny Cash*
G.O.M.D. - *Sickick*
Raise Hell - *Dorothy*
Susie Q - *Creedence Clearwater Revival*
Bleach Blonde Bottle Blues - *Larkin Poe*
Trouble - *The New Respects*
Ring of Fire - *Social Distortion*
Blitzkrieg Bop - *Ramones*
Down with the Sickness - *Richard Cheese*
Volcano Girls - *Veruca Salt*

Come Out and Play - *The Offspring*

I Believe in a Thing Called Love - *The Darkness*

River Water - *The Spencer Lee Band*

Whatta Man - *Salt-N-Pepa ft. En Vogue*

Zombie - *The Cranberries*

She Lit a Fire - *Lord Huron*

Stuck in the Middle with You - *Stealers Wheel*

It's Called: Freefall - *Rainbow Kitten Surprise*

Love Is Alive - *Louis The Child ft. Elohim*

Show Me How to Live - *Audioslave*

Find Your People - *Drew Holcomb & The Neighbors*

Loser - *Beck*

Schism - *Tool*

Bodies - *Drowning Pool*

Powerful - *Major Lazer ft. Ellie Goulding and Tarrus Riley*

Coming Undone - *Korn*

What I Got - *Sublime*

The Weight - *Aretha Franklin*

Your Touch - *The Black Keys*

Black Hole Sun - *Soundgarden*

Fade into You - *Mazzy Star*

Try a Little Tenderness - *Otis Redding*

Narcolepsy - *Third Eye Blind*

Comedown - *Bush*

Down - *311*

Mannish Boy - *Muddy Waters*

Wannabe - *Spice Girls*

Lonely Day - *System of a Down*

Drive - *Incubus*

Ghost - *Josiah and the Bonnevilles*

Symphony No. 5 in C Minor, Op. 67: I. Allegro con brio - *Ludwig van Beethoven*, performed by *Wiener Philharmoniker, Carlos Kleiber* directing

Heavy - *Birdtalker*
Come as You Are - *Nirvana*
Sympathy for the Devil - *The Rolling Stones*
Sabotage - *Beastie Boys*
Seek & Destroy - *Metallica*
War Pigs/Luke's Wall - *Black Sabbath*
Rest in Peace - *Dorothy*
Living Dead Girl - *Rob Zombie*
Highway Tune - *Greta Van Fleet*
Good Day - *Jax Anderson ft. Mister Wives and Curtis Roach*

CONTENTS

PART THREE
BRAINS

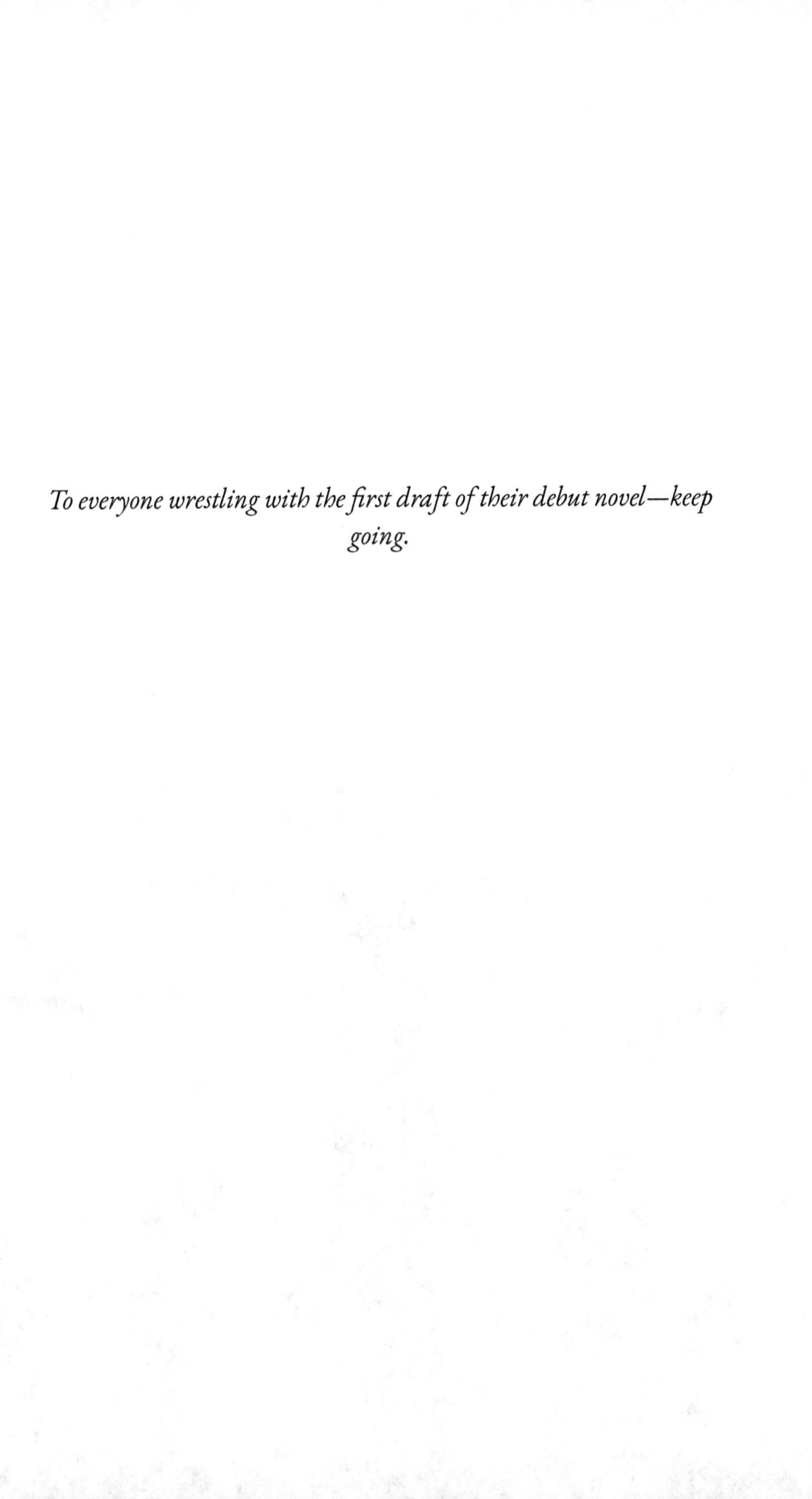

*To everyone wrestling with the first draft of their debut novel—keep
going.*

PROLOGUE - OUTBREAK

March 1, 2025 - *The Global Times* (Excerpt)

"Mysterious Flu Outbreak Hits Europe: Health Officials Urge Calm"

A peculiar strain of flu has swept through several European countries, leaving health experts scratching their heads. Early symptoms include fever, fatigue, and a curious hunger for flesh. While the European Center for Disease Prevention and Control (ECDC) emphasizes that the situation is under control, they do recommend that citizens stay indoors, stock up on canned goods, and avoid biting their neighbors.

Just in case.

———

March 5, 2025 - CDC Address to the Public (Transcript)

Dr. Lisa Redfield: The CDC advises vigilance and urges individuals to report any concerning behaviors to their local authorities. Do not take matters into your own hands. Those infected are considered dangerous and highly volatile. Are there any questions?

Reporter: "What caused the outbreak?"

Redfield: "We don't know."

Reporter: "Is it a virus?"

Redfield: "We don't know."

Reporter: "Are the infected people still alive?"

Redfield: "We don't know."

Reporter: "Do you know anything?"

Redfield: "We've confirmed it spreads through their bites. The contagion is concentrated in their gums and transmitted via saliva into open wounds—similar to how venom is delivered by snakes."

Reporter: "What steps are you taking to stop it?"

Redfield: "We're exploring every available option— containment, treatment, eradication. No resource is off the table in our search for a countermeasure."

Reporter: "Have you made any breakthroughs?"

Redfield: *[Pauses]* "No comment."

———

March 10, 2025 - *The Evening Observer* **(Excerpt)**

"Emergency Declared: Citizens Urged to Stay Indoors"

As the "flu" spreads, governments worldwide have declared states of emergency. Reports of widespread violence and unprovoked attacks have emerged in major cities. Authorities urge everyone to stay indoors and refrain from using the phrase "apocalypse" on social media. It's up to you to not spread paranoia.

———

March 11, 2025 - Discord (Excerpt)

@BiteMeNow: Y'all believin' this!? The "flu" my ass! Lock your doors! Hide your family! Stock up on food! APOCALYPSE IS GOING DOWN! #survivalofthefittest #outbreak #cannedgoodlife #governmentconspiracy #washyourhands

@InfectedFan1968: I told you all that this would happen! All my apocalypse training is finally going to pay off. Take that high school bullies! #surviveatallcosts #apocalypseishere #suppliesnolies #iwillsurvive

@sleepychaz: So does this mean I don't have to go to work tomorrow??? #whatsthepoint #undeadeverywhere #noworknoplay #imgonnastayin

———

March 13, 2025 - Snack Attack Jack (Blog)

"Apocalypse Canned Food Chili"

2 cans of chili beans
1 can of corn
1 can of diced tomatoes
1 can of chicken or beef (your choice)
1 can of tomato sauce
1 packet of chili seasoning mix (if you got it)
Salt and pepper to taste (again, if you got it)

Instructions:

Open all the cans (drain the corn and meat if necessary) and seasoning mix then dump into a large pot. Place the pot over medium heat or roaring fire and bring the mixture to a simmer. Let it cook for about 15-20 minutes, stirring occasionally. Add salt and pepper to taste. Serve quickly.

Enjoy your chili with a side of canned bread or crackers (if you're lucky).

Stay safe and keep your energy up!

———

March 15, 2025 - Drama Club President Randy Jenkins's Address to the Student Body, Springboard High School (Delivered atop a Cafeteria Table)

My fellow teenage thrivers,

We are gathered today not just as students, but as survivors. Yes, we come from different cliques, clubs, and chaotic lunch tables—but today, we unite under one cause: not dying.

The world as we knew it is gone, replaced by one overrun with the undead and questionable cafeteria meat. Our mission now is clear: to forge new alliances, adapt, and—dare I say—thrive amidst the apocalypse.

Let us not waste time bickering over locker space or prom dates. Instead, let us rise above, hand in hand, and build a future where the living and the formerly-living coexist . . . awkwardly, but peacefully.

So I ask you now, with courage in my heart and glitter in my soul—who's with me!?

([A long beat.] Only Frankie and Travis raise their hands. One of them is eating a pudding cup.)

———

March 20, 2025 - Spray-Painted Message in Downtown Lawrenceville, VA

Hell is Upon Us,
`I'll Bring the Snacks`

PART ONE
BLUSHES

DON'T BITE ME THERE!: A ZOMBIE SURVIVAL GUIDE

BY EARL RUSSO

Tip #1: Aim for the head, dumbass.
Shooting arms or legs might slow the infected down, but it won't stop them. Want a permanent solution? Destroy the brain. Shoot it, stab it, bash it—whatever works. Just make sure you're hitting the nail on the head. *Literally.*

Tip #18: Plans will change—so should you.
If you're stubborn or allergic to change, good luck out there. As my wife lovingly reminds me, flexibility is key—a trait I apparently lack. Things never go according to plan (even the ones you stayed up all night obsessing over), so be ready to pivot fast and roll with the chaos.

Tip #30: Think like the infected.
Yeah, you read that right. To beat them, you've gotta understand them. They follow noise. They move in packs. Use that. Firecrackers, car alarms, loud distractions—they're your new best friends. If you're feeling bold, turn the horde into a weapon. *Just be ready for the fallout.*

ONE
START WITH A BANG!

LYLA

"I JUST WANT to officially state, once again, that this is the dumbest idea ever. Your survival odds are as tiny as a snail's. And did I mention you're crazy? . . . Over."

I smirk, bringing the walkie-talkie to my lips. "And didn't I tell you I don't care? Over."

"Yes, but I wish you'd care more about staying alive. I need someone to talk to. Who else will listen to my endless rants about sparkles, rainbows, and kittens? The fuckin' brainless, cannibalistic, balls-to-the-wall nuts walking dead? Over." Jo's voice crackles through the static, each word dripping with disbelief.

I pull back the yellowed curtains of the second-floor apartment where I'm hiding, peering down at the boarded-up market across the street. I would bet my entire food stock Jo is pacing between the empty aisles, her dark curls bouncing on her wiry frame as she gestures to an imaginary audience. I hold my hand up as if she can see me and start to count. Pointer finger. "Joanie, first, keep your voice down." Middle finger. "Second, I know you're fourteen and the world's gone to hell, but don't say 'fuck.' " Ring finger. "Third, you hate all things cute, so no one will ever listen to you ramble about that crap." Pinky. "Fourth, you know why I have to do this." Thumb. "And fifth, I told you not to get attached to people. They'll likely end up shot, eaten, torn apart, turned—or did I mention eaten? If I die, I die. You'll move on. Over."

The curtain slips from my fingers, the fabric falling back into place with a whisper-soft swish. The air inside the room feels heavy, thick with the scent of mildew and old wood. Sweat slicks my palms, and I shift my grip on the radio, its worn plastic casing digging into my skin.

"Yeah, but do you know how hard it is to find someone who doesn't snore? It's one of your best features." She huffs into the mic.

A small, breathless chuckle escapes me, sharp and sudden against the tension coiling tight in my chest. It's absurd, laughing now. What I'm about to do could easily get me killed—*will* probably get me killed. But in a world where the dead walk and humanity has rotted from the inside out, my plan barely registers on the insanity scale.

Jo's sarcasm works its usual magic, cutting through the anxiety and easing my racing thoughts. When everything around us has been stripped down to survival—hunger, thirst, death—her no-bullshit attitude has been my anchor.

In a handful of months—through starvation, sprints from the undead, and fights against people worse than monsters—Joanie has become family. The little sister I never had.

I scoff, imagining the hell she would've raised if she'd ever met my dad. God, he would've hated her mouth.

But he would've respected her heart.

"Look, boss. I know you've got business to handle and that this d-bag deserves what's coming to him. Just be careful and try to make it back in one piece." She hesitates before whispering, "I—I don't want to be alone. Over."

Jesus, Joanie, way to throw on the guilt trip. I wish this weren't her reality. I wish she hadn't lost her parents to the virus. I wish I didn't have to ask so much of her.

No one should face the death of their parents at such a young age, especially not in such a horrific way. I wish I could have pulled the trigger myself for her just so she didn't have to walk around with the weight of being the one to end their lives.

I glance at my watch. It's half past noon, and the tension in my chest tightens as I look down main street, scanning for any sign of danger. I click the walkie on. "Love ya too, kiddo. We're almost there. You know what to do, right? Over."

"Lyla. Please. We went over it a hundred times. Ye of little faith—"

We both hear it—the rumble of the transport bus's engine approaching. Jo rushes at a lower volume, "I won't let you down. See you on the other side, boss bitch. Over."

If I survive this, I swear I'm going to wash that girl's mouth out with soap.

I place the walkie on the windowsill for Jo to retrieve once I'm gone. The room is dimly lit, the only light coming from the sun filtering through the curtains. Dust particles dance in the air above the worn furniture and the makeshift barricades we've set up over the past few weeks. This place has been our sanctuary, but now it's time to move on.

BANG!

The transport bus screeches to a halt right outside my window. The sound is deafening, echoing through the empty streets, guaranteed to bring a horde. My heart pounds in my chest as I peer through the blinds. The bus is old and battered, its once-bright paint now faded and chipped. The windows are cracked, and shadows move inside.

The blinds slip from my fingers, settling without a whisper. I pivot, the worn doorknob warm against my palm as I twist and push the door open, leaving it ajar for Jo.

My footsteps glide over the scuffed floor, each one light, swift, practiced. The hallway feels endless, the air thick with that stale, abandoned scent. The side entrance looms ahead. My shoulder brushes the door as I slip through, the alley swallowing me whole.

The world outside hits hard—stench first. Decay, foul and rancid, curls in my nose and sticks to the back of my throat. My knees bend instinctively, dropping me into a crouch, muscles coiled tight. My boots skim over the pavement as I creep toward the alley's edge, every nerve buzzing.

The street beyond is a canvas of ruin—crumpled cars, shattered glass, and the grotesque carnage of the world's collapse. Limbs, torn and forgotten, rot where they fell. Trash flutters across the cracked pavement, whispering the stories of a life long lost.

The weight of my drop-point knife is a promise against my thigh. My fingers find it, sliding it free with a soft hiss of steel.

The bus door creaks open, and I tighten my grip on the knife.

Here we *go*.

Three men slink onto the street, each one armed to the teeth. Their greasy hair clings to their foreheads, and their clothes are a patchwork of sweat and grime. One sports a brown, scraggly beard with bits of food tangled in it, or at least I hope it's food. Another is rail thin with a rat's tail, while the third flashes yellowed teeth whenever he sneers, throwing his shotgun around like he's a big shot. They move to the front of the bus, surveying the damage with narrowed eyes. Seizing the moment, I creep behind the bus, my heart pounding as I keep my eyes locked on them.

"You've gotta be *fucking* kidding me." The one with the shotgun spits, kicking at the dirt in frustration. His words carry an edge of impatience, like this isn't the first shit luck they've run into today.

The other two don't respond, just exchange a look before ducking back onto the bus. A moment later, a tire rolls down the steps with a hollow *thunk-thunk*. They don't waste time. One crouches low, already working to pry off the damaged rubber, while the other hauls the spare into position. Their movements are practiced, efficient—quicker than I expected from men who look like they spend more time looting corpses than fixing vehicles.

Shotgun Guy paces, gun slung over his shoulder, his gaze flicking up and down the empty street. His fingers twitch at the strap, restless. On edge. "This is bullshit," he mutters, low and sharp. "We shoulda been there an hour ago."

Rat Tail, the one tightening the lug nuts, grunts. "Maybe if someone hadn't driven straight into that mess of debris, we *woulda* been."

"The hell was I supposed to do? Float over it?" Shotgun Guy snaps back, jerking his chin toward the road, where the shredded remains of their old tire lie in a heap. "Some asshole laid that trap on purpose."

The second man, the quietest of the three, wipes a grease-streaked hand on his pants and stands, cracking his neck. "Less talk, more fixing. Ain't like we got time to bitch."

I shift, grabbing ahold of the handle and hoisting myself up just enough to peer through the back window of the bus.

Six passengers. Four women, one man, and—*shit*—a little girl. No older than ten. Scattered across separate seats, backs stiff, eyes locked forward, as if looking anywhere else might draw attention.

One guard inside. A potbellied bastard with greasy white hair hanging in limp strands down his back, like some junkie Santa Claus gone to hell. He moves slowly, pacing the aisle, his heavy boots thudding against the floor in an unhurried rhythm. Not searching for threats. Not watching the road.

Watching *her*.

My grip tightens around my knife, blood roaring in my ears. Oh, I'm going to enjoy killing him.

I slide back down to the ground and face down the street. I check my watch, feeling my pulse tick in sync with the second hand. Timing is everything.

Three. Two. One.

The second the minute turns over, the front window of the bank down the block detonates. Glass erupts in a shimmering spray, catching the firelight as flames burst outward, devouring the air with a hungry roar. Heat ripples through the street as fire claws its way up the second story, licking at the bricks like a living, breathing beast.

Showtime.

I shift, tracking the men's movements through the dusty glass front of the shop to my left.

"*Fucking hell!*" Shotgun Guy bellows, voice sharp with panic. He whirls, shotgun snapping up, his wild eyes darting across the empty street, searching for an enemy that isn't there.

Moans and screeches start to make their way down the street.

Perfect.

The two fixing the tire stop, gaping at the flames down the block, their hands hovering uselessly over the wheel. Shotgun Guy smacks them both upside the head. "Pick up the pace, boys." He strides toward the open bus door and hollers, "Hey, Charlie!"

A low growl rolls out from inside the bus. "Nobody fucking moves unless you want a bullet in the back of your head!" The voice is thick, scratchy, phlegm-clogged.

A second later, Santa's reject steps off the bus, his potbelly jiggling with each step. "What the hell was that?" His yellow teeth flash, and he clutches his gun to his chest like a lifeline. The sight of him almost makes me gag.

Shotgun Guy spits to the side. "Does it *look* like I know? Go check it out."

Charlie sneers, the folds of his neck shifting like raw dough. "Why me?"

Come on. My leg jiggles with anticipation, the pent-up energy coiling tighter with every second. I press my back against the bus, my fingers flexing around the hilt of my knife. *Breathe.* Deep inhale. Slow exhale. *Steady, girl.*

Shotgun Guy steps up, jamming the barrel of his weapon into

Charlie's chest. "Listen, fat man," he sneers. "You're lucky I don't carve you up right here and leave you for the runners. But since the boss *tolerates* you, I won't. As long as you *do. What. I. Say.*"

Each word is punctuated with a hard jab to Charlie's sweaty forehead, and the way he winces makes it clear this isn't the first time Shotgun Guy's put him in his place.

Shotgun Guy is built like a scarecrow—tall, lanky, all sharp angles with a gaunt face that makes his hollowed cheeks look even more severe. Dirty-blond hair sticks out in tufts, greasy strands matted together in places like he hasn't washed it in weeks.

And yet, the elves are running the show because *Santa* grumbles but obeys. With an exaggerated huff, Charlie starts a waddling shuffle toward me.

Step.

Step.

Step.

His boots scuff against the pavement, his breath a ragged wheeze. *Damn, is he already winded?* The closer he gets, the stronger his stench—sweat, rot, something stale clinging to him like a second skin, and I force my stomach to stay put.

Almost there.

My breathing evens, syncing with his sluggish pace. *Inhale. Exhale. Inhale.*

Step.

Step.

Bye-bye, Charlie.

The moment his foot crosses the threshold of the back of the bus, my hand clamps over his forehead, yanking him back until his spine collides against my chest. A startled grunt rumbles in his throat, but it never has the chance to form into a scream.

I drive my knife into the left side of his thick, sweat-slick neck. His whole body seizes, a violent shudder rippling through his bulk as steel bites through flesh.

A wet, sucking sound fills my ears as the blade carves its way across his throat, severing muscle, sinew, everything that keeps him breathing. Warm blood bursts over my knuckles, gushing in thick waves, coating my fingers, my wrist, my arm. The scent of iron crashes over me in a suffocating wave. His choked scream gurgles into nothing as his own blood drowns him.

His hands claw at me, sluggish and weak, nails scraping against my forearm in a pathetic attempt to fight back. I keep him upright, pressing into him, letting gravity do the work as his weight sags against me. His life drains fast, each failing breath rattling, struggling, until—nothing.

I hold him a second longer, feeling the last tremors of his existence flicker out. Then, with a sharp yank, I rip my knife free and let him drop.

He crumples in a heavy, wet heap at my feet, blood seeping into the cracked pavement, pooling around the edges of my boots. The tips of my long blond hair drip crimson. Loose strands cling to my face, my neck, soaking into my clothes. The warmth of his death attaches to me, seeping into my skin.

I don't wipe it away. I don't move. I just breathe—steady, measured—as the world steadies with me.

Not done yet, Charlie boy. Gotta sell it.

The image of the little girl's tear-streaked face burns behind my eyes, fueling the fire in my veins. I lunge forward, straddling Charlie's lifeless body, and let loose a raw, unhinged scream that rips through the morning like an animal gone rabid. My blade arcs high, then plunges deep, over and over, the sickening crunch of steel meeting flesh and bone drowned beneath my frenzied howls. Blood sprays hot across my face, splattering my lips, my chin, dripping from my lashes, but I don't stop.

Hell, I should've been an actress. My throat burns from the force of my screams, but I keep wailing, painting the perfect picture of a crazed survivor gone completely off the rails.

The pounding of boots barely registers before I'm yanked off the body, tackled hard into the pavement. The air whooshes from my lungs as my cheek smacks against the burning asphalt. I thrash, kicking wildly, snarling through gritted teeth, but one of them drops his weight onto my legs, pinning me down. Another twists my arms behind my back, wrenching them at an angle that makes pain bloom up my shoulders.

Cold steel presses against my temple, biting into my sweat-damp skin. My breath heaves, ragged and manic, as Charlie's dead, vacant eyes stare back at me, blood still pouring in sluggish waves from his shredded throat.

Boots—scuffed, brown, worn from miles of violence—step into my line of sight, stopping just inches from my face.

"Well, lookee here, boys. We got ourselves a crazy one. And she's a looker too—under all that mess."

The shotgun barrel lifts from my temple, giving me just enough room to suck in a breath before a fist tangle in my ponytail and yanks back, hard. My neck strains, my scalp stings, but I don't flinch. Shotgun Guy crouches close, and his yellow-toothed grin spreads, lazy and lecherous, eyes raking over me like I'm nothing more than a prize to be claimed.

"You know, I should thank you," he muses, his grip tightening as he leans in. "I've been wanting to gut that piece of filth for a while."

An easy, sweet smile stretches my lips, and I meet his gaze with something far sharper than fear. I summon every ounce of spit I can muster and hurl it straight into his face.

The glob lands with a wet smack, sliding down his cheek toward his sneering mouth. He recoils, cursing, his grip slipping from my hair as he wipes at his face like he can scrub away the humiliation. Laughter rips from my throat, wild and unhinged. I let it echo, let it crack the air around us like gunfire.

A boot slams into my ribs, knocking the breath from my lungs. Pain explodes through my side, sharp and unforgiving.

"Think you're funny, bitch?" Shotgun Guy snarls, his voice tight with rage. Rough hands grab at me, yanking my arms back. Thick, coarse rope coils around my wrists, biting into my skin as they yank it tight, securing the knot with jerks meant to bruise. My fingers tingle from the cut of the rope, but I don't struggle. Not yet.

Underestimating me will be their biggest mistake today.

My hair yanks back again, harder this time, my scalp burning as strands threaten to tear free. The pain sharpens, but I grit my teeth, refusing to give him the satisfaction of a reaction.

"You're gonna regret that," Shotgun Guy sneers, his teeth flashing as he jerks my head back farther, his grip like a vise in my ponytail. He motions to the others with a flick of his head. "Get her on the bus."

The weight on my back vanishes, and rough hands haul me to my feet. The bearded one shoves me forward, forcing me up the metal steps. My balance wavers, and before I can brace myself, I'm hurled into a seat. My temple smashes against the steamed window, the impact rattling through my skull. A sharp sting radiates through my cheekbone, but I barely register it because a tiny whimper behind me sends a bolt of ice through my spine.

The little girl.

A single inhale steadies me as my gaze scans the other passengers—expressions hollowed out with fear, ages ranging from early thirties to late sixties. An older man's face is smeared with dried blood, some of it tangled in his graying hair.

Shotgun Guy saunters onto the bus, his swagger dripping with arrogance. His gaze locks on to me, heating with something ugly.

Before he can take another step, a rustling at the back of the bus draws his attention.

The older man slowly rises. Determination hardens his features as he pushes himself upright, swaying slightly but standing firm.

"Let the women and child go," he demands, his voice rough but steady. "You don't need them. Do what you want to me, but let them go."

"Sit down," Rat Tail snarls, driving the butt of his rifle into the older man's shoulder with a sickening thud.

A chorus of gasps ripples through the bus. The man staggers, his face contorting in pain, but he doesn't go down. He reels back, eyes blazing with defiance, ready to charge despite the odds.

The guard cocks his gun and swings the barrel toward the head of an elderly woman sitting across the aisle. "Try it," he taunts, his finger ghosting over the trigger.

The older man freezes. His fists clench so tight his knuckles go white, his whole body taut with rage. But the woman—kind eyes set deep in a wrinkled face, cropped white hair trembling with each shallow breath—lifts her hands as if to help him.

He gives her a sharp look, a minute shake of his head. A warning.

She swallows hard and slowly retracts her hands, curling them into her lap as though folding in on herself. The fear in her eyes flutters to resignation.

The older man lowers himself back into his seat, fists still clenching, his jaw grinding like he's holding back an explosion. But he keeps his gaze moving, protective, watchful over the others and me.

A choked hiccup breaks through the tense silence.

"Mom."

The woman across the aisle from me moves instinctively, long chestnut hair tumbling over her shoulders as she reaches toward the little girl. Her smoky eyes flash with desperation, her fingers stretching as if sheer will alone can bridge the distance between them. She shifts in her seat, her body tense with the urge to move.

"Let me hold her," she pleads, voice wobbly.

Shotgun Guy stiffens, his dirty-blond hair falling into his face as he turns on her. His mouth flashes in an ugly sneer. "Did I fuckin' say you could speak?" His voice is sharp, laced with cruel amusement.

"Please," she says, her chest rising and falling with quick, shallow breaths.

He steps forward, his shotgun dangling at his side, but his free hand lifts. His palm hovers, poised midair, a silent threat hanging between them.

"You deaf, sweetheart?" he growls. "Or just stupid?"

The woman's eyes spark, defiance fighting against the fear tightening her features.

Shotgun Guy's lip curls, his fingers twitching like he's deciding whether or not to bring them down across her face.

Screw this.

"Hey," I snap, my voice cutting through the tense silence like a blade.

He whips his head toward me, his expression twisting with irritation and something darker. "So, the little psycho finally speaks?"

I tilt my head, keeping my tone cool, almost lazy. "How about you try fucking with someone who'll actually fight back?" I lean forward, my teeth flashing like a predator about to pounce. "Or are you afraid to be beaten by a woman, little boy?"

His grip tightens on the shotgun, the muscle in his jaw twitching, my words obviously striking a nerve. Typical fragile masculinity. *What else is new?*

While he's busy glaring, the mother takes her shot. Quick and quiet, she slides into the seat beside the little girl, wrapping her in her arms, shielding her. Shotgun Guy hesitates, catching the movement too late. His nostrils flare, but he must decide she isn't worth the effort. He lets it slide, shifting his fury back to me.

He steps in, closing the space between us, his fingers biting into my chin with bruising force. My jaw aches under the pressure, my head forced back as his rancid breath spills over my face—hot, sour. His gaze slithers over me, and when he leans in until our noses nearly brush, his voice drops low, thick with malice.

"Too bad you're just his type. Otherwise, you and I would've had some fun tonight, sugar."

Revulsion coils deep in my gut, but I shove it down, locking my stare on to his. I force my lips to move against the grip crushing them. "Whose type?"

I need confirmation. No one else on this bus can be sent to him. *Just me.*

His grip loosens just enough for him to smirk before he shifts, caging me in with his arms. The seat presses into my back, his presence suffocating as he leans down, voice barely above a whisper.

"Da Vinci."

Bingo.

He pulls back, triumphant, mistaking my silence for fear. He thinks he has me. He thinks I don't already know exactly who he's talking about—the monster I thought was finally lost to the outbreak. My lips curl into a feral grin, sending a look of confusion across his face.

Before he can react, I rear my head back and slam it forward.

Crunch.

His nose explodes in a spray of blood. He howls, stumbling back into the driver's seat, hands clutching his ruined face. His features contort with agony, shock, and something even better—humiliation.

His eyes go dark, murderous, and then he lunges. His hand clamps around my throat, squeezing hard before I can react. My air vanishes in a flash. *Okay . . . maybe I pushed him a little too far.*

"I'm gonna make you regret that, bitch," he snarls, blood dribbling from his lips as he slams my head against the back of the seat.

He glances around the group, snarling at Rat Tail, "Get this bus moving." Then he locks eyes with me, a cruel smile spreading. "I've got plans for this one."

He turns toward the front, waving the others on.

Oh, I've got *plans* too, sweetheart. Just. You. Wait.

TWO
CATCH UP

THERE IT IS.

I ease off the gas, yanking the rig off the road and into the dense cover of the woods. Dry branches screech against the sides of the van, scraping like skeletal fingers, while sunlight filters through the canopy, casting jagged patterns of light and shadow across the windshield. The terrain shifts beneath the tires, uneven and riddled with roots, the whole vehicle lurching as we carve a rough path through the undergrowth. In the side mirror, I catch a glimpse of Leon's truck veering in behind us.

Inside the cab, Trish braces a hand against the dashboard, the other on the door handle in a death grip. "Jacob," she warns, voice tight, "I know you're panicking even if you won't say it, but can you please stop treating my van like a damn bumper car?"

Even in a crisis, she's trying to keep it together, but the sickly green tinge creeping up her dark skin tells me her stomach is doing somersaults. Trish never lets anything shake her, but I'm pushing it.

"Oh, I'm sorry," I bite out, yanking the wheel hard to the left, the tires grinding to a stop in a semi-open clearing with a narrow line of sight to the jail through the trees. "Would you rather I ease in at a casual twenty-five miles per hour while our people get marched off to be tortured, killed, eaten, or worse by whoever the hell took them?"

Trish swivels to glare at me, eyes burning hot enough to melt steel. "No, dumbass, I didn't say slow down. But do you wanna roll into town like it's a damn parade and lead every starving corpse straight to us?"

Point taken.

I clench my jaw, my pulse hammering in my ears as I try to shove down the sick feeling twisting in my gut. Trish keeps her stare locked on me, unflinching, then reaches out, her fingers steady as they grip my shoulder. "Jacob. We're all freaking out, but we need to stay frosty."

I exhale sharply, forcing my shoulders to drop. My grip on the wheel loosens, the tension in my knuckles fading from bone white to something closer to human. Trish watches me, waiting, her body mirroring my own—tight, coiled, running too hot. We both take a second to shake it off, to let logic shove emotion aside.

When it comes to the people I love, I lose my edge. I let panic creep in. I let fear drive the wheel. And right now, fear is a luxury we can't afford.

A few more measured breaths. My pulse is still hammering, but steadier.

So, naturally, I turn to humor, my go-to defense against the kind of pressure that could crush bone. "Did you really just quote *Aliens*?"

Trish shrugs, casual as hell, but the corner of her mouth twitches. "Of course. Right now, you're Hudson, and I'm Hicks."

I scoff, peeling my hands off the wheel and rubbing my palms against my jeans. "I have my shit together more than Hudson did."

A door slams outside—Leon's truck. His heavy footfalls crunch over sticks, moving toward us.

I know I shouldn't ask, but I can't help myself. "And Leon is?"

Trish chuckles, popping her seat belt with a flick of her wrist. "Why, the spunky Ripley, of course."

I groan, pushing open my door, muttering as I hop down, "Leon's always been your favorite." I drag a hand down my face, exhaling slowly. "All right. I'm calm. And I'm sorry for snapping earlier."

Trish tilts her head, considering.

I huff out a laugh. "Next time we're chasing down a transport van to a prison in the middle of nowhere, you drive. Good?"

She grins and pats me on the damn head like I'm a child. "Yes, Chief."

I bat her hand away. "You know you're getting that head pat back tenfold."

She just smirks, already walking ahead. "You can try."

I shut the door and shake off the tension that's been coiling in my muscles since the second we found out they were taken. The anger sits heavy, a burning coal in my gut. I should've been there. Should've done something—anything—to stop it.

We'd come back to camp from a supply run, expecting to see familiar faces, the comforting sounds of life in the apocalypse: the clang of supplies being sorted, quiet conversations, Earl bickering with Edith over another one of his conspiracy theories. Instead, we found *nothing*. Just silence and overturned crates where a camp should've been.

According to Pete, the coward, a transport bus had rounded them up like cattle at gunpoint.

He just cowered and watched while our people were forced onto that bus. He didn't lift a finger to stop it.

Pete only slithered out from whatever hole he'd been hiding in to tell us what had happened because I was tearing through camp, yelling loud enough to shake the trees, not giving a damn who heard me.

And the only reason that son of a bitch is still breathing?

Because he at least had the decency to read the damn bus. Lawrenceville Correctional Center. The only clue we've got. The only thing that kept me from putting a bullet between his eyes and calling it a day.

I move to the back of the truck, flipping down the tailgate, metal clanking loud in the quiet morning air. The scent of damp earth and old gasoline lingers as I start pulling out the guns, the familiar weight of steel centering me. Leon is already there, moving with his usual quiet efficiency. He taps my shoulder, drawing my attention. The sunlight catches in his ginger beard, making it blaze like fire against his otherwise unreadable expression.

"*What's the plan?*" he signs, his hands quick and precise.

Leon's always been the cool head to my impulsive streak, the stable hand to my unrestrained determination. While I throw myself into the fire, he watches from the edge, calculating, waiting for the right moment to strike. We balance each other out, and it's why we work so well together.

I inhale deeply, steadying my pulse. You're Hicks, Jacob. Time to take control.

Strapping a knife to my thigh, I grab my handguns, loading each one with a satisfying click before slipping extra magazines into my holsters.

"We walk the perimeter," I say. "Check for guards, figure out their numbers. We find a weak spot in the fence, cut our way in. Sneak through the outer buildings toward the main structure. Once we've cleared enough ground and found our people, we get the hell out. If they chase us"—I slide the last magazine into place and snap it shut, meeting Leon's sharp gaze—"we lead them into a herd of the undead and let them do our dirty work. Thoughts?"

Leon steps up beside me, already zipping up his Kevlar vest. He loads his crossbow, the familiar creak of the string stretching taut as he slings it over his back. A quiver of arrows follows, secured in one easy motion. His hatchet hangs at his side, its handle worn from years of use, as much a part of him as his own hands. His eyes flick to the gas canisters in the truck bed, sharp and calculating.

His hands move, fingers slicing through the air. *"I say we light one of the buildings on fire, draw them out."*

I hesitate, my fingers tapping against my thigh. Gas is precious. Hard to come by, harder to replace. Every drop is a step closer to whatever safety we're scraping together. But a fire? A fire could turn this hellhole into a frenzy, force them to scatter, give us the chaos we need to slip inside unseen.

Risk versus reward. The usual gamble.

My gut clenches. There's always a cost. But hell, if there's one thing I know, it's that fire is as much a weapon as any blade or bullet. And it's always helped me focus.

Screw it. Let's burn something.

I glance at Leon, the tension easing from my shoulders. "Grab one." My lips curl, something dark and reckless creeping into my voice. "Let's cause some destruction."

Leon's dark green eyes gleam with mischief, a familiar glint that always means trouble—the good kind. With his red hair and beard, he looks like some devil from an old war story, a man built for battle, for destruction. He hefts the gas canister with ease, saluting with two fingers before striding toward the van. Trish is already stepping down, rifle slung over her shoulder, her stance braced like she's expecting a fight to land on our doorstep any second.

I swallow hard and exhale through my nose, trying to ground myself. "I don't know what shape they'll be in when we get them back." *If* we get them back. The thought claws at my gut, but I shove it down. "I want supplies ready to treat them the second they're out." I pause, glancing past her to the open stretch of land, the distant fence line barely visible through the trees. "And keep an eye out for the infected."

Her gaze sweeps the tree line, sharp and assessing. "You better bring them back, Jacob," she mutters, her voice low and unwavering.

Leon moves his hands, *"We'll get them back."*

Trish watches, then sighs, nodding her head. "Of course you will, Ripley."

Leon gives me a deadpan look and shakes his head while moving his hands. *"She's been quoting* Aliens *again, hasn't she?"*

I grin. "Game over, man."

Trish chuckles, the tension in the air thinning just enough to breathe. Just enough to believe that when we come back, we won't be coming back empty-handed.

Leon rolls his eyes but doesn't bother responding, already moving toward the tree line, his steps light despite the weight of the gas canister.

Trish moves in the opposite direction, climbing up onto the roof of the van with practiced ease. "All right, boys," she calls out. "Make them pay."

She lies flat on her stomach, rifle in hand, and snugs the butt against her right shoulder. The scope glints in the dim light as she adjusts her position, settling in, ready to take out anything that moves the wrong way.

I turn after Leon, pushing forward into the woods. The scent of pine clings to the air, mingling with the distant stench of decay—the ever-present reminder that the dead are never far.

The trees around us are thick, their canopies casting shifting shadows that dance across the ground. Plenty of coverage to stay hidden, but also plenty of places for something—or someone—to be hiding. Every snap of a twig, every rustle of leaves sends my pulse hammering. My grip tightens on the wire cutters, my other hand hovering near the knife strapped to my thigh.

Leon moves like a ghost beside me, his long strides effortless, his breathing even. He belongs in this setting—hunting, tracking, blending into the wild like he was made for it. His sharp eyes scan ahead, always searching, always knowing what to look for.

The closer we get, the heavier the air feels—thick with the eerie silence of a place that should be teeming with movement. The fence looms ahead, rusted chain links stretching high, topped with razor wire that glints under the weak afternoon sun. We crouch low, moving through the dense underbrush, our boots sinking into damp soil. Every shift of leaves, every scrape of metal against my gear, sets my nerves on edge.

No one in the guard towers. No patrols pacing the perimeter. Just empty space where there should be men with guns, scanning for threats. The front lawn sprawls ahead of us, cracked pavement and patches of overgrown grass reclaiming the once-manicured prison yard.

It's wrong. Too quiet. Too still.

As we creep closer to the compound's entrance, my gut tightens. I raise my fist, signaling Leon to stop. He halts instantly, lowering himself deeper into the brush. I can feel his eyes on me, waiting for my next move, but I can't tear my gaze away from the sight ahead.

The air shifts, heavy with the stench of burnt flesh, thick and cloying, coating my tongue like ash. Thirty yards ahead, a blackened crater scars the earth, twenty feet wide. Charred remains are stacked in the center, twisted and fused together in grotesque shapes.

The bile rises fast, scorching the back of my throat as I clamp my jaw so tight my teeth groan under the pressure. The sheer number— bones piled like garbage, discarded, meaningless—

What if we're too late?

The thought is a blade, slicing through my composure, embedding itself deep. What if this is them? What if we're standing in the grave of the people we came to save?

I glance at Leon, searching for that unshakable presence, but even he looks rattled.

Breath too fast, pulse hammering against my ribs. God, I miss my anxiety meds.

A sharp whistle cuts through the tension, slicing into my spiraling thoughts like a blade. My head snaps toward Leon just as his hand grips the back of my neck. He pulls me forward, pressing our foreheads together, his touch grounding me like a damn anchor.

He begins breathing deeply. In and out. In and out.

I squeeze my eyes shut, forcing air into my lungs, but my chest still feels like it's caving in. Focus. The sound of birds chirping. The weight of Leon's palm, solid and sure. *You're here. You're not alone.*

I let the breath out slow, my ribs aching with the force of it. My forehead lifts from his, and I meet his waiting gaze.

I'm back.

Leon studies me for a beat longer before giving a firm pat to the side of my face.

He crouches low beside the fence, fingers running over to find the best spot to cut in, but his hand meets the edge of a jagged tear in the metal. His usual mask of indifference is still there, but beneath it, something else lingers. Concern. Unease.

His hands move swiftly. *"Someone's been busy."*

I step closer, scanning the damage. Not just one cut—multiple slashes, uneven and wide, running down the length of the perimeter. I grind my teeth, confusion dulling the rough edge of my nerves. "Question is, why?" The words slip out more to myself than to him.

Anyone or anything could slip through. A mistake? Unlikely.

Leon exhales sharply, the ghost of a shrug lifting his shoulders. His fingers flick in a quick sign, *"We'll find out."*

He slips through the opening first and I follow, my gun raised, senses stretched thin, every muscle braced for the worst. The air inside the fence feels different—thicker, heavier, like the world's holding its breath.

The first building looms ahead, its dark windows gaping like hollow eyes. I force myself to look forward, to keep moving, to ignore the blackened pit of bodies behind me.

They're still alive.

They *have* to be.

THREE
SAD LITTLE BOY

LYLA

WELP, I *didn't* expect this.

With my eyes still closed, I try to get my bearings without drawing attention. All right, I'm in a chair, arms tied in the back. Not the worst position, to be honest. Shuffling reaches my ears so someone must be in the room with me.

Okay, Lyla. What was the last thing you remember?

We were about to pull up to the jail, the assholes stopped the bus, got out, huddled, and discussed something. Shotgun Guy gestured widely, but then they all shook hands. Shotgun Guy came back on the bus, and by the throbbing in my head, he must have knocked me out with the butt of his rifle.

Sweet. All right. But where am I?

"The big man's not gonna like this," a familiar male voice mutters.

I can make out the press of the button as something clicks into motion. Suddenly the room fills with the opening chords of "Susie Q."

What is it with psychos and CCR?

Wait.

What does he mean the big man isn't going to like this?

I swear, if I'm not in front of da Vinci right now, I'm going to—

Suddenly I can feel the ends of my hair being played with while another hand brushes the strays away from my damp skin. I keep my head loose, lolling it forward, pretending to be lost in the oblivion of unconsciousness.

One thing at a time, Lyla. Get free, subdue whoever is touching me, figure out where I am, and then get back on track. Cool.

Calloused fingers grip my chin, shifting my head up.

"Time to wake up, sugar." A thumb strokes the curve of my jaw. "We've got a lot to do . . . and not a lot of time to do it."

The music plays on, guitar thrumming, the guttural vocals echoing against the walls.

Steady, girl. You'll get your chance. You just need to—

All thoughts leave my mind as a warm tongue drags up the side of my face. My body jerks, my eyes blow open.

This motherfu—

Shotgun Guy's grip tightens on my chin. "Shh." He slaps a strip of duct tape over my mouth before I can make a sound, smoothing it down.

"There we go." His voice drops to a purr. "That's a good girl."

I thrash, trying to yank my head away.

"Let's get to know each other before all the fun begins, yeah?" He leans in, lips brushing my ear. "Just pretend this is a first date."

First date, my ass.

He leans back into his chair, watching. Waiting.

I jerk my arms, muscles straining against the ropes. Again. And again. The sound of fibers creaking under pressure fills the air, giving me a moment to assess the room.

No windows. The only light is coming from a lantern next to the metal door. Four cement walls. So we must be in the isolation wing. A boom box is on the floor next to the lone worktable, which is covered with various blades and tools.

And no da Vinci.

Great. I love that for me.

"You can keep trying," he taps my knife against his thigh, "but it's no use." His grin widens, sharp and taunting. "Many before you tried. Many fought. Many cried." He drags a finger across his throat. "Guess how that ended?"

Oh, right. I should be frightened right now.

My chest rises and falls too fast, creating the sound of muffled whimpers seeping through the duct tape. My movements turning desperate. Oh no! I'm a scared little woman. Please don't hurt me, mister. *Pfft.*

He motions toward me with the tip of the knife.

"Name's Lars," he says, voice dripping with false warmth. He twirls the blade between his fingers, letting the light catch the metal. "I'll be your torturer for the day. Please keep all hands and arms inside the ride at all times. Feel free to scream, cry, and beg for mercy, but do keep in mind . . ." He pauses, leaning down so his breath ghosts along the side of my neck. "We are severely understaffed and won't be able to promptly address your complaints."

Do not roll your eyes. Do not roll your eyes. Do. Not. Roll. Your. Eyes.

"I'm going to make you beg," he murmurs, his gaze sweeping over the worktable.

No, honey. I'm going to make *you* beg.

My eye catches on a rusty filleting knife.

His eyes turn back to me, raking over my body.

Gross.

"We're going to take our time." His voice thickens with hunger. "Because I deserve this. This world—this beautiful, broken world—was made for people like me. And people like you?" He tilts his head. "You exist to serve us. That's your only purpose now."

He stands and walks over to the table, his back to me.

Rookie mistake.

"You should count yourself lucky." He chuckles as his hand hovers over a bowie knife and a hacksaw. "If I'd given you to da Vinci, you would have *pleaded* for me. He's a true artist of pain." He trails his fingers over the hacksaw. "He doesn't just kill—he creates. Every scream, every drop of blood, orchestrated. A masterpiece of agony."

Oh trust me, Lars, I know exactly who *he* is.

I whimper, covering up the sound of my movements and the quiet pop of my thumb.

The rope falls from my wrists.

His hand grips the saw. "And you? You would've been his greatest work yet. Trust me, sugar, you wouldn't have survived an hour."

He turns around and freezes when he sees me standing right in front of him. His eyes widen as I pull the duct tape off my mouth.

"Boo." I smile and before he can react I snatch the filleting knife from the table and drive it up through his jaw, lodging it deep into the roof of his mouth.

A scream tears from Lars's throat but dies before it can escape, choked by the blade.

He drops to his knees. Blood bubbles past his lips and flows down the hilt onto my hand. His hands fly to his jaw, to the foreign metal stabbing through flesh, but before he can even attempt to pull it out, I twist the handle.

A fresh bolt of agony detonates behind his eyes. His vision darkens at the edges, body spasming, hands clawing at my grip, desperate to pry me away, but I hold true. My fingers tangle in his hair, wrenching his head back, forcing him to look at me and see my satisfaction.

My mouth curves. I lean in close so that our noses touch. "Stop. Talking."

Then I rip the knife free.

A guttural roar bursts from his shredded mouth, a fresh spray of blood splattering down his chin and across his hands as he clutches at the wound.

Before he can get up, I yank his head forward, slamming it against the table.

His limbs go limp, heavy, useless. My boots smear the puddles of blood on the floor.

My breath ghosts over his ear. "Nighty-night, *sweetheart.*"

I slam his head against the table one more time, knocking him unconscious.

I glare at the crumpled heap of filth sprawled on the floor, his unconscious body slack, his face half-buried in his own blood.

Well, I feel *much* better.

I pop my left thumb back into place and rub the joint. I'm lucky he didn't tie the ropes so tight that I couldn't slip my hand out. A fun little trick I picked up at the academy.

Deep breath, Lyla. Focus. Need to rearrange the order of the plan. But real quick—

I kneel, my fingers curling around his ankle. He's nothing but dead weight as I drag him across the floor. His limp body thuds against the stained concrete, a sick, rhythmic sound that feeds my fury. Each impact is a small burst of satisfaction.

A smirk tugs at my lips.

I tighten my grip, yanking him harder, watching his head loll to the side. I hoist him up and slam his ass into the chair, his weight settling with a sickly squelch.

Let's see how smug you are when you wake up, asshole.

I yank the ropes tight, each knot cinching down, unyielding, cruel. His wrists, his ankles, his chest—bound so tight his circulation will give before I leave. For good measure, I grab the roll of duct tape. A sharp, satisfying rip. The sound alone makes my lips twitch. I wrap it around his mouth, yanking it behind his head, locking it in place. His face tilts at an unnatural angle.

I step back, arms crossed, studying my work.

Not bad.

One glance at my watch. One hour down. Thirty minutes to go.

Okay. This is doable. I was hoping to take out da Vinci first and then get the hostages, but that won't work now. All right, switch the order and hope to God this works better.

Fingers crossed.

I stride forward.

Crack. My palm smacks across his face, sharp and loud, in the silence.

"Hey!"

No response.

Crack. Harder this time. "Wake up, dipshit."

A twitch. A flutter. His eyes flutter open—glassy, unfocused, lost.

Then recognition.

Then fury.

He thrashes, muscles jerking, the chair creaking beneath his weight. A trapped animal, rabid and useless.

Muffled screams pour from behind the tape, his rage a pathetic, garbled mess.

I chuckle, low and dark, leaning in until my face hovers just inches from his. "You can try," I taunt, throwing his own smug words back at him, "but it's no use."

His eyes snap to mine, blazing.

I grip his jaw, fingers digging into bruised, bloodied skin. Hard enough to make him squirm, to remind him exactly who's in control. "What a sad little boy you are," I murmur, my voice laced with contempt. His body tenses, muscles bunching like a coiled spring. But he can't do shit. Not anymore.

I lean in, my lips brushing his ear, my breath a whisper of heat. "Men like you," I murmur, "never take it well when a woman proves she's better."

His muffled roar vibrates against the tape, furious and pathetic.

"I've been watching you," I continue, voice smooth, lethal. "Your gang. Your routines. Your weaknesses. Every mistake. Every blind spot. This wasn't luck."

His thrashing pauses. The cornered rat finally recognizes the trap.

"This," I say, razor-sharp, final, "has been coming for a long time. You didn't catch me." I lean back, watching the truth dawn in his wild, desperate eyes. "I caught you."

I release his jaw, stepping back, letting the weight of my words sink into his bones. "Before all this, I'd have put scum like you behind bars." A wicked smile breaks across my face. "But there's no law anymore."

His breathing stutters.

I grin, feral, unyielding. "So I've invited some hungry friends." I flick his nose as his face drains of color.

"And they're just *dying* to meet you."

He thrashes harder, the chair rattling against the floor, but there's no escape.

"I'd love to stay," I murmur, voice dripping with mock regret. "Watch them tear you apart piece by piece. See how long you last before you stop screaming." I tilt my head, studying his sweat-slicked face. His wild, bloodshot eyes plead with me. "But I've got a date with your boss."

His muffled scream rips through the gag. Desperation pours off him, thick and frantic. He bucks against the chair, the wood groaning under his weight, his wrists straining against the ropes.

"Wish me luck, *sugar.*"

His body shudders violently. Panic claws at the air between us, but I'm already turning away, already making my way to the table where his little collection of horrors gleams beneath the dim lantern light.

My drop-point knife sits among them. Hello, beautiful. I grab it, securing the sheath to my thigh.

Then my gaze flicks across the rest. Knives. Blades of every shape and size, each one kissed by rust and old blood. I pocket six and then my eyes catch on the real prize.

His shotgun.

Polished wood. Oiled steel. A true beauty. I pick it up, flipping it open. Two shells. Not enough. I scan the room. Come on, come on . . . bingo. A small bag near the workbench, tossed aside like an afterthought. I kneel, unzip it, and grin. Two whole boxes of shells.

Praise all that is holy.

Slinging the bag over my shoulder, I move to the cell door, pressing my back against the cool metal as I ease it open just enough to peek into the hallway.

Candles line the hall, their light shining weakly, painting the stained walls and cracked floor with nervous shadows.

Empty.

My pulse ticks faster, every second stretching thin, each breath a countdown. Time isn't on my side. If I hesitate, I lose my shot.

Behind me, his muffled screams reach a fever pitch even muffled under the tape.

I glance over my shoulder to see his entire body trembling, veins bulging in his neck, eyes wide with sheer, unfiltered terror. A dark stain spreads across his pants, fear soaking through the fabric.

I cock my head, clicking my tongue in mock sympathy.

"Poor *baby*."

His panic intensifies, head shaking frantically, muffled wails breaking into choking sobs.

I toss him a lazy salute.

"Try not to scream too loud," I murmur, stepping into the hall, leaving the door wide open.

FOUR
TIMING

LYLA

GOTTA MOVE. *Gotta move. Gotta move.*

My heart beats in sync with the thought as I make my way down the dim corridor. I need to get to the main office. If I know da Vinci —and unfortunately, I do—that's where he'll be. Holding court like some twisted monarch, relishing his reign over this festering hellhole.

But first, the hostages.

I stop and take a moment to orient myself. Okay, based on the plans Joanie and I found at city hall—one of the many benefits of an apocalypse, no request form needed—the main office should be on the other side of the cafeteria, which is accessed near cell block A. And I'm in . . . I look around and find a *C* in black paint at the end of the wall up ahead.

My mind sorts through the layout, piecing together every bit of intel I've gathered from my study of the outside of the buildings, every scrap of logic that fits da Vinci's sick, methodical nature. He'd want them close. Not just for security—*for pleasure.* He'd want to hear their screams.

Cell block A it is.

I roll my shoulders, exhale slowly through my nose. No room for nerves. No room for mistakes.

Each footfall lands with precision as I move down the corridor, my senses sharpening, stretching out like a net, catching every whisper of sound, every hint of movement.

Images of the passengers flash—overlapping my mental map of the halls. The little girl's tear-streaked face burns behind my eyes, her cries echoing like a haunting melody that won't let go.

Back against the wall at the intersection, I hold my breath and listen. The air hangs heavy, stale—like the walls themselves suffocate under the weight of what they've witnessed. Sweat slicks my palms despite the chill bleeding from the concrete. My grip tightens on the knife.

There.

Voices. Faint. Just a tremor—muffled, strained. Crying. Soft, choked sobs slicing through the stillness like tiny blades.

Desperation coils in my gut, twisting like barbed wire. They're close.

I ease forward, footsteps brushing the ground. Each one, a gamble. Each breath, a risk. My pulse pounds in my throat—louder than sense allows.

The sounds grow sharper. Raw. Anguished. Each sob cuts like a dagger.

At the final corner, I freeze and peer around. Two guards flank a heavy metal door, rifles slung over their shoulders. Their postures are loose, focus drifting as they exchange crude jokes. Screams behind the door cut through their laughter, a sick contrast that roils my stomach.

Back against the wall, adrenaline spikes.

Think, Lyla. *Think.*

Fingers curl around the knife. I draw it free, its weight grounding me, a reminder: one shot at this. No screwups.

The shotgun lowers in my grip with a solid thunk that echoes through the hall.

The guards stop laughing.

"Hey, did you hear that?" one asks, voice low, suspicious.

"Yeah." The other scoffs. "Probably just Hank again, trying to cut in line."

Footsteps echo down the hallway, growing louder. My grip tightens on the knife, the rough handle biting into my palm as anticipation floods my veins.

"Hank," the guard calls, irritation creeping in. "You know the rules. Wait your damn turn."

The steps stop, just around the corner. I steady my breath. Muscles tense.

He rounds the corner and before he can yell, my hand covers his mouth and I yank his body to mine as the knife slices into the right side of his throat, cutting off his airflow. His body slumps instantly and before I can catch it, his rifle hits the concrete hard.

"Phil?"

Footsteps inch closer. "Phil? You all right, man?"

I drag his body deeper into the shadows, boots sliding in the slick pool spreading beneath him.

Crouched at the corner, I press tight to the wall. My heartbeat pounds in my ears.

The barrel appears first.

I snatch it—twist it up and away—yanking his body forward with the motion.

His breath catches right before I drive my fist into his gut. A choked grunt escapes him as the air rushes from his lungs.

No pause. I slam my forehead into his nose. Cartilage shatters against my skull, the wet crunch sickening. He stumbles, blood streaming down his face.

I drive the blade deep into his throat. His eyes widen, hands clawing at my wrist. I twist and slice across his neck in a brutal arc.

A fresh burst of blood sprays against the cement, painting the walls in violent red strokes. He gurgles, staggers, knees folding under the weight of death. I wrench the rifle from his weakening grip as he drops. He twitches, fingers uselessly pressing against the gaping wound in his throat. The fight drains from him in seconds, his body going still.

His lifeless eyes stare up at the ceiling, glassy and unseeing.

Two down. Many more to go.

"Thanks for the rifles, boys," I whisper, scooping up the second gun. A quick pat down yields a handful of ammo. I pocket the rounds, sling the weapons, and move to the door. I crack the door, just enough to peek inside.

My breathing stops.

This isn't just a cell block—it's a hellscape.

Open-bar cages line the walls, each one a stage for suffering. The prisoners sit trapped in their own nightmares, just close enough to hear each other scream.

At the far end, a young girl curls in a chair, light brown hair tangled around her face. Hazel eyes—wide, terrified—shimmer with unshed tears.

A few feet away, her mother strains against her restraints, chained to a chair in the next cell. Dark brown hair falls in loose waves around her face, softening the lines etched by fear. But while the girl trembles, her mother's matching eyes burn with desperate defiance.

Chains rattle as she leans forward. "Poppy, sweetheart, look at me." She forces a shaky smile. "It's okay, honey. Just keep looking at me, all right? We're going to be okay."

Down the line, a white-haired woman thrashes against her bed restraints, wrists raw and red.

"Earl! Wake up! Earl, please!" she cries, each word soaked in desperation.

In the next cell, the older man—gray hair, heavy frame—slumps against the floor, motionless. Chains bind his ankles to the ground, his head twisted at an unnatural angle.

Across from him, a woman sags in her chair, her body so thin she barely fills the space. Crimped, dirty-blond hair hangs forward in tangled curtains, hiding her face. Her knees bounce in an erratic rhythm that doesn't match the eerie stillness of her upper half.

At the final cell, an older woman—bruised and battered—lies crumpled on the floor, her hands tied in front of her. Her silver hair is speckled with blood.

Above her looms the bearded man from the bus, his presence oppressive, the knuckles on his hands cracked and bleeding.

My fingers tighten around the knife until they go numb.

"Shut the hell up, all of you!" he bellows, voice echoing through the corridor. "You're ruining the mood."

He turns back to the woman sprawled on the floor, fingers curling into her shirt like she's nothing but trash. With a violent yank, he hurls her against the back wall. Her body hits the cement with a sickening thud. A grunt escapes, but she doesn't crumple. She plants her spine against the wall, legs bent, arms limp—but not broken.

Then she lifts her head.

The glare she throws him burns with heat. Not fear. Not surrender. Fire. Sharp. Unyielding.

It punches jealousy through my ribs.

I slip into the cell like a shadow. Pulse pounding, hands steady. She glances past him—just once—brown eyes locking with mine. They flash like embers before cutting back to her attacker.

Her voice drops, low and satisfied. "I'm going to enjoy this."

He scoffs, his broad frame relaxed, completely oblivious, fingers toying with his buckle.

"Oh really?" His voice drips amusement. "And what exactly are you gonna enjoy, darlin'?"

She leans forward, smile curling into something predatory. "*This.*"

He doesn't even register the shift.

I'm behind him in a blink. One hand clamps over his mouth, cutting off the sharp inhale. The knife slides through his throat—smooth, deep—slicing flesh and artery in a single, merciless drag. Man, I'm on a *roll* today. His body jolts, muscles spasming as hot blood pours down his chest. I lower him to the floor, silent. Not even his gear dares to rattle.

The woman doesn't flinch.

Yeah. I like her even more.

She shifts her sharp gaze to me, brown eyes sweeping over me like she's weighing, measuring.

I step close and cut the ropes binding her wrists. The fibers snap, and she immediately rubs at the raw skin, wincing. Before she can sway, I grip her arm and steady her until she plants her feet.

She rolls her shoulders, a pop cracking in her hip as she straightens, and sizes me up with a smirk that's more amusement than gratitude. Taller than I expected. Lean. Strong. The kind of strength built from survival rather than comfort.

"Had a feeling you weren't actually crazy," she murmurs, voice low and even—like an inside joke. Her head tilts as she studies me. "At least, not in the way you wanted them to think. Although . . ." Her brown eyes glint with something close to admiration. "Takes a special kind of nuts to willingly get on that bus."

A quiet huff slips out as I kneel and wipe my blade on the dead man's shirt. "You'll have to be more specific. I've made plenty of questionable choices lately."

She strides past before I can say more, heading straight to the next cell. Without hesitation, she begins untying the mousy woman slumped in the chair. Efficient. No nonsense. She throws a look over her shoulder that says, *Aren't you going to help?*

Would it be weird if I asked her to be my mom?

I move to the bed where the elderly woman shudders against the restraints. The ropes fall under my blade, and she pulls me into a bone-crushing hug, blood on my clothes be damned. Tears streak her cheeks as the words pour out.

"Oh, thank you. Thank you. Thank you. Thank the Lord for you, sweetie."

She plants a kiss on my cheek before hurrying to the next cell. Kneeling beside her husband's limp body, she shakes him gently.

"Earl, honey, wake up." Her voice cracks.

Behind me, my new mom moves with purpose—steps steady, hands sure. She makes quick work of the ropes binding the mousy woman, who immediately curls in on herself, arms wrapping tight, rubbing at the red lines carved into her skin. No words. No sound. Just blank eyes fixed to the floor, bracing for whatever comes next.

New Mom doesn't press her. Doesn't waste breath on comfort that won't land. She pivots to the little girl still trembling in the chair, her chest rising in short, uneven gasps.

Crouching low, she makes herself small, nonthreatening. Her voice stays soft—too quiet to hear—but whatever she says works. The girl's gaze, still glassy with fear, begins to thaw. Her shoulders drop, a fraction of the tension slipping away.

Gently, New Mom wipes the tear tracks from her cheeks, her thumb gliding across freckled skin smudged with grime.

A sharp voice cuts through the moment.

"Earl! Wake up!"

A slap cracks against skin. Then another.

I move to the mother still struggling against her chains. I start searching around for the keys but can't find anything.

"The keys are in his pocket," the mother says quickly, nodding toward the dead man.

I move fast, patting him down until my fingers close around the metal in his back pocket. The keys clink as I rush back, unlocking her cuffs, then tossing them through the bars to the woman near the girl. Chains fall away, and the mother bolts upright the second she's free.

The little girl launches into her arms.

"Mom!" she cries, burying her face into her mother's shoulder. Her small body shakes as her mother wraps her up, holding her like she'll never let go.

Tears carve silent tracks down the woman's face as she meets my eyes over her daughter's head. She nods once—no words, just raw gratitude, heavy and humbling. I nod back. A beat shared in silence. Real. Unshakable.

Behind me, the old man jerks upright, fists raised, eyes wild—pure instinct. The mother and daughter scramble to him, dropping to their knees to work the cuffs off his ankles.

I sweep the room, pulse ticking faster.

At the door, I scoop up the rifles, sling one over my shoulder, and chamber a round in the other. My watch glints in the low light.

Ten minutes.

I turn—and every set of eyes is on me.

The weight of expectation crushes my chest—thick, suffocating. They wait. For orders. Direction. Anything.

New Mom steps forward, hand extended.

"Barbara." Her grip stays firm, voice steady despite everything she's endured.

"Lyla," I reply, shaking her hand with a small nod.

She lets go and gestures toward the mousy woman, who stiffens under the attention, arms locked across her chest like a shield. "That's Jessica."

Jessica doesn't speak. Doesn't nod. Just studies me with wary, unreadable eyes.

Barbara shifts, motioning toward the older couple. "Earl and Edith."

Earl pulls me into a bear hug that knocks the air from my lungs. He releases me, but keeps his hands on my shoulders, deep brown eyes locking with mine. "Young lady, you have my deepest thanks. When we make it out of here, I'm treating you to dinner for the rest of our lives." He winks, earning an exasperated eye roll and a playful smack from Edith.

Barbara's hand sweeps toward the mother and daughter. "Clair and little Poppy."

Poppy clings to her mother's hand, lifting a small tentative wave. Clair's gaze softens. "I second what Earl said."

Silence settles, heavy and expectant.

Here we go.

"It's nice to meet you all, but we don't have much time. Who here's best with a gun?" My voice slices through the tension like a blade.

Earl and Barbara raise their hands without pause.

"Good." I hand them the rifles and extra magazines. Earl checks the chamber with practiced ease. Barbara grips hers like she was born for it.

I face the rest. "Search the cells. Grab anything you can use."

They scatter, urgency driving their steps. Chair legs. Pipes. It's not much—but it'll do. They return quickly, clutching their weapons with varying degrees of confidence.

Poppy clings to a hammer, arms locked to her chest, hands trembling.

I hand out extra knives from Lars's stash, keeping one for myself.

"Stay close." I scan each face. "If you see one of them—don't wait. Don't hesitate. They won't."

Nods ripple through the group, fear giving way to focus.

"For now, we wait for the signal."

I glance at my watch. Five minutes.

Clair tightens her grip on Poppy's hand, knuckles white. "You stay with me, okay?"

Poppy glances at me, worry etched in every line. She leans into her mom, voice a whisper. "What signal are we waiting for?"

I wink. "You'll see."

FIVE
RING OF FIRE

JACOB

WE MOVE FAST, hugging the perimeter. The compound sprawls larger than I anticipated, with wide-open spaces leaving us very little cover.

We weave between two small buildings, our boots silent on the dirt-packed ground. The air shifts—voices, sharp and agitated, slice through the quiet. I throw up a fist, signaling Leon to stop. We press ourselves against the wall, staying low, listening.

Two men pace near the entrance of a large metal shed.

"Man, I can't wait to have my turn with this batch," one grumbles, rolling his shoulders. His thick arms are littered with faded tattoos, his voice hoarse from years of chain-smoking.

The other guy scoffs. "Yeah, yeah. Just don't touch the mom. I call dibs on her." His lips twist showing off his gold grill. "She's got that fight in her—gonna be fun breakin' that."

My breath comes hard and fast, blood roaring in my ears. I turn to Leon to sign my plan to approach them from behind, but he is already marching around the corner, death in his eyes as his fist connects with the wiry guy's temple in a brutal arc, sending him into the shed. The man crumples into the dirt without so much as a groan.

I rush around the corner, hand snapping out and locking around the other man's throat as I press my knife against his side. He stiffens, a strangled noise escaping before I clamp his mouth shut. He starts to thrash, panic overtaking instinct.

"Quiet," I hiss into his ear, my tone low and lethal. The bastard quivers beneath my grip, his pulse hammering against my fingers as I dig my knife into the soft flesh of his arm. The metallic scent of blood fills the air, mingling with the damp musk of the shed. His breath comes in ragged gasps, eyes darting, searching for some miracle that won't come.

Behind me, the wet, sickening thud of knuckles meeting flesh echoes like a drumbeat. Leon straddles the other guard, fists a blur, turning his face into a shattered mess of blood and bone. Gurgled sounds spill from the man's throat as his gold teeth fly through the air, glinting in the sun.

The man flinches with every impact. I haul his rigid body backward into the shed and shove him into a rickety wooden chair that rattles beneath his weight. My boot slams between his legs, locking him in place, the knife still pressed to his arm.

"Let's make this simple," I crouch to his level. "How many people are in the facility?"

Leon's final punch lands with a wet crunch. A gurgle. Silence.

Out of the corner of my eye, Leon grabs the gas canister and walks out.

The man clenches his jaw so tight his teeth grind. His fists grip the armrests.

I tilt my head, a mocking smile curving my lips. "That wasn't a rhetorical question."

The blade glides up, pressing beneath his jaw. He swallows. A bead of sweat trails down his temple. Still silent.

Stupid mistake.

The knife slams down, pinning his hand to the armrest. My other hand clamps over his mouth, muffling the scream. His body jerks, the chair wobbling as blood pours from his wrist.

I lean in, breath brushing his ear. "You're gonna want to talk."

His eyes dart toward the shed door again, hope flickering in their depths like a dying ember.

I sigh, long and slow, shaking my head like this is all a damn inconvenience. "All right then."

Before he flinches, I rip the knife free and drive it into his left knee. The blade tears through skin, muscle, tendon—straight into bone. His body convulses, a strangled scream ripping into my palm. Blood spreads fast, soaking his pants in a dark bloom. He slumps in the chair, panting, eyes blown wide, skin draining to ash.

I pull my hand from his mouth and grip his jaw, forcing eye contact. "Speak."

"O-okay," he gasps, voice barely above a whisper. "Thirty . . . about thirty in the main building."

"And the hostages?"

His chest heaves. "They're in cell block A. Main building. Everyone's in the main building." He sucks in a wet breath, pain twisting his face. "Th-that's it, I swear."

"Good." I yank the knife free.

Blood drips thick and slow, pooling at the hilt before sliding over my fingers. I wipe it clean on his shirt. He crumples forward with a broken sob, shoulders quaking, spittle threading from the corners of his mouth, breath wet and shallow.

"See?" I pat his cheek, the smack echoing in the cramped space. "That wasn't so hard, was it?"

His glassy eyes lift to mine, a silent plea buried under the pain.

Leon's boots scrape behind me. He steps up beside me, drops the body like trash, then douses it in gas. The stench swells in the air, clinging to my skin, sinking into my clothes, my lungs.

Leon straightens, fingers twitching slightly before his eyes find mine. *"We good here?"*

I unclip the rope from my belt, my fingers moving on autopilot as I loop it around the bastard's ankles and wrists, pulling tight. He flinches but doesn't resist.

When the last knot is secured, I rise, meeting Leon's gaze. Leon arches a brow. I give a single nod.

He lights the match.

Flames roar to life with a hungry snap, racing the trail of gas like a fuse. Fire swells, curling up the shed's walls in greedy waves. Wood pops. Smoke thickens.

We turn for the exit. The weight in my chest eases—just a fraction—knowing we're one step closer to getting our people out.

"Hey! Hey! Wait! STOP!"

I don't slow. Don't speak. My grip tightens around the blade at my side, every step deliberate, controlled. Fury stays leashed—barely.

Behind us, the screams climb. Ragged. Choking. The fire answers louder.

We move, swift and silent, slipping through the shadows.

Outside the next building, we crouch low behind a rusted ATV, weapons drawn. Smoke curls skyward, thick and black. It'll bring them out. That, and the screams.

The shed's burning like a goddamn bonfire, flames clawing at the surrounding buildings, spreading fast across the dry grass. I keep my gun raised over the side of the ATV, waiting for the first face to appear. Beside me, Leon draws an arrow, calm as ever.

Boots crunch through the dirt.

"Shit! Fan out, check the perimeter!"

Three of them. First guy rounds the corner—barely registers the fire before I put a bullet through his forehead. He drops like a stone.

Leon's bow twangs. Second man stumbles, clutching the shaft sticking out of his throat before collapsing in a gasping heap.

The third turns to run. Smart. But not smart enough.

I rise, pivot, and fire twice. He hits the dirt, twitching.

Leon taps my arm and jabs two fingers toward the main building —more movement. The fire and gunfire did exactly what we wanted.

Doors slam open across the clearing.

More men spill out. Five, six—maybe more. One's got a sniper rifle and is heading for the guard tower.

Shit.

I motion to Leon—circle wide. He nods once, already rounding the burning shed, and disappears like smoke on the wind. I stay low, moving in the opposite direction. One shot, then another. Purposeful. Loud. Drawing their attention toward me.

Gunfire cracks the air as bullets whip too close to my chest. I drop flat, roll behind the transport bus, and return fire.

"Over here!" one of them shouts. "He's flanking left!"

Good.

Let them think I'm alone.

While they spread out toward me, Leon moves like a ghost, picking them off from behind. One guy gurgles and drops. The rest don't even notice.

I pop up, fire twice, then duck and sprint toward the building for cover.

They chase.

Idiots.

I spot Leon again through the flames—he raises a hand, motioning me to move.

I nod, then toss a rock toward the opposite side of the shed. It clatters, draws the sound chasers that way. Leon uses the distraction. He lunges out of the dark, silent and surgical—hatchet in one hand, bow slung over his back. Two go down before they can make a sound.

A figure crouches at the base—scope flashing in the sunlight, rifle slung tight to his back. If that sniper reaches the high ground, we're screwed.

Each heartbeat closes the distance. He's halfway up the ladder, boots scraping metal.

I lunge, grab his ankle, yank hard.

He slams back-first against the ladder, metal echoing like a gong. His hands flail, boots kicking—but I'm already on him, machete in hand.

One jab under the ribs—clean, silent.

He goes still.

I cock the rifle and move toward the fire. Leon's already in motion, arrows cutting through the smoke. Two bodies hit the ground before I reach them. I zero in on the last man. He turns just in time for my bullet to punch through his chest.

Smoke curls through the clearing. The fire's still raging. But the ground's quiet again.

Bodies everywhere.

Leon emerges from the shadows, wiping blood on his sleeve. He meets my eyes, then flicks his head toward the building.

We move in tandem, fast and low, toward the entrance. Guns up. Breaths steady.

Then something shifts.

A low, rhythmic thump cuts through the silence—deep, pulsing, carried on the wind like an afterthought.

I stop dead. My head tilts, straining to catch it beneath the roaring blaze. It doesn't belong here, doesn't fit, yet something about it claws at my memory.

"What the hell?" The words slip from my lips, barely more than a breath.

Leon stiffens beside me. His gaze locks ahead, fixed on the front gate. Brows furrowed. Mouth parted. Hands start to move.

"Is that the Ramones?"

I barely have time to process before a bright yellow Hummer bursts from the tree line, barreling down the dirt road like a battering ram. Dust churns in its wake, swallowing the headlights in a thick haze. My pulse slams against my ribs.

No. Fucking. Way.

The Hummer plows forward with single-minded ferocity, aimed directly at the front gate. Then—*impact.*

Metal shrieks, groaning under the force as the steel gate crumples inward, twisted beams snapping in half. The sound is deafening, an unholy mix of grinding metal and shattering glass. The chain-link fence warps, parts of it torn from the posts, flailing wildly in the wake of destruction. Shards of steel slice through the air, embedding into the dirt with deadly force.

I jerk forward, hand flying to my sidearm—then I see her.

A young girl grips the steering wheel. Her face—equal parts steel and recklessness—screams inexperience, the kind that charges straight into danger without understanding the cost.

But she's not alone.

My gaze shifts.

Blood chills.

They follow. Dozens—no, more. A seething, writhing surge of rot and rage crashes forward, bodies slamming into each other in blind pursuit. Flesh dangles in shredded ribbons, torn by time, by teeth, by death's steady hand. Some sprint, limbs flailing wild, broken bones jutting like blades. Others drag ruined legs, jaws locked open in endless, silent screams.

The air thickens with snarls—wet, guttural, ravenous.

A sick twist coils deep in my gut as the Hummer tears through the compound, its tires chewing up the dirt, its battered frame rattling with violent momentum. The undead pour in behind it, a relentless, unstoppable wave, tumbling over the ruined gate, bodies smashing together in a desperate bid to reach fresh meat.

She's a twisted piper of the apocalypse, and we're standing squarely in her path.

SIX

HEY HO, LET'S GO!

THE OPENING CHORDS of the Ramones detonate across the compound. Each drumbeat slams through my veins, syncing with the adrenaline surging under my skin.

"Now!" I shout, voice lost in the storm.

We burst from the hallway, fury and desperation wrapped in flesh and grit. Chaos reigns—guards yelling, boots thundering over concrete. We move through the bedlam like smoke, slipping past blind spots, striking hard and fast, taking advantage of their divided attention.

Earl's rifle cracks, the single, deadly shot dropping a guard midstep. Barbara rushes ahead, blade punching deep into a man's side. He writhes, clutching the wound, scream swallowed by the pulsing bass. She doesn't flinch, but instead snaps up her rifle and starts firing.

Hell yes. *Let's go!*

I lunge, knife flashing before it buries deep into the throat of the man on my left. His gurgling choke vibrates against my blade, blood pooling around my fingers. I rip it free, already turning as another lunges. I slash across his throat—clean and fast. Arterial spray streaks the wall.

To my left, a burly guard grabs for Clair. She spins, pipe cracking against his ribs with a sickening thud. He doubles over—gasping. Poppy strikes, her hammer slamming into his shin. Bone cracks. He screams, his knee buckling, and Poppy swings again.

Clair brings the pipe down onto his skull, the wet crunch of bone shattering under the force. He drops like a stone.

Another man charges—a blur of rage and muscle wrapped in tattered camo, but I reach him first. My knife buries deep in his gut. He folds around it.

Behind me, Jessica stands frozen beside Edith, her shoulders locked with fear. A guard lunges at them, snarl curling his lips—

Edith moves.

Her knife flashes, steel driving into his throat with brutal force. His eyes bulge, a garbled choke slipping past his lips as he crashes to the floor, twitching as blood pools beneath him.

She bends down, yanks the blade free, wipes it on her pants, then looks up and grins like we're at a Sunday barbecue.

"Took notes from your fight with that fat man on the bus. Thanks, sweetie!" She winks and shuffles behind Earl, who's reloading like he's done it every day of his life.

Who the *hell* are these people?

Barbara fires. Her rifle kicks, the shot punching clean through a guard's skull. He drops.

The path to the main office opens.

"Move!" I bark, waving the others forward.

Barbara and Earl flank me, rifles up, eyes like stone. Clair keeps Poppy close, her grip tight around the girl's hand. Jessica and Edith hold the rear—tense, alert, teeth clenched like they're ready to bite someone.

We're bloodied, bruised, barely standing, but . . .

A smile tugs at my lips. We're having fun. Well, most of us are.

The twisted truth sinks in—pride and grief curling in my chest like smoke.

I think I found my people.

Too bad I won't see them again.

Joanie's face flashes in my mind—that wild, reckless grin, the fire in her eyes, the sharp snap of her voice when she calls me an idiot.

The ache spreads deep, hollow and sharp.

I won't see her again either.

But there's no room for regret.

I shove it down and press forward. One step. Then another. The future can wait. I've got a job to finish.

The warden's office door looms ahead, a final threshold, a promise of whatever hell waits on the other side.

I grab Barbara's arm and yank her toward me. "Listen," I shout, cutting through the gunfire and distant, hungry moans.

Her eyes snap to mine—wild, sharp, lit with adrenaline. Fingers white-knuckled around her rifle. Breath ragged.

"You need to get them to safety." My voice slices through the noise, each word clipped and biting. "Take everyone. Head for the entrance. Save your ammo for the infected. Look for Joanie—she'll be in the yellow Hummer. Flag her down and give her the code word: Romero. She'll know. Tell her I said to get everyone out."

Her lips part. The protest builds.

I tighten my grip. "Tell her I'll meet you at the safe house."

A lie. But it lands clean.

Barbara's jaw clenches. Breath hisses through her teeth.

I ease—just a fraction. "*Please*. I need you to do this."

"All right," she says. Voice tight, trembling, but steady enough. She turns to the others like a switch flipped—snapping into command. "You heard her. Let's move!"

The group follows without question, ducking between bodies

and bullets, slipping into the smoke like ghosts. Some glance back. Confused. Hesitant. Waiting for me to fall in line.

I don't.

Then there's Poppy.

She pauses. Turns. Hazel eyes lock on mine. She lifts a small hand and gives a small wave.

The simple gesture hits harder than a bullet.

I nod, fist curling tight at my side. *Please, let them make it.*

I face the door. Fingers tighten around the knife. Each breath drags deeper. Rage coils with fear, winding tighter around my ribs, my chest, my heart, until I feel like I might explode.

Mark's face flashes. That carefree grin. Those warm, hazel eyes. The memory punches the air from my lungs.

A chair scrapes behind the door.

Someone hums. Slow. Rhythmic. Tapping in time with the distant pulse of the Ramones.

One breath.

Another.

The knife bites into my palm.

I kick the door open.

The impact cracks like thunder. Wood splinters. Hinges shriek. The force shudders through the room. Candles gutter. Shadows leap, stretching jagged shapes across the battered desk and yellowed maps.

There he is, planted behind the warden's desk like a king on his rotting throne. At ease, like he's been expecting me. A twisted smile creeps across his face. It crawls like mold over wet stone.

No flinch. No surprise. Not even a blink.

He leans back, soaked in smug calm. Fingers fold over his stomach. Every inch of him a mockery.

"Well, well."

The voice slides over my skin, slow and smug, every syllable oozing with condescension.

"If it isn't the infamous Agent Matthews."

He says it like a joke. Like my name's the punchline.

My pulse hammers harder.

Head tilts. He drinks in the moment like it's his last meal.

"I was wondering when you'd show up."

SEVEN

THE ARTIST

LYLA

NAUSEA CRASHES through me as the walls close in.

Paintings cover every inch—women bound and broken, frozen midscream. Crimson streaks glisten in the dim light, thick and raw, smeared with surgical cruelty. The air hangs heavy with iron, the stench of dried blood soaked into the canvas.

Faces twisted in agony. Eyes stretched wide in silent, unanswered pleas. Every brushstroke, a crime scene. Every smear, a confession. Bodies contorted and tied in positions no human should endure—rendered in sick, meticulous detail.

Not art.

A shrine. A temple of suffering.

My pulse pounds, visions slamming into my skull, unrelenting.

Case files. Names. Faces.

I know these women. Studied them. Searched for them. Looked into the hollow-eyed stares of their parents, their friends, their lovers—all of them grasping at hope only to be destroyed with another found body.

And here they are.

Reduced to brushstrokes and blood.

My hands ball into fists, nails digging into my palms so hard I half expect to bleed. The bastard didn't just take their lives. He made them his legacy.

Rage coils in my chest. Thick. Suffocating. Bile burns my throat. *Not here. Not now. Not in front of him.*

"Admiring my exhibit?" His voice slices through the suffocating silence, smooth as silk yet oozing with malice. It's a voice that revels in the power it holds.

He sits behind the desk, dressed in black. The fabric hugs his lean frame, tailored to perfection. Fingers tap the armrest—steady, patient. A countdown in motion.

His face is a contradiction—sharp, almost elegant, high cheekbones carved like a sculpture, a jawline that could cut glass. The kind of beauty that deceives. The kind that makes you lean in—right before the teeth sink in. No wonder they followed him.

But the eyes ruin it. Empty. Measured. Storm colored and inhuman.

"I've been wondering . . ." His voice lilts, light, amused. Like he's talking about a wine vintage. Not murder. Not mutilation. Fingers flick toward the paintings. "What your face would look like when you saw my masterpieces."

His teeth flash as he tilts his head, watching me as if my every breath, my every flicker of emotion, is a note in a song only he can hear.

"What do you think?"

The grotesque portraits leer from the walls—twisted faces frozen in agony, every detail carved into memory. I scan them once more, then shrug.

"Amateur at best."

His smile falters, just for a heartbeat, a tiny twitch at the corner of his mouth. But I see it. Satisfaction blooms in my chest, even as I brace for the counterstrike.

He leans forward, fingers laced, chin resting on the cage of his hands. Soft. Calculated. "Would you feel the same if you were looking at your partner's painting?"

Breath locks in my chest. The room shrinks.

He tilts his head. That scalpel stare slices straight through me. Precise. Premeditated. A surgeon dissecting fear.

"Too bad I didn't have time to gather my materials," he adds, tossing a wink like a match into gasoline.

Rage ignites—fast, blistering. My fingers clamp the knife. Muscles wind tight. The name detonates behind my eyes.

Mark.

His blood. His broken body. The unblinking stillness of his eyes.

I swallow the fury, let it settle like burning coal—hot, contained, feeding something colder. The mask holds, edges honed to razors.

"I don't see your latest victim here." I don't see a portrait of the last woman he killed, the one that brought me to this state in the first place. The one who led me to Virginia.

He hesitates, calculating. "She was a surprise."

"That's it?" I scoff. Maybe I can goad him into a confession just to make sure she was really one of his. "You love the sound of your own voice. Surprised you're not begging to describe every sick detail."

He grins. "Now that I have your full attention, I guess I'm speechless."

Sick son of a bitch.

"I only wanted *your* attention, Agent Matthews," he says, voice dipping into something soft, worshipful. His gaze slides over me— slow, dragging. "You're my muse."

"You're sick." The words snap loose, trembling with rage that coils tighter, begging to be unleashed. I hold my ground, spine straight, breath sharp. He feeds off reaction—I won't give him that.

Not yet.

I tilt my chin, voice cool as steel. "You and your little art club— Monet, van Gogh, Pollock, Dalí—you stole their names to mask what you are. Frauds. They thought they were untouchable too. But they all bled." The knife bites into my palm, grip locked tight. "Just like you will."

He hums, smooth on the surface, but there's a hitch beneath it. "So. What happens now, Agent Matthews?"

His head tilts, studying me like a puzzle he hasn't quite solved.

"You've already torn apart my little kingdom here." He waves at the door, as if the carnage outside is nothing more than a minor inconvenience. "Is this where you kill me? If so, I must say . . ." His brow lifts, faux casual. He reclines, steepling his fingers in mock calm —but his knuckles blanch, fingertips white. "I won't make it easy."

I let the silence stretch, watch the way his pupils contract just slightly, and enjoy the moment before I shatter his world.

I step forward until my legs press against the desk. My voice drops, low and lethal. "I was counting on it . . . *Franklin.*"

The name lands like a gunshot, clean and sharp.

His eyes flare—just for a second—before the mask slams back into place.

I smile. Sharp. Knowing. Cruel. "Didn't see that coming, did you, Frankie?"

His composure cracks. Rage bleeds into his features as he struggles to keep it together.

"You didn't think I'd dig up your real name?" My voice slices through the space between us. His jaw locks. Fingers twitch, hungry for a weapon. "Lucky me that two years of chasing and researching gave me the answer I was waiting for—right before the world fell to hell. I admit, you hid your tracks well."

His shoulders coil, tension winding tighter with every word.

"When I learned your actual name was Franklin Schmidt. I'll admit . . . I felt a little *disappointed.*"

I stalk around the desk, a wolf closing in. He stays seated, but I see it in his eyes—he's the one cornered now.

My fingers trail the wood. Nails tap a slow rhythm, taunting as I round the corner. "To share a name with a man who dressed up in women's clothes to commit murder?"

His nostrils flare.

I drop my voice to a whisper, piercing and intimate. "What. A. Shame."

Rage curdles in his eyes—humiliation twisted into something feral.

I step into his space, forcing him to tilt his head to meet mine.

"Tell me, Franklin," I murmur, voice soaked in mock concern. "Do *you* have mommy issues too?"

His jaw tics. Shoulders lock. Fists curl.

I straighten, letting the derision drip from my voice as I drive the final nail in. "What a cliché you turned out to be."

His face contorts into something feral as he lunges, a letter opener flashing in his grip. I sidestep the opener, but his other arm swings up and catches me in my jaw, sending me backward. The desk slams into my ribs like a battering ram, driving the air from my lungs in a violent gasp.

He vaults the desk. Canvases crash, smeared faces raining around us.

My knife arcs up. Metal kisses his arm—crimson blooms. He grunts but keeps coming. His hand clamps around my wrist. The twist is brutal—white-hot pain flares through my arm. My grip shatters.

The blade falls.

My other hand snatches it middrop. I twist. Drive the steel into his thigh.

It sinks deep.

His roar shreds the air—raw, guttural. His knee slams into my gut, a wrecking ball to my ribs.

I hit the floor hard. Vision blurs. Black creeps in.

He crashes down, pinning me between his legs. My spine slams against the concrete. Breath gone.

Pain detonates in my skull—his fist crushes my eye, then my jaw. Stars explode. Ears ring. Another blow, then hands clamp around my throat.

He squeezes.

My nails dig into his wrists, clawing, scraping, trying to tear him off. Spots bloom in my vision, the edges darkening, creeping inward.

His eyes gleam—wild, certain. He thinks it's over.

My fingers scramble wildly against the floor, searching, desperate. Cold. Metal. My fingers close around it and I drive it upward, feeling it tear through fabric, skin, and muscle.

He jerks, a strangled sound ripping from his throat. His grip breaks. I roll, coughing, gasping. Air crashes back into my lungs.

He writhes, clutching his side—letter opener embedded, blood soaking his shirt.

Then I see it.

My knife, still in his leg.

I lunge and rip it free.

I push to unsteady feet, blood-slicked fingers tightening around the hilt of my knife. My ribs ache with each inhale, but I don't take my eyes off him.

He stumbles up, hand pressed to his side. Blood seeps through his fingers, dripping in thick, sluggish trails down his shirt.

I move.

Fast. Precise.

The blade slashes his chest. He grunts, slamming back into the desk before his knees buckle, sending him crashing to the floor. Blood spreads beneath him, a dark, glistening pool against the faded linoleum.

A glint of silver—a flash of motion.

Pain erupts through my side.

I suck in a sharp breath, a cry ripping from my throat as the blade bites deep into my abdomen. Fire explodes through my nerves, the wound burning hot and merciless.

The world tilts.

No.

I stay up. I won't fall.

He lunges again, but I'm faster.

Not today, fucker.

I pivot and drive the knife into his chest. The sound—wet, final.

His body jerks. Breath catches. A silent gasp freezes on his lips. Fingers twitch, reaching—then fall limp. His arm drops.

I twist the knife.

He crumples. A puppet with cut strings. Blood spills fast, mixing with mine, soaking through fabric, seeping into skin. Heat presses down, thick and suffocating. Smoke slithers through the air, its acrid scent stinging my nose.

Where did the fire come from?

The knife slips from my grasp, clattering uselessly onto the blood-slick floor. The room spins. My breath stutters. A sharp, shallow inhale. A wheezing exhale. I blink down at the blade still embedded in my flesh, the handle jutting from my side. My fingers twitch at my side, useless. My knees hit the ground first, the impact rattling through my bones before I collapse fully, landing just inches from Franklin's corpse.

My vision wobbles, the edges swimming, curling inward like burnt paper. My pulse slows, every beat sluggish, my body sinking into the growing void. I take a small piece of paper out of my back pocket, softened by my hands and time, and drop it on his chest.

It's over.

He's dead.

But something's off.

A gut-deep unease coils in my stomach, a glimmer of doubt scraping against my exhaustion.

I force my head to turn, muscles sluggish, my body heavy with blood loss. My gaze lands on Franklin's still form, his lifeless eyes staring up at the ceiling. His chest unmoving. Or is it—

Instinct gnashes at the edges of consciousness. Something's not right.

I strain, try to rise—nothing. Limbs deadweight. Blood soaks into the floor beneath me.

The room tilts. Darkness creeps closer.

I sink into the growing pool of my own blood.

I'll just take a little nap right here. Yeah. On this nice, sticky, blood-soaked floor. Perfect spot. Real cozy. Then I'll get up. Make sure he's dead. Crawl out. Save the day. Great plan. Solid.

That's the lie I cling to—until I hear footsteps.

Fast.

Urgent.

A shadow appears in the doorway, blurred and indistinct, rushing toward me. A voice slices through the haze.

"Lyla! Hang on!"

Barbara?

Hands grip my arms, lifting, dragging me through the slick mess. I slump against her shoulder, my body limp, every nerve screaming but too tired to fire. My cheek presses against the warmth of her collarbone—steady, alive—but my mouth won't move. The words burn in my throat, trapped.

No. No, wait. He's—

The world sways. Colors smear like paint in water. Darkness curls at the edges, creeping in with greedy fingers.

Then—

A sound.

A breath.

Faint. Almost imperceptible.

A sharp, rasping inhale.

The world goes dark.

EIGHT
THEY'RE COMING TO GET YOU, BARBARA!

JACOB

SHE TEARS through the courtyard like a demon unleashed, Hummer tires shrieking, gravel and dirt kicking up in a blinding storm. Music blasts from the stereo—louder than the flames, louder than the undead's guttural groans. It's a chaotic symphony of rebellion, her laughter slicing through the madness.

Flames leap higher, adding to the already blazing summer heat, consuming the buildings in the courtyard's perimeter. Smoke billows, dark and choking, shrouding the scene in a haze of destruction. The horde surges after her, a writhing mass of rot and snapping jaws.

Their bodies are in various grotesque stages of decay—skin hanging in tatters, bones exposed, eyes clouded yet locked on their target with horrifying focus. The stench hits like a punch to the gut, a rancid mix of decomp and death carried on the hot wind. Groans rise into a chorus of hunger, clawed hands grasping just inches from her as the Hummer whips out of reach.

Beside me, Leon watches the scene with a bemused shake of his head. He signs, *"Gutsy kid."*

"More like crazy," I mutter, though the edge in my voice carries something closer to respect. Reckless, sure. But it's working. The distraction is perfect. Still—*why* the hell is she here?

Men pour out of the building, shouting and firing. The girl jerks the wheel and swings the Hummer wide, cracking shots from her window. Her hair streams like a war banner, the courtyard her battleground.

Gunfire flares. Muzzle flashes light up the smoke. Bullets slam into the infected, others ping off the Hummer's reinforced frame.

The vehicle swings wide, its tires screeching against the pavement as the girl circles the courtyard like a predator. Every bullet finds a mark—one man drops, screaming, blood pouring from his thigh before an infected in a shredded navy suit tackles him and bites into his neck. Another takes a bullet to the shoulder, his gun spinning away. A third, rat tail and all, drops like a stone, shot clean through the skull. More and more fall, crumpling to the ground as she carves a path of destruction.

We move fast, low, dodging corpses already bitten. Minutes, maybe less, before they rise and join the hunt. Fire crackles behind us, heat licking my back as we close in on the rear of the group.

I raise my handgun. Target locked. One clean shot, center mass. He drops to his knees with a strangled cry, fingers clawing his chest before going still. Undead mechanics still in their coveralls swarm him, making quick work of tearing his flesh from his body.

Beside me, Leon moves with effortless precision. He nocks an arrow, the bowstring singing as he releases. The shot punches a man's eye socket, dropping him before he can even turn.

More infected pour through the breach, dozens, limbs twitching with unnatural speed. Milky, bloodshot eyes lock on to us, their rotting faces contorted with insatiable hunger. Then they sprint.

"Shit." I raise my gun.

The first one's fast. Its mouth stretches open, blackened teeth snapping, decayed fingers reaching. I shoot and its skull explodes like a popped balloon. Brain and bone splatter across the pavement.

"They're fast today." I reload.

Leon looses another arrow. It slices a woman's neck, her long black braid bouncing, but she doesn't slow.

"So, he *does* miss sometimes," I mutter. I lift my pistol and drop a bullet clean through the forehead of a bloated jail guard, walkie dangling from his belt.

Leon looks over. Brow raised as though saying, *Oh really?* Without breaking eye contact, he draws and releases. The bowstring thrums. A thud follows. Black-haired woman collapses, arrow buried deep in her eye socket.

Leon flicks imaginary lint off his jacket with his middle finger. I bark a laugh and fire again, chest thrumming with adrenaline. God, I love this fucked-up life sometimes.

The horde peels away from the Hummer, drawn to easier prey—the men still outside the doors. Gunfire's got them rattled, fear making them clumsy. They're scrambling to fall back inside.

If they make it, we're screwed. Our people won't get out.

A shadow flickers, peripheral movement. A man rounds the corner, rifle raised—

Leon moves first.

He lunges, hatchet flashing in the firelight. The blade cuts deep into the side of the man's skull, bone cracking under steel. A sharp gasp escapes his lips before Leon yanks the blade free, sending a fresh spray of crimson onto the ground. The man slumps, eyes already glassing over.

I step over it. Boots crunch through blood-slick dirt. Every sense is razor sharp.

Another shape stumbles into view.

Its face is a grotesque ruin, strips of flesh peeling from its cheeks, jaw slack, milky eyes locked on to mine. It snarls—wet, guttural, hungry—and lunges. It jerks, fingers twitching, grasping blindly. I twist, bone scraping against steel as I rip it free.

It drops.

But more are coming.

They shamble through the slits in the fence, one after another, locked on to the scent of fresh meat. No question who cut those gaps.

Is she here for our people?

Fire rips higher behind us. Whatever Leon rigged, it's working.

The Hummer keeps circling, tires kicking up gravel and ash as she fires sporadically. She's shouting now, taunting the men who try, and fail, to aim at her. There's something wild about her, almost joyful, like she's feeding off the madness.

And honestly? I get it as I take my pistol and start firing at the last few men blocking my path. There's a strange liberation in the wreckage.

The entrance looms ahead, the heavy doors forced wide open. The fight's spilled into the yard—blood, smoke, teeth. But the men aren't retreating.

Wait.

Is that—

Earl rushes out the doors, rifle clipping, his face focused as he drops a guard and two infected women in matching hot-pink track suits in quick succession. Edith follows, blade swinging, eyes locked on an undead reaching for Earl. One quick slice—head gone. The head separates cleanly, black blood spraying as the body collapses in a twitching heap at their feet.

Further back, Jessica and Clair fight side by side, their movements jerky as they swing to keep the undead at bay with Poppy crouched between them. Jessica's pipe caves in a skull. Clair's knife stabs fast and clean. Blood sprays. Bodies fall.

Poppy grips her hammer with both hands and slams it into an

infected's leg. It lurches, Clair finishes the job, blade through the temple. Brain matter hits the dirt.

How *the fuck* did they get out? *Where* did they get weapons?

"Get to them!" My shout rips from my throat, smoke coating the words. I point, and Leon yanks an arrow from a corpse's skull, his gaze snapping to Clair and Poppy, determination blazing in his eyes.

We charge forward, blades and bullets clearing a path. One step at a time. Through fire. Through blood. Through hell.

A pack of well-dressed undead seniors lurch into our path, sagging flesh, mouths gaping wide with hunger. I slash and shove, blade cutting through brittle bone, each strike fueled by desperation.

Leon's hatchet cleaves through a neck. He kicks the body aside, already raising his bow. The arrow flies, punching into the skull of an infected inches from Clair and Poppy.

"Keep going, you Legolas badass!" I yell, jamming my blade through another skull as it lunges.

Leon surges ahead, locked in. His eyes snap between the horde and Clair. Another arrow whistles, spearing an infected woman in a checkered red dress. She crumples just as her claws swipe for Poppy's arm. The girl flinches but doesn't stop, her small blade stabbing a twisted leg. Jessica smashes her pipe into the infected's skull, bone crunching loud.

The horde thickens, flooding through fence gaps like a tidal wave. The air is thick with the stench of death and smoke, every breath burning my lungs.

I swing again. Again. Blade sinking into flesh, splintering bone. Blood sprays, ours, theirs, doesn't matter. No time to think. No time to process. Only move.

"Edith!" My voice cuts through flame and moans.

Her eyes meet mine—relief, fleeting—before she spins, blade slamming into a guard's chest. The spear clatters from his hand.

She shouts something, my name, maybe, but the horde swallows it whole.

Earl fights beside her, blade flashing, face streaked with sweat and black blood, his graying hair matted, soaked red.

Leon's arm whips back. He hurls the hatchet. It spins once—twice—buries itself deep in a sprinting corpse's forehead that was about to chomp down on Clair's exposed arm. Its legs fold midstride, its body hitting the ground in a twisted heap.

He reaches them and yanks Clair into his chest just as an infected crashes down inches from her, clawed fingers slashing empty air. Jessica slams her pipe into its skull.

Clair's breath stutters, chest rising and falling in quick, frantic bursts. She turns and locks eyes with Leon, both sharing a look of terror and relief.

Poppy stumbles, her small frame folding from exhaustion. Leon catches her before she hits the ground, steady, firm, careful. She blinks up at him, hazel eyes wide, stunned. He motions for them to follow.

Another one charges. Leon pivots, arrow already nocked.

The body drops at their feet, a wooden shaft buried deep in its eye. Clair exhales, scoops Poppy up. The girl clutches her mother's bloodstained shirt, knife dangling from weak, trembling fingers.

"Get them to Trish!" I shout through the gunfire.

Leon hesitates for a fraction of a second, just long enough for me to see the war in his eyes. He doesn't want to leave. Doesn't want to abandon me. But he nods, jaw tight, and grips Clair's arm, steering them toward the fence.

I shove Earl and Edith after them, urgency coiled in my gut. "Edith, where is—"

Movement.

My stomach knots. Instinct slams through me.

I turn—

And the world sharpens to a single point.

A figure slips into the building, darting through the smoke and pandemonium. Jessica follows close behind, arms reaching, trying to stop her.

Mom.

The ground might as well vanish. My pulse hammers, drowning everything—the gunfire, the screams, the groans.

She's alive.

And she's running straight back into hell.

NINE
A MEET CUTE?

JACOB

THEY DISAPPEAR INTO A ROOM AHEAD, smoke curling through the doorway like a living thing. I burst through after them, and the outside chaos pales compared to what waits inside.

Mom crouches in the center, gripping an unconscious, bloodied body, struggling to drag her toward me. Sweat streaks her face, eyes wild with raw determination.

A second body lies sprawled nearby, male, lifeless, his form twisted unnaturally on the floor. Jessica stands beside them, caught between frustration and panic, voice raised over the roaring fire and distant screams.

"Barbara, leave her!" she shouts, coughing, eyes darting to the groaning walls as flames lick the edges. "We don't have time! She's a lost cause!"

Mom spins toward me. "Jacob! Help me! We can't leave her!"

Her face stops me cold.

Bruises bloom across Mom's cheekbone and jaw like dark accusations. A cut near her temple bleeds into the lines of exhaustion carved into her skin. My chest tightens. Rage flares white-hot.

I'm going to find the bastard who did this and peel the flesh from his bones until he begs for mercy.

I reach out to her, but Jessica steps into my path, her fingers clamping on to my arm with surprising strength.

"Jacob, listen." Her voice rushes out fast. "She's done. If we stay, we die. You can't save her—she'll only slow us down."

Mom turns, fury blazing in her eyes. "If it weren't for her, none of us would still be breathing! We owe her this—we owe her everything!"

Jessica freezes, mouth open to argue, but I push past her, eyes locked on Mom and the woman she's desperately trying to pull from the fire. I drop low, grab the woman under her arms, careful to avoid the switchblade jutting from her side.

Shit.

She stirs as I lift, her head lolling against Mom's shoulder. One ice-blue eye cracks open, paralyzing me in place. Blood streaks down her face and trickles out the corner of her mouth—still curved in a grin. Mischief twinkles behind the pain.

"Hello, gorgeous," she murmurs, voice smoky, low, and edged with something playful. "I'd fight off a horde just to see that face. Whaddya say, want to go out sometime?"

I blink.

She's bleeding out, semiconscious, clinging to life—and she's flirting?

"See? Delirious. Too much blood loss," Jessica spits.

Mom whirls, snapping with that fire I grew up fearing. "Shut it!"

The woman lets out a weak, breathy laugh that crumbles into a harsh fit of coughing. Blood spatters across her already ruined shirt as she slumps harder against Mom.

She locks those wild, unfocused eyes on to mine, her lips curving, "I call 'em like I see 'em," she rasps, the words slurring together. "What would you call me?"

The answer slips out before I can stop it, along with the smile spreading across my face. "Trouble."

Her grin widens. More blood spills down her chin. And God help me—I'm turned on.

What the hell is wrong with me?

Then her head tips back, eyes rolling shut as she crumples. I lunge just in time to catch her before she hits the floor. She's dead weight, heavy and limp, her warmth bleeding into my hands.

"We have to go!" Jessica barks, slicing through the moment.

"She saved us." Mom's voice is steel, cutting through the havoc. I haven't heard that tone since the night she dragged me home after the cops found me drinking in the school parking lot.

Her eyes lock on mine. "If we leave her, you might as well leave me too. I'd be dead without her."

Well. Fuck.

When she puts it like that—

I shift my grip and haul the woman over my shoulder, same as I've done with too many others.

Her head rests against my back. Her blood soaks through my shirt, hot against my skin. Time's running out.

I yank my machete free, grip tightening as I stalk past Jessica, boots scraping over blood-slick concrete.

"We're not leaving her." My tone is final. No debate.

Jessica stiffens, arms crossed, frustration etched deep. I brace for the argument—but she just exhales, shakes her head, and heads for the exit.

Mom falls in beside me, pulling my pistols from their holsters.

"You know," she mutters, flipping a safety off, "sometimes, I really want to punch that girl in the face."

A short laugh escapes me. "You know, that's exactly what you said before you decked Aunt Jill on New Year's." I raise an eyebrow.

"Well," she says, tucking a pistol into her waistband, "she asked if my resolution was to lose weight. I'd say she deserved it, don't you?"

"Hell yes."

Mom cocks the second pistol. "Let's move."

I nod, tightening my hold on the woman's legs.

As we leave the office behind, I murmur low, just for her, "Hold on, Trouble."

Smoke claws at my throat, thick and acrid. Every breath scorches like fire.

Her breath is a whisper against my back, each rise and fall shallow. If she stops breathing, if she—

A sharp pinch on my ass snaps me out of the downward spiral.

"Nice view," she mutters, her voice slurred and hazy before she slips back into unconsciousness.

Of course she'd cop a feel while bleeding out.

A laugh slips out, dry and disbelieving. "Down, girl," I mumble, shifting my grip as I charge forward.

We explode out of the building, open air slamming into me. For a split second, it feels like salvation—until reality crashes back in.

Screams tear through the air, a mixture of human and inhuman, gunfire punching through the madness. The fire rages higher, its glow casting shadows across the gore-soaked ground.

Near the entrance, Leon, Earl, and Edith stand ready. Heads snap toward us, their eyes locking on the bloodied, unconscious woman hanging from my shoulder.

Edith waves us forward, blade gleaming, soaked. Her other arm slices through the air in sharp, frantic signals.

"Where's Clair and Poppy?" Mom shouts, her gun still smoking from the last shot.

"They're with Trish! We came back to help!" Edith yells.

The roar of the horde closes in, swelling like a crashing wave.

Earl pumps his fist in the air. "Let's go!"

We bolt. The ground beneath us vibrates with the relentless pursuit of the dead. Their groans turn to shrieks as they pick up speed. The air shifts—a clawed hand swipes at me, fingers grazing my back.

Mom fires beside me, her gun kicking back, the sharp cracks ringing. Every pull of the trigger drops another rotting corpse, but for every one that falls, three more push forward, climbing over their own to reach us.

Leon bursts ahead. His hatchet rips through flesh, bone, cartilage—clearing a path one corpse at a time. Blood splashes wide, hot and wet. A severed hand hits the dirt near my boot.

The others form a barrier around me and the woman, weapons raised, bodies tense.

The woods loom ahead, the jagged gap in the fence barely visible through the shifting sea of rotting bodies.

"Stay tight! Move as one!" I shout, every muscle straining, adrenaline burning through the fatigue.

A blur lunges at Leon, rotted skin, snapping jaws, clawing hands.

He spins, hatchet already swinging. Bone cracks. The blade sinks deep. He yanks it free, turns, and buries it in the next one.

Mom's gunfire is relentless, each shot ringing out in brutal succession. Empty shells hit the ground. She switches to pistols, movements smooth despite the trembling in her fingers.

The gap narrows.

"Go, go, go!" she yells.

We crash through the opening, the horde's rancid breath nipping at our heels. Branches tear at my skin, leaves lash my face as we hit the tree line at full speed.

Then, like a beacon through the nightmare, the vehicles come into view.

Atop the ER van, Trish stands, rifle raised, legs braced. Her shots are lethal, every bullet a lifeline.

She catches sight of us, and despite the undead and the sheer insanity of this day, her lips pull into a fierce grin.

"No guts, no glory!" she shouts.

To her left, Clair and Poppy work from the back of the truck bed. Clair fires at will, while Poppy stands beside her, ready to hand over a fresh clip.

"I see you finally found your inner Hicks, Jacob!" Trish calls, voice riding the gunfire like a battle cry.

I flip her off without breaking stride.

Her wild laughter rings out over the pop, pop, pop of her gun.

The van door's already open. With a grunt, I lower the woman onto the stretcher.

Her chest rises in shallow, wheezing breaths, each one sounding more like a struggle than a victory. Her forehead glistens with sweat, her blond hair drenched with blood.

Trish scrambles down from the roof and her eyes widen the moment she sees the woman. "Hot damn." She reaches for an IV, hands moving with experience.

The front doors slam and Leon slides behind the wheel, Mom in the passenger seat.

"Are the others okay?" I ask.

Leon nods, motioning, *"Earl's driving the others. Hold tight."*

He kicks the engine on and we peel out, the wheels kicking up dust as we leave the compound behind, the roar of the undead fading into the distance. The van jolts and bumps along the forest floor, the suspension groaning with every uneven stretch.

My knees jam into the stretcher as we lurch. Trish crouches, hooking up the IV.

"Blood and fluids," she mutters, more to herself than anyone else. She pulls the other end of the tubing, her gaze flicking to me. "All right, O neg. Show me your veins."

I shove up my sleeve. "Have at it."

The needle stings as it slides into my arm. My eyes stay locked on the woman's face. Her cracked lips still curve in that faint, reckless smile, even though she's comatose.

The van hits a pothole, jostling us both. "Careful, Leon!" Trish snaps as she steadies the IV. Blood fills the tubing, snaking toward her arm.

Then—headlights.

A blur of yellow swerves into view. Leon slams the brakes. The van jerks to a stop, tires screaming. The smoking Hummer skids to a crooked halt. Music cuts off.

The driver's door swings open.

A teenage girl with dark, curly hair jumps out of the destroyed vehicle, gun raised, her eyes scanning us. She hurries to the back of the van but before she can grab the door handle, I kick it open. Gun raised while keeping the IV untangled.

She doesn't flinch. Her stance shifts, weapon trained, eyes hard. "Where is she?" she demands, scanning every face in the van.

Her hardened expression cracks when her gaze lands on the woman. Her eyes widen, fear and shock fluttering across her face. "Holy shit."

"Are you Joanie?"

The girl's head snaps toward Mom, gun now pointing at her.

Nope. Don't like that.

"Maybe," she says, tone edged with sass and suspicion.

Before I can redirect her aim, Mom says, "Romero."

What the hell?

Mom nods to the woman on the stretcher. "Lyla said to tell you to take us to the safe house."

Joanie's face shifts, suspicion melting into something softer as her gun lowers. She nods once, sharp, then leaps into the van.

"I'll give you directions," she says, slamming the door. "Just keep driving straight down this road until you hit Main Street. Once you reach Anderson Road, take a right."

Leon punches the gas, and the wheels spit gravel as we lurch forward.

Joanie moves to Lyla's other side, dropping into the seat beside the stretcher. Her fingers curl around the woman's hand, gripping it tightly as she leans in close.

"Hey, boss," she whispers. Her leg bounces with anxious energy. Her other hand lifts, shaky fingers brushing blood from Lyla's cheek. Her thumb moves slow, careful. "You better not fuckin' die."

Lyla's breaths are too damn weak, a reminder of how close to the edge she is. She shifts on the gurney, her skin white and clammy beneath my hands. So much blood. It soaks into the sheets, sticks to my fingers, a stark contrast to the heat still radiating off her like she's fighting hell itself.

Trish tears into the trauma kit and grabs gauze, clamps, a roll of pressure bandages, but she stops short at the sight of the blade lodged in Lyla's side.

"I can't pull it," she says, voice tight. "If I do it wrong, she'll bleed out before we hit pavement again."

My stomach twists. "So what do we do?"

"We stabilize it," she says, already moving. "Pack around the wound, keep pressure on the bleed, and pray we hit a flat road soon."

She grabs a wad of gauze and gently presses around the embedded knife. Blood oozes around the edges.

"Joanie, I need you—hold the base of the knife steady. Don't let it shift."

Joanie slides in, hands ready, eyes wide with fear but focused.

I press my hands to Lyla's shoulders, grounding her as her body twitches and her eyes flutter open. "You're okay," I whisper. "We've got you."

Trish works quickly, padding gauze around the handle, wrapping it tight with torn strips of cloth and medical tape to keep it from moving, hands slick with blood.

Lyla shudders against me, her head lolling forward, her breath barely there as Trish continues to work on her side.

Everything tunes out as I press my forehead to hers, my voice barely a whisper.

"Keep fighting."

And I swear she gives me a wink before she passes out in my arms.

Again.

TEN
IS THIS REAL LIFE?

LYLA

OUCH.

Everything hurts. My mind drags, thick and slow, wrapped in fog. Pain pulses—constant, heavy, like my body's been fed through a grinder. Muscles scream. Bones ache. Each breath stabs deep.

I blink against the grit in my eyes, my vision swimming as the world slowly sharpens. Timber walls surround me. Smoke clings to the air. Dust drifts through the light slipping in from a narrow window.

Not the compound. Not hell.

The safe house.

But how did I get here?

The second I move, pain rips through my side like a serrated blade. A choked groan slips past my lips, as my body reminds me in no uncertain terms that I am very much alive, but barely. I instinctively reach for the wound, but there's a metallic clink that stops me.

There's a handcuff gripping my wrist, the other end locked around the iron frame of the bed.

"Seriously?" I mutter, my throat dry like I've chain-smoked since birth.

A voice cuts through the stillness, smooth and almost amused. "Well, hello, beautiful."

My head snaps toward it. Pain explodes up my spine. I wince, eyes clenching shut as the room spins.

When my eyes finally focus, I see a woman lounging in a rocking chair like she owns the place—or maybe the whole damn world. Her boots rest on the bed frame, one hand holding a romance novel with a shirtless pirate on the cover, the other draped lazily over her knee. Her chocolate-brown eyes meet mine, sharp and amused.

She's gorgeous. Short, almost buzzed curls frame high cheekbones. A small hoop nose ring and matching earrings gleam against her dark skin. She looks like she could kill a man and then read a book over his corpse. I like her already.

Crap.

"Rough night?" she asks, smile never wavering.

I don't answer. Too busy taking her in—and ignoring the fact that I'm cuffed to a damn bed like a lunatic. She's dressed in standard apocalypse chic—fitted maroon shirt, black jeans, boots. But what really catches my eye is the black EMT jacket slung over her chair. The patch on the sleeve glints in the low light.

My jaw tightens as my free hand balls into a fist. "Not to sound ungrateful for the whole keeping-me-alive thing," I rasp, "but who the hell are you?"

She doesn't answer right away. Just slides a worn-looking receipt into her book, shuts it, and leans back, still watching me.

I take in my surroundings again, the faint beeping and the tubes running from my arm. I'm hooked up to some kind of medical rig— a crude setup, IV fluids and a monitor hooked to a small gas generator, all carefully arranged to keep my heart ticking.

"I'm Trisha," she says at last. "Friends call me Trish. I'm the one who dragged your ass back from death's door."

I huff a weak breath, shifting against the mattress, wincing as my side protests the movement. Yeah, no shit. "I can see that," I grunt. "But who the hell are you?"

Her head tilts, assessing, before finally saying, "I'm part of the group you saved back at the prison."

My heart kicks. I jerk up—only for the cuff to snap me back down with a dull clank. A fresh bolt of pain shoots through my ribs, but I don't care. "The others," I rasp. "Are they okay? Did they all make it out?"

Trish leans back, her smirk softening into something almost reassuring. "Yes, thanks in large part to you."

A pause. Then—

"And Joanie."

Tension eases in my chest—just a fraction.

She reaches for a steaming mug on the nightstand. My attention snaps to it. The rich, bitter scent hits, and my stomach growls.

I nod toward the mug, raising a brow. "I was saving that, you know."

Trish pauses midsip, one brow lifting in a perfect mix of challenge and amusement. "Payment. For my excellent medical services."

She takes a long gulp, hands cradling the mug.

"Besides, I only stole a little. Instant coffee's not exactly gourmet. Makes me miss the real stuff." Her eyes flick back to mine, still glinting with mischief. "But if you want a cup, I can make one for you, Mizz . . . ?"

"Lyla. Lyla Matthews."

She repeats it under her breath, testing the sound, then leans back, fingers tapping the chair's arm. "See? Now we're friends."

I take a moment to really look her over. Trish is fit, not bodybuilder fit, but the kind of fit that screams efficiency. She looks like the type who could run a 5K at sunrise, whip up breakfast from scratch, and knock out half of her to-be-read list before even starting her day. Lean muscle frames her compact build, her buzzed hair drawing attention to her sharp jawline and those unnervingly large brown eyes.

Even sitting, I can tell she's shorter than me by at least four inches. That thought sparks a brief moment of confidence. If it came to a fight, I could take her.

Probably.

Maybe.

Trish tilts her head, studying me with a mix of curiosity and amusement, her lips twitching like she knows exactly what I'm thinking. "If you're wondering if you could take me in a fight I have to warn you that I may be small, but I'm mighty. Besides, you wouldn't stand a chance in the condition you're in."

She may have a point there. So instead of confirming her suspicions, I burrow further into my pillow. "What happened?"

Her gaze grows distant, thoughtful, as she rocks slowly, taking another sip. "Jacob and Barbara dragged you out of that hellhole of a prison," she says, her tone matter-of-fact but not unkind. "You were bleeding like a stuck pig, but they got you to my van in time. I patched you up—basic emergency procedures for a blood transfusion and fluids, plus clamping and stitching the wound on your side. Lucky for you, Jacob's O negative. Universal donor."

She pauses, a small smile tugging at her lips. "And you've had a lot of visits from a certain mouthy teenager."

Relief and joy charge through my body. Joanie must be okay if she is visiting me all the time.

Trish nods, her eyes glinting with amusement. "Oh yeah. She's been here every day. Got a mouth on her, that one. Hasn't stopped talking to you in hopes that her voice will magically wake you up."

I can't help the faint smile that tugs at my lips. Joanie's tough, scrappy, and loyal in the way only someone with something to prove can be. She's rough around the edges, sure, but she's got heart.

But then my gaze shifts downward, landing on the cuff locked tight around my wrist. The metal is cool against my skin, a stark reminder of where I am—and what they think of me. My grin fades as I glance at Trish, raising an eyebrow. "Why am I handcuffed to the bed?"

Trish chuckles. "That's all Jacob." Her tone carries a mix of exasperation and understanding. "Can't say I necessarily agree, but he made a good point."

She tilts her head, her gaze curious. "See, we don't really know you. Not yet."

I clench my jaw, irritation flaring in my chest. "I saved all those people," I snap.

Trish leans forward, dropping her feet to the floor, elbows resting on her knees. Her demeanor shifts, her eyes sharpening, but there's no hostility—just a careful, considering calm. "You were on a suicide mission, Lyla. And we don't take kindly to 'risk takers.' " She raises her fingers, throwing air quotes around the phrase. "Don't get me wrong—I think what you did was badass. But I also see Jacob's point."

Whoever this Jacob is, I swear to God, I'm going to knee him in the groin so hard his balls will pop out his ass. And who the hell does this woman think she is? I force my voice to stay even. "And what's his point?"

Trish doesn't flinch. "If you're so careless with your own life, how careful are you with others?"

The question lands like a punch to the ribs, sharp, direct, impossible to ignore. "I didn't think saving people was something to question."

Trish tilts her head, unimpressed. "Is that why you got on that bus? Just to save people? Or were you using them for your own agenda?" She shifts, folding her arms. "Because from what I heard, you could have left with the rest of the group. Instead, you stayed behind to 'take care of something.' It nearly cost Barbara, Jessica, and Jacob their lives to pull you out."

Welp, there it is.

Guilt.

Right on top of the simmering anger already bubbling in my gut. I don't need this. I don't need a damn lecture from someone who wasn't even there. I didn't go into that jail with the plan of sacrificing anyone just to get my revenge. But yeah, I can see how it might not look great from the outside, considering the shitshow Joanie and I stirred up.

I force myself to breathe. "I didn't ask them to come back for me."

Trish leans forward, her stare sharp, unyielding. It's the kind of look that makes it clear she's not buying my bullshit. "No. But we don't leave people behind. Or give up on them. Even when it's clear they're dead set on sacrificing themselves—and damning everyone else who gets in their way."

My mind flashes to Mark. His face, the moment his life bled out in front of me. The weight of his body in my arms, the finality of it.

Something inside me twists, sharp and relentless.

I did the same thing with him, didn't I? Screw the consequences. As long as I got to kill da Vinci, nothing else mattered. Except it wasn't da Vinci who died.

And now?

Did I just do it again?

My stomach churns. Was I so blinded by revenge that I didn't consider the fallout? The fact that someone might come back for me?

Yes, I killed him this time. But at what cost?

Would it have been worth it if the others had died trying to escape—while I wasn't even there to help them?

I chose him over them.

Again.

My throat tightens. The words I want to say, the defense, the excuses, die before they can form. Because what if she's right?

I press my lips together, my gaze dropping to the rough wooden floor, suddenly unable to meet Trish's eyes.

She shifts, the chair creaking as she leans forward like she's about to say something else. But before the silence can stretch further, the cabin door bursts open with a loud crack, the hinges groaning under the force.

Pain explodes down my neck the second my head snaps toward the sound, a sharp, unforgiving reminder that I need to seriously stop doing that.

But the pain fades fast as my attention locks on to the man stepping through the doorway.

Something shifts in my brain. A weird sense of déjà vu settles over me like a heavy fog. Have we met before?

His face is set in a grim scowl, those deep brown eyes stormy and unreadable, shoulders stiff with tension. He moves with confidence, each step measured, like someone who doesn't waste energy on unnecessary movement.

And holy shit.

This man is gorgeous.

Like, *distractingly* gorgeous.

And I look like a trash panda that got beat with a baseball bat. Awesome. Great. Just *great*.

I take one second, just one, to admire him, because why the hell not? Tall, lean, built like someone who knows how to throw a punch. His short, dark brown hair is slightly messy, just enough to look effortlessly good.

But it's the tattoos that grab my attention.

Intricate designs of trees, flowers, and woodland creatures weave up his forearms, disappearing beneath the rolled-up sleeves of his black Henley.

Is the rest of him covered like that?

Focus, Lyla.

Behind him, Joanie practically leaps in, the sharp sound of her boots snapping me out of my thoughts.

"—didn't even wait!" she shouts, her words laced with fury. "You just left me standing there, you ass!"

He doesn't flinch. If anything, his scowl deepens, frustration rolling off him in waves. He jerks his head toward me, clearly done with whatever argument they've been having.

"Can you get this one to shut up?" he asks, his tone flat, but also deliciously deep.

Hello.

My eyes flick to Joanie, who's staring at me with a megawatt smile.

I glance back at him, my voice dry as desert sand. "I've been trying for months."

Trish snorts, hiding her amusement behind a sip from her mug. The corner of Joanie's mouth twitches, clearly relieved I'm able to make jokes.

He just stares, one eyebrow ticking up slightly, like he's not sure whether to laugh or groan. "Perfect," he mutters, dragging a hand through his hair. "I'm surrounded by comedians."

Joanie comes over and sits on one side of the bed and gives my hand a squeeze. "Hey, boss bitch." Her eyes glisten with unshed tears.

"Hey, kiddo." I grin because damn, it's so good to see her. "You okay?"

She scoffs, blinking the moisture away. "I should be asking you that, ya fuckin' loon."

"Nah, this is just a typical Tuesday." I wink and give her hand a reassuring squeeze.

My smile fades when I turn back to who I guess is Jacob.

But I'm slightly less annoyed about being tied down now.

I lift my wrist, jingling the cuffs with emphasis, the iron clanking against the bed frame.

"Look," Jacob says, his voice gruff, his tone dropping as his eyes stay locked on mine. "We appreciate what you did more than we could ever say, but we don't know you. We've been burned before by people we thought we could trust."

Okay. Fair point, but it doesn't mean I like it. The tension in the room thickens, pressing down on all of us.

He nods toward my arm. Matter-of-fact. Unapologetic. "Just a precaution until we know more about you and your real interest in that prison."

Joanie huffs, crossing her arms as her glare sharpens. "This is still bullshit."

Jacob doesn't even glance at her. His eyes stay on mine, unwavering, waiting for my reaction.

I hold his gaze, the ache in my body almost forgotten as something else rises—anger, sure, but also exhaustion and understanding. I let out a breath, forcing myself to push past the frustration. "Fine," I say, my voice firm. "But I'm not a fan of chains. At least, not in this sense."

Just for a second, his mouth twitches. Almost like he wants to smile but won't let himself. And his eyes flood with heat. "Noted," he says, voice dropping even lower. How is that possible?

Joanie rolls her eyes, muttering under her breath. Her hand squeezes mine as her eyes meet mine, the sharpness softening.

"You okay, boss?" she asks, her voice quiet, almost hesitant.

I nod, though it's a small, tired gesture. My body feels like it's been run over by a truck, but I manage to meet her gaze. "Yeah," my voice cracks as I grip her hand tightly, reminding myself that she is okay. "I'm right here with you."

For a moment, silence settles over the room, broken only by the sound of the wind rattling the cabin walls and the faint creak of Trish's rocking chair. She leans back, her eyes flicking between us, her expression unreadable but attentive.

Jacob clears his throat, cutting through the quiet. I barely have time to turn toward him before another figure steps into the room, stealing the air from my lungs.

This guy is huge—built like a damn bear—his massive frame filling the doorway like a blockade. Fiery red hair tied back in a low bun, a thick beard that matches. Bulkier than Jacob, though his arms lack the intricate tattoos that coil up Jacob's skin like living art.

He doesn't speak. Doesn't acknowledge the tension in the room. Just moves across the space and leans against the wall, his arms crossing over his chest, his biceps flexing just enough to make me believe he could rip the bedframe in half if he wanted to.

His stare locks on to mine.

Unyielding. The kind of look designed to unnerve, to press, to see what I do next.

Naturally, my first instinct is to see how far I can push him.

However, Jacob doesn't let me.

His presence pulls me back in, reclaiming the room without even trying.

Trish stands, motioning for Joanie to follow. "Come on. I'll get you set up with Earl. He needs another set of hands for making traps."

Jacob reaches for the chair Trish just vacated, dragging it closer to the edge of my bed before sinking down.

Joanie doesn't budge. Instead, she looks at me, waiting.

Her unspoken question is clear: *You good?*

I nod. "I'm good. Give me half an hour. If they don't leave by then, you can come storming back in with Sweetness."

Joanie's lips twitch, and then a devilish chuckle escapes her. She turns on her heel and heads for the door, her shoulders shaking with silent laughter.

Three sets of confused eyes swing toward me.

I shrug. "Sweetness is the name of my knife."

Silence.

A good, solid ten seconds of unmoving, blank stares.

Then, Trish snorts, barely managing to cover her mouth before wild laughter bursts free. She turns on her heel, shaking her head as she disappears down the hall.

Bear Man gives me nothing. Just stands there like an immovable wall.

Jacob, on the other hand?

His gaze tilts skyward, and he pulls in a deep, restrained breath—the kind of exhale that screams irritation. "Lord, give me strength."

From down the hall, Trish's voice echoes back in a truly terrible Austrian accent. *"I'll be back."*

Jacob lets out a sharp huff—a noise that sounds suspiciously close to a laugh.

Then, just like that, the amusement vanishes.

His posture shifts. He leans forward slightly, resting his forearms on his knees, his expression sharpening.

"Lyla."

Just my name. That's all. And yet, it sends a delectable shiver down my spine.

Jesus.

I need to get my shit together. Now is not the time to get excited.

"We have some questions," he says, voice light but carrying just enough of an edge to tell me this isn't a request. His eyes lock on to mine, pinning me in place. "And we need answers."

So that's how he wants to play it? Hmm.

Let's make this more interesting.

A slow grin creeps across my lips.

"Only if you say *please.*"

ELEVEN
SMALL TALK

JACOB

OF COURSE she's going to make this harder than it should be.

Her good eye locks on to mine, sharp, aware. Tough. Smart. Calculating. She's the kind of person who doesn't just survive—she fights, adapts, refuses to yield. And man, is that hot as hell. The tension. The challenge.

Leon's gaze flicks between us, cool and detached, taking in every detail like the silent observer he is. I can feel the judgment radiating off of him.

Do not show you're enjoying this. Do not show you're enjoying this.

I exhale, schooling my features into something neutral, unbothered, like this is just a friendly conversation and not a battle of wills.

"All right, Lyla," I say, keeping my tone casual, unhurried. "Why don't you tell me what you were thinking, going into that prison alone?"

Her smile spreads even more—dangerous, full of mischief. My pulse spikes before I even realize why.

"I don't even know your name," she says, tilting her head, voice smooth as silk, laced with defiance. "So why should I answer any of your questions?"

This woman is going to be the death of me.

I take a breath, ignoring the very real and very inconvenient reaction happening below my belt. If she's going to be a brat—which I apparently like more than I should—then fine. I'll be a smartass right back.

I plaster on a mockingly polite smile. "Where are my manners?" Sarcasm drips from every word. "I'm Jacob." I jerk my chin toward Leon. "That's Leon."

Her gaze shifts to him, curiosity flashing in her eyes.

Leon, ever the enigma, gives a single, brief nod.

"Does he ever talk?" Lyla asks.

"No. Car accident when he was thirteen left him mute."

She winces. "Shit. Sorry."

Leon shrugs.

She gestures toward him with a lazy flick of her thumb. "Is he supposed to be the bad cop?"

"Yes," I say flatly. "And I'm the one trying to help you out. So, I'm going to ask you again—why did you go into that prison alone?"

She shrugs, casual as ever. "I wanted to save some people and kill some bad men in the process," she states like it's just another day in the apocalypse.

I lean back in my chair, crossing my arms over my chest, mirroring her nonchalant expression. "See, we're not used to people going out of their way to save strangers," Pause. "Not anymore." My gaze locks on to hers, searching, pressing. "Around here, we like to know who's running into the fire and why. Nowadays, the *why* matters most."

For the briefest second, her smirk falters—a pause just long enough to tell me she's weighing her next move. Her eyes dart toward Leon, her expression sharpening, assessing. Trying to piece him together.

Leon doesn't give her an inch. Just watches, silent, unreadable.

"He isn't going to give you anything," I tell her, voice cool. "I suggest you keep your focus on me."

Her gaze snaps back, and I catch it—the glint of annoyance in her eyes.

"Why'd you do it?" I ask, my voice dropping lower, more serious now. The room feels heavier, the air thick with expectation. "Clearly you and Joanie had something planned by the way she stormed in with a bright-ass yellow metallic steed. You had planned to get on that bus no matter who was on it. So, why did you need to get into that prison?"

Her expression shifts, the faintest crack in her armor before she smooths it over. Her eyes grow guarded, her tone breezy, almost dismissive. "Let's just say I was overdue for a visit with a certain individual who deserved to die."

I narrow my eyes. Her gaze avoids mine. There's subtle tension in her shoulders, the way she leans just slightly away, like she's trying to keep the truth at arm's length. Why won't she tell me who she needed to see?

Leaning forward, I press her, my voice sharper now. "So you thought the only way to get to this person was by taking on an entire compound of psychos with nothing but a knife, a fourteen-year-old in a souped-up Hummer, a blaring Ramones soundtrack, and a horde of the undead?"

Her lips twitch. "Well, when you put it that way . . ." she drawls, her unbruised eye locking on to mine, challenge sparking in the blue depths.

Before I can retort, a voice cuts through the tension from the doorway.

"Personally, I like her sense of humor better than yours, Jacob," Trish quips, leaning against the frame, her eyes alight with amusement, clearly enjoying the show.

I shoot her a look, patience thinning. "Aren't you supposed to be helping Earl? Not her?"

She shrugs, a grin spreading across her face. "This is more fun."

Figures. I turn back to Lyla. "The problem I have with your plan, Lyla, is that you used my people to help you settle your score. Which tells me you're reckless with others as long as you can get what you want."

The shift is instant. It's like watching steel slam into place behind her eyes. The teasing, the amusement—it's all gone, replaced by something chillier, something lethal. *Deadly.*

"Look, asshole," she says, "I am reckless. But that doesn't mean I don't give a shit about people." She leans forward, eyes darkening, her entire body coiled tight despite her injuries. "Yes, I got on that bus so I could get to a man who deserved to die. However," she pauses, her glare searing into me, "I fought to save your people. I didn't leave them there so I could go finish what he started. I got them out first. I gave them a fighting chance. Which, by the way, you would've been too damn late to do."

The words land hard, and I know she's right. She saved them. If she hadn't been inside that prison when she was, I'd be digging graves right now.

She leans back into the pillow, but her gaze stays locked on mine, burning with the fury of a raging bull. Then, just to twist the knife, she adds, "And I don't owe you any more details as to *why* I went in there. So, with all due respect—since you did help save my life— kindly fuck off."

Silence stretches between us, thick and unyielding.

Leon shifts in the corner, his hands moving. *"I think you met your match, brother."*

I exhale through my nose, rubbing a hand over my jaw, pushing down the laugh that's dangerously close to breaking free. My focus stays on Lyla, but I give Leon the smallest nod, a silent concession.

She doesn't miss it. Her eyes narrow. "What'd he say?" she demands, voice edged with warning.

Yeah, I'm not about to tell her the truth.

I shrug. "He says you're a pain in the ass. I happen to agree with him."

Lyla's glare shifts to Leon, eyes burning with the kind of challenge that makes men rethink their life choices. But Leon? He doesn't so much as blink. Instead, his lips quirk at the corner.

Holy Mary and Moses. I can count on one hand the number of people that can make Leon smirk. I guess I'm going to have to add another finger. *Dirty.*

He holds her stare, daring her to make a move.

Trish snorts from the doorway.

I sigh, pinching the bridge of my nose. Fantastic. Now they're all feeding off each other.

Lyla's lips twitch, just enough to show that spark of amusement creeping back in. She locks on to me again, and I already know what's coming before she even opens her mouth.

"Are you done being an ass?"

Behind me, Trish lets out a low chuckle. "I take it back," she mutters, and I don't even have to turn to know she's grinning at Leon. "She's Ripley."

Lyla's gaze flicks to Trish, amusement behind those sharp blue eyes. Just for a second. Then she snaps back to me, waiting.

I stand, taking a step back, sliding the chair against the wall as I put some space between us. "We're grateful for what you did," I say, letting some of the tension ease from my tone. "You and Joanie can stay with us—if you want. But understand this." I pause, letting the words settle, making sure she hears me. "No more reckless plans. We work as a unit. We trust each other to have each other's backs. Can you do that?"

Her good eye gleams with something entirely too mischievous. "Yes, sir," she replies, throwing in a mock salute. "Of course that's *if* we decide to stay. We're not looking for a handout. I've got supplies —good ones. You can take half as thanks for pulling me out." Her eyes narrow. "But I need time to think about the rest."

I roll my eyes, biting back a grin as I turn on my heel, heading for the door. Behind me, Trish steps aside, mirroring Lyla's salute with an exaggerated flourish. She gives Lyla a wink over my shoulder before striding down the hall.

Leon steps forward and pulls a key from his pocket. The faint metallic click echoes in the quiet room as he unlocks the cuff around Lyla's wrist. She rubs her wrist absently, watching him with a guarded mixture of curiosity and appreciation.

He pockets the cuffs, his face unreadable as he turns toward the door. His boots make soft thuds against the wooden floor as he heads after Trish, his broad shoulders almost disappearing through the doorway.

But then he stops.

Pausing just inside the frame, he turns back to Lyla, his posture relaxed, his expression calm. For a moment, his dark eyes meet hers, and then he places his fingers over his chin and pulls them away, palm up.

A simple phrase.

Lyla's gaze follows the motion of his hand, her brow furrowing.

She looks at me, silently asking for an explanation.

I nod. "He said thank you."

A small, almost reluctant smile touches her lips. She nods, the tension in her shoulders loosening ever so slightly. "You're welcome, dickhead," she says, her tone light but carrying an undertone of sincerity.

Leon snorts, before turning and stepping out the door, leaving just the two of us.

"Look, Lyla," I say, my voice quieter now, more measured. Her gaze sharpens, meeting mine head-on as I take a step closer. "You may have a death wish, but thank you for what you did for the others. I don't want to think about what would've happened to them if you hadn't stepped in."

My mom's bruised face flashes in my mind. I swallow hard. "For that, I owe you."

That's all I'm willing to give, and I turn toward the door, ready to leave it at that. But just as I step over the threshold, her voice stops me.

"Jacob."

I glance over my shoulder. She's propped herself up more, her expression fierce despite the bruises.

"Now was that so hard to say?" A coy smile tugs at her lips.

Yep, a challenging woman is definitely my kink. "Not at all, Trouble."

Her brow furrows. "Trouble?"

I tilt my head, leaning against the doorframe. "You don't remember our first meeting?"

She shakes her head slowly. "Noooo."

I press a hand to my chest. "You wound me." My lips curl. "You don't remember calling me gorgeous, pinching my ass, or asking me out?"

Her eyes widen, mouth opening and closing as she tries to piece together my words. "I thought that was a dream."

Oh, this is going to be fun.

"No, Trouble. It was very much *real.*"

Before she can fire back, I turn away, throwing a wink over my shoulder.

"Don't worry. I'll give you my answer in due time."

TWELVE
ON THE MOVE
LYLA

FOR THE PAST TEN DAYS, the cabin has been both my prison and my refuge. Ten days since the compound. Ten days since I nearly bled to death. Ten days of healing, of breathing in the musty scent coming off the quilt lying over me and listening to the others chattering outside while my ribs try to piece themselves back together.

Ten days of Joanie's nonstop talking.

She's barely left my side, popping in and out of the room like my own housemaid with far too much energy. She's taken it upon herself to educate me on everyone in the group, even though I told her I met most of them already. I don't have the heart to tell her I don't want to get close to them. In this world, the likelihood that all of them will survive is slim to none. It's better to not get attached, but I will let Joanie talk away if it makes her feel better.

"Earl and Edith are the old married couple," she says now, her tone bright and animated as she sits cross-legged on the floor beside my bed. "They're in their seventies. Edith was a librarian."

Huh. How did a librarian become such a badass?

Joanie continues. "Earl used to be a firefighter, retired before all this crap went down. That's how they know Jacob."

"So Jacob was a firefighter?" *Of course* he was.

My mind conjures the image—him carrying me over his shoulder, smoke swirling around us, his jaw set with determined focus as flames rage in the background. My hand . . . and his very firm backside.

Heat creeps up my neck, spreading to my cheeks.

I smack my hand over my eyes with a groan.

"Hey, you okay?"

"Yeah," I mutter, clearing my throat and forcing my hand back down. "Sorry. Keep going."

Joanie grins. "So Jacob wasn't just a firefighter," she says, her voice dipping into a conspiratorial tone. "According to Earl, he was the fire *chief*. Says Jacob was the best firefighter he had in years." She pauses, then deepens her voice, pitching it into an impressively gruff imitation of the old man himself. " 'In my unbiased opinion.' "

"Not bad," I admit, giving her a mock-serious nod. "You might have a future in voice acting if this apocalypse thing ever blows over."

Joanie beams and leans back on her hands. "Told ya I've got range."

I raise an eyebrow, my lips curling into a small, amused smile. "Is that right? And then there's Clair and Poppy?"

Joanie nods enthusiastically. "Clair grew up in the same town and used to be an elementary school teacher before . . . you know." She waves a hand, as if the apocalypse is just a minor inconvenience. "And Poppy's ten. Loves to draw."

She pauses, her expression faltering. "I, uh . . . might not have been keeping my swearing down around her though."

A laugh bursts out of me before I can stop it. The movement sends a bolt of pain tearing through my ribs. I clutch at my side, groaning as I try to catch my breath.

Joanie's face drains of color, her wide eyes fixed on me in panic. "Shit! You okay?"

I grimace. "I'm fine. Just swell. Keep going."

Joanie hesitates, her eyes scanning my face for any sign that I'm bluffing. When she seems satisfied, she continues. "Well, there's Pete and Jessica."

Her face twists into an expression of distaste, and I can't help but grin. "Oh, I remember her." How could I forget the woman who called me a lost cause? I may have been in and out of consciousness, but I still heard that loud and clear.

"Yeah," Joanie mutters, her eyes narrowing. "She's a real *treat*. I don't know what her problem is. Whenever Leon gives me food, she just glares at me."

My smile disappears. "She hasn't done anything to you, has she?" I have no problem knifing someone, ribs or no ribs.

Joanie shakes her head. "Nah, she's just a bitch."

"Joanie, for the love of—"

She rolls her eyes. "Okay, fine! She's a piece of a stinking pile of poo. Better?"

"Smartass," I mutter.

Joanie grins, her eyes twinkling. "I learn from the best. Anyway, the rest of them, you already know. Trish, Leon, and Barbara, Jacob's mom."

In the depths of my mind, tires screech, followed by the unmistakable sound of a fiery car crash.

"Barbara," I repeat slowly, my voice slightly strangled. "Badass Barbara. The woman I have seriously considered asking to adopt me . . . is *Jacob's* mom?"

Joanie blinks. "Yeah? Why do you sound so shocked?"

Oh, I don't know, *Joanie*. Maybe because I shamelessly flirted with her son and asked him out, while looking like a punching bag, *right in front of her*.

See, this is why I never drink or do anything that might

compromise my filter. Because, apparently, the second my brain takes a hit, I become painfully blunt and terrifyingly honest. Normally, I have at least *some* self-restraint. But no—semiconscious, bleeding-out Lyla? She shoots her shot without hesitation.

Nope. Not sharing that humiliation.

"Nothing," I say quickly. "It's just surprising. I wouldn't have guessed Barbara had a son like Jacob."

Joanie eyes me. "A son like how?"

"Just one that looks like him."

She pauses, tilting her head, her eyebrows inching up.

Then it clicks.

"Oh my God," she breathes, her voice full of disgust. "Please tell me you're not thinking what I *think* you're thinking."

If she's going to be nosy, I might as well lean into it. "I don't know what you mean," I say, stretching back against the pillows. "But I will admit he is one gorgeous stack of pancakes." Even if I do want to drop-kick him in the throat.

Joanie gags, shoving a pillow over her face. "I hate you."

I chuckle, but the truth is, Jacob has been stopping by my room every morning and night. Always checking in. Always watching. Making sure I'm healing or, more likely, making sure I'm not plotting with Joanie to drive off in the middle of the night with all the supplies.

The man has serious trust issues.

Joanie groans, throwing her head back in mock agony. "Also, please don't say pancakes. I miss them so much." Her dramatic despair lasts all of two seconds before a sly grin spreads across her face. "But, you know . . . I might start calling him that. Just to piss him off."

I raise an eyebrow.

"He's so funny when he gets all angry. Like, his jaw tightens, and his eyebrows do this twitchy thing." She attempts to mimic it, but she just ends up looking like she's having a stroke.

I bite my lip to keep from laughing. "That's not even close."

"It *is*!" she insists, doubling down. "Yep, 'Pancakes' from here on out. It's perfect."

If she actually starts calling Jacob "Pancakes," I'm half-convinced she'll be running for her life within the hour.

Joanie's eyes glaze over, and I realize she's not thinking about Jacob anymore. She's practically drooling at the thought of actual pancakes, her expression turning wistful in a way that's both adorable and mildly concerning.

"Joanie," I say, my tone sharp enough to snap her out of it. "You're starting to look like you might cry over syrup."

She blinks, startled, then laughs, the sound bright and unapologetic. "Fine, fine. But pancakes, Lyla. *Pancakes*. I'd trade my soul for one right now."

I can see some dribble starting to form at the corners of her mouth and I'd rather not get drenched in syrup-loving memories. I shift, steering us back to reality.

"Joanie, is he really dead?"

I've avoided asking her this since I woke up. Trish hovered the first few days, always checking vitals or reminding me to drink more water, which made privacy a joke. Then Jacob started showing up— never announced, always full of questions.

But the truth is, I already know the answer.

I've known since I opened my eyes.

I just didn't want to hear it out loud.

Her smile falters, the mischief draining from her face. She looks away, her fingers finding a loose thread on her sleeve and twisting it absently. "Probably," she says after a beat. "I went back a couple days ago with Leon and Jacob. Just to make sure no one survived or was following us. We didn't see anyone in the office."

She pauses, her shoulders tightening. "If he was there, he was eaten. Or turned."

"If that happened, there'd be evidence."

She shrugs, gaze sliding away. "There was blood everywhere. No way he walked out of that."

I study her face, searching for cracks in her story, or in her resolve. "You're sure there was nothing left in the office?"

Her eyes lock on mine. "Yeah. Nothing."

If he had been eaten or turned, the note I left would still be there. *Fuck.*

The asshole must still be alive. If he's still breathing, I can't leave. Not yet.

The door creaks open, the sound slicing through the quiet. My head snaps toward the noise, tensing automatically, but it's just Trish.

She steps inside, her sharp eyes sweeping over me and Joanie like she's gauging us for damage.

"Hello, Sunshine," she drawls, amusement lacing her tone. "Since you don't look quite as ghostly anymore, it's time we get moving."

I shift, propping myself up on one elbow, wincing as my ribs protest. "Where are you going?"

"We're heading to my family's farm in Montana."

"Montana?" They can't be serious. "We're in Virginia, and you want to trek through a sea of infected, trigger-happy psychos, collapsed highways, and whatever other nightmares are out there . . . instead of hunkering down here? Why risk it?" I pause, shaking my head. "That could take weeks—months—if you can't find gas along the way."

Trish stays calm, her voice hopeful but guarded. "Yes, it will take time to get there, but the reward at the end is worth it. My parents own hundreds of acres, and big enough to house survivors. Some can stay in the barns for now, but there's room to build houses, grow food, raise livestock. It's not perfect, but it's a chance to find some normalcy. It gives people something to live for. And it's remote. Low population means fewer infected. Cold winters will slow them down." She shrugs. "Plus, you know, I want to see if my parents are still alive."

Oh, yeah. That. Touché.

"What's the plan for getting there?"

Trish sketches a rough path in the air. "We're taking the northern route up through Maryland, cutting across Pennsylvania, then west to northern Ohio. From there it's a trek across the Midwest and finally home to Lavina, Montana."

She adds, "We'll avoid major cities and highways. Stick to the back roads, hit small towns for supplies."

Every part of this plan is a gamble. Small towns, supply runs—each stop is a loaded gun. All it takes is one bad hand to lose everything. One swarm. One ambush.

Joanie grins, eyes gleaming. "We get to loot at every stop? Awesome."

Trish grins, crossing her arms. "Sounds fun, right?"

"Sounds crazy," I counter.

Trish lifts a brow. "This coming from the woman who stormed a prison full of lunatics?"

Joanie doesn't even try to hide her snort.

Trish continues, "It's a crazy that's necessary. I'd think you of all people would appreciate that."

Point for Trish. "Why didn't you go there sooner?"

"We've been busy helping people. We stayed behind to find survivors, get them to safety, and gather supplies. We sent others ahead of us in smaller groups, thinking they'd have a better chance of making it if they moved under the radar. Each group took a different path for the same reason—stay off the radar, stay alive. The goal is to reach the farm with enough food, meds, and fuel to keep us going for a while. We're the last group to leave."

I tilt my head, narrowing my eyes. "And how do you know they'll make it?"

She shrugs. "We won't know until we get there."

"How many groups did you send?"

"Six," she says. "Ten people in each group. They were made up of people we knew in our town. People we can trust."

Joanie shifts, her voice small. "Do you think they all made it?"

Trish hesitates, her jaw tightening. "I hope so."

She perches on the edge of the bed, crossing her legs. "Look," she says, her voice quieter now, almost earnest. "If you and Joanie are up for it, we'll take you with us. You're free to leave anytime you want, but," she pauses, meeting my gaze head-on, "I highly suggest you stick with us. You know, the whole 'strength in numbers' thing."

I arch an eyebrow, my voice sharp. "And why exactly should I trust you?"

Trish laughs, the sound low and unbothered, as if the question is the most predictable thing she's heard all day. She shakes her head, leaning back. "Hell, if I wanted you dead, I wouldn't have gone to the trouble of saving your ass."

Well, she's got another point there.

"Thanks, but I don't think I'm the settle-down-with-a-group type," I say. "I'll head out on my own once I'm healed."

Because if I go with you, I'll miss him. He's out there. He has to be close.

Joanie interjects, "Lyla, what the fuck?"

I blink, startled. "What?"

She steps forward, arms crossed, eyes blazing. "You're seriously thinking of staying behind? After everything?"

I glance at Trish. "Can you give us a minute?"

Trish nods, stands, and heads toward the door. She pauses before leaving, her expression softer but firm. "You might not trust us, and we might not trust you, not fully. But we take care of the people who help us. Jacob pays back his debts. Always. And you saved the group, including his mother. So, like it or not, he's trying to pay you back." Then she's gone.

Her words hit harder than I expect, slipping past the armor I've spent years fortifying. I hate that. Hate the way my chest tightens, the way my throat thickens with something dangerously close to emotion.

Damn it.

I can't afford this.

Joanie already got in. That alone terrifies me more than I want to admit. Letting anyone else in? It's a risk I swore I'd never take again.

Not after Mark.

Joanie's still staring at me, hands on her hips now. "Are you seriously pulling this lone-wolf shit?"

"I need to finish this. I need to make sure."

She scoffs. "No, you *want* to finish it. Big difference. He's gone, Lyla. You need to let him go and live your life. Or at least the best you can in this shithole."

"You don't get it." She doesn't understand that he will come for them all if I don't stop him. Da Vinci doesn't take kindly to people who best him.

She steps back. "You said we were in this together. You dragged me into your world and now you're ready to dump me to chase some psycho ghost while I ride off with strangers?"

"I want you to stay and help me. I'm not dumping you."

"That's exactly what you're doing." Her voice cracks. "And I can't do this again with you. You almost fucking died, Lyla, and I'm not going to stick around and watch it again."

My chest constricts like a vise. "Joanie—"

"No." She holds up a hand, her chin trembling but high. "I'm not asking for your permission. I'm going."

She's going. They all are.

And da Vinci . . . he's not going to let this go. They beat him. They humiliated him. He'll want revenge, and he'll come for them whether I'm with them or not.

I could tell them. Warn them that he's still alive. That he'll be hunting us. But I know what Jacob will do—he'll pack up, change direction, scatter the group, and make sure da Vinci never finds them again.

And I'll lose him. Lose my shot at finishing this for good.

If I stay behind and miss him, he could destroy them before I even get close.

And Joanie, she'll be on the front line.

I can't risk that.

"Fine," I say, voice rough. "I'll go."

Joanie freezes midstep. Then she whirls and launches at me with a bone-crushing hug that punches a whimper from my mouth.

"Oh shit! Sorry!" She pulls back with a sheepish grin. "I'm just so happy you're done being a stubborn dickhead."

"Ha. Ha. Now go tell Trish and let them know they can pack *all* the supplies."

She skips out of the room, already yelling down the hall.

I'll go. Not to play house. Not to belong. But to keep them safe. To make sure when he shows up—and he will—I'll be there, waiting.

THIRTEEN

FIRST STEPS

THE CLEARING outside the cabin thrums with movement. The group loads supplies, secures weapons, and checks vehicles—spurred into action the second Trish got Lyla's go-ahead. Every sound bleeds into the rhythm of departure: truck doors creaking open, crates thudding against dirt, voices overlapping in a chorus of urgency to make sure nothing vital gets left behind.

I'm at the back of the ambulance with Leon, sorting through a crate of canned goods. The sunlight filters through the trees, dappling the ground in shifting patches of light and shadow.

I still can't believe Lyla's actually coming with us. After a week of dodging, deflecting, and pretending I didn't exist every time I checked on her, she's chosen to stay. I try not to grin at the image of her face, red, horrified, absolutely wrecked with secondhand embarrassment at the mention of what she *really* said to me at the prison. But damn, it's there , bubbling up anyway. She looked like she wanted to melt into the mattress.

This road trip just got a hell of a lot more interesting.

Leon glances toward the cabin, where Joanie's voice drifts

through the open window, sharp with irritation. His fingers move quickly. *"I like that kid."*

Shaking my head. "You've always had a soft spot for troubled kids."

He gives me a deadpan look, his expression unreadable except for the slight arch of his brow. Then signs, *"Weren't you a troubled kid when we first met?"*

The faint twitch at the corner of his mouth betrays him. Smug bastard.

I was thirteen when Mom brought Leon home, introducing him as my new older brother. I was already pissed off at the world—at Dad for walking out and Mom for pretending we were fine.

I spent that first week being a complete dick. But it wasn't until the cops dumped me on our doorstep one night after catching me spray-painting the brand-new windows of Watkins' Grocery Store that everything shifted.

Mom dragged my ass to the store, made me apologize, then handed me a bucket and a sponge.

An hour in, I was dying—sweat dripping down my back, arms aching, my punishment baking me alive on the sidewalk. That's when I heard footsteps and the quiet *thud* of another bucket hitting the ground.

Leon crouched down, grabbed a sponge, and started scrubbing, never even glancing my way. His stitches were still fresh against his throat, dark against his pale skin.

"You didn't do shit. Just go home," I muttered, irritated.

He rolled his eyes and pulled out the small notebook, scribbled something, and turned it toward me.

We're brothers now, whether you like it or not. So when one of us screws up, the other helps them fix it. End of story.

"We're not brothers."

He wrote again. *Not by blood, but since I have no one left, you'll have to do.* Then added one last word, underlining it twice. <u>*Shithead.*</u>

Then, like it was nothing, he went back to scrubbing.

I shake off the memory, rolling my shoulders. "Yeah, well, if I remember right, you weren't exactly a *great* influence once you got to high school."

The ladies loved Leon. Strong, silent type, built like a damn tank, always jumping in to help people like some brooding superhero. Plus that ridiculous red hair of his made him stand out. Not exactly fair competition for the rest of us mere mortals. All of them noticed Leon.

Well, except one particular girl.

The corner of Leon's mouth quirks up as his hands move. "*Do as I say, not as I do.*"

The van eventually fills with supplies from the cabin, each item a testament to the scavenging efforts of Joanie and Lyla.

The stuff they managed to pack in this place is impressive—canned food, cheesecloth, electrical tape, whistles, blankets, deodorant, matches, and more I wouldn't have thought to grab. No wonder the nearby houses came up empty when we searched.

Leon lifts the last box into the van and slams the back doors shut. My eyes drift to the cabin and linger. How is she feeling today?

A tap on my shoulder. Leon's questioning gaze hits me as he signs, "*Are you having second thoughts about them joining us?*"

"No. I just think there's more to her," I say finally. "She went into that compound like she had a death wish. And maybe she did. But . . ." My mind turns over the memory of Lyla lying on the office floor, bleeding out. "There's something else driving her."

Leon's gaze bores into the side of my face, waiting.

I exhale, my voice dropping. "I don't think she's done fighting yet." And I don't want our people to get hurt on her crusade.

Leon's expression is unreadable, his eyes scanning the clearing before flicking briefly to Clair, who's talking to Mom by Earl's truck. Her gaze cuts over Mom's shoulder to Leon, a small smile spreading across her face.

His hands are fluid but weighted. *"None of us are ever done fighting."*

Leon glances back at me, his expression softening just enough to remind me why I trust him—his instincts, his way of seeing people for who they really are. He's always been my compass when my own gut starts to falter.

Jessica rounds the corner of the ambulance, her face set in that familiar hard expression, like she's already bracing for a fight. She stops beside me, her gaze flicking to Leon.

"Can we talk?" she asks, her voice low but urgent.

Leon meets my eyes for a moment, then shrugs, pushing off the side and stuffing his hands into his pockets as he heads toward the others.

Jessica waits until Leon is out of earshot before stepping in, her fingers curling around my arm, pressing just a little too tightly.

"You can't be serious about taking them with us," she hisses, her eyes locking with mine, sharp and insistent. "We don't know them. You saw what she's capable of. Do you really think she's the kind of person who will put the group first?"

I drag a hand through my hair as irritation tightens my chest. Jessica's quickness to judge has always rubbed me the wrong way. "She saved all of you, Jessica. I don't know why you're so dead set against them joining us. She's a fighter. A damn good one, from what I heard. And yeah, maybe she's got her own reasons, but that doesn't mean she's a threat."

Jessica scoffs, her grip tightening. "You *think* she's not a threat."

I shoot her a look, my jaw ticking. "I *know* she's not the enemy."

Her lips press into a thin line, but the fire in her eyes dims for just a second. "I just don't want you to get hurt again."

It's not the words themselves that catch me off guard—it's the way she says them. Soft. Raw. I stiffen.

"I know what happened with Sheila hurt you—"

The name lands like a punch to the gut, hollowing out my ribs. My teeth clench so hard my jaw aches. "Stop."

Jessica flinches and releases my arm. I won't drag this into the light—not here, not now.

Her lips part like she wants to argue, but after a beat, she exhales, stepping back, tension coiling in her shoulders. I don't give her a chance to say anything else. I turn away, my fists clenching at my sides, shoving down the past before it can sink its claws into me.

The creak of the cabin door is the only thing that keeps the anxiety from closing in completely.

Joanie and Trish step onto the porch, half carrying, half supporting Lyla between them. She looks like hell—her face pale, her movements sluggish, and the bruise around her eye has deepened into an ugly smear of green and yellow. But even in this state, her jaw is set, her expression edged with determination.

Stubborn ass.

They move carefully down the steps, and I'm already striding toward them, my eyes narrowing.

"What do you think you're doing?" My words cut through the murmurs of the others.

Lyla's head snaps up, her gaze colliding with mine. A defiant smirk curls at the edges of her lips. "Oh, you know, just going for a lovely stroll on this nice summer day, which I *can* do on my own." She casts a pointed look at Trish and Joanie before shifting her attention back to me. "What about you?"

I drag a hand down my face, forcing down the immediate urge to roll my eyes.

Can she make anything easy?

I close the space between us, my irritation simmering beneath the surface. "You're not funny."

"Debatable. People tell me I'm hilarious."

I arch a brow, crossing my arms. "Oh really? And who says that?" She opens her mouth, but I cut in before she can speak. "Besides these two." I nod toward Trish and Joanie, who both shrug, clearly enjoying the show.

Lyla presses her lips together, honestly pondering her answer, then her face lights up with an idea. "I bet your mom thinks I'm a *delight*."

I tilt my head. "Oh, I bet. She did have a front-row seat to your romantic ways."

Lyla freezes. The horror on her face is priceless.

Joanie's head snaps so fast toward her that I hear a pop. "Oh my God. Lyla, noooooooo."

Before she can retaliate, I step in, ignoring Joanie's squawk of protest as I reach out and take Lyla from their hold. My arms curve around her, cradling her effortlessly against my chest. She stiffens slightly, her breath catching as the warmth of her body presses into mine. Her wide blue eyes lock on to mine, the quick rise and fall of her chest brushing against me. There's a subtle hitch in her breath, and her fingers twitch against my shoulder like she's resisting the urge to grab on.

Oh yeah. She feels it too.

"I told them to let me know when they were moving you," I say, voice low, my gaze on her.

She scowls, a look that could probably scare off a weaker man. "I can walk on my own."

I shake my head, adjusting my hold on her. "I'd rather not have you bust open a stitch and bleed all over people again. Supplies aren't exactly easy to come by these days."

Her scowl slips, and the shift in her expression sends an unexpected pang of regret through me. Maybe I didn't need to say it like that.

But before I can find something to soften the blow, the moment's gone. Her grin returns, shameless, like she never felt the sting at all.

"Face it," she says, her voice dripping with sarcasm, her eyes sparkling with mischief. "You just wanted an excuse to hold me close, eh, *Gorgeous*?"

Trish's soft laugh cuts through the air. I shoot a glare at her, but she doesn't even have the decency to look guilty. She just continues toward the ambulance with Joanie.

I sigh, turning back to Lyla. "You're pretty cocky for someone who looks like she got into a brawl with a pack of hyenas and lost."

Lyla arches a brow, her full-blown smile making my heart stutter. "That's because I know my glowing personality is enough to dazzle you."

Damn her.

"More like blind me," I mutter.

By the time we reach the ambulance, her weight feels like it's pressing a little heavier against me, her posture relaxed. I pull open the passenger door, setting her down gently in the seat. Her sassiness fades, replaced by something quieter, almost vulnerable, as she watches me buckle her in. I keep my movements careful, afraid she might shatter if I handle her too roughly.

"There you go," I say, stepping back to give her space.

She frowns, her gaze darting around the cab. "I thought I was going in the back."

I shake my head. "I need you where I can keep an eye on you." I pause, leaning in just enough that to make her breath hitch, her body go still. "Besides, this way, we'll have plenty of time to get to know each other. And for you to tell me who you needed to see in that prison."

Her lips part as fire sparks in her gaze, and she straightens, arms crossing. "Well, get ready for a quiet car ride. I hope you have some good music to drown out the silence."

The bright smirk she flashes me does something low in my stomach, heat curling in my core. But just as I'm about to push her a little further, Mom steps up beside me, her quiet presence dousing that heat like an ice bath.

I clear my throat, shifting aside as she reaches out, her hand settling gently on Lyla's arm. The change in Lyla is instant—her frustration fades, the sharp edges of her expression smoothing as her good eye meets Mom's with a kind of warmth I haven't seen from her before.

Mom smiles, her voice warm as though she doesn't want to spook a wild animal. "How are you holding up, sweetheart?"

Lyla hesitates, the usual fire in her gaze faltering, her walls lowering just enough to reveal the cracks underneath. "I'm better," she says, her voice quieter than usual. "Thanks to you."

Mom chuckles, shaking her head. "Oh, don't give me too much credit. You're the one who kept fighting."

Lyla glances down at the hand on her arm, her fingers twitching like she's not sure what to do with the contact. When she looks back up, there's something raw in her expression. "You came back for me," she says, and it's not just gratitude—it's disbelief. Like the idea of someone choosing her, of coming back for her, still doesn't quite make sense.

Mom's brows scrunch with confusion. "Lyla, you saved my life. Of course I came back for you. That's what we do. We look out for each other."

Lyla just stares at her, like she's trying to process the words, to believe them. "Well, thank you," she murmurs, like she's not used to saying it. "For not leaving me behind."

Mom gives her arm a gentle squeeze, her own smile turning knowing, almost amused. "You remind me a lot of Jacob." She glances at me with that mix of pride and fond exasperation she's had my entire life. "Stubborn as hell, always acting like you don't need anyone. But deep down, you've got a good heart. You just don't like showing it."

Lyla snorts, rolling her eyes as she gestures toward me. "Great. Just what I needed, to be compared to him."

Mom leans forward in a mock whisper. "Oh, don't worry. You're tougher than he is. But don't tell him I said that."

Lyla chuckles. "Your secret's safe with me."

I cross my arms as I look between them. "All right, enough bonding time. We've got to start moving if we want to make good time today."

Mom tuts at me, then winks at Lyla before heading to the truck, leaving the two of us alone.

The silence stretches, and when Lyla turns her head toward me, her eyes playful and knowing.

"What?"

She tilts her head, pretending to think. "Just wondering, does it bruise your ego a little? Knowing your own mom thinks I'm tougher than you?"

I huff a laugh, stepping closer, resting one hand on the open doorframe. "You think I need her to tell me that?"

Lyla blinks, caught off guard for half a second, and I use the opening, leaning in just enough to watch the goose bumps spread across her arms, the way her fingers twitch against her lap.

"You're impossible." she says.

I tilt my head a little closer. "And you love it."

This close I catch whiffs of woodsmoke and rain-drenched earth. It clings to her like she belongs out here, something wild, untamed.

I like it. *A lot.*

I lock her my gaze with hers, my voice low. "Besides, if I decide to take you up on your offer for that date, I might just let you see how *impossible* I can be when we're alone."

Color blooms high on her cheeks, her pupils darken, and her eyes flick—quick, instinctual—to my mouth. Her lips part, but before she can fire something off, I straighten and shut the door.

I smirk, satisfied.

Through the window, her voice rings out, loud and indignant, "I take back the offer!"

"Too late," I yell back.

Her glare sharpens, lips moving fast, no doubt throwing every insult she can think of, but I don't stick around to hear them.

I just turn, heading back toward the clearing, my grin stretching wider.

Leon is leaning against his truck, my camper already reattached, with his arms crossed. As I approach, he raises his hands, signing, *"I saw that."*

"Don't you have something better to do?"

Up ahead, Earl stands by the hood of his beat-up red Ford, a map spread out across the dented surface. He's squinting at it, one hand braced on the hood, the other gripping a pencil. Hopefully, he doesn't notice the faint cup stain I left on one of his precious maps.

I stride up beside him, leaning over the hood to get a better look at today's route. "What's the verdict, Earl?"

Earl jabs the pencil at a crooked line on the map. "This one here's faster—cuts straight through the back routes up toward DC—but there's a good chance it'll dump us into a nest of walkers or worse." He shifts the pencil to another line. "This one's safer. Follows the old highways, but will take longer. And we sure as hell don't have unlimited gas."

"True, but safety is what we need, especially after this past week." I'm not risking our people again. If that means we have to hit smaller towns with fewer supplies, so be it.

"US Route 301 it is then," Earl mutters, rolling up the map.

I head back to the ambulance, pulling open the driver's door. Joanie and Trish are already in the back, their voices a faint hum.

Behind us, Leon's truck rumbles to life, Clair and Poppy already settled inside their own car. Beyond, Jessica and Pete are climbing into her beat-up Volkswagen.

Earl's truck kicks up dust as he rolls out of the clearing, and I follow, the ambulance bouncing over the uneven dirt road.

We don't even make it a full minute before Joanie's voice drifts up from the back.

"So, what snacks do we got for this trip?"

Un-freaking-believable.

PART TWO
BANTER

DON'T BITE ME THERE!: A ZOMBIE SURVIVAL GUIDE

BY EARL RUSSO

Tip #8: Don't be a loner.

Your odds of survival skyrocket when you've got a crew—especially one you can tolerate. Divide up responsibilities, play to your strengths, and take turns keeping watch so you can finally get some damn sleep. Just don't hesitate to cut the weak link if it comes to that. One bad decision can get all of you killed. *Trust me.*

Tip #13: Always know your exit strategy.

If a place only has one way in and out—skip it. You want options, because the undead don't knock. They crash in swinging. Always have a way out and be ready to fight like hell to reach it.

Tip #22: Stock up on those essentials.

Water. Food. Medical supplies. That's your holy trinity. If you find it, you take it. *No questions.*

Wife's suggestion: Use rain barrels or buckets to collect clean water. She's the smart one, obviously.

```
Memo to self: Find out who left the coffee ring
on my map.
```

Blood seeps through the shredded fabric, hot and steady. The sting barely cuts through the haze of rage boiling just beneath the surface. Her face is still burned into the backs of my eyes.

She thinks it's over.

Thinks she won.

The taste of blood lingers, thick on my tongue. Metallic. Familiar. Fuel.

Pain pulses with every heartbeat, but it's distant. Background noise. A warning light ignored.

The passenger door creaks open. The engine's already running—rumbling like it knows who it serves. The idiot behind the wheel shifts nervously, hands twitching on the steering wheel. Like a mutt waiting for approval.

Pathetic.

Still, he dragged me out—kept me from burning or turning. For now, that earns him his life.

He doesn't matter. None of them ever mattered.

Only one thing matters now.

I turn my head. Eyes burning holes through him.

"Find her."

No need to explain. No room for questions.

He swallows and nods, the tires already crunching over gravel, the car slipping into the dark like a shadow with teeth.

FOURTEEN
ROAD TRIP

HOURS CRAWL BY, marked only by the steady hum of the van as it jostles over cracked roads and gravel shoulders. Three supply stops broke the monotony—though Jacob insisted I stay behind, which gave me some time to hobble to a nearby gas station to get paper, pens, and nails—but otherwise, it's been nothing but silence.

Giving me plenty of time to think of the notes I'm going to leave for da Vinci to find.

Outside, the trees blur together, shadows stretching across the dirt path. Inside, the only sounds are the low growl of the engine, the occasional clatter of shifting supplies, and the unspoken weight hanging between us.

The most thrilling thing we've seen? An undead farmer in faded overalls, repeatedly body-checking a black-and-white cow statue in the middle of a cornfield like some undead square dance. It was weirdly hypnotic—and tragically on brand for our lives now.

Talk about entertainment.

Jacob's grip on the steering wheel is firm, fingers flexing every now and then, like he's working something out in his head. His eyes stay locked on the road, jaw tight, muscles in his forearm taut. The soft glow from the windshield cuts across his face, tracing the sharp edges of his profile, making it impossible not to look.

I shift in my seat, forcing my eyes away. The air between us feels stretched, taut, like a string pulled too tight.

I never get a chance to find out which one of us will break the silence because from the back, Joanie's voice slices through the quiet.

"Sooooo," she drawls, dragging out the word as long as humanly possible. Her knee bounces, fast and restless. "What kind of fucking music do ya got?"

Clearly she didn't listen to me when I told her the basics of interrogation. I turn in my seat and shoot her a sharp look. "Language."

She shrugs, unbothered, leaning back against the wall of the van with her legs stretched out in front of her. A piece of her dark, curly hair drops into her eyes.

"Do you ever not run your mouth?" Jacob asks, his voice dry, eyes flicking to the rearview mirror to meet hers.

Joanie sticks out her tongue at him. "You're just grumpy because I don't take your shit."

Trish snorts, her eyes blazing with amusement. "Aww, she's like a mini me."

Jacob's lips quirk up. It's fleeting, just the ghost of amusement, but it loosens the tight knot I keep wound around my heart.

My eyes drift, drawn to the tattooed black forest inked across his forearm, the dark lines stretching over muscle. Strong. Defined. The kind of arms built for holding, protecting. Damn. I was always an arm girl, and Jacob's? Well, they're very nice.

His fingers flex against the wheel, veins shifting beneath his skin, and heat flickers low in my stomach. My gaze trails upward, catching on the sharp cut of his jaw, the faint stubble that I know would feel rough against my fingertips. Then, his eyes.

Deep, chocolate eyes. The kind that shouldn't be able to pull a person in the way they do. There's something unreadable in them, something that feels like a challenge and a secret all at once.

The slow widening of his smile tells me I've been caught.

Shit.

I snap my gaze forward, heart kicking up a notch.

Jacob chuckles under his breath, and I swear I can hear the smugness in it.

Yeah. I'm in trouble.

"So," he says after a moment, his tone more conversational now. He rubs the stubble across his jaw. "What's your story, Trouble? You and the kid. What were you doing before everything went to hell?"

I hesitate, my fingers brushing against the edge of the door handle, the weight of his question pressing against me. But his tone isn't probing—it's genuinely curious.

"I was an FBI agent," I say finally, keeping my voice matter-of-fact, ready for the inevitable surprise reaction I get when I say this.

However, Jacob just hums, a knowing look crossing his face as though he's just slotted a puzzle piece in place in his head.

Joanie adds, "She was badass too. Some of the stories she told me are wild." Her fingers fiddle with the hem of her shirt as she leans back against the wall.

My eyes squeeze shut at her dramatics. "She likes to make it sound more exciting than it actually was." The way Joanie puts it, I sound like the coolest person ever, but she couldn't be farther from the truth. "I was tracking a specific group of criminals."

"What group?" Jacob asks.

I sigh. Might as well give him this. "They called themselves the Artists. Each one took the name of their favorite painter and used . . ." I pause, searching for the least horrifying way to say it. ". . . distinct methods in their kills."

Jacob glances at me, brow furrowed. "What kind of methods?"

I take a deep breath. "Van Gogh specialized in amputation. Pollock? Splatter art, only with blood. Dalí had a thing for power tools. Called them 'transformative.' " My voice flattens. "There were six in total. One ringleader."

A beat of silence.

"Did you get them all?" Trish asks.

I pick at a loose thread on the hem of my shirt, my fingers working mindlessly as my thoughts drift to the life I had before all of this. Before everything I thought I knew was ripped away.

"Almost," I whisper.

I could blame da Vinci for how everything unraveled, for the isolation that's sunk into my bones like rot, but the truth is, I was always a loner. Dated when it suited me. Spent time with Mark and his family when I felt like it. But after my dad died, I stopped showing up. Didn't have much family left, and I convinced myself that was fine.

I was self-reliant. That was enough.

Or so I thought.

Then Mark was taken, and the ground vanished beneath me. No warning. No chance to brace. Just free fall.

The weight settles in deep, thick and frigid. I clamp my jaw tight, trying to swallow it down, but it clings, refuses to let go.

I just need to hold out until he shows. Once I finish what I started, this emptiness will go with him.

Jacob looks at me, obviously waiting for me to continue, so I say, "I was investigating a case when everything went sideways."

"What kind of case?"

I shrug, eyes locked on the blur of trees outside the window. "Doesn't matter now." I can't bring her back, but I can make damn sure the monster who took her stops breathing.

He nods, gaze sliding to Joanie, clearly catching the hint that I'm done sharing. "And you, kid? What's your story?"

Joanie shrugs, the usual spark in her eyes dimming. "I was a freshman. I was at school when the emergency broadcast went out. They sent us all home on buses."

She hesitates, the air between us shifting. "Unfortunately, some of the buses didn't make it home."

Her voice wavers, just enough to crack through the mask she always wears.

Joanie never talks about the time before I found her. Anytime I ask, she freezes up, her whole body going still, or she deflects with some half-assed joke. I don't push. I should, but I don't.

Because I worry about her.

She buries her pain under humor, grinning through the cracks, pretending like the past can't touch her if she doesn't acknowledge it. But grief doesn't work like that. It festers. It lingers. It eats at you from the inside out.

She won't heal if she doesn't talk about it. But who am I to say differently?

I do the exact same thing.

She continues, "Anyway, Lyla found me. Saved my ass. And she's been stuck with me ever since."

Trish's voice is gentle. "And your folks?"

Joanie stares ahead, eyes locked on the wall, but she's not seeing it. She's back in that living room, gun in hand, crouched between her dead parents, tears streaking down her face. Her usual fire's gone, snuffed out and replaced with a hollow, faraway look.

Jacob notices. His voice drops, steady and soft. "I'm sorry, kid."

No teasing. No sarcasm. Just quiet understanding.

No one speaks for a while. Trish watches Joanie with quiet sadness, like she knows the shape of this kind of grief all too well. Jacob keeps glancing in the rearview, worry etched deep across his jaw.

Fantastic. He's not just built like every terrible decision I've ever wanted to make, he's got a good heart too. The universe is mocking me. Loudly.

I clear my throat, needing to shake off whatever this is. "What about you?" I ask, breaking the silence. "Where were you when it started?"

Jacob's hands tighten on the wheel, knuckles paling slightly. "On the job. Putting out fires—literally. We got a call about an explosion at the edge of town, and when we got there . . . people were running. Screaming. Then we saw them, the dead, moving, chasing. Coms went down soon after, and we were on our own."

His voice is even, but there's something underneath it. Something sore.

I turn to Trish.

She exhales sharply, raking a hand through her short hair. "Same. I was responding to 911 calls in the emergency van. It was madness, people begging for help, not understanding what was happening. We kept going until we couldn't. Until it was just us."

No one says it out loud, but I know what she means. *Until everyone else was dead.*

I shift in my seat, wincing as my ribs remind me they're still in recovery. Joanie is leaning back in the rear corner, her legs crossed at the ankles, picking at her nails like she's trying to act unbothered, but she sneaks glances at Jacob through the rearview mirror.

"So," I say, breaking the quiet. We all really need to pick a new word to break the silences. My gaze shifts to Trish. "What's the routine and pace on this fun journey?"

Hopefully, not too fast.

Trish leans forward. "We drive until we hit a small town. Stick to the main roads long enough to scope out the infected levels. If it looks clear, we scavenge—shops, houses, cars. Three-hour limit. Then we regroup, pack up, and move on."

"Once it gets close to nightfall," she continues, "we post up near the next town, sleep, then hit it fresh in the morning. Same pattern every day. Quick meals. No long breaks. Just steady progress before winter hits."

It's late August, which gives us maybe three months to make it to the farm, if we keep pace.

Jacob cuts in. "Basically, we favor the slow-and-steady mindset."

Score.

He glances at me. "Unlike you."

Our eyes meet, and there it is again, that spark of challenge in his gaze, the one that gets my blood pumping. Then he winks, the bastard, and tingles spread across my body like a live wire snapping to life.

"All right," I say, eyeing him. "Where to next?"

Jacob's grin turns downright sinful, voice dropping an octave, thick with amusement. "Next?" He drags it out, glancing at Joanie, who's practically vibrating. "Stony Creek, where we're getting you ladies some wheels."

Good. The more we stop, the more time da Vinci has to catch up.

Joanie lights up like the Fourth of July. "Oh, hell yes!" she yells, punching the air like she just won the apocalypse lottery.

I arch a brow, shifting my gaze to Jacob. "Since we didn't pick up a car earlier, I assumed you wanted me riding shotgun for the rest of this trip, *Gorgeous*."

His grin widens, smug, cocky, dangerous. "Just wanted to see if I could get more information out of you. And I did."

You didn't get all the information, bud.

"Don't worry. I plan on enjoying your company for many, many miles. But you need your own space. Somewhere to crash. Somewhere to stash gear." His eyes rake over me, lingering in a way that has zero to do with logistics.

"Besides, I plan on having you ride shotgun on something else, *Trouble*." He winks.

Heat curls low in my stomach.

Joanie makes her classic gagging noise. Trish snorts from the back.

"Careful, Jacob," I say, tone light, edged with warning. "You might regret giving me that much freedom."

His eyes snap back to mine. For a beat, everything stills. Thick air. A spark caught between us.

Then he looks away, eyes on the road, voice low, sure.

"Looking forward to it."

FIFTEEN
NETWORKING

LYLA

WE'VE CHOSEN a small clearing for the night—a patch of mossy ground cradled by towering pines. The sky is a fading masterpiece of orange and purple, the last light slipping into the grasp of twilight. The air hums with a chorus of insects, blending with the low crackle of our fire, the flames dulled by a tall ring of rocks to keep us hidden.

As the group settles in, I force my body to move despite the exhaustion dragging at me. Every muscle aches, a dull throb beneath my skin, but staying still isn't an option.

I scan the perimeter, taking in the quiet rhythm of survival.

Earl rubs his ankle while Edith fusses over him. Trish organizes supplies, her movements methodical. Leon sharpens his hatchet, the scrape of steel against stone filling the air.

And then—just beyond the fire's reach—I see *him.*

Jacob moves through the trees like a man who's done this a hundred times, his presence seamless with the night. The firelight catches on the edge of his jaw, the strong curve of his shoulders as he strings metal cans between low branches.

I watch him work, his movements practiced and efficient. Even in stillness, there's tension in his shoulders, a quiet alertness that never fades. He doesn't seem to do *relaxed.* Not really.

I've noticed it more over the past week—the way he carries the weight of everyone's survival like it's second nature, the way he watches over the group without making a show of it. The way he *watches me.*

And maybe I watch him too.

Okay, I *definitely* watch him too.

I don't realize how long I've been staring until he glances up, catching my gaze across the clearing.

His eyes hold mine for a beat, unreadable. Then he tilts his head toward the trees, a silent invitation.

My pulse skips.

I push off the log I've been leaning against, making my way over. My boots crunch softly against the forest floor, the firelight dimming behind me until it's just me and him, wrapped in the shadows of the trees.

"Old-world security system?" I ask, nodding toward the cans.

"Crude, but effective against the undead." Jacob's fingers finish off another knot. He tugs the wire tight, testing it. "If anything gets too close, we'll hear it before they get the drop on us. Plus, you should see the stakes." He nods into the darkness and I can just make out Leon and Earl driving clusters of wooden stakes, clearly made from thick tree branches, into the ground.

"We put these up every time we set up camp. Helps slow down a horde just in case we need to make a quick getaway."

Efficient. Tactical. Always thinking ahead.

"Anything else I should be aware of out here?" I ask.

"There are also some bear traps beyond the barriers, so it's best to stay within the perimeter unless either Leon or I are with you." He winks and continues hanging cans.

My gaze catches on the calluses lining his hands—earned, not inherited.

I nod, glancing back at the camp. Small clusters of people sit around lanterns, voices low, laughter sparking through the stillness. It feels . . . foreign.

Soon, I'll need a way to stay awake at night. Keep watch. He'll come—bruised, maybe broken, but alive. I'll use that window to prepare. Volunteer for security setup, figure out the blind spots. Maybe pitch a few extra measures, make the place harder to breach. Make it harder for da Vinci to slip in unnoticed.

Jacob misinterprets my hesitation because his voice dips lower, smoother—more knowing. "They won't bite."

I huff. "Nice joke, Dad."

He chuckles, but when I glance over, his expression has softened into something serious. "I mean it. You don't have to hang back. You saved them. That matters."

I grab the end of the wire he's threading, anchoring it to a low branch. If he knew I was dragging danger straight to their doorstep, he might not be so quick to hand out gold stars. "Saving people is easy. Talking to them is the hard part."

Jacob studies me for a beat, then tilts his head. "You scared of networking, *Trouble*?"

I snort. "I'm not scared of anything." I yank the knot tighter. "I just don't like to get attached."

He says nothing. Just waits for me to continue. Annoying.

"I don't like to have friends."

Jacob hums, thoughtful. "Could've fooled me with all that overconfidence, the snappy remarks, and the way that kid follows you around like a damn shadow."

My gaze flicks toward Joanie, who's laughing at something Trish said, her voice bright and unbothered.

It's weird how much she's wormed her way into my life in only a couple of months.

"She's more like an annoying kid sister."

Jacob chuckles, shaking his head. "Sure."

He finishes tying off his end of the wire, then holds out another length of it toward me. When I reach for it, he doesn't let go, forcing me to meet his gaze.

His fingers are warm against mine and I swear I can feel my pulse there, in that single point of contact.

"In this world, you don't survive alone. You might think you can, but eventually, you'll end up stuck—shuffling around, lost, just like them." His head tilts toward the tree line, where the faintest groans of the undead still linger in the night air. "It's other people that'll keep you moving forward. They'll give you light in all this shitty darkness."

His fingers tighten—just for a second. Then he lets go, expression shifting. Something haunted flashes in his eyes before the mask drops back into place.

"Trust me," he says quietly. "I know."

The words settle like gravel in my chest. I look away, but the truth clings to me—sharp, familiar.

He must see it written across my face, because his shoulder bumps mine as he nudges me toward the clearing. His voice shifts—dropping into something downright playful. "Now, be a good girl and go make some friends."

My breath catches.

The heat hits low and hard—unexpected and far too effective. Why did my body react so quickly to those two words?

Memo to me: *unpack that later.*

I roll my eyes and shove past him, ignoring the grin stretching across his face. He knows exactly what he's doing. Bastard.

I square my shoulders and step back into the firelight, heading toward Edith and Earl, both of whom are tucked under a worn red checkered blanket.

They seem like good choices to start with.

Edith is fussing over Earl, who tells me that he twisted his ankle all because of a rabbit burrow while hunting with Leon yesterday. Of course Edith mentions how he also bruised his ego.

The warmth of the exchange seeps into my bones.

I haven't felt this in a long time. Like I finally belong somewhere.

The conversation drifts through the night, easy and effortless. Edith tells a story about how Earl once tried to fight off a raccoon with a spatula—a tale that earns a loud, cackling laugh from Joanie and a sheepish grin from Earl.

Eventually, I leave Joanie with them, my body dragging like dead weight. As I step away, Edith murmurs something conspiratorial to Joanie—her voice low, teasing.

Joanie snorts water up her nose. Trish smacks her back, cursing.

I shake my head, a small smile tugging at my lips as I head for Lucy, the beautiful, dinged-up maroon Trailblazer Joanie and I picked out earlier in a high school parking lot.

But a few steps away, Barbara sits cross-legged beneath a stunted pine, her back pressed against the rough bark as she sifts through a modest pile of supplies—bandages, a few cans of food, a small sack of clothes.

The firelight dances across her face, tracing the tired lines around her eyes. She glances up as I approach, tucking a loose strand of brown hair behind her ear.

"Mind if I join you?" I ask, lowering myself onto the mossy ground beside her.

She shakes her head. "Free country."

We both laugh at the absurdity of it.

I nod toward the supplies scattered in front of her. "Taking inventory?"

"Something like that."

Barbara picks up a can of peaches, turning it over in her hands before setting it aside. "Figured I'd see what's worth keeping, what we can trade if we run into friendlies."

"Smart," I say, studying her in the firelight.

She's got that quiet kind of strength—the kind that doesn't need to announce itself but is impossible to ignore. Unshakable. I can see where Jacob gets it.

She shrugs. "Just doing what I can." Then her eyes flick to mine, assessing. "Can I ask you something?"

"Well, since you did save me . . ."

She doesn't take the bait. "Who was that man in the office with you?"

My body goes still. So that's where Jacob gets his bluntness.

"He was a man who destroyed many lives." The words scrape out of me—raw, bitter. I hesitate, weighing how much of myself I want to give away. "He took someone close to me. Just to punish me. I owed a lot of people his death."

The truth hangs in the air between us. Solid. Unshakable.

I think of every family I had to face. Every mother I had to tell, *your daughter's gone.* Every promise I made that justice would come.

And now, it will.

A jolt runs through me at the warmth of Barbara's hand on mine. She squeezes my hand, pulling me back. When I meet her gaze, there's only comfort.

"I'm glad you got him," she says simply.

My chest tightens. I wish I could tell her he's really gone. That he isn't still out there, breathing, watching, waiting. But soon. I won't let da Vinci tear apart another family.

Movement catches my eye.

Jacob steps into the clearing, heading toward the camper hitched to the back of Earl's truck.

I nod toward him, eager for the shift. "What's his story?"

It's low, I know—asking his mom—but who better to offer insight than the woman who raised him?

Barbara follows my gaze.

Firelight softens her features, and for the first time, I catch something unmistakable in her eyes—love. Fierce. Unshakable. The kind I used to dream my father might show me. The kind he never did.

"He's always taken responsibility for the family," she says, voice steady but laced with something heavier. "Protects us at all costs."

Her shoulders drop with the sigh that follows. "He blames himself when things go sideways. When someone gets hurt. Carries it all like it's his cross to bear—never asks for help, never lets anyone carry the weight with him."

She pauses, eyes on the flames. "When his father walked out, Jacob convinced himself it was because of him. Thought maybe if he'd loved harder, been better, his father would've stayed."

She shakes her head, frustration flickering beneath the surface. "I've told him a thousand times it wasn't his fault, but he still won't believe it."

The words hang between us.

I don't have a response. What could I possibly say to that?

Before I can pin it down, her eyes land on me. My pulse jumps.

Oh *no.*

"He might just need someone else to make him see differently," she says, going back to organizing supplies like she didn't just drop a grenade in my lap.

Did Barbara just encourage me to go after her son?

Cool. Now my face is on fire.

I pretend not to notice the heat crawling up my neck and steer the conversation toward safer ground. We talk logistics—where we might head next, how to stretch what little we've got. She jokes about teaching Joanie some manners, and I snort, picturing Joanie trying to sip tea while stabbing an infected through the eye.

It's moments like these—easy laughter, quiet companionship—that make something in my chest shift.

Is this what it feels like to belong again?

The idea is reckless. I should know better. Comfort gets you killed. Attachment gets you gutted.

And yet, sitting here with knees pulled in, firelight dancing across familiar faces, I feel it—those invisible threads weaving between us. Fragile. Tentative. Real.

Something close to family.

Then his face flashes in my mind.

Mark.

That crooked smile. The teasing glint in his eye. The way his body fell—

No.

I shut the door on the memory before it can crash down like a wave I'll never swim out of.

My fingers curl into my palms, nails biting into skin. The laughter, the warmth—it all feels *stolen*. Like something I don't *deserve*.

Before Barbara can clock the shift in my face, I shove to my feet and brush the dirt from my hands.

She studies me. Clearly, I'm not as good at hiding my emotions as I think because her face softens with concern.

Luckily, she takes pity on me.

"Get some rest," she says, voice gentle.

Joanie's laugh rings out, bright and reckless. In the firelight, she looks like a kid again—soft edges, unguarded. For once, she isn't carrying the weight of the world on her spine. The apocalypse stole a lot from her, but not this. Not completely.

Leon hangs at the edge of the light, half-shadowed. His attention drifts toward Clair and Poppy's vehicle, gaze lingering a second too long before flicking away.

Then there's Jessica.

Standing near the camper, her figure a dark silhouette against the trees. Eyes locked on Jacob.

I tense, hackles rising.

She senses it. Her gaze slices toward me, sharp and territorial.

Seriously?

She turns back to Jacob—who, of course, is completely oblivious to her admiring gaze.

Nope.

I don't have the bandwidth for this adolescent power play, Jessica.

I exhale sharply, the warm night air sticking against my skin, and turn back toward Barbara—who is very clearly trying not to laugh.

Guess she caught my eye roll.

"Night, Barbara," I mutter, already walking.

She lifts a hand in parting, voice filled with barely concealed amusement. "Night, Lyla."

I nod and turn toward Lucy, ready to shut out the world. I'll deal with the others later. Right now, my social battery is shot, and my body's screaming for rest.

I reach for the SUV door, already dreaming of the quiet inside, when a voice slices through the camp noise.

"Hey, uh—Lyla?"

Damn it.

I turn, slow, already bracing.

Pete.

Of course.

Tall, lanky, twitchy as hell. His greasy hair's been slicked back like that helps, but it only makes him look more like someone you wouldn't want near a school zone. His shoulders hunch like he's trying to disappear into himself, eyes flicking around like he's prepping for an escape.

My internal alarms start howling.

Warning. Warning.

"Yeah?" I cross my arms.

"Pete Clarks," he says with faux casualness. "Just wanted to, uh, officially introduce myself. Figured we'll be seeing a lot of each other now that we're, y'know, traveling buddies and all."

He shuffles his feet, hands twitching like they don't know where to land.

"I was gonna say hi earlier, but I didn't wanna, like, overwhelm you or anything. Figured you needed space."

He adds a halfhearted chuckle, trying to read as shy and thoughtful. But it's all bullshit. I've seen better performances from decapitated walkers.

I let the silence stretch. Let it work on him.

One of the oldest tactics in the book.

His Adam's apple bobs. He scratches the back of his neck. "I'm a friend of Earl's. He's always tried to help me out, give me a place, some purpose." Then, like it's the grand finale of his pity parade, he mutters, "Anyway, uh . . . thanks. For saving me. By saving everyone else, I guess."

I stare at him. "I didn't do it for you. I did what was right."

Pete's eyes dart. His hand now starts to pick the back of his neck, fingers twitching, like they can't find a place to land.

He starts again, quieter, more conspiratorial. "Jacob, though? He's been on my ass ever since we got out. Acting like I could've done something. Like I let those guys take everyone. But what was I supposed to do? Get killed trying to be a hero? That would've helped no one."

My jaw clenches, a sharp grind of teeth.

Pete watches me carefully, then sighs, his expression taking on a pitiful slant. "He doesn't know how it really went down."

There it is.

The real reason he's here.

He wants me to vouch for him. Tell Jacob he's not so bad.

I step in, slow and steady.

"You want sympathy?" My voice slices clean. "Wrong person."

He swallows hard.

"I would've died for those people." I jab a finger toward Clair and Poppy's car. "I would've ripped out every throat to save that little girl."

Poppy's terrified cries ring through my head like an echo I can't shake. The way she clung to her mother, tiny hands wrapped around Clair like she could hold her together. The way she whimpered, tied to a chair, too small, too innocent for the nightmare she was forced into—while this pathetic excuse of a man stood by and did nothing.

The rage inside me is white-hot, desperate to get out and burn the man in front of me.

"Forgive me if I don't want to hear how unfair Jacob's being," I say, venom lacing every word. "He sees you for what you are."

I step even closer.

"A coward."

Pete's eyes blaze—something dark, something defensive—but he doesn't argue.

Maybe he knows there's nothing he can say to change what he is.

Or maybe he's just too weak to defend himself.

He lets out a breath through his nose. "Guess I shouldn't have wasted my time. You've already made up your mind. Just like the rest of them."

I shrug. "Guess so."

He turns and disappears into the dark, shoulders tight with frustration.

As soon as he's gone, I let out the breath I've been holding.

My talking meter? Officially tapped out.

I climb into Lucy and slam the door, letting the quiet press in.

My body hums with residual rage, nerves buzzing under my skin and I can tell sleep isn't coming anytime soon.

Damn it.

Fine. If I can't rest, I might as well make the insomnia useful.

I reach for the notepad and pen I snagged earlier and flip it open.

The words pour out in jagged ink, bleeding anger across every page. Each line is a weapon. A breadcrumb. A challenge.

This time, I'm not chasing him.

I'm *leading* him.

Every detail I leave behind is bait. A map. A way to lure da Vinci straight to me—on *my* terms.

For once, I get to be ready.

And I'm going to make it count.

SIXTEEN

WELCOME CAMPERS
LYLA

THE CAMP'S SILENT.

Edith and Earl slump in their chairs, heads at broken angles. Clair's sprawled in the dirt, arm outstretched toward the truck bed, where Poppy's small hand hangs limp.

Footsteps. Slow. Measured.

Da Vinci steps into the firelight, face dripping red. Behind him, Jacob kneels, da Vinci's fist in his hair, blade catching the glow.

"Missed you, Lyla," he purrs. "Thought I'd save you a front row seat."

The knife slices. Blood sprays. My scream tears loose—

—and I spring up in the SUV, chest heaving, knife clenched in my hand.

The images cling, Jacob's body collapsing, blood pooling around the people I swore to protect. My pulse hammers. My grip tightens on the blade.

I won't let that happen.

Joanie's snoring, a faint, rhythmic sound, drags me back to reality as my breathing evens out. I look over the dim interior of Lucy, shadows stretching long across Joanie's sprawled-out form. She's draped over her makeshift bed like a crime scene chalk outline, mouth slightly open, one arm flopped over my stomach.

Typical.

Her brow furrows for a second, like she's dreaming something bad, and her fingers twitch against my stomach before relaxing again. It's fleeting, but strange enough that my eyes linger on her face a beat longer than usual. Then she mutters something low, too soft to catch, and flops onto her side, still snoring with the same determined energy.

I sigh, dragging a hand down my face. There's no point in trying for another round.

Carefully, I shift upright. My muscles protest, stiff and sore from pushing too hard for too long, but I grit my teeth and move anyway.

I need to walk this nightmare off.

With practiced ease, I slip on my boots, crack my neck, and tuck Sweetness into my belt before quietly crawling to the driver's seat.

The door creaks as I push it open, muggy morning air rushing against my face. I step onto the dirt, stretching until my spine pops, shaking off the stiffness.

The sun is just cresting the treetops, spilling golden light through the branches, chasing away the last shreds of night. The air is damp, thick with the lingering kiss of morning dew, the scent of pine and earth mixing into something almost clean. Almost peaceful.

Leaning against Lucy's trunk, I rub a hand over my face before scanning the camp.

Earl leans against his truck, a huge stack of paper maps spread across the hood, muttering to himself as he traces routes with a calloused finger.

People still have those?

Near the van, Clair sits with Poppy, carefully brushing through the little girl's tangled curls while Poppy scribbles in a small notebook, her tongue poking out in concentration. Clair's dark-circled gaze keeps glancing over to Leon, who is crouched by a pile of gear, sharpening a knife with slow, methodical strokes. Sunlight glints off his weapons, bow, arrows, hatchet, handgun, all strapped into place.

Now where is he going?

I grab my gun from Lucy's driver's seat, slipping it into the chest holster. My fingers double-check Sweetness at my waist before I head toward Leon.

"Where ya headed, *friend*?" I ask, aiming for casual.

Leon doesn't even glance up. Just keeps adjusting the strap on his quiver.

I cross my arms, arching a brow. "You know, I get the whole strong, silent routine. Which, for you, is just called existing. But a little acknowledgment wouldn't kill you."

Finally, he looks up. No smirk, no twitch of amusement. Nothing.

Tough crowd.

"Listen," I say, voice quieter now. "I've got all this energy and nowhere to put it. Can I help with whatever you're doing? I'll go nuts if I don't have something to do."

His grip on the strap loosens, his sharp gaze assessing me in a way that feels less guarded.

He nods once, then jerks his chin for me to follow.

We weave through a small cluster of trees, slipping between thick trunks until we reach Jacob's camper. Leon raps his knuckles on the door twice, short and sharp.

A beat later, it swings open, revealing Jacob with a sawback machete strapped to his back, Lars's shotgun resting easy in his hands. *So that's where that went.*

His brows lift when he spots me lingering behind Leon.

They start signing to each other, fast, fluid movements of their hands, an unspoken language I don't understand.

And I hate that.

Being left out of a conversation is one thing. Knowing it's about *me*? That's a whole other level of annoying.

I clear my throat, tilting my head. "You know, I'm getting real sick of these private chats about me right in front of my face."

Jacob's gaze slides to me, one brow lifting in amusement. "How do you know we're talking about you?"

"Oh, please." I roll my eyes, arms crossing tight over my chest. "You both keep looking at me like I'm some lost puppy." I level him with a pointed look. "Newsflash, I'm bored. So unless you want to find me climbing the damn trees, I need something to do. So," I gesture at the both of them, "what are we up to? Because I'm tagging along."

Plus, if we're moving through new ground, I can use the time to lay some tracks. A scratch here, a subtle mark there—nothing too obvious, just enough for the right eyes to follow. Da Vinci's eyes. He'll think he's hunting me, but really, I'll be setting the path. Drawing him closer.

Jacob steps out of the camper, closing the door with a firm click. He exchanges another quick set of signs with Leon before turning back to me.

"We're hunting. Lead the way, Trouble."

Stepping past them, I toss a smug grin over my shoulder and call back, "Let's go find us some wabbits, boys."

———

THE CAMPFIRE CRACKLES in the dusk, its warmth a sharp contrast to the creeping night chill. Smoke curls into the sky, mixing with the mouthwatering aroma of roasting venison.

The deer we downed earlier sizzles on a spit, juices dripping onto the coals in small bursts of steam. The scent stirs something primal in me, an honest hunger I haven't felt in ages.

Earl and Edith handle the meal with skill, dried spices, a pinch of salt, and whatever canned vegetables they dug up.

When Edith ladles portions into mismatched bowls, quiet appreciation ripples through the group. People lean in, inhaling the smoky fragrance, shoulders loosening.

The murmurs, the laughter, the way they settle into each other's company, it tugs at something I refuse to name. It'd be too easy to lean into this, to pretend it's safe to belong. I know better. The second you get comfortable, the world takes it away.

Not everyone's at ease though.

Jessica sits beside Jacob, posture stiff, eyes darting. Possessiveness rolls off her in subtle waves—in the way her fingers tighten around her bowl when he speaks, in the way she watches him like she's waiting for confirmation.

Jesus.

I exhale, tongue pressed to the roof of my mouth to keep my eyes from rolling so hard they get stuck.

Because really?

After everything we've survived, after the blood, the loss, the constant fight to stay alive, *this* is what she's focused on?

Jacob, for his part, doesn't seem to notice.

He can't be that oblivious, can he?

Earl clears his throat, eyes twinkling. "All right, let's liven things up with a quick round of questions." He rubs his hands together, leaning forward like he's about to reveal some great mystery. "What's the food you miss the most from the old world?"

Trish doesn't hesitate. "Movie theater popcorn," she sighs, glowing at the memory. "With the fake butter oil that'd clog your arteries."

Barbara chuckles. "Mine's mint chocolate chip ice cream."

Jacob leans back, a smirk tugging at his lips. "Only the green kind, right?"

Barbara grins wider, pointing at him. "That's right."

Poppy's voice is a timid whisper. "S'mores."

Clair, beside her, murmurs, "Frosted brown sugar cinnamon Pop-Tarts."

Trish grins. "Oh, this is going to get interesting." She nudges Leon. "He swears by frosted strawberry Pop-Tarts. Best flavor. Would die on that hill."

Leon's jaw tightens.

Clair's gaze flicks to him, curiosity sparking, the smallest of smiles playing at her lips.

Joanie, ever the little savior, jumps in. "Buttermilk pancakes."

All eyes turn to me.

This should be good.

"Cinnamon gummy hearts."

The reaction is instantaneous.

Groans erupt from the group, a unified sound of horror and betrayal. Even Poppy, sweet, innocent Poppy, gasps like I've personally ruined her childhood.

"Cinnamon gummy hearts?" she squeaks, her tiny nose scrunching up like I just suggested we eat dirt.

Joanie takes it further, clutching her chest like she's been mortally wounded. "Of all the treats left in the ashes of civilization, that's what you miss? Not chocolate? Not donuts? Not pizza-flavored anything?" She fake-gags for emphasis.

Poppy giggles, sudden, bright, and completely unexpected.

Clair startles, her wary eyes flicking between Poppy and Joanie, as if waiting for the moment to vanish. But then, as if it's contagious, she starts to laugh too, soft at first, then growing.

I glance at Leon. His lips are curved in a rare grin as he watches them, like he's seeing something worth remembering.

Well, well, well.

I shrug. "What can I say? I like a little bite."

Joanie groans, shoving my shoulder. "You're so lame."

"I like what I like, and I won't apologize."

Across the fire, Jacob's gaze locks on to mine, amusement shimmering in the dim light. "Oh, I bet you don't apologize for much, Trouble."

The low, teasing tone sends a thrill down my spine. My pulse kicks up, heat prickling my skin.

I clear my throat. "All right, hot shot. What do you miss?"

"Pulled-pork nachos."

I bark a laugh. "Pulled-pork nachos? You couldn't pick something more apocalypse-friendly? At least mine comes prewrapped and lasts forever."

Jessica chimes in. "I also would choose pulled-pork nachos."

Of course you would.

"See?" Jacob's grin spreads. "Also, what was it someone just said?" He taps his chin, feigning deep thought. "Oh, right. 'I like what I like, and I won't apologize for it.' "

I huff, narrowing my eyes. "Good luck finding a pig for your nachos."

Trish chuckles from across the fire. "Jacob would be the type to try and domesticate a javelina for the sake of his nacho cravings."

Jacob laughs, all cocky charm. "Damn right."

"Okay, but if we ever come across a pig, we have to name it Nacho," Joanie adds.

Earl, clearly enjoying the energy around the fire, claps his weathered hands together. "All right, it's the moment of truth, Lyla." He strokes his scruffy chin, and I swear I can hear the wheels turning in his head. "Since you're fed, was it the government who killed JFK? You must know."

Edith groans, already massaging her temples like she's had to endure this conspiracy theorist nonsense for decades. "Please don't start."

Earl ignores her. "Come on, you can't tell me those documents just vanished when the world went to hell. You know something."

I smirk. "Oh, I know plenty."

Earl leans in, rubbing his hands together like he's about to unearth some great, long-buried truth. "See? Knew it."

"You wanna know the truth?" Everyone leans in, barely breathing. I deadpan. "The moon landing was real."

A beat of silence.

Joanie groans, throwing her head back. "Oh, come on!"

Jacob chuckles, while Trish straight-up snorts into her bowl.

Earl crosses his arms, feigning deep offense. "I don't trust you, Agent Lyla. That's exactly what a government plant would say."

Edith pats his knee. "Let the woman eat her chili in peace."

Earl slumps. "Fine. But I'm keeping my theories wide open, and you and I are gonna talk more."

I grin, scooping another bite of food. "You do that, Earl."

Laughter ripples, warm and easy. It seeps under my skin before I can stop it. Almost makes me want to let it stay. Almost. But warmth like this comes with a price I've already paid.

Earl's next question catches me off guard. "What's the best thing about this apocalypse, if you had to pick?"

Some shift uncomfortably, others stare into the fire, searching for an answer. It's easy to talk about what we've lost. Harder to admit that some things might actually be better now.

Trish stretches her legs out, tapping the cover of a worn paperback beside her. It's different from the one I saw her with last week—this one has a dragon breathing fire at a knight. "More reading time."

Joanie grins, raising her hands in mock praise. "No more school. Permanent summer vacation, baby."

"No more chores." Poppy beams.

Clair chuckles, tucking Poppy's hair behind her ear. "No more overbearing parents," she says, a shadow in her voice.

"The company," Edith says warmly.

Earl chuckles. "I'm finally useful! Took the world ending, but my cartography skills are paying off." He pats the folded map on his knee.

Leon signs. Jacob translates. "Hunting."

We all raise our bowls in a toast.

"No work," Pete mutters.

Jessica, however, speaks with more conviction, "Friends." Her eyes jerk to Jacob's profile.

I swallow the snort that is fighting to break free.

Jacob's gaze slides to me. With a lazy smile he says, "New friends."

The way his eyes linger makes my pulse stutter.

I hold his gaze, refusing to let him win whatever unspoken game he thinks we're playing. My lips part, a retort already forming, something to wipe that self-satisfied look off his face, but before I can, he stands and stretches, his muscles shifting beneath his shirt as he rolls his shoulders.

"Tomorrow, we head into town for supplies." His tone shifts to command. The warmth fades, replaced by responsibility. "Rest up."

One by one, people peel away from the fire, murmuring quiet goodnights as they slip into vehicles or tents. Trish hooks Joanie into a headlock, dragging her toward the ambulance while Joanie shrieks in protest, laughing between gasps. Leon lingers just long enough to sign something to Jacob before melting into the dark like a ghost.

I rise, stretching sore muscles. "Hey, Jo, I'm heading to bed."

Her muffled voice carries from under Trish's arm. "Be right there! Just grabbing a book."

I narrow my eyes. "Trish, she's fourteen. Make sure it's appropriate."

Trish cackles, already vanishing into the ambulance. "Yes, Mom!"

I shake my head. Walking toward Lucy, the firelight dancing in her windows, I feel it—lightness. Rare. The night is warm but not muggy, laughter still hanging in the air. For once, just for a moment, everything feels *almost* normal.

Then Jessica steps into my path.

Son of a biscuit-eating bulldog.

The shift is instant. Warmth gone. The night feels sharper, hostile. She plants herself in front of me, rigid. Her eyes lock on mine, chin tilted in territorial challenge.

"Back off," she murmurs, low enough for only me to hear.

I blink, deadpan. "Excuse me?"

She moves closer, not touching, but close enough to make her intent clear. "He's been through a lot. He needs people who understand him."

"I'm not doing anything to him."

She scoffs. "He lost his fiancée right before the world went to hell," she hisses. "It was brutal." She lets that hang, like bait on a hook. Waiting to see if I'll bite. "It was hard for him to see her displayed like that. Broken. Butchered. Taken from him. From all of us."

The words are designed to hurt, to plant doubt. And damn it, they succeed, just for a second. Something inside me tightens, a flicker of hesitation winding its way through my ribs.

Jessica notices. She likes it.

She leans in, smug now. "Don't think you can replace what he lost."

Ah. There it is.

My pulse kicks up. "Why? Because that's what you're trying to do?"

Jessica's head snaps back like I slapped her.

I step forward, forcing her to hold my gaze. "I'm not here to replace anyone. And don't threaten me, Jessica." My voice drops, blade-sharp. "Because I will show you just how threatening I can be."

For a moment, uncertainty flares in her eyes. Then her lips press into a thin, bitter line. "Just stay out of my way."

She turns and disappears into the shadows.

I stand there, fists clenched so tightly my nails bite my palms, heat prickling the back of my neck.

What is it with assholes confronting me before bed?

First Pete. Now Jessica. If one more person tries their bullshit before I sleep, I might actually snap.

I breathe out slow, but Jessica's words keep circling back, laced with something venomous. *Jacob's past. His fiancée. Taken from him.*

She wanted to rattle me. To make me second-guess everything. And dammit, I hate that it worked.

I'm not angry he hasn't told me. I haven't exactly spilled my own truths. But the thought worms in, what if I'm just a distraction? What if this pull between us is just something to fill a void?

My jaw tightens.

Stop.

What the hell is wrong with me?

I exhale sharply, forcing the tension out of my shoulders. Whatever game Jessica is playing, I'm not here for it. I've got more important things to worry about.

But she's right about one thing, there's more to Jacob's story. And if I want to be the person he trusts with it, I have to be willing to give something, too. I just haven't decided *when* or *if* I'm ready to share.

My resolve hardens. As I head for Lucy, every step feels heavier.

I veer off the path for just a moment—just long enough to duck behind a thicket of trees near the edge of camp. The bark is rough beneath my fingers as I nail another note into place, low enough to avoid the wind, high enough for the right eyes to see.

The low metal hum of the nail against wood makes something in me settle. Control. Choice. A reminder that I'm not waiting for the storm.

I am the storm.

WE'RE TRYING something different today. After a week of striking out on supply runs, empty shelves, ransacked homes, more risk than reward, Joanie tossed out an idea that actually stuck.

"A high school," she said, eyes bright. "I mean, who loots a high school? You have *no* idea how much shit people kept in their lockers."

She wasn't wrong. The more I thought about it, the more it made sense: vending machines in the cafeteria, first aid kits in the nurse's office, cleaning supplies from janitor closets, maybe even extra clothes in the locker rooms. Hell, the lost and found alone might be a gold mine.

So when we hit our next stop—Stafford, VA—that's the plan. No neighborhood crawl. No scouring gas stations. Just a direct hit on *Springboard High School*.

The camp hums with nervous energy, the kind that coils in your gut and sharpens every sense. Movements are quick and efficient, straps cinched, weapons checked, low murmurs exchanged in case things go south.

Across the clearing, Lyla weaves through the group like she's always been here, part of the mismatched family. She tightens Joanie's pack strap, bumps Trish's shoulder, tosses a remark that makes Earl bark out a laugh.

Then she turns, eyes locking on mine with a mischievous glint. Every muscle tightens, the tension shifting to something electric.

She nods at my rifle. "You sure you're not compensating for something, Gorgeous?"

I slide a clip into place, the click slicing through the quiet. My grin is slow, knowing. "Not at all, Trouble." I tilt my head, letting my gaze drag over her like a challenge. "Sounds like you're projecting. Something you want to share with the group?"

Her laugh is light, teasing, but with a hook meant to pull. And damn if it doesn't.

"You wish," she tosses over her shoulder.

I shouldn't, I really shouldn't, but my gaze drops anyway, tracking the curve of her ass, the easy confidence in her stride. Two weeks ago, she was on death's door. Now I'm standing here like a teenage idiot, watching her walk away like she's the last bit of pleasure left in the world.

A muttered curse slips out.

She glances back, catching me in the act. Her brow arches before she adds just enough sway to her hips to make sure I notice.

I shake my head, biting back a groan. She's gonna kill me.

A heavy hand claps my shoulder. "Didn't you hear me calling your name? Are you ready?" Earl's gaze is steady under bushy brows.

I shake off the images burning in my head. "Always."

Adjusting my shotgun strap, and other things south, I let my fingers trace the cool metal, mind settling into what's ahead.

We move in tight formation, each step deliberate, breaths measured. Even Joanie keeps her mouth shut. Jessica, Edith, Mom, and Poppy stay behind to guard the vehicles. The rest of us push toward the high school, the air thickening with every step.

An old rusted car slumps near the curb, windshield shattered, a faded honor roll bumper sticker peeling off.

The school looms in the distance, a skeletal husk of faded brick, cracked windows, the gaping front entrance swallowing the light. Vines climb up its walls, making it look half-consumed, like nature is trying to erase what happened here.

As we draw closer, my stomach knots at the sight of the words spray-painted in jagged black letters across the entrance doors:

ALL TURNED INSIDE. ENTER AT YOUR OWN RISK.

"Well, hell," Earl mutters.

Joanie squints. "That sounds promising."

Lyla tilts her head. "I mean, at least they warned us, so kudos to them."

Trish snorts, but Leon and I both give her a look.

"What?" Lyla throws up her hands. "All I'm saying is someone took the time, after getting out, mind you, to warn people. That's practically a love letter in today's world."

Even Clair chuckles, though her eyes stay locked on the abandoned cars in the parking lot.

I turn to Trish. "Think there's anything worth taking?"

"If people stayed out, maybe," she says, studying the doors. "Could still be medical stock, nonperishables."

"Or a damn death trap," I counter.

Pete huffs, nerves already fraying. "You can't be serious. This screams bad idea."

A grin spreads across my face. "Thank you, Pete. You just volunteered to go first."

Color drains from his face. "Screw you. I'm not going in."

I step close, voice low. "If it were up to me, I'd have left you a long time ago. Edith and Earl vouched for you, so I let you stay, even after your stunt with the bus. Now? You've made it clear I can't trust you to guard the vehicles. So congratulations—you're coming in, with me watching your every move."

His breath hitches, shoulders curling inward. "This is horseshit."

I can tell he's contemplating fighting me on this, weighing his options. But we both know how that would end.

I turn to the group. "All right, democracy time. Who's going in?"

Trish and Leon raise their hands without pause. No surprise.

Joanie's hand shoots up like we're handing out free candy.

Then Lyla, of course, throws both hands in the air, wiggling her fingers like she just won the grand prize.

I pinch the bridge of my nose. Beneath the exasperation, though, is a flash of appreciation. Pete's not wrong, this place does scream bad idea, but she meets it with that reckless fire, refusing to let the world take one more piece of her.

Clair hesitates, eyes darting between us and the woods. "I have to think about Poppy," she says.

Leon's shoulders loosen.

I press a walkie into her hand. "Stay here at the doors. If anything moves out here, call us."

She grips it tight, knuckles white, wanting to do more but knowing where she's needed.

Trish tosses a couple of empty gas cans beside her feet, the metal clattering against pavement. "When we get out, we'll check the cars for fuel."

Clair nods, stepping back.

I tighten my grip on the shotgun. No turning back now.

Pushing the doors open, we pause.

Silence.

A prickle runs down my spine.

Beside me, Lyla steps in, her whisper curling with dark amusement.

"Welcome to hell."

———

THE STENCH HITS FIRST, thick, cloying, a mix of rot, mold, and the sweet tang of old blood. It coats my throat, settles in my gut like a warning.

The hall stretches ahead, swallowed in shadow, littered with crumbling textbooks, torn notebooks, scattered test papers—remnants of a world that once cared about GPAs and homecoming games. Now it's just another graveyard.

Our footsteps echo too loud. The silence here listens.

A faded banner curls on the wall:

LET'S GO BOBCATS! DISTRICT CHAMPS!

The words feel wrong—frozen cheer for an audience long dead.

Leon leads, bow raised, posture razor-sharp, Pete behind him. Then—movement.

A handful of undead goth teens drag into view, bodies stiff, moans dry and rasping. Too long without fresh meat.

They're sluggish. Desperate. Predictable.

An arrow punches through an eye socket. Earl follows, his blade flashing, splitting the skull of a young girl with piercings lining both ears. One by one, they fall.

Leon braces a boot on a corpse, yanks his arrow free, wipes it clean.

Pete's another story, breathing too fast, hands shaking, eyes darting.

"We shouldn't be here," he mutters. "This is bad."

I turn, voice low. "Shut it. You want to draw more? Keep talking."

He swallows, goes quiet, but the tremors stay.

I watch him carefully as we push forward, sweeping the hallways, our movements tight.

Lyla keeps her knife ready, steps measured, eyes daring the dark to make the first move. Joanie shadows her, quiet for once. Trish sticks close to Pete, our biggest liability.

Leon and Earl take point, silent as ghosts.

The admin office looms ahead with the nurse's station attached. Probably our best bet for whatever medical supplies are left.

The door is intact, but the glass panel is smeared with dried blood, rust-brown streaks painting a history of panic and loss.

Leon tests the handle. Locked.

Lyla taps her knife against it. "Quiet or fast?"

"Fast."

"Okey dokey, artichokey."

She wedges the blade, wrenches hard. Wood splinters. Lock gives. And we're in.

Inside's a mess—cabinets hang open, their contents looted long ago. Drawers half-ripped from their tracks, the desperation of past survivors etched into every overturned bin, every scattered supply.

A hospital bed sits in the corner, mattress stained, sheets bunched. Someone tried to make a stand here, but by the smears of dried blood all over the floor, it didn't work.

We spread out. Searching. Hunting for anything useful.

Joanie yanks open a cabinet and immediately groans. "Oh, great, gauze! Because that's exactly what I was hoping for when risking my life in a creepy-ass high school."

Trish pulls down a bottle of aspirin. "Take what you can get, kid."

The haul is modest, a couple of bottles of aspirin, some bandages, a nearly full box of tampons that has Joanie fist-pumping, and a few rolls of medical tape.

The others slip out into the hallway, their footsteps fading into the quiet ruin of the school. I move to follow, but Lyla lingers.

She's crouched by the cot, rolling a Band-Aid between her fingers before setting it down.

It's such a small thing. Insignificant. But something about it makes me pause.

"What's that about?"

She doesn't answer right away. Just studies the bandage for a second longer before finally standing, brushing dust from her hands.

"I always leave one thing behind," she says simply. "In case someone else comes looking. You never know, this could be the thing that saves them. Or at least gives them hope."

I don't know what to say to that.

I should brush it off, throw out some sarcastic remark about how one Band-Aid won't fix a damn thing in this world.

But the truth is, she's right.

And just like that, I feel the cold rush of guilt.

"What?"

I blink, forcing my features into something neutral. "Nothing. You just reminded me of someone."

She hesitates. "Was it your fiancée?"

My jaw tightens. "How do you know about her?"

"Jessica told me in an attempt to scare me off." She shrugs and shuffles toward the door, pausing when she gets close, close enough that I can catch the quiet sincerity in her voice. "I'm so sorry you lost her."

She doesn't ask for details. Just acknowledges the loss, gives it weight, and moves on.

If only she knew the whole truth.

Would she look at me differently?

"What do you mean Jessica tried to scare you off?"

Lyla gives an exasperated look. "You can't be that blind, can you?"

Shit.

I've had my suspicions for a while, but I was hoping I was wrong about Jessica. I hate to turn her down since she has been such a good friend to me, and Sheila, but I just don't see her that way.

"I suggest you take care of that before it gets worse," she adds.

I nod, stepping aside as she moves past me, following the group toward the cafeteria. The eerie silence of the school presses in, only broken by the occasional scuffle of boots against dust-coated floors or the distant echo of something shifting unseen.

Lyla falls into step beside me, her presence a strange mix of lightheartedness and quiet resolve, like she belongs here in this darkness, yet somehow manages to bring a spark of something lighter with her.

She thrives in the unknown.

I should ask her for some pointers. Might help regulate my anxiety in these moments.

The cafeteria looms ahead, its doors slightly ajar, but before we can advance, a sudden movement catches my eye.

Pete. Veering away toward a different door down the hallway.

Of fucking course.

His fingers curl around the handle. My gut twists, a deep, primal warning.

"Pete, stop—"

The doors burst open with a groan of rusted hinges, and then—hell spills out.

A wall of undead surges forward, teens and faculty led by an infected clutching an empty pudding cup. They're a relentless, rotting tide—grotesque hands clawing, blackened fingernails cracked and jagged from mindless scraping. Sunken, milky eyes lock on to fresh prey, their hunger a physical force, teeth clacking, jaws stretching unnaturally wide as if already tasting flesh.

The smell hits next, the rank, putrid stench of rotting meat, festering wounds, and stale, death-thick air. The horde crashes into Pete like a battering ram, slamming him backward with the force of a wrecking ball. His arms pinwheel wildly as he chokes out a strangled cry and hits the floor hard, scrambling like a trapped animal. He finally finds his footing and sprints back to us.

I yank Lyla behind me as gunfire erupts.

"MOVE!" I shout, my voice barely cutting through the noise.

Earl swears, and Leon is already a blur of deadly efficiency, his hatchet cleaving through decomposing skulls of uniformed basketball players. Joanie's revolver booms, her shots ripping into the first wave, bodies crumpling with sickening, wet thuds.

Muzzle flashes strobe through the dark, lighting up blood-slicked floors and swaying, ravenous corpses.

Trish and Lyla stand shoulder to shoulder, their pistols kicking back as they unload round after round into the oncoming horde.

Joanie fumbles with her chamber. A shadow lunges for her. My shotgun booms, the blast turning a rotted skull of a girl with bright pink braces into a spray of gore that paints the lockers and my arm. *Gross.*

I sling the shotgun over my back, unsheathing my machete in one smooth motion.

The dead crash against us in an unrelenting wave—gnashing teeth, clawing hands, the guttural moans of hunger filling every inch of space. Their bodies crush together, spilling through the doorway like floodwater, pushing forward even as they're cut down.

The air is thick—gunpowder, rot, coppery blood. The stink clogs my throat, but I shove it down, swinging my blade in tight, brutal arcs. The first strike carves through the throat of a snarling woman with purple glasses. The second takes another's jaw clean off, leaving the basketball coach snapping uselessly, black fluid spilling from the wound onto his hanging whistle.

I catch the heels of Pete's boots out of my periphery bolting down the hall. The coward's legs pump, eyes wild, leaving the rest of us to fight for our lives.

A hand clamps down on my arm.

I pivot hard, slamming the shotgun stock into the face of a young girl wearing a green hoodie. Bone cracks like a splitting log. She stumbles, jaw hanging loose, but before she can collapse, another one takes its place.

Too many.

Too fast.

Joanie fires again—the sharp crack of her pistol slicing through the crowd. But she hesitates just a second longer before pulling the trigger.

She's running low.

We need to move. Now.

"Fall back!" I yell.

Trish and Lyla hold the rear, their weapons barking out controlled shots, dropping any that get too close. Leon's blade is a flash of silver in the dim light. Earl and Joanie cover our flank, moving fast, reloading on the run. I keep my shotgun poised for any necessary close calls, pumping a round into the chamber.

But the halls feel smaller. The tide of undead rolls closer.

Up ahead, that twitchy, spineless bastard stands at the intersection of three hallways, his fingers clawing at something mounted on the side of the wall. His movements are jerky, panicked, like a rat cornered with no escape.

Lyla pants beside me, her breath sharp with adrenaline. "What the hell is he doing?"

Then, Earl's flashlight swings up, the beam catching on the object in Pete's hands.

Oh, you've got to be shitting me.

"Pete!" I bellow, but he doesn't flinch. Doesn't even fucking hesitate.

CLANG!

An old security gate slams closed, rattling the walls, sealing him safely on the other side.

Rage flares hot. I pound the barrier, roaring his name, but he's already running.

Lyla stumbles, her boot catching on a loose textbook, slamming her head hard into a locker. Trish pulls her up with an iron grip, hauling her forward even as she checks her head.

Earl and Joanie fall into position, guns barking out their last few shots, each bullet a desperate, final attempt to hold the line. The spent casings ping against the tile, tiny echoes swallowed by the unholy sound of the horde.

We're backpedaling now, forced into a tighter formation. Their moans build into a horrific crescendo, like the world itself is screaming.

My breath shortens.

My pulse pounds.

We're out of time.

I shove past the panic and force my mind to calm.

What would Hicks do?

EIGHTEEN
SCHOOL'S OUT FOREVER

LYLA

THE THUNDER of snarls and pounding feet churns the air into something charged, rattling down to my bones. Earl's flashlight strobes over the hallway, guttural moans bouncing off tile and dented lockers, weaving into a terrible melody of hunger and despair.

Jacob's voice cuts through the clamor, sharp and commanding. "Split up! Draw them away! Do what you have to do to get outside and find Clair!"

Leon and Joanie tear down one corridor, Trish and Earl down another. Their footsteps vanish under the rising tide of the undead. Jacob and I take the last one and sprint. Each step sends a shot of pain to my head.

Behind us, the horde surges like a black wave, slamming lockers, tripping over rotting limbs, never stopping.

The hallway stretches ahead, flashlight beams slicing the dark, illuminating bloody handprints smeared across the walls. My lungs burn, but there's no room for it—only *run*.

A blur—something lunging from a side door.

Decomposing fingers swipe for Jacob's throat.

His machete carves through the air, the blade hissing before it crunches through bone. The skull splits like overripe fruit, black gore splattering. The thing collapses midstep, its body crumpling with a grotesque *thud.*

"Keep moving!" Jacob barks, shoving the twitching corpse aside.

We round the corner, three more undead teens stumble into our path.

The closest lunges, lips peeling back in a grotesque snarl. Instinct takes over. I meet it halfway, driving my knife deep into the mush of its skull. Wet crunch. Twitch. Dead weight drags me down.

Jacob's machete flashes—clean, efficient. Heads roll.

We push past the fresh corpses, boots squelching in congealed gore.

The moans behind us swell.

"Left!" Jacob shouts.

I glance back and regret it instantly.

The hallway writhes with rotting faces and clawing hands, eyes locked on us with mindless hunger. Bodies slam lockers, feet scrape cracked linoleum.

They're close enough I can almost feel their rancid breath on my neck.

Move, Lyla. NOW.

I yank Jacob toward an open doorway.

We burst into a science lab, slamming into desks in our desperation to put something, anything, between us and the clawing hands reaching for us.

Jacob throws his weight against the door, shoving it shut just as the first body slams into the other side.

We move as one, muscles straining as we drag a metal cabinet across the entrance.

BAM.

The impact rocks the frame, the hinges groaning under the force.

BAM. BAM.

The horde piles up, their weight pressing, their clawed fingers scrabbling against the wood, nails splintering as they tear at the barrier.

The cabinet jerks. Jacob braces his back against it, breath harsh, fury rolling off him.

"I'm going to kill Pete," he growls.

I drag the teacher's desk over, legs burning, adrenaline flooding every vein, a headache burning behind my eyes. We wedge it in place. "Get in line."

His dark chuckle holds no humor.

We shove more lab desks into the barricade, my pulse hammering, every nerve buzzing from the fight, from the too-close teeth snapping at my throat just seconds ago.

Outside, the pounding grows wilder.

The furniture jerks with another violent thud. We don't have much time.

I exhale, pressing the heel of my palm against my side, only to pull it away slick with blood.

Jacob's gaze drops to it, his expression hardening. He grabs supplies from our earlier haul and crouches beside me.

"Quick, let me see." His voice is low, gruff, threaded with concern. He lifts my shirt just enough to reveal the soaked bandage on my ribs.

Shit.

He peels it back, fingers careful. "You popped a few stitches. Give me a second to clean and tape them so the others don't go along with it and you bleed out."

The antiseptic stings as he dabs it over the wound, his fingers brushing against my skin as he secures the gauze in place, with duct tape. His touch is warm, reassuring. My chest tightens, heat curling in places that have nothing to do with pain.

His jaw tics. His eyes flick to mine, something unreadable swimming in that dark pool of chocolate.

I watch him work, unable to look away.

There's an intensity to him when he's like this—all precision and control, his full attention locked on me, on making sure I'm okay.

The air between us shifts, thickens. Suddenly, the world outside this room, the snarling, the death, the inevitable horrors waiting on the other side of that door, fades to nothing.

All I see is *him*.

Up close, I catch the little gold flecks in his eyes, bright against their dark depths. The way his stubble darkens his jaw, the curve of his lips, the quiet heat behind every lingering glance.

I wish I could let myself fall, let him wrap me up and never let go. Let myself *want* something for once without fear gnawing at the edges. But the voice in my head, the one that's always stopped me, whispers its usual warnings.

What if I lose him? What if I let him down?

The what-ifs harden my resolve. Da Vinci dies. No matter what. Getting close will only make it worse.

We reload in silence, the air between us thick with what neither of us says.

I nod toward the door. "What's the plan?"

He heads over to the wall of windows behind us and smashes one open with the handle of the machete, glass raining down.

"There may be some infected out there, but we kill them and circle to the main entrance," he says.

Adrenaline hums under my skin. "Sounds like a blast. You ready?"

He holsters his gun, cracks his neck. The door rattles with pounding fists.

Then his eyes darken, not with strategy, but with something else.

Liquid fire curls low in my stomach.

"One more thing," he murmurs, stepping in close.

I open my mouth, half a breath away from saying how now is *really* not the time for small talk—

But his hand slides behind my head, fingers threading into my hair, and everything stops.

My breath catches.

His lips brush mine—soft, slow. A question. A warning. A challenge.

Then he claims me.

NINETEEN

RECKLESS
JACOB

THIS, right here, is paradise.

I push closer, tongue sweeping into her mouth, devouring her like a starving man, because I am. Want coils low in my gut, sharp and consuming. My hand grips her hip, dragging her closer, taking more, stealing whatever I can before the world rips it away.

She moans into me, the sound hitting like a drug.

I snap.

I drive her back until she slams into the wall, glass crunching beneath our boots. Reckless. Insane. Perfect. Her grip tightens in my hair, a jolt of pain shooting down my spine, straight to my cock.

I groan into her lips, pressing until there's nothing between us but heat, breath, and the electric thrum of want. My hand wraps her throat, the other skimming her waist, memorizing every curve. I grind against her, slow and hard, the friction deliberate. She gasps, arching into me, pleasure and danger blurring together.

We break just enough to breathe, foreheads touching, chests heaving. I rake my eyes over her face, branding her into my memory. Then she grins—that devastating smile that could break hearts or save souls.

"Just in case we get eaten," I rasp.

A breathless laugh escapes her, wicked and knowing. Her fingers fist my shirt. "If we're doing final requests," she purrs, voice dripping with sin, "I want your head between my thighs." She nips my lip.

Jesus Christ Superstar.

"If there was time," I growl in her ear, "I'd drop to my knees and show you exactly why I was always late to class."

A hum slips from her throat, nails biting my scalp before she lets go. "Shame," she murmurs, that one word dripping with disappointment.

Fuck.

Her eyes drag over me like she's already plotting how to get me alone.

Oh sweetheart, if you only knew the filthy things I want to do to you.

I consider saying screw it, let the world burn while I take her apart piece by piece.

But then, the pounding against the barricade. The moans of the dead. Our people fighting for their lives.

I suck in a breath, shaking off the haze, every muscle still vibrating with need. "Later."

Because *fuck yes*, we are *definitely* getting back to this later.

She twirls Sweetness between her fingers, catching it with ease. Great, now I'm using the damn knife's name.

What the hell is this woman doing to me?

She takes a steadying breath, gives a firm nod. "Ready when you are."

Trish's voice crackles over the walkie at my hip. "Jacob? Lyla? You there? Over."

I pull it free, locking eyes with Lyla. "We're here. I see you made it to Clair before us. Over."

Relief colors Trish's voice. "Technically, Leon and Joanie beat us to her." Joanie's gloating comes through in the background.

"Please tell me you're both okay. Over."

"Banged up but alive. How's everyone else? Over."

"All good here," Trish says, then adds, "Earl twisted his ankle. Again." Static hums for a second before she comes back on. "We were damn lucky, Chief. Over."

My fingers tighten around the walkie, my jaw flexing. *Damn lucky* indeed. "Do you see Pete anywhere? Over."

"No, but you need to get here. Leon's about to start breaking shit. Over."

Fucking hell. *What now?* "We're heading your way. Coast clear? Over."

There's a pause, then Trish's voice returns, softer now. "Mostly. We'll make some noise to clear the rest. Just get to the entrance. Over and out."

I clip the walkie back onto my belt. Lyla's ready despite the exhaustion in her shoulders.

"Let's go."

We move fast and quiet out the broken window and across the campus quad. Stragglers groan and stumble toward us, but they don't make it far. My machete carves through bone, slicing clean through the rot. Lyla moves just as efficiently, her knife puncturing skulls with ruthless accuracy.

We stay close, steps in sync—protective, but not crowding. When Lyla rushes ahead to smash open a classroom window, I cover her, then follow. We climb through the jagged opening and slip into the dark hall beyond.

Our footsteps echo faintly as we move, careful and quick. Then, up ahead, the main entrance comes into view.

Outside once more, Joanie slams into Lyla, arms tight around her waist, nearly knocking her over. "I knew you'd make it! I was beginning to worry." She breathes, scanning her for injuries like she doesn't quite believe it.

Trish grabs my arm, flicking a penlight to my eyes. "Iris looks good. Not cloudy. No sign of infection." She holds it there for thirty seconds, watching. Then she's already moving, hustling toward Lyla for the same check.

Earl claps my shoulder. Small, fleeting reassurances. *We're okay. We're alive.*

Lyla winces under the penlight. Trish mutters, "Figured you had a concussion from that fall."

Then I see Leon pacing next to Clair, fury rolling off him in waves.

Earl leans against a rusted-out car, cringing on his ankle.

I move to Clair. She's slumped against the wheel well, blood streaking her temple, fists clenched, breath shallow. I kneel. "What happened?"

Leon's hands fly in sharp signs, anger etched into every motion. *"He smashed his gun against her temple."*

Heat spikes in my chest, molten.

Leon starts pacing again, rage looking for somewhere to land.

Lyla kneels beside me. "What did he say?"

My voice comes out low, dangerous. "Pete blindsided her." Saying it feels like taking a hit to the ribs. "Did you see where he went?" I grind out.

Clair's eyes drop. "No. I went to help him, to ask what was going on. I heard the gunfire and tried to pull him back in, but then he—" Her voice breaks.

Lyla grips her shoulders. "This isn't your fault. How could you have known?"

But the guilt crushes my ribs. I should have been there. Should have protected her. Why can't I protect the people I care about?

Clair whispers, "I told myself I wouldn't make the same mistake twice."

The air shifts. Expressions harden. Leon's knuckles whiten around his hatchet, so tight I swear the handle might splinter. His whole body is rigid, vibrating with fury—but his eyes, when they land on Clair, are heartbreakingly soft.

Lyla sends me a look of confusion, the silent question written all over her face. *What does she mean?*

I give her a look that says *I'll tell you later.*

Right now, we have a more pressing issue.

I stand, pacing like Leon, rage burning under my skin. "Lyla's right. This isn't on you, Clair. It's on me."

Earl shakes his head. "Now, son—"

I don't let him finish. "I should have kicked him out before. I knew he was a problem. But I didn't."

They still look at me like I'm someone worth following.

They shouldn't.

Earl exhales. "He should never have been part of our group at all. And that's on me." He turns to Clair, voice soft. "I'm sorry, darlin'." Then to the rest of us, "I'm sorry to all of you."

Clair stands, moving until she's in front of him, waiting until he meets her gaze. "There's nothing to forgive, Earl." Her voice is firm. Then, she turns to me. "Let's get back before the others start to worry."

I nod once before turning on my heel, striding toward camp.

Trish catches up, adjusting her gun strap. "Where do you think Pete will go?"

"I don't know, but if he comes around, he'll regret it."

Leon rolls his shoulders, falling into step beside me.

TWENTY
THE FINAL STRAW

LYLA

THE CAMPSITE BREAKS through the tree line, Earl's red truck glaring like a beacon. If we're keeping this place secure, we'll need to find him something less obvious.

We step into the clearing, nerves still strung tight, muscles coiled even though we're "safe."

Edith spots us first. Her eyes lock on Earl's limp, and she's moving before anyone else can speak. "Oh, thank God! You're all okay."

She collides with him, arms wrapping tight, face buried against his neck. No protest. No teasing. Just his grip tightening like an anchor. She cups his face, presses a kiss to his lips, rests her forehead against his. "You scared me," she whispers.

I look away.

"Mom!"

A small, choked cry—Poppy. Her tear-filled eyes lock on Clair, and she runs. Clair drops to her knees, arms wide, catching her midstride. "I'm here, honey," Clair breathes into her hair, holding her like she'll never let go. Poppy's shoulders shake with silent sobs.

Clair rocks her, murmuring reassurances, then carries her toward their car.

Edith turns back to the rest of us. "Pete came running in, saying there was a swarm at the school. That you all got separated and—"

"Where is he?"

Jacob's voice cuts through like a blade—low, controlled, lethal.

Edith freezes. Her eyes flick toward the far side of camp.

Oh, Pete. You should've kept running.

Jacob's stride is swift, shoulders rigid, every muscle coiled with barely restrained fury. Violence thrums off him in waves. He reaches Earl's truck, Pete hunched in the driver's seat, fumbling with wires, desperately trying to hot-wire the damn thing.

Are you fucking kidding me?

Jacob's hand clamps on to Pete's collar, yanking him out so hard that he practically flies from the truck. Pete stumbles, boots scraping against the dirt, but before he can get his balance, Jacob's grip shifts, fingers wrapping around his throat, dragging him into the center of the clearing, and slams a fist into his jaw.

CRACK.

Pete drops like a sack of bones, gasping, spitting blood. No one moves.

Edith's face drains of color, her wide eyes darting between Jacob and Pete, confusion bleeding into fear.

Barbara and Jessica rush from the van, Barbara's voice sharp. "What the hell is going on?"

Pete's hands come up, trembling. "Jacob, wait—I panicked—"

Another punch. Then another. Bone crunches. Skin splits. The wet, grotesque smack of skin splitting under impact.

Pete's body jerks with every brutal hit, his head snapping back, blood streaking down his chin, his nose, his mouth.

Jacob doesn't stop. Not until Pete is a barely conscious, gasping heap on the ground, his face a mess of swelling and red.

Fisting Pete's shirt, Jacob hauls him close. "You put lives in danger. I can do whatever I want to you, you piece of shit."

He shoves Pete back.

He hits the dirt with a grunt, dust rising in frantic little clouds as he scrambles away, his limbs weak and useless.

A single, chilling sound cuts through the thick, pulsing silence. *Click.*

The safety comes off. Jacob levels the gun at his head. For a breathless moment, I think he's going to pull the trigger. I'm not sure I'd stop him.

Pete is frozen, barely able to blink, his chest rising and falling in shallow, panicked bursts. His entire existence hinges on the pressure of Jacob's finger against the trigger.

And then—

A single hand.

Resting against Jacob's shoulder.

Barbara doesn't try to force him down. She just stands there beside him.

Jacob's jaw flexes, the tendons in his neck pulling tight, his fingers twitching against the grip. Tension hums like a live wire, crackling, dangerous. Then, with a measured breath, he lowers the gun. "Leave."

Pete staggers to his feet, but Jacob steps forward, his voice a quiet death sentence. "And if I so much as *hear* that you're headed toward Trish's family farm, I *will* shoot you on sight."

Silence grips the clearing.

"What did you do, Pete?" Edith whispers.

"He locked us in," I say.

The words land like a blow. Edith staggers back, disgust in her eyes. Pete scans the crowd for pity. Finds none.

Pete looks up, his bloodied face searching the crowd for anything —sympathy, pity, even a begrudging defense. But all he finds is a wall of cold, unyielding stares. He shifts, his mouth opening like he wants to say something, to plead his case, but there's nothing left to say.

Leon steps forward, yanks Pete up, shoves him toward the tree line. I envy the controlled rage in Leon's body as he tries to keep it in check because I have a feeling that if we all weren't here, Pete's body would never be found.

A flash of silver glints in the fading sunlight as he tosses a small knife at the dirt near Pete's feet. One weapon. No food. No water.

Leon flips him off, his expression carved from stone, positioning himself between Pete and the rest of us. The message is clear: if Pete so much as twitches in the wrong direction, he'll have to go through Leon first.

Pete snatches it up. The silence stretches, pressing in around him like the creeping darkness at his back. And then, without another word, he turns and disappears into the trees, swallowed whole by the branches.

No one speaks or moves.

Jacob's fists drip red, knuckles raw. His whole body vibrates with barely contained rage.

And I can't look away.

It's brutal, honest, familiar. The hunger for justice without rules or mercy. It matches mine. I want to tell him it's okay to be a weapon when the world demands it.

I know what other people would say. That it's twisted. That watching someone unleash their wrath and knowing, deep in my gut, that I would have done the same—that it makes me a monster.

Maybe they're right.

But when you've spent your life hunting serial killers, tracking them down, seeing the aftermath of what they leave behind, you start to see yourself as something else.

A necessary evil.

An executioner where the law fails. Or, in this case, where there is no law at all. Justice lives in my hands. And I'm perfectly fine with that.

Jessica moves toward him. Her arm outstretched, reaching for him. Before she can take another step, Trish cuts in.

Her body is a barrier, planted firmly between Jessica and Jacob, and the look she shoots is a warning.

Don't.

Jessica freezes.

Her hand pauses midair, fingers twitching. For a second, her gaze shudders—uncertainty, hesitation—but then it hardens.

Bitter. Calculating. But she takes a step back.

Trish lays a hand on Jacob's shoulder. "Come on, Chief. Let's get you cleaned up."

He lingers, eyes locked on the tree line where Pete vanished, like he's memorizing it, branding it into his mind. But then, finally, he exhales and lets her lead him toward the van.

People drift toward their own vehicles, retreating into small pockets of comfort. I stay rooted. So does Jessica. The scent of blood lingers.

I try to make him look back. To see me standing here. To know I understand the weight he's carrying, because I carry it too.

But he doesn't.

He keeps walking, letting the night pull him farther away.

TWENTY-ONE
MAYBE TRISH IS RIGHT

JACOB

THE EMERGENCY VAN reeks of antiseptic and exhaustion.

Trish doesn't speak as she yanks open the first aid kit. Metal clatters. The bite of alcohol burns the air. I flex my fingers.

Bad move.

Pain rips across my knuckles, raw and throbbing, crawling up my arm to settle behind my eyes. Skin shredded. Blood caked. Bone-deep ache in every joint.

Worth it.

But I should've seen this coming. I always should.

Why do I keep screwing it up? Hurting the people I'm supposed to protect? Always hitting back too hard, too late. Never in time to stop the damage.

"Sit."

Trish's voice cuts through the silence. No softness.

I drop onto the cot, elbows on my knees, head low. The weight in my chest hasn't moved since my fists started swinging.

Outside, the camp's quiet. Maybe they're giving me space. Maybe they don't want to see me like this.

I don't look at my hands. Can't.

Did I go too far? Or not far enough?

Trish moves with the quick, sure hands of someone who's done this too many times. Gauze. Tape. Disinfectant. But her jaw's tight. Eyes hotter than the sting of the alcohol she pours over my knuckles. It burns like hell. I suck in a sharp breath, jaw locked. She presses a cloth to the mess, the gauze blooming red.

"You don't always have to do this."

That's the thing about Trish, she never lets anything slide. Calls us out. Keeps us honest. Especially when it hurts. It's one of the many infuriating things I love about her.

The mind-reading part's less cute.

"You don't always have to be the one bleeding," she adds, softer.

But I do.

I owe these people everything. My mom kept me steady after my dad bailed. Edith and Earl pulled me back more than once. Leon beat the arrogance out of me. Trish has been the mirror I can't look away from. Jessica, even after Sheila died, made sure I didn't fall apart.

So I give what I can. And when it's not enough, I give blood.

"You think I don't see it?" Trish's voice tightens. "Every time shit goes sideways, you take it all on yourself. Like carrying it makes it better for the rest of us." She tugs the bandage tighter. "You did the right thing."

"Did I?"

Her hands pause. Then keep moving, wrapping my hands like she's trying to patch the cracks in me. "That bastard locked us in and left us for dead. He's lucky you let him walk away. I was ready to shoot him myself."

The weight in my chest doesn't move. "Everyone saw, Trish. They saw the part I bury. The part that always got me in trouble."

That part's been with me since my dad walked out—rage, sharp and hot. I used to control it. Fight fires, drag people out, spar with

Leon until I bled. That pain had purpose. Now it builds until I can't keep the lid on.

And when I let it loose, it scares me.

I should've done it differently. Quiet. Out of sight. Leon would've understood. But the others? They weren't supposed to see the version of me that doesn't stop. The version that doesn't want to stop.

I should've been better. For Sheila.

That guilt sits in my ribs like stone.

As if reading my damn mind, Trish pulls back, eyes fixed on mine. "What happened with Sheila wasn't your fault."

I freeze. Breath locked in my chest. "You don't know that."

"I know you, Jacob."

She's wrong. She doesn't know what I did. What I *didn't* do.

The thought creeps too close to the surface. I slam the door on it before it spills out.

"You can't change the past," she says. "But you can stop letting it bury you."

I huff a bitter breath. "Got a manual for that?"

"Nope." She shifts, leaning on the counter. "But I've got a question. What do you want?"

"For people to stop making stupid decisions."

She rolls her eyes. "No, dumbass. I mean, what do you want—for you."

I blink. The question feels foreign, like I lost the right to it. But Trish doesn't let me run.

"I've only seen one real spark in you since all this started," she says, nodding toward camp. "And it sure as hell wasn't Pete."

My heart kicks.

Lyla's fire. Her sharp tongue. The way she moves like she'll burn the world to protect what's hers. She lives in the quiet corners of my mind. The kiss earlier—heat, weight, the pull I haven't felt in a long time—slams into me.

I want her.

Trish sees it on my face before I say anything. "Tell me I'm wrong."

I don't.

Lyla *sees* me, the parts I keep locked away, and she doesn't flinch. It's like her demons recognize mine. And instead of running, they reach out.

For the first time in too long, I want to be seen.

Then—Sheila.

The guilt slides in fast. I don't deserve this. I failed her. And I'm afraid I'll fail Lyla too.

No one knows what really happened before Sheila died. They think she was ripped away from me. They don't know what I said. Why she was alone that night.

I press my eyes shut. The worst part? I don't know if I'll ever be able to tell them.

"You ever think about what comes after this?" I murmur.

"All the time," she says.

I trace circles over the ink on my wrist—the roots of the tree. The one I got when I thought I was finally growing out of the anger. When I thought I was finally grounded. "I don't know if I get to have an after."

"Why the hell not?"

I don't answer. How do you explain carrying something that broke you while pretending you're still whole?

She exhales, rolling her shoulders like she's shaking off the bullshit. "Look, Jacob. I don't know what kind of demons rattle around in that thick skull of yours. But I do know this, you can't spend your life carrying a ghost while you still have breath in your lungs." Her gaze sharpens. "You want to live? Then live."

When I let myself picture it, I see Lyla—smirk sharp enough to cut through fog, eyes that see every shadow I hide. She challenged me from the moment we met.

I flex my fingers against the fresh bandages. I'm not free of the past. The guilt's still there. The truth no one else knows. But something cracks open.

And I think, maybe, I want to *try*.

With Lyla.

If she'll take me, broken pieces and all.

TWENTY-TWO
BONFIRE

LYLA

THE CAMP HUDDLES beneath a star-scattered sky, their light dim, like even they're too tired to shine tonight. Everyone cleaned up after the shitshow at the school, taking turns washing in a nearby creek. We look refreshed, even though my head is still pounding like crazy, but the silence that followed us through the day isn't peaceful—it's hollow, stretched thin by everything unsaid.

Leon moves like he's done with it. Like he refuses to sit in the ruins of the day a second longer. He gathers scraps of wood, stacking them with care. The fire crackles to life, licking at the darkness, warming the chilled air. Shadows gleam across worn faces, chasing away the edges of grief.

Then he pulls something from his pack, and my breath stumbles —a bag of marshmallows, a box of graham crackers, and chocolate bars appear like magic.

The sight is so absurd, so achingly familiar, I almost cry. My brain rejects it outright, like my eyes are playing a cruel trick.

Poppy's sharp inhale snaps the spell. "Are those real?" she whispers, like he conjured them from thin air.

Joanie clutches her chest, gasping with mock drama. "Leon. You beautiful, silent bastard."

And for the first time tonight, he grins.

Clair presses a hand to her mouth, her shoulders shaking with a breathy laugh—part disbelief, part gratitude.

"Where the hell did you get those?" My voice comes out softer than I mean it to.

Leon taps the side of his nose. A silent *wouldn't you like to know.*

Trish grins. "I don't even care. Let's eat."

Earl, quiet since Pete's exile, chuckles, low and warm. "Never thought I'd see the day roasted marshmallows would feel like a miracle."

No one disagrees.

Leon spears a marshmallow on a stick and hands it to Poppy, who takes it with the reverence of someone holding an ancient relic. She scurries back to Clair, excitement buzzing off her in waves.

Clair kneels on a worn blanket, arranging the graham crackers and chocolate like the fate of the world depends on the perfect crunch-to-melt ratio. She glances at Leon, and for a moment, something sparks in her gaze. Gratitude, maybe. Or something else entirely.

Leon watches them, his expression unreadable, except for the way his eyes catch on Clair a beat too long.

I step beside him, arms crossed. "You know," I murmur, low enough for only him, "you *could* talk to her."

A sidelong glance. Blank stare.

I nudge him with my elbow. "Right, mystery-man act. Forgot you save the silent treatment just for me." I mime a drumroll, then wink. Nothing.

"Okay," I say, voice dipping, "but you could write it down. Let her know how you feel. I know there's a heart in that fortress of yours. I see how you are with Trish and Jacob. Hell, even Joanie."

His gaze stays on Clair and Poppy. The only sign he's listening is the slight tightening of his jaw. His fingers flex at his side.

A laugh breaks through the night. Poppy yanks her marshmallow from the flames just before it disintegrates. Clair blows on it, gentle, patient, while Poppy giggles and reaches for another.

Joanie swaps her perfectly toasted marshmallow for Poppy's charred one without hesitation. "I love the burnt ones," she declares, then yelps, fanning her mouth, eyes watering.

Leon shifts, pulling a small notepad and pencil from his pocket. He scribbles, then hands it to me without looking away from Clair and Poppy.

They're guarded. I don't want to push.

The words settle heavy in my chest. When I look back at him, I catch it—softness. A crack in the armor. A quiet battle behind his eyes, buried beneath years of silence.

"Do you know why they're guarded?"

A single nod. Another quick scribble. *Someone hurt them.*

His hands curl into fists, chest rising in angry breaths. Whatever truth he's holding, it's enough to shake even him.

I hope whoever hurt them is dead. And if not, if Leon finds them, they will be.

By the fire, Clair tucks a strand of hair behind Poppy's ear, listening to her chatter between bites of gooey marshmallow. Her fingers smooth Poppy's jacket, protective, fierce. Like she's willing the world itself to stay soft for her kid.

I step closer to Leon and whisper, "Don't wait too long."

He holds my gaze, nods once, then heads for his truck. Too solemn.

So, I decide to fix that.

I cup my hands around my mouth. "I'm honored you came to me, Leon. That thing on your ass doesn't sound normal, so make sure you have Trish take a look at it. No need to be embarrassed."

His shoulders snap tight.

I bite back a grin as he stops, turns, and glares. His lips press into a razor-thin line, but I catch the twitch at the corner of his mouth.

Trish howls. Joanie's eyes widen, Barbara snorts into her cup, and Edith shakes her head with a grin. Earl's hand drifts to his own backside, brows furrowing, as if he's just now questioning whether he, too, might be suffering from this mysterious affliction.

Clair gapes at me, cheeks pink. I know exactly where her thoughts went.

You're welcome, bud.

Poppy, mercifully oblivious to my antics, stays hyperfocused on her marshmallow. Brow furrowed in determination. As if achieving the perfect golden toast is the only mission in the world that matters.

Leon stands there for a beat, then slowly flips me off with both hands.

The camp erupts louder. I blow him a kiss.

He signs something fast, definitely not polite.

A low chuckle rumbles behind me. Jacob's there, arms crossed, patched-up hands on display, watching me with that amused fascination that makes my pulse stumble. His gaze drops to my mouth, and the memory of our kiss slams into me—hard.

My breath catches.

The fire crackles, but the real heat is here, in the space between us. His eyes darken, sharp, knowing. He tilts his head like he's weighing something.

And God help me, I hope it's kissing me again. Or more.

"What did he say?" I ask, aiming for casual and missing.

"Leon said thank you," he drawls, then, with a lazy grin, "and suggested you get that third nipple checked out. The green tinge isn't a good sign."

Earl sputters so hard he almost topples off his camping chair, hacking on his water. Edith, ever patient, pats his back with the kind of practiced ease that says *this isn't my first rodeo.*

The camp roars with laughter. Trish groans like she's developing a migraine in real time, one hand rubbing her temples.

I spin, flipping off Leon's retreating figure. He salutes without turning, shoulders shaking.

Trish mutters, "I'm not checking anyone's weird growths or third nipples," which only fuels the chaos.

Then Poppy asks, "Mom, what does a third nipple look like?"

The camp loses it all over again, laughter rolling through the night like thunder. Clair shoots Leon a half-amused, half-exasperated glare, while Poppy watches us all, wide-eyed, clearly delighted but utterly lost as to why.

———

THE NIGHT DRIFTS ON, soft and unhurried, the sharp edges of the day smoothing into something quieter.

Joanie and Poppy sprawl on their backs, full of s'mores and sleep heavy, their giggles dissolving into murmured nonsense. Poppy curls closer to Clair, fingers sticky with melted chocolate.

Joanie, stubborn as ever, fights sleep like it's a battle she refuses to lose, mumbling about not being tired even as her eyelids betray her.

As the fire burns low, Jacob stands and says goodnight. Before he turns to leave, his eyes catch mine and hold for a beat longer, like he's saying *see you soon*. He winks and heads toward his camper, his silhouette framed in fading firelight.

I wait. Just long enough to pretend I wasn't.

Then I push to my feet, murmuring a quick, "Night," to whoever's still lingering, slipping past the fire as if my destination isn't already decided.

But my pulse betrays me, hard, fast, each step echoing something inevitable. The memory of his kiss from earlier crackles through my head like a live wire—the way his hands gripped me, the way he took like consequences didn't exist.

I almost died today. Again.

Near-death changes a person.

Yes, I'm afraid of losing more people. Yes, I'm terrified I'll hurt the ones I care about, or worse. But right now? I want to be selfish. Wanted. Needed. I can punish myself later. Right now, I want him.

Don't wait, I told Leon. Now it's my turn.

Jacob's camper is dark.

I stop at the door, pulse hammering. Did he go to bed? Did I misread him? No. *Stop being stupid, Lyla. Don't second-guess.*

I raise my hand to knock—

The door swings open.

Jacob fills the frame, broad and consuming, eyes shadowed but glinting. That grin says he knew I'd come. Smug, sexy bastard.

His gaze drags over my face, dips to my lips, then back up. Slow. Unapologetic. Heat prickles over my skin.

Neither of us moves.

Exhaustion softens the edges of his face, but his eyes stay locked —focused, intense. Like I'm worth studying. Worth *keeping.*

No one's ever looked at me like this. And somehow, it starts to mend something I didn't know was broken.

I part my lips, but he beats me to it.

"I'm finally ready to take you up on your offer."

I blink.

He studies my face like he's waiting for me to catch up. "I'd like to have dinner with you. Next week."

Wait. *What?* "You do realize the world ended, right?" I arch a brow. "Social rules and etiquette died with it. Flesh-eating monsters kind of killed the whole *dating* concept."

His smile stretches, confident, knowing. He leans against the doorframe, arm braced above his head, looking like he has all the time in the world to tease me. "I guess I'm old-fashioned."

"Then why a week? Why not now?"

"You got a concussion today." His voice dips, rough. "Yeah, I heard from Trish. You should heal before taking on any other"—his eyes flick down, then back up, dark with intent—"strenuous activities."

Heat curls low in my stomach, frustration biting at its edges. I huff, shaking my head. Patience is not my strong suit.

Fine. If he wants to tease, so will I.

I turn, tossing my words over my shoulder. "Maybe I'll go see what Leon's up to. I bet he won't make me wait."

I barely make it two steps.

Strong hands grab me, yanking me back against heat, solid and unyielding. His arms cage me, pressing me flush to him, pulling me into the shadows. Bonfire smoke, sweat, and something sharp and male sinks deep into my veins.

His breath is hot at my ear. "Try that again," he murmurs, dark, dangerous, "and see what happens."

The words curl down my spine, pooling heat between my thighs. One hand grips my hip, fingers digging in. The other traces the bare skin above my collar, fingertips grazing my pulse before resting at my throat.

A spark ignites, sharp and liquid, spreading like wildfire.

Oh, *I like this.*

His fingers tilt my chin back, forcing me to bare my neck, a silent dare. My pulse pounds against his palm, and I know he feels it.

A low tsk rumbles from his chest, wicked and indulgent. My breath stutters, my body caught on the tightrope between defiance and surrender.

"There's a lot of messed-up things in this world," he murmurs, voice like smoke and sin. "So I'm going to date the hell out of you. Court you. Make you feel special."

His lips brush my neck, barely a touch, but it ignites me, sets off a sharp ache.

"I'll cook for you, we'll get to know each other . . . and in a week, when Trish gives you the all-clear, if you let me," his mouth follows the curve of my throat, tongue flicking out before dragging back up to my ear, inhaling as he goes, "I'll make you scream my name while you ride my face."

A shudder rips through me so hard I forget to breathe.

Holy. Hell. Yes.

He kisses the hollow of my neck before pulling back, his hand tightening on my throat.

"Does that itinerary suit you, Lyla?"

The way my name rolls off his tongue sends a chill straight to my center.

I shift, grinding against the unmistakable hardness straining against his jeans.

He hisses through clenched teeth, sending a wicked thrill through me.

"Depends," I murmur, meeting his eyes. "How good of a cook are you?"

A low chuckle vibrates against me. His hand leaves my hip, pressing between my thighs, palming me through denim.

His grip on my throat tightens just slightly. A moan slips out before I can stop it.

"Not nearly as good as I am in bed."

My pulse pounds, control slipping through my fingers. "Damn," I murmur, shifting again to hear that sharp inhale. "I really love a good meal."

His grin is all teeth as he drags his mouth along my jaw. "I'll work on that." His lips hover over mine, barely touching. "What do you say? Do you want that date?"

Do I have a choice? The man's a sexy devil playing my body like a demented fiddle.

I nod slowly, brushing our lips—a fleeting, electric touch that has both of us breathing hard.

"Good girl."

Ding, ding, ding. Congratulations, Lyla! You've just unlocked the praise kink. Only two hundred points to the hand-necklace fetish.

His teeth catch my earlobe, tugging lightly, playfully, but the effect is anything but playful. A sharp surge of want pulses straight to my clit, my body tightening in response.

"And since you're being so good, I think you deserve a gift."

The rasp of my zipper sliding down sends chills racing over my skin. My mind loops the same desperate mantra—*please don't stop, please don't stop.*

He guides me into the side of the camper, the cold metal searing against my front, a jarring contrast to the heat radiating from him behind me. His body shields me from view. My palms flatten against the siding, bracing, as his hand slips past my waistband, fingers gliding over the thin barrier of my underwear in slow, deliberate circles. His other hand stays wrapped around my throat, holding me in place.

"Oh, Trouble," he murmurs, voice dark with promise. "The filthy things I'm going to do to you."

My thighs tremble. Anticipation winds hot and tight through my veins. His mouth brushes my neck, lips and teeth coaxing shivers down my spine.

A moan escapes before I can bite it back. I press into the sensation, my head tipping against his shoulder.

His fingers slide my panties aside. The first touch of pressure sends a sharp jolt of pleasure shooting through me, and I whimper.

"Shh," he breathes against my ear, fingers stroking through my slick heat. "You don't want the others to hear, do you?"

I bite my lip, swallowing the sound building in my throat. His hardness presses firm against my ass, and I arch into it just as his finger presses against my clit.

His hand leaves my throat, covering my mouth instead, trapping the sounds he drags out of me. My hips jerk against his hand, chasing the friction, every muscle strung tight. I'm already close—too close.

His fingers work faster, each stroke hitting that spot with ruthless accuracy. Heat coils low in my belly, sharp and insistent, winding me tighter with every pass.

I try to breathe, to steady myself, but the rhythm of his hand is merciless. My nails dig into the camper's siding, searching for something solid while everything inside me comes undone.

"That's it," he growls against my ear, his breath hot against my skin. "Take it. Don't hold back."

The words push me closer, my body arching into him, his chest a solid wall at my back. I can feel the power in him, restrained but threatening to snap, as his other hand presses harder over my mouth, a silent order to stay quiet even as pleasure surges higher.

Each stroke sends another shockwave through me, my thighs shaking, knees threatening to give out. I grind back against him, feeling the hard length of him throbbing against my ass, a wicked reminder of everything he's still holding back.

The coil inside me tightens to the breaking point. My breath comes in short, desperate bursts through his fingers. My vision blurs. The rest of the world falls away until there's nothing but his hand, his body, and the unbearable, perfect pressure building until—

The wave crests fast, too fast, and then I'm shattering, quaking against the camper, clutching the back of his head for something to hold on to as my orgasm tears through me. My breath stutters, hips twitching until I'm left weak, melting into his hold while the aftershocks pulse through me.

He turns my head and kisses me as he pulls my zipper up. Then, just as suddenly as he had me, he's gone. The emptiness rushes into the space between us, brutal and biting, and my body protests violently. Every nerve still thrumming, still on fire, still aching for more.

Dazed, I stand there, my head turned, watching him stride up the steps to his camper. His movements are too controlled, too precise, like he's forcing himself to walk away.

But just before disappearing inside, he pauses.

His fingers grip the frame, knuckles whitening, tension coiled tight in his stance. His eyes, dark, hooded, hungry, lock on to mine.

Then—

That devastating smile.

"Goodnight, Trouble."

My pulse slams against my ribs, my throat. I barely find my voice. "Night, Gorgeous."

He steps inside, and the door clicks shut behind him.

I stand there, heart pounding, heat curling low, my body still thrumming with the ghost of his hands, his lips, his voice.

Then, with legs far less stable than I'd like, I turn and head back to Lucy.

Next week can't come fast enough.

TWENTY-THREE
SHOPPING

LYLA

SINCE THE HIGH SCHOOL, supply runs have stayed small —tiny convenience stores, quiet neighborhoods, and gas stations. No big risks. Everyone's still raw from too many close calls.

Like Jacob is with me.

Since the bonfire, he's been full of questions—favorite fruit, favorite movie, what my parents were like. If I could be one inanimate object for the rest of my life, what would it be? Each answer pulls me in further, and the way his eyes track me makes it harder to pretend I'm not attached.

And after that orgasm against his camper? Yeah, I'm in dangerous territory. Falling fast. I even went back a few nights ago to return the favor, only for him to lock the damn door and talk to me through it.

His voice was low, tight, vibrating through the metal like it physically hurt him to say no. "You're testing my control, Lyla. I shouldn't have even touched you. Not when you have a concussion."

Talk about a hit to the ego.

And now? I'm jumpy. Frustrated. On edge. I shouldn't be getting this close. Not when I've been leaving clues in the woods, markings and notes I hope da Vinci finds. Breadcrumbs meant to lead him back to me. Back to *us*.

I told myself it was the only way to end this.

Now I'm not so sure.

"Woo hoo, Lyla?" Trish snaps her fingers in my face.

I shake my head, adjusting the straps on my pack, and force my brain back to reality.

Trish and Joanie flank me as we continue our sweep of the small downtown area of Libertytown, MD. Joanie keeps scanning the rooftops, her eyes flicking down alleys.

One hour. Grab what we can. Try not to die.

Trish's eyes light up at the next shop sign, *Margaret's Books and Trinkets.*

Inside, the air hangs heavy with the musk of old paper, dust coating every surface. Light filters through a skylight, illuminating rows of shelves stacked with forgotten stories. It looks untouched. Guess books aren't top priority in an apocalypse.

Shocking.

I'm about to leave, but Trish bolts down the main aisle toward the back.

"Two seconds!" she calls over her shoulder.

I chuckle as she beelines for the romance section.

Joanie drags over a stepstool, stretching to scan the high shelves. A minute later, she plucks down a handful of comic books and picture books.

"For Poppy," she whispers when she hands them to me.

I take them, fingers brushing the worn covers, a lump forming in my throat. *God, I love this kid.*

We sweep the shelves, first-aid guides, survival manuals, road maps, even a pocket dictionary, because why the hell not? Joanie tucks away a comic.

I'm skimming a gardening manual when Trish heads toward us,

her backpack bulging, straps digging into her shoulders. No way she's carrying fewer than twenty books.

"That was more than two seconds," I say.

She rolls her eyes. "Oh, hush. Mama needs her spice fix."

Spice, you say? "Got a collection in your van? Might need to stop by."

Her grin explodes. "Please tell me you're also a reader of the delectable genre?"

I shrug. "I've dabbled here and there. Might be nice to get back into it now that I have some free time."

Joanie snorts.

"Well, my library is your library." Trish points a warning finger. "Just don't dog-ear the pages. I draw the line there."

"Noted."

She starts for the door, but a question itches at the back of my mind. "Trish."

She pauses, curiosity flashing in her eyes.

"Can I ask you something?"

Trish perches in front of a section of battered cookbooks, arms folding over her chest. "Sure."

Here goes nothing. "What's Jessica's deal?"

The warmth from seconds ago cools, strain creeping into the space between us. Joanie inches closer.

Trish exhales, rolling her lips together like she's measuring her words. "Jessica is complicated."

Understatement of the freaking year.

She pulls a dusty book off the shelf, flipping through the pages like she's searching for the right words. Or stalling.

"As you know, she was a schoolteacher. Lost her family early on. She was friends with . . ." She hesitates, clearly uncomfortable.

"With who?" I press.

"Someone close to her. And Jacob." Her voice tightens. "That's all I'll say."

A weight drops in my chest. "I know about Jacob's fiancée."

Trish's head snaps up, surprise lighting her face. "Did Jacob tell you?"

"No. Jessica did. Jacob just confirmed it." And said I reminded him of her a little, which I keep to myself.

Trish's eyes darken. "What did she say?"

I fill her in on the conversation, and by the time I finish, Trish's fingers are digging into the edge of the table, knuckles white.

Trish shakes her head, jaw clenching. "Jessica's always been protective of Jacob, and it annoys the shit out of me. I had a feeling she had a thing for him but never acted on it because, well—her best friend was his fiancée. Now?" Her voice runs cold. "She's seizing an opportunity."

"Well, that's fucked up," Joanie mutters.

Trish lets out a dry laugh. "Yep. You can say that again."

Joanie doesn't miss a beat. "Well, that's fucked up." She grins like she's proud of herself.

I groan. "Really?"

Joanie throws up her hands. "What? She said it. You can't expect me to not follow through on a classic."

Trish shakes her head, rubbing her forehead. "I did walk into that one."

Joanie sticks her tongue out at me. "See?"

Trish's gaze snaps back to me, serious again. "You asking because you care about Jacob?"

I nod.

Trish's eyes bore into mine. "Jacob's like a brother to me. He's come a long way from the angry kid I grew up with. He deserves someone who cares about him for who he is—not just for what he can provide."

Heat creeps up my neck. "Would it help if I said I'm looking for that too?"

"A little. But if I'm being honest, it's Leon's approval you'll need in the end." She winks.

Super.

"Just make sure you're all in before you start something with him," she adds, voice dropping lower. "Jacob loves hard when he lets someone in."

My mind flashes to his grin, his steady hands, the heat of his kiss. Something hot, dangerous, but tender rolls through me like a warm ocean wave, settling somewhere deep in my chest. "I will."

Trish nods. "And let's both keep an eye on Jessica. Might be worth giving Jacob a heads-up—so he can let her down gently."

I nod. "Already done, T-Dawg."

"Yikes." Trish sighs.

Joanie claps her hands together. "All right, enough of the heavy shit. Let's wrap this up and move on. We've got an hour, remember?"

The door creaks as we step onto the street, the exit bell giving a soft jangle, a sound that feels absurdly out of place in the hollow quiet of a ruined world, but makes me smile all the same. I reach up and pull it down, stuffing it in my bag. This will be good for the stringed cans.

Joanie shades her eyes, scanning the block. "Clothing store up ahead. Think we've got time to snag a few outfits?"

I glance at my watch. We should if we hurry.

Then an idea sparks.

"Hey, Trish?"

"Yeah?"

"Did Jacob fill you in on our 'date' plans?"

She nods. "Yeah, why?"

"Wanna help me torture him a little? You know, for making me wait a whole week?"

Joanie grins. "I'm in if it means messing with him."

Trish raises a brow. "What do you have in mind?"

I turn back to them, my grin wicked.

"Let's go shopping, ladies."

TWENTY-FOUR
DATE NIGHT

JACOB

INSIDE MY CAMPER, candlelight flickers across the cramped space, the air warm and scented with melted wax and vanilla.

I move in restless circles—adjusting, straightening, second-guessing.

I rake a hand through my hair, exhaling.

A knock breaks against the door.

With a quick breath, I light another candle, placing it at the center of the table. My hands hover for a second before I force myself to step back. It's fine. It's good enough.

Maybe waiting a week was a mistake. Too much time to think, to overthink. It's not like I haven't done this before.

Just breathe.

And don't jump her the second you see her.

I move to the door, forcing my nerves down, ready with something cocky, something to set the tone, but the second I swing it open, the words die in my throat.

Lyla stands framed by the night, a vision I have no business looking at. No boots, no cargo pants. A sapphire satin dress clings and flows, catching candlelight and shimmering like liquid moonlight. Strappy black wedges make her legs look endless. Her hair falls in loose waves down her back. The makeup sharpens already dangerous eyes.

A breeze carries her perfume, warm and faintly sweet. *Lethal.* My pulse stutters. The low-dipping neckline teases her delicious curves, her smooth, creamy skin illuminated by the glow of fireflies dancing around her. She looks unreal.

Heat surges through me, blood rushing south so fast it's almost painful. My fingers twitch, aching to touch, to ruin whatever fragile composure I was pretending to have.

What was that about being a gentleman?

Fuck.

"Holy shit." The words slip out low.

Her smile is pure trouble. "Well, hello to you too, Gorgeous."

I shake my head, trying and failing to clear the haze she's thrown me into.

I drag my gaze over her, restraint hanging by a thread. "You're . . . everything."

Something softer crosses her eyes before she blushes, barely visible in the dim light. A-fucking-dorable. "Thank you. You clean up pretty well yourself." Her gaze takes in my dark green Henley and jeans. Her teeth catch her lip. *Sweet Moses.*

I drag a hand over my jaw, trying to ground myself. Trying not to think about how easily I could back her against the doorframe and kiss that smirk off her lips.

Do we really need to eat first?

Stop. This is not about you, dumbass. It's about the goddess in front of you.

Pull it together, bud.

Her eyes flick past me to the table and candles. "Are you going to let me in?"

Right. The date. The date with Lyla. The date with Lyla that I *insisted* on having.

That date.

I step aside, holding out my hand. "Please, come in." I shake my head like that'll somehow knock the sheer need for this woman out of me.

She brushes against me as she passes, satin against my arm, warmth bleeding into my skin. Vanilla curls into my lungs. My pulse hammers.

This night is going to ruin me.

And I can't fucking wait.

"You went all out," I say, shutting the door, then regret it. The dress dips low in the back, stopping just before the curve of her ass. I clench my jaw, resisting the very real urge to drag my mouth along the exposed line of her spine, to hear what kind of sound she'd make if I did.

She grins over her shoulder. "You insisted on a date. I wanted you to see how I would've shown up if the world hadn't ended."

A low chuckle rumbles from me. "I appreciate it. This is perfect."

She circles the space, stopping at the wall over the sink lined with Polaroids—Mom, Leon, Trish, and me, from childhood to just months before the collapse. She laughs at one in particular. Leon is smacking the back of my head while Trish spits water out of her nose midlaugh.

Her gaze softens. "I've never asked—how'd you grow up with Trish when her parents are in Montana?"

I lean against the counter. "Ah. Well, Trish and her parents lived in our town for as long as I can remember, but her mom's family owns a big farm in Montana. When the current owners retire, they pass it down to their kids. Trish's mom, Anna, was their only child, so she runs it. But by then, Trish was already in college. They moved out there while she stayed to finish school, working to help pay off tuition before heading out to join them."

"When was that?"

"Six years ago."

Lyla tilts her head. "Why did she stay so long?"

I rub the back of my neck, exhaling. "She stayed for a guy."

Her eyes widen, lips parting. "What happened to him?"

Anger tightens my chest, a long-buried frustration surfacing. "Honestly? No one knows. They were happy. I was sure he was going to propose, but then one day—poof. Gone."

Lyla's brows knit together, her gaze shifting back to the photos, landing on one of Trish holding up a bass on a fishing line, grinning. "What a bastard."

"If you want a shot at him, get in line behind Leon and me." I gesture toward the small booth. "Come on. Can't have my date standing all night."

She slides in, satin whispering over the seat. I set a steaming plate of spaghetti in front of her, the rich scent of tomato, herbs, and pasta filling the small space. She inhales, eyes widening.

"Spaghetti and wine?" she muses, tapping a finger against the rim of her glass. "I'm impressed."

I slide in across from her. My leg brushes hers beneath the table, sending a jolt straight to my chest. "Only the best for you."

Her pupils darken. "Careful, Jacob. Keep making me feel like this and we won't make it past the wine."

"You promise?"

She contemplates, lips parting enough to allow her tongue to swipe across her bottom lip, making my brain short-circuit. "Nah. Like I said. I love a good meal."

I chuckle and raise my wine. We clink mason jars, because that's as fancy as it gets around here.

I tilt my glass toward her. "So, what brings a beautiful woman like you to a place like this?" I gesture at the cramped camper, the dim candlelight, the end of the world.

She laughs, twirling her fork. "Oh, you know, heard the neighborhood had good scenery and interesting neighbors. Always looking for a little excitement."

"Well, I can't promise Michelin-starred meals, but I can guarantee there are no lines at this establishment." I wave a hand around, showcasing my five-star camper experience, complete with peeling wallpaper, a rickety table, and exactly one working burner.

She hums, tapping a finger against her chin in mock consideration. "No wait times? Decent ambiance? A chef who's easy on the eyes? I'll leave a review in the morning."

"I only ask that you wait to leave a review till after all the night's festivities." I wink.

She lets out a sound, somewhere between a snort and a laugh, that feels like the stars just rained down into my soul and lit it the hell up. It's my life's mission now to make her laugh like that every damn day.

We fall into something easy. Trading stories, glimpses into who we were before the world collapsed.

She tells me about a diner back home that had the best pies, the kind so good you'd want to bathe in the gooey centers. I admit I once considered entering a professional eating contest before realizing I lacked both the stomach capacity and any actual life direction for it.

She laughs, full and real, and I watch her, soaking it in. The way her lips curve. The way her eyes light up. I store it all away for the bad days.

As she twirls pasta around her fork, lips twitching in amusement while throwing another sarcastic remark my way, I realize something dangerous.

I've never felt this at ease with a woman before. Not like this. Not where it feels effortless.

When the plates are empty, I push away from the table, moving toward the counter. I feel her eyes on me—curious, waiting. I rummage through a paper bag beside the sink, the edges crinkling under my fingers. I turn back and set it in front of her.

"What's this?" She asks.

"Dessert."

She opens the bag, blinking. She lifts her gaze to mine, something like awe in her eyes. "You remembered."

She pulls out a bag of cinnamon gummy hearts, fingers brushing over the plastic like she doesn't quite believe it.

"I found them this morning at the gas station, buried in some forgotten corner. Who would've thought a tiny-town gas purveyor would be a fan of these?"

Her fingers tap against the edge of the bag, her teeth sinking into her lower lip.

She needs to stop doing that because I'm this close to reaching across the table, pulling her lip free with my thumb, and replacing it with my mouth.

She tears it open and pops one into her mouth.

The sound she makes is cruel. A low, husky moan of satisfaction, rich and indulgent—the kind that has no business being made over candy. Heat licks up my spine. My grip tightens around my mason jar. I watch her, stunned, utterly ruined by something so simple.

She meets my gaze, knowing and amused, delighted by my reaction just as much as the candy itself.

I'm going to make her pay for that.

"Come on," she teases, pushing the bag toward me. "One won't kill you."

With an exaggerated sigh, I pluck one from the bag and pop it into my mouth.

Instant regret.

The artificial cinnamon burns across my tongue like a crime against humanity. My face contorts before I can stop it, and Lyla loses it, head thrown back, full, rich laughter spilling into the small space like music.

I force myself to swallow, shaking my head like I've survived something catastrophic. "Nope. Never again."

She grins, eyes bright. "I appreciate you trying."

I lean back, letting the warmth settle between us. My pulse

pounds, not from adrenaline, not from fear, but from something sweeter. Something dangerous in a different way.

She looks at me, really looks, and for once, I don't feel like a man unworthy of love.

Silence stretches. Comfortable. Charged. Then her voice dips, sultry, laced with danger. "So, on a normal first date," she muses, "how would this end?"

I tilt my head, watching her in the candlelight. "Typically?" I let the word drag. "I'd drive you home. Walk you to your front door, hold your hand the whole way just because I could. I'd lean in slow, kiss you goodnight—just enough to leave you thinking about it long after. Then I'd message you as soon as I got home, tell you I had a great time, and ask when I get to see you again."

Her lips curve, wistful, like she's letting herself imagine that world, one where we met before everything burned. "And now?" she whispers.

Heat coils low, tight and unrelenting. My fingers curl on the table. "Now," I murmur, voice rough, "I want to take you to bed and show you what would happen on the typical third date."

She exhales a soft laugh, eyes glinting with mischief. "As a responsible adult, I have to ask"—she lifts a brow in mock sternness —"do you have protection, sir?"

A sharp laugh escapes me. Before she can blink, I'm up, crossing the camper in two strides. I yank open a drawer, pull out a box of condoms, and set it on the table with a quiet thud.

"Sure do. Had to hide them while shopping with my mother present. Not my proudest moment."

She snorts. "I wonder what we'll do once all the condoms in the world expire?"

I shrug. "I guess we'll go back to the ancient technique of pulling out."

Tears stream down her face as she clutches her side, laughter spilling out. But then it shifts. The sound fades, replaced by uncertainty.

She reaches out, fingers brushing mine. "Jacob," she murmurs, voice low and intent, "I need to tell you something first."

The warmth tilts into stillness, tension curling at the edges. My stomach tightens—not with desire now, but with something else.

Anticipation. Concern.

Candlelight casts shadows over her face, making her look vulnerable and determined all at once.

I slide back into the booth, covering her hand with mine.

"Okay. I'm listening."

TWENTY-FIVE
YES. PLEASE.

LYLA

THE SILENCE STRETCHES THIN, taut, like a wire ready to snap.

Here's the moment of truth.

I've dreaded this all day.

And it's not just this. The real truth coils in my gut, rotting—why I joined them, how I've been laying breadcrumbs for da Vinci. I've told myself I'll confess eventually, that I just need the right moment, but every day makes it harder. And now? With Jacob looking at me like that? It feels impossible.

So I go with something else.

"I don't produce a lot of lubrication," I blurt, too loud.

The urge to smack my forehead is so strong I sit on both hands. I'm a coward.

"It's not that I'm not into it—my body just doesn't cooperate. And some guys take it personally. Like I must not be attracted to them. Like I don't want it. And that messes with their ego. Now I'm rambling way too much for a first date, so I should shut up now."

I clamp my mouth shut, heat crawling up my neck.

"Lyla. Look at me."

Quiet authority in his tone makes my stomach flip. I hesitate, then force myself to meet his gaze.

"First," he says, voice brimming with conviction, "there's nothing wrong with you or your body. You're gorgeous, Lyla. Those assholes who couldn't figure that out? That's on them. Fuck them."

The words land hard. Like a gavel slamming down, final and absolute.

I blink, caught off guard by the sheer certainty.

"Second," he continues, leaning forward, forearms on the table, "this doesn't scare me. Not even a little. Unlike the gems you've had the misfortune of dealing with, I care about my partner's feelings and"—his eyes darken, heat igniting beneath his tone—"pleasure."

That word drags through the air like a physical touch. My breath hitches.

"And third," his gaze drops, tracing my torso, lingering, burning, before sliding back up. "I don't shy away from a challenge, sweetheart."

My heart kicks into high gear.

He leans in, close enough to make the tiny table between us feel laughable, a barrier that could, and maybe should, be shattered.

Then he smiles, and I feel it everywhere. "So I only have one question for you."

My pulse stutters. My voice barely escapes. "What's that?"

"What do you need from me to make you come, comfortably?"

The air crackles. I reach into my bag, pulling out the small bottle of lube. I set it between us. "I need you to use this whenever you want to enter me."

His expression doesn't change. "Anything else?"

I let my gaze roam over his chest, lingering, before dragging back up to meet his.

"I like my body to be played with." I let the words stretch. "Slowly."

He picks up the bottle, rolling it between his fingers, and gives it a light squeeze. "Is this all you've got?"

I narrow my eyes, deadpan. "I'm not the Sahara Desert, Jacob. It's not that bad."

His smile turns sinister as he leans back, crossing his arms over his broad chest, gaze locked on to mine like a challenge.

"No, Trouble," he says, voice rich with promise, "I mean, we'll need more than this little bottle because I plan to take you many times, for many nights going forward."

My eyes widen. *Oh.*

My foot moves on instinct, sliding up his leg, toes skimming over denim, feeling the tightness in his muscles, the sheer power beneath.

His pupils darken, hunger sharpening in his gaze. He leans in, voice dropping to something rough, dangerous. "You say the word," he murmurs, each syllable deliberate, almost a growl. His fingers ghost over my thigh, just enough to make my breath hitch, "and I'll make sure you never feel less than again."

His words sink into me, threading through the cracks I pretend don't exist, sealing over old wounds with something hot, undeniable.

And God help me, I'm about to shatter for him.

I should be scared by how easily he gets me. Most men shy away when I push, when I test, when I sharpen my edges to see who's willing to bleed.

But not Jacob.

He doesn't just take it, he matches me. Meets me head-on like he sees me, every stubborn, messy, scarred part, and doesn't blink. He sees everything and still wants me.

And that's the problem. I want to be one of his people. I want to be part of this strange, stubborn, tenacious family. The thought of losing it, losing him, guts me worse than any bite would. Which makes what I've been doing even more unforgivable.

My pulse pounds.

My body burns.

"Yes," I breathe, the word slipping out.

"Thank fuck." He stands in one swift motion and pulls me up, crushing his mouth over mine like he's been ravenous for this, for me. His hands are everywhere, firm, strong, memorizing every inch of me through touch alone. My fingers tangle in his shirt, gripping tight as I sink into him, the heat between us burning hotter than the surrounding candles.

The taste of wine and spice lingers on his tongue, blending with the faint smokiness of the air. The wool of his shirt brushes my skin, familiar yet new, every sensation heightened, amplified. My back collides with the kitchenette counter, rattling a spoon, but I barely notice. I only register the press of Jacob's body, the way he holds me like I'm something worth worshipping. Like I'm whole.

He pulls back just enough to look at me, his gaze molten, pupils blown wide with need. But there's no rush in his touch, no desperate urgency to claim.

There's just intention.

His lips brush the curve of my jaw, slow, reverent. A gentle press at the hollow of my throat. A careful, lingering kiss just below my ear.

Every touch is controlled, sending a shiver rolling through me, coiling low and tight.

He's unraveling me with patience.

I close my eyes, drowning in him—the scent of clean soap, faint spice, and something undeniably, dangerously Jacob.

A low hum of pleasure builds in my chest. My body melts beneath him, surrendering to the aching way his fingers roam, unhurried, claiming every inch.

When his lips return to mine, his tongue sweeps in, coaxing, teasing, tasting, like he has all the time in the world.

"Lyla," he breathes against my mouth, his voice a quiet whisper that flips my stomach. "We take our time, okay? Whatever you need, we do that."

The softness in his words, the lack of expectation, makes something deep in my chest tighten—raw, unfamiliar.

I slide my hands into his hair, nails grazing his scalp, pulling him closer, anchoring myself in the solid weight of him.

"I trust you," I whisper.

The words land heavy. I do trust him. Too much. But the truth wedged between my ribs makes them sharp edged. It's a lie wrapped in truth, and the guilt slides in right behind the warmth.

His lips curve into a grin against mine. "Good," he murmurs before his arms tighten, lifting me onto the counter like I weigh nothing.

He steps between my legs, body flush to mine, heat radiating, consuming. His hand grips my neck, firm, possessive, tilting my head before he takes my mouth.

The kisses are raw, devouring, pulling me deeper into something unhinged.

Hands roam, squeeze, explore. His hard length through denim presses against my center, tormenting, sending a molten ache through me. I grind against him, chasing friction, reveling in the hitch of his breath, the way his grip tightens like he's barely holding on.

He yanks me closer, fingers digging into my hips with a bruising grip that sets me on fire. His hips roll—slow, precise—and the sound that tears from my throat is pure need. His groan rumbles low and dark, vibrating against my lips.

One hand grips my ass, lifting me, the other locking across my back, keeping me pressed to him as he carries me toward the bed. He lowers me onto the mattress, and the blankets are softer than I expect, a careful detail I hadn't noticed before.

He stands between my legs, palms on my thighs, thumbs tracing hypnotic circles that light my skin.

Then—he stops and just looks. The admiration in his eyes is raw, unfiltered.

My chest tightens. I want to hoard this moment, keep it, live in it. Before the truth strips it from me.

"I want to see all of you," he says. "Please."

A teasing smirk tugs at my lips. "I could get used to you begging."

His eyes darken, candlelight sparking in them. "Darlin', I'll get on my knees right now if that's what you want."

My breath stutters. Fuck. I lean in, my voice a smoky promise. "Soon, Gorgeous. Since you're being such a good boy, I'll give you what you want soon enough."

His groan is low, rough, vibrating against my skin. His hand fists the front of my dress, pulling it down just enough to reveal more of my breasts. His grin is destructive and pure Jacob.

He sinks to his knees between my legs, lips pressing to my shoulder where the strap of my dress has slipped down, heat lingering in his wake.

His fingers ghost up my calf, tracing higher, over my knee, beneath the hem of my dress. I let out a breath, my mind silencing the voices that whisper doubts.

His fingers move with exquisite care, a slow discovery that makes my breath hitch. Each brush of his knuckles, each press of his lips behind my ear, layers sensation until my body hums with an ache that feels as natural as breathing.

This is Jacob.

Focused. Unshaken. So attuned to me that for the first time, I don't feel like something to fix.

I just feel.

The bottle of lubrication waits on the table, but my body already responds—softening, opening to him in a way I didn't think possible. He's here, with me, for me. That realization sends a shiver down my spine. And the guilt comes with it, whispering that he doesn't know everything. That he's letting someone into his bed who's been leading danger straight to his door.

I shake my head, as if I can scatter the thoughts loose.

I can't keep risking them for my plan.

No more clues. No more notes.

Just this.

Jacob pauses. His hand cups my cheek, his thumb brushing along my jaw. His brown eyes search mine, soft. "You okay?"

No, but I will be. "Yeah," I murmur. "Just nervous."

His mouth tugs into a crooked smile. "Didn't think you could get nervous."

"I'm just nervous you won't be as good in bed as you think you are."

That makes his brow lift, mischief flaring in his gaze as he reaches for the bottle. "Oh, really?"

His gaze locks with mine as he warms the liquid between his fingers, eyes dark with focus. Slowly, he slides his hand beneath my dress.

The first glide of his fingers is gentle, a teasing press that makes my breath catch.

His eyes stay on mine, watching, adjusting, learning, the intensity making my pulse stutter.

Then he tilts his fingers—

And the sensation changes.

Not just good.

Perfect.

A rhythm builds, my spine arching, lips parting on a shaky exhale, pleasure blooming like fire under my skin.

His groan is low, rough with restraint.

"So good," he murmurs, kissing my temple. "Perfect. Like you were made for me."

I feel it, the truth in his words.

For the first time, the past falls away.

Only this exists.

The heat of his palm. The rough touches. The way he watches me, like every reaction is sacred.

He captures my mouth, tongue coaxing mine into a lazy, intoxicating rhythm.

I melt into him, arms looped around his neck, fingers threading through his hair.

His weight presses into me—hot, hard, ready—a promise against the barrier of his jeans. His forehead rests against mine, breath uneven, control fraying.

Jacob stands in one swift motion, taking my dress with him, stripping me bare except for my black lace thong and heels.

His body locks.

Muscles flex, chest rising and falling in deep, controlled breaths. Pupils blow wide, lethal want etched in every line of him.

I can see the battle, restraint against desperation, the urge to slam inside me warring with his need to take his time.

His gaze meets mine after what feels like forever, though it's only seconds.

His voice is rough, wrecked. "I will never make you wait again."

He pulls my legs wide, his grip bruising, a silent warning. Then he descends, lips tracing a slow path down my body.

He lingers at my breasts, lips wrapping around a nipple, tongue flicking, lapping, while his hand pinches the other, a sharp pleasure that has me writhing beneath him.

"That's what you get for teasing me," he murmurs against flushed skin.

Mental note: tease him more often.

I'm about to retort when his mouth keeps moving, sliding lower, lower—

Until his lips press a kiss through the lace of my thong, right over my throbbing center.

A moan escapes me.

He groans, the vibration sinking into me, rattling bone. "You smell so fucking destructive.

Then he kneels.

His fingers hook the thin fabric, tugging it aside before his tongue finds me—hot, slick, devouring.

My head slams back into the mattress, spine arching at the first stroke of his tongue.

He settles in, throwing my legs over his shoulders, my heels digging into his back as he eats me like I'm the main course.

A rough groan vibrates against my clit, sending shockwaves through me. He doesn't let up—licking, sucking like he'll die if he doesn't wring me dry.

I've never come from this alone before.

But Jacob is relentless.

Heat pools low, coiling tight, unforgiving. Darkness creeps at the edges of my vision.

Then—he pulls away, mouth leaving me with a slick pop, and before I can protest, he slides two lubed fingers inside me, deep, curling just right.

"Fuck." My voice breaks, thighs trembling.

He kisses along my inner thigh, murmuring soft worship, tracing delicate paths with his lips. I'm right there, so close, legs fighting to stay open, not to crush his hand.

Then he presses his thumb hard to my clit.

I break.

His name rips from my throat in a choked, ragged cry as my body shatters, pleasure crashing so hard I forget to breathe.

My thighs quake, my pussy clenching around his fingers, dragging out every last pulse as he works me through it, coaxing every drop from my overstimulated body.

I'm a sweaty mess, barely clinging to reality.

He presses one last kiss to my inner thigh before gently pulling out his fingers. Then, fuck me, he leans down, brushes a featherlight kiss over my still-sensitive clit, making me jolt.

Jacob chuckles, straightening to his full height. "Good girl."

Then he drags his tongue over his fingers in deliberate licks, eyes locked on mine.

Holy shit.

Heat flares again, rekindling despite the fact I should be a heap of jelly.

I prop myself on my elbows. "Your turn. Take off your clothes."

Jacob grins. "So bossy."

My tongue drags over my bottom lip. "No, honey. Just want to return the favor."

His brows lift, amusement sparking in his darkened gaze. "Well, in that case . . ." He winks, grips the back of his shirt, and yanks it over his head—golden skin, hard muscle, and intricate ink revealed in one motion.

I sit up, my fingers itching to trace the art carved into his skin.

Twisting roots, sprawling trees, delicate flowers intertwined with woodland creatures. Vibrant colors shaded with exquisite detail—a story painted across his body.

I press a kiss to his chest, trailing lower, following the ink, tasting the heat of his skin as my lips glide down his stomach.

By the time I reach his jeans, I can feel the tension in him, the way muscle tightens beneath my touch.

I pop the button, unzipping slowly, dragging his jeans and briefs down, finally freeing him.

Damn.

He's thick, hard, flushed, like he's just as desperate for me as I am for him.

Beautiful. Dangerous. Mine.

My fingers wrap around him, stroking, pumping, savoring the way his breath hitches, the way his jaw clenches, the way every part of him reacts.

Jacob hisses, his head tipping back, a guttural growl tearing from his throat. "Lyla." He says my name like a prayer.

The foil crinkles in his hands, a promise. That cocky, teasing smirk curves his lips, and it hits harder than his touch.

"Never thought I'd miss the sound of foil tearing," he murmurs.

I laugh, breathless, warmth blooming in my chest. The tenderness beneath the heat makes something deep inside me ache, makes the truth I'm hiding feel heavier. The closer I pull him, the more it feels like I'm setting fire to something I'm desperate to keep.

Then his expression shifts.

Softens.

"As much as I'd love to come in your mouth," he says, voice low and rough, "I want to hear your moans the first time I enter you."

My stomach tightens, heat surging through my veins.

He grabs the lube, pops it open with his teeth—God, that's hot—and squeezes it into his palm, warming it before sliding his hand down, parting my thighs, coating me with slow strokes.

I whimper, thighs quivering, needing more.

He watches everything, how I glisten, how my hips arch to meet him, how I can't hide the way my body responds to him.

The intimacy is suffocating and intoxicating. I want to drown in it, even knowing that if he knew what I've done, why I joined them, he'd rip this away in a heartbeat.

He pours more lube into his palm, stroking himself, slicking every inch until he's impossibly harder.

His gaze darkens, chest rising and falling with barely leashed control. "Ready?" His voice is strained.

I nod, wanting him more than air. And hating myself for thinking that when I'm one word away from destroying it.

Jacob moves over me, bracing on his forearms, his body solid above mine. Then he pushes inside, stretching me open, filling me inch by inch.

Pressure. Ache. Perfect.

I exhale sharply, adjusting, taking him in, and his lips brush mine, whispering soft encouragements.

"That's it," he murmurs, voice rough. "Fuck, Lyla. You feel so good."

We move together like it's muscle memory, like this is where we were meant to be all along.

His hands map me, fingertips tracing my sides, a thumb skimming my jaw before tilting my chin up for another deep, searing kiss. He reads every shift, every breath, adjusting when I tense, groaning when I moan his name.

The cramped camper turns it into something almost unbearably intimate—the bed creaking, our breaths mingling in the close air.

Outside is ruin. Inside is life. Inside is him. Inside is this.

And then it hits.

That heated coil, winding tight, pulling me toward the edge.

"Lyla," he groans, grip tightening on my hip.

Then he throws my leg over his shoulder, sinking deeper, hitting that devastating spot.

"I need you to let go. Right." Hard thrust. "Fucking." Hard thrust. "Now." Hard thrust.

His hand slides between us, fingers pressing to my clit, rubbing fast, precise circles. White-hot pleasure floods me, my body clenching around him.

"Yes. Yes, Jacob. More. More." My hands brace against the wall above my head, driving him deeper.

His mouth drops to my nipple, nipping just hard enough to make me jolt, then soothing with his tongue—pain and pleasure blending until I break.

Pleasure detonates, ripping a raw scream from me.

Jacob follows, shuddering, my name breaking from his lips as his body convulses, his release dragging mine out until I'm limp beneath him.

He buries his face against my neck, breath hot, lips dragging open-mouthed kisses along my collarbone.

I shiver, still feeling the aftershocks, still clinging to the shape of him inside me.

For a long moment, we don't move.

I feel him everywhere—his weight, his warmth, the way his fingers draw lazy circles on my hip without thought.

He shifts just enough to meet my gaze, thumb brushing my cheek. His expression is soft in a way that destroys me.

Then he grins, lazy, satisfied, completely mine.

And now I know exactly what I stand to lose. The terror of it is worse than any monster waiting outside these walls.

TWENTY-SIX
OPEN THE FLOOD GATES

LYLA

MARK IS ON THE GROUND.

Sprawled in a pool of his own blood.

The warehouse is dark, cavernous, the air thick with rust, rot, and something far worse. Flickering fluorescent lights buzz overhead, casting erratic shadows across the concrete. His breath comes shallow, lips trembling around words he'll never get to say. His green eyes are wide with pain—but there's something else. Acceptance.

"No, no, no—Mark, stay with me," I sob, pressing hard on the wound in his stomach, but the blood keeps coming, hot and slick between my fingers. Too much. I can't stop it.

His fingers twitch, gripping weakly at my sleeve. His lips part, but all that escapes is a choking gasp, a desperate, dying sound. "Lyla," he manages, voice barely a whisper. "Run."

I shake my head, tears streaming. "I'm not leaving you! Just—hold on, dammit! You're gonna be fine, I promise."

A laugh cuts through the darkness. Amused. Cruel.

The sound slithers down my spine like ice. The air shifts behind me, a presence looming just out of reach—vile and all-consuming.

"Such devotion," da Vinci muses, his voice a velvet-coated blade. "You always were his little shadow, weren't you?"

My breath stutters. Terror crawls through my limbs.

"Funny thing about shadows," he continues, stepping closer, voice dipping into something almost gentle, almost mocking. "They fade in the dark."

Pain explodes through me. White-hot agony as cold steel tears through my back and bursts from my chest.

I gasp—no sound. Only a wet, choking noise as the air is ripped from my lungs.

My eyes drop.

The blade glints—gleaming, slick, soaked in red. My red.

My blood.

My hands twitch at my sides, still sticky with Mark's, useless now. Numb.

I can't move. Can't breathe. The world lurches sideways, warping into a nightmare haze.

Time slows.

My pulse pounds in my ears—fast, erratic, fading.

Then I feel him.

His breath ghosts against my skin, warm and wrong. I want to scream but my body won't obey.

His voice is soft. Almost tender.

"I win."

———

I JOLT AWAKE, gasping, the scream lodged in my throat. Sweat drenches my skin, my heart slamming hard enough to crack ribs.

I bolt upright, breath ragged, ears ringing with the phantom echoes of the nightmare.

So much blood.

Jacob's already there. His hands find me—firm, gentle, steady.

"Lyla," he says, voice rough from sleep but calm. Solid. "You're safe. I got you."

He holds me like I'm worth protecting, and I'm sitting here with blood on my hands, waiting for the moment he realizes it.

I squeeze my eyes shut, trying to banish the image of Mark choking on his own blood. It clings anyway.

Jacob says nothing else. He just pulls me into him, one hand cupping the back of my neck, massaging slow circles. His other hand glides up and down my back.

"Talk to me, Trouble," he murmurs, voice soft enough to slip past my defenses.

I want to lie. I want to shove the nightmare into a corner of my mind and lock it there. But tonight I'm done carrying it alone.

I trace absent patterns across his chest, centering on the steady rhythm of his heartbeat.

"My partner's name was Mark Valentine."

The name hits me like an avalanche I've been outrunning for years.

I don't deserve this safety, not when Mark's dead and buried by a system that never gave him peace. At least Mark knew what he'd signed up for. They don't.

Jacob's arms tighten like he can feel the weight, the guilt, the self-loathing I can't shake.

It would be so easy to tell him now. Rip off the bandage, show him the rot underneath. Explain the marks, the clues, the notes I've left behind.

But first, he needs to understand *why*.

Why I would risk them.

Why I couldn't stop chasing this ghost.

Why I couldn't let it go.

If he knows that, maybe he can forgive the rest.

"I'm here," he says, voice like gravel and warmth, something to hold on to when the world spins.

I breathe in deep, clinging to his scent. Letting it settle me. Letting myself believe, for one second, that maybe I'm not too far gone.

"We worked together for three years," I say. "Mark and I. Hunting serial killers. The worst of them. Monsters hiding behind everyday faces."

Every name. Every scene. Every body.

"But no matter how bad it got, we always caught them. Because it was Mark and me. Always together."

My fingers dig into his skin like a tether. He doesn't speak, but I feel him shift, grip tightening at my waist. A silent I'm here.

"Until *he* showed up."

The name sticks in my throat.

"Da Vinci," I whisper. It tastes like poison. "He abducted, tortured, and murdered his victims in ways so grotesque, so deliberately twisted, that law enforcement didn't realize it was the same man at first. Every scene looked like a different killer." My throat tightens, nausea crawling up it, but I push through. "By the time they connected the dots, thirteen women were already dead."

Silence swells between us.

"They were all between twenty-five and thirty-three."

Another beat.

"All blond. All blue-eyed." I force the words out. "Just like me."

A muscle tics in his jaw. His grip on my waist hardens, not to restrain, but like he's trying to hold me together.

"The sad part?" I press into him, chasing his warmth. "The bureau only got involved when he sent a letter." I can still see it, delicate script describing atrocities.

"He wanted attention. Said we were missing the 'art.' Described the killings like masterpieces." My breath shakes. "He wanted us to see him. To know that even with a task force on his heels, he could still make people vanish. After Mark and I joined the case, he . . . noticed me."

Jacob stills. "Noticed how?" he asks, voice low.

"He started writing directly to me. Addressing every note by name. Every taunt, every new murder—'gifts,' he called them—for me. He'd write, 'I thought of you the entire time,' or 'Hope you admire my work up close.' He was fixated."

Jacob's arms lock like steel, his body a shield.

A shiver runs down my spine, not from fear, but from the way he holds me. The way he absorbs my unraveling without flinching, like he wants to carry the rot so I don't have to.

I bury my face against his shoulder, breathing him in. Without a word, he shifts, pulling the blanket over us in one motion, wrapping us in a cocoon.

"He can't get to you," Jacob murmurs, voice firm against my ear. "Not now. Not ever."

If only he knew the truth.

"What we didn't know," I whisper, "was that he wasn't just some lone psycho. He was part of something bigger. A network—an underground ring of serial killers. They helped each other vanish. Hid each other's tracks. We weren't hunting monsters, we were chasing ghosts. Always one step too late. And every crime scene," I go on, hollow, "was like looking in a mirror."

Jacob's thumb sweeps my cheek, the softness cracking something deep inside me.

"Ten more women died because of me," I choke out. "Years of chasing him. Obsessing. Losing everything for one man. And I couldn't do it. I couldn't stop him."

The tears come hot and silent.

"I failed. Over and over again."

It would be so easy to tell him now. To let him see all of it. Both outcomes—understanding or exile—feel cleaner than this limbo.

Jacob kisses my temple like he's pressing courage into my skin.

"We almost had him," I whisper. "New Orleans. A year ago. Our informant said the artist was in town. We were so close. I didn't wait for backup. I didn't think. I had to end it. I shouldn't have pushed for us to go in alone," I rasp. "But I was tired of waiting."

Tired of staring into the lifeless faces of women he destroyed and seeing my own reflection. I couldn't take it anymore. I was reckless. Obsessed. Selfish. We split up. Mark took the front. I took the back. We were going to trap him between us. But he knew. He always knew.

"Our informant didn't know he'd been compromised. Da Vinci used him to feed us exactly what he wanted."

My stomach twists. "We found what was left of him the next day."

His organs were strung across a rusted chair like some twisted art installation.

"Mark and I walked right into the trap. Mark was on the ground. Trying to hold himself together. His hands pressed to his stomach, but he was bleeding out, and there was nothing I could do. I was too late. And da Vinci—"

I see it again, sharp as the day it happened. "He was already halfway out of the room. Paused at the door, looked back at me like it was a joke. He winked. Blew me a kiss. All he ever wanted was my attention. To tear away every person I cared about until he was the only thing left. Mark was still alive. Barely. And I—" The words crack. "I almost left him. I almost chased after that monster and left my partner to die alone."

Jacob lifts my chin. "But you didn't," he says, certain.

"I didn't. I stayed." I tried to stop the bleeding. I begged him to hold on. But we both knew.

"His last words—he made me promise to tell his wife he loved her. To tell their unborn child to be good and that their daddy loved them very much."

The sob rips through me, jagged and uncontrollable. Ten years of it in one breath.

Jacob holds me tighter, absorbing the pain.

"The crime scene team found a note in Mark's jacket. From him. Addressed to me."

"What did it say?"

"*See you soon.* I carried a copy every day. Waiting to shove it down his throat."

"How did you find him again?"

"Luck. I was sent to confirm whether a woman's murder in Virginia matched his signature." Her body was posed, carved, displayed like some grotesque masterpiece.

"Before I could meet with local PD, the outbreak hit. Two months later, there he was. Walking down Main Street with a group of men. Joanie and I tracked him. Stayed in the woods, off-grid, until we reached the prison."

If it hadn't been for Joanie, I'd have stormed in guns blazing. She grabbed my hand, wouldn't let go while I rage-sobbed in the woods.

"What I didn't expect was to find more of them."

Thirty men—armed, organized, coordinated. They moved like soldiers. Predators.

"For three days, we watched. Tracked shift changes, memorized guard rotations. Then on the fourth day, he appeared. A prison bus rolled in. Eight people shoved out—four men, four women. Broken already. Huddled like animals waiting for slaughter."

He prowled around them like a wolf. Grinning. Taking his time. He yanked a brunette by the hair, dragged her face into the light, stared like she was a trophy.

Then he pistol-whipped her. Dropped her like garbage. The others followed suit—each one picking someone, dragging them inside.

"They never came back out. Not until two days later. At sunrise, they dragged what was left into the yard and set them on fire."

They cheered. Laughed like it was a celebration. The flames lit up the sky. I can still smell it—burning hair, skin, bone. I clutched a tree like it could hold me together. Joanie threw up behind me. They were laughing.

"Something in me snapped. Everything went quiet. I stopped thinking like a fed. If I had to be a monster to kill one, so be it. I would end them all, even if it killed me to do it. As long as da Vinci burned with them, it'd be worth it."

Mark had a family. I have rage. Nothing left to lose.

Jacob cradles my face. "You don't deserve to die. That monster did this. Not you."

I want to believe him. But monsters wear human skin—and mine still fits too well.

"You tried to stop a killer," he says. "You acted because you knew another woman would die if you didn't. Another family would be shattered."

The words ease the barbed wire I've wrapped around my heart.

"He's gone because you didn't give up," he murmurs, then kisses me. The guilt returns, coiling around my ribs and sinking deeper than ever, turning the kiss into ash. I can't keep risking them for my plan. No more clues. No more notes.

I just want this. I want Jacob and this crazy bunch of people to be *my* family. I want to spend nights wrapped in his arms, enjoying my life for once.

Jacob slows the kiss, pulling away suddenly. His arms tense, eyes boring into mine.

"Lyla?" His voice is too calm. Controlled.

"What is it?"

"The woman you were supposed to investigate. Right before the outbreak. What was her name?"

"Sheila Tatters," I say. "Why?"

He goes still. His hand clenches against my spine.

"Sheila Tatters was my fiancée."

TWENTY-SEVEN
SMALL WORLD AFTER ALL

JACOB

THE REALIZATION SLAMS into me like a freight train, knocking the air from my lungs.

Sheila.

Lyla was investigating Sheila's murder.

What are the fucking odds?

I jolt upright, the bed creaking beneath me, pulse hammering in my ears. The camper walls close in, suffocating.

I need air. I need to move.

I swing my legs over the edge, feet hitting the floor as I push up, pacing in nothing but my underwear. The space feels too damn small to contain this.

Behind me, the sheets rustle.

"Jacob." Lyla's voice cuts through the fog, but beneath it, something fragile.

I turn. She clutches the sheet to her chest, shoulders rigid, eyes dark with concern.

"Explain." Her voice doesn't waver. "Please."

I drag a hand through my hair, gaze flicking anywhere but at her.

"It's . . . complicated," I mutter, gripping the kitchenette counter like it's the only thing keeping me upright.

"Then uncomplicate it."

A bitter laugh escapes—sharp, humorless. It's never that simple.

Lyla waits, patient in a way that twists my stomach.

I take a breath. "Sheila," I start, her name foreign on my tongue. "She was one of my best friends."

Lyla's expression softens. "Tell me about her."

I close my eyes for a second, enough for the memories to flood in, unstoppable. "I met her at the local elementary school. Trish and I were giving a fire safety and first aid assembly. Sheila was a second-grade teacher. Sweet. Kind. Lit up a room just by being in it."

Lyla stays silent, watching with quiet intensity.

"Trish introduced us. They were in the same book club. That's how I met Jessica too, they'd grown up next door to each other."

I shake my head. "Sheila and I . . . it was easy. Easy to talk to, easy to be with. We dated over a year. I proposed. She said yes." A hollow chuckle slips out. "Wedding plans started almost immediately."

I still can't look at Lyla. Not while my head drowns in what-ifs and the cruel joke the universe just played.

Because Sheila Tatters, the woman I was supposed to marry, had been one of his. And Lyla had been chasing her killer.

"But as the months went by, things changed." My jaw clenches. "Or maybe I changed. We grew apart. I got bored."

The words scrape like glass.

"Sheila wanted stability. A house, kids. Me? I wanted adventure. Excitement. Anything but the routine we'd fallen into."

My throat tightens but I force myself to continue. "I couldn't give her what she wanted. I sat her down, tried to make her see reason. She refused. Stormed out—hurt, confused, furious." My nails bite my palms. "That was the last time I saw her."

I glance at Lyla. Her expression holds understanding, not pity.

"The next day, the police came to the station. The way they

looked at me . . ." My jaw locks. "They found her body in the alley behind the grocery store on Main."

Images flash, the words *Sheila Tatters is dead* leaving the detective's mouth, the world tilting.

"They questioned me, asked where I was, when I'd last seen her. Then they showed me the pictures."

Her body crumpled in the alley, limbs bent wrong. Bruises, so many bruises, violent against pale skin. Deep lacerations, carved into her like she was a jack-o'-lantern. Her lavender dress soaked dark, clinging like a second skin.

And her eyes—once bright and laughing—empty.

Bile burns my throat.

"I couldn't believe it. Knowing it was my fault she was out there alone." My voice breaks. "I threw up in the station."

Lyla doesn't flinch. She just watches, steady, as I pace.

"The police grilled me for hours. It took two weeks for them to look anywhere else. A rookie profiler suggested they contact the FBI. Thought the posing matched another killer. They kept details out of the papers, just a brief notice. But by then the world was already unraveling."

I drop onto the edge of the bed, elbows on my knees, head in my hands.

"I didn't pay attention to any of it. I shut down. The flowers, the memorial, the sympathy looks—all a blur. People talked at me. Hugged me. Cried. I just stood there, hollowed out and nodding like a coward."

The guilt hasn't loosened its grip since.

"A month later, the world fell apart. Riots. Panic. The infected. The news shifted. Sheila became another name lost in the noise."

The awful part? I liked it. The chaos kept me moving. No time to drown in guilt.

"I never told anyone Sheila and I broke up," I admit. "To everyone else, she was still my fiancée. When the world went to hell, I went on autopilot. Saving people. Fixing things. Doing something. It was easier than thinking. Easier than remembering."

I know it makes me sound like an asshole, but I say it anyway. "I needed to forget. Otherwise, I'd lose someone else."

The mattress dips. Lyla's arms wrap around my shoulders, chin resting on my right one. She says nothing at first, just stays, cutting through the storm like a lighthouse.

"I'm so sorry, Jacob," she whispers. "I read about her. Before they sent me out here."

Her breath brushes my skin.

"Her case crossed my desk. But I didn't get far before—" She stops. Before the world burned.

I turn slightly. "Why did you get her case file?"

Her arms tighten. "It matched da Vinci's MO," she says. "But something felt off. He never targeted small towns, always big cities where his 'art' made headlines. Sheila's murder didn't fit. I thought maybe it was a copycat. Or he was shifting patterns. But now, knowing he was here, right before the outbreak—" She stops, fingers flexing against my chest. "It makes sense now. Killing her in a quiet town bought him time."

Her voice cracks. "I'm sorry I didn't stop him before he got to Sheila."

I turn fully to face her. The grief, the guilt, the fire in her eyes, it slams into me. "You couldn't have known," I say, voice low, rough. "None of this is on you."

"And it's not on you either," she says, cupping my face. "You didn't know what would happen. You did what you thought was right. She needed space. You didn't know what would happen that night."

Her thumbs press into my jaw.

"You didn't kill her. You couldn't control it. You can only control what you do now, for the people you still have." Her eyes mist, but her jaw is set as though she is talking to herself too.

The words soak in, slow, reaching places I've kept sealed. I shake my head, faint smile tugging. "We're quite the pair, huh?"

"Both carrying guilt like it's a backpack we can't take off. Maybe our guilt together will cancel out?"

A rough chuckle escapes. "I don't think that's how it works."

"Worth a shot."

Silence settles—heavier, but steadier. "So, what do we do now?"

Her thumb brushes my jaw like she's burning my face into her memory, like she's still not convinced she gets to keep it.

"Now," she says, tracing my face, "we help each other let go. It doesn't matter what we did before tonight. We move forward. We do better together."

I search for hesitation. There's none. "Together, then?"

She nods. "Together."

She settles back against the pillows, still watching me, softer now.

I lie beside her, tracing the curve of her face, the candlelight gilding her cheekbones and lips, lips I want back on mine.

Outside, rain taps the roof—a steady heartbeat. Something shifts inside me. The weight's still there, but it's lighter with her beside me.

I pull her close, fingers slipping into her hair, stroking down her back. We stay like that, skin to skin, letting touch speak where words can't.

My body comes down from the adrenaline. My eyes start to close.

Then—

"So, I remember the itinerary tonight included me sitting on your face."

My eyes snap open. She's grinning, her wicked gaze dark with hunger.

A smirk tugs at my lips. "I'm all yours."

PART THREE
BRAINS

DON'T BITE ME THERE!: A ZOMBIE SURVIVAL GUIDE

BY EARL RUSSO

Tip #3: Save firearms for emergencies.

Guns are loud. Loud means attention. And attention means a horde of undead—or worse, other survivors with bad intentions—headed your way. Stick to silent weapons like a bow, hammer, or anything that doesn't go bang. *Silence is a weapon.* Use it. And tell your chatty crew to shut up while you're at it.

Tip #6: Mental health matters.

The apocalypse isn't just hard on your body, it's hell on your brain. Make time for small routines, quiet moments, and joy where you can find it. Read a book. Sketch. Watch the stars. Hell, take up cartography. (No bias here—I just happen to be very good at it.)

Tip #11: Use fire wisely.

Fire is essential, but it's also a beacon. Keep it small, keep it controlled, and keep it hidden. Build fires with low smoke output, and for the love of all that's uninfected, put them out when you're done. The last thing we need is a forest fire on top of everything else.

Leon's tip: At night, surround the fire with rocks or branches to hide the glow.

Bonus Tip: <u>Don't</u> let others borrow your maps!

The farmhouse reeks of damp wood and rot, the kind that soaks into your lungs and never leaves. Candlelight dances along cracked walls, casting jagged shadows that twitch with every glimmer.

My knife spins against the table. Thunk, thunk, thunk. A rhythm to keep the rage from bleeding out.

The door creaks.

My grunt shoves a ragged man forward like trash. He stumbles, drops to his knees, dirt smeared across his face, sweat streaking down his temples.

"Caught him near the edge of the next town," the grunt says. "Claims he used to run with the group you're looking for."

The knife stops spinning.

Interesting.

I stay seated, watching. Quiet. Calculating.

Then I smile—warm, disarming, the kind that makes prey think the wolf might pet them.

"Well," I murmur, setting the knife down, "looks like fate finally threw me something useful.

He blinks, startled by the calm.

I rise, slow, deliberate. Extend a hand like we're about to strike a deal. "I'm da Vinci."

He hesitates, then grips my hand. "Pete."

I nod. "Strong name."

His chest puffs a little. Pathetic.

"Tell me," I say, casual as smoke, "was there a blond woman with your group? Sharp eyes. Quicker tongue. Name of Lyla?"

His scoff is instant. "Yeah. Real pain in the ass."

I slap him.

Hard.

His head whips sideways. He groans, clutching his jaw.

The silence swells.

I wipe my palm with a rag. "Sorry, friend. I don't like people talking about my things like that. You understand?"

He nods fast, blood spotting his teeth. "I'm sorry."

"Good." I pat his head. He stays down.

"Now," I say, "tell me about your group. Who leads?"

"Jacob," Pete spits. "He's the one who did this." He gestures to the bruises on his face.

I crouch beside him. "Let me guess—he turned everyone against you and tossed you out?"

His snort flares with heat. "Exactly. Thinks he's noble, but he's a control freak. Everything has to go through him. And now?" He hesitates. "He's got eyes for Lyla."

My Lyla.

Her name coils around my chest, makes the air vibrate. My body hums with the thought of her—how her fear tastes.

I pace behind him, knife back in my hand, casual as if we're sharing a drink. "She's been leaving me breadcrumbs, you know. Not obvious to them—just enough for me to follow. Clever, my girl. But sloppy. She wants me to find her."

Pete glances up, frowning. "Breadcrumbs?"

"In the woods," I say, smiling at the memory. "A broken branch pointing the wrong way. A boot print just where it shouldn't be. A mark on a tree only I'd notice. She's calling me, Pete. She thinks she's the hunter." My voice drops into a purr. "But she's always been the prey."

Pete swallows hard.

"People like Jacob," I continue, "pretend it's about loyalty. Honor. But it's control. They forget who kept them alive."

Pete nods, leaning toward me now. "That's what I'm saying. I kept them alive. Me. And they threw me out like I was nothing."

I rest a hand on his shoulder—light, reassuring, a leash tightening. "They were wrong about you, Pete."

He exhales. "What do you mean?"

I grip his jaw, force his eyes to mine. "I want Lyla."

His eyes widen.

"She belongs to me."

He freezes. "What do you plan to do?" he blurts.

I tilt my head, grin spreading slow. "I'll take what's mine and kill anyone in the way." I let go, watching my fingerprints fade from his skin. "And you, Pete, are going to help me."

"I— I don't want—"

I slap him across the other cheek, harder. Blood drips from his lip. "You think you have a choice?"

My grunt fists Pete's hair, holding him steady.

I press the flat of my blade to his cheek, lean in, voice a whisper soaked in malice. "Now. What route are they taking?"

TWENTY-EIGHT
PLAY TIME

JACOB

A SLIVER of dawn cuts through the thin curtains, casting gold over the crumpled blankets and the woman sprawled across my chest. Lyla's warm, soft limbs and tousled hair drape over me like she belongs there. Her steady breathing soothes something deep in me.

I stare at the ceiling, replaying the night before—the confessions, the raw edges, the slow burn of something far more dangerous than attraction. Telling her about Sheila felt like slicing open a wound I hadn't touched in years, but now the weight feels lighter.

I tighten my arm around her, pulling her closer, breathing her in, warm skin, faint vanilla. My hands roam, sliding lower—

"If you start something, you better finish it."

A grin pulls at my lips. "Is that a challenge?"

She lifts her head, one eye open, a lazy smirk curving her mouth. "Always."

God, this woman. I drag my fingers up her back, brush hair from her face, trace my thumb along her jaw. "Can't back down from that, can I?"

"I'd be disappointed if you did."

I kiss her—slow, methodical. She melts into me, her fingers

grazing my jaw before cupping my cheek. She tastes warm, soft, sweet from sleep.

In one motion, I shift us, pinning her beneath me. Her back presses into the blankets, her body pliant against mine. Golden light spills over her face, highlighting the slope of her cheek, the full curve of her lips, the shy flush on her skin. I drink her in.

"Stunning."

Without breaking eye contact, I lower my mouth to her jaw, then down her throat. Her pulse flutters under my lips. Her breath quickens as I trail lower. Her fingers tangle in my hair, holding me close as I take my time.

My hands explore, mapping every curve, every tremor.

I slide between her legs. She parts them, easy, trusting. *Mine.*

I press a kiss to the dip between her hip and center, then lower, just above where she wants me. Her nails dig into my shoulders, grounding us both. I hum against her thigh, kissing lightly before lifting my head.

Her eyes are closed, lips parted. I brush my thumb over her cheek. She stirs, lids heavy.

"Why'd you stop?" Playfulness laces her voice.

She tries to pull me back down, but I stand between her open thighs. Before she can protest, I hook her knees, dragging her to the edge of the bed. Her gasp—half yelp, half laughter—hits me low and hard.

Keeping my gaze locked on hers, I lick my fingers slow, deliberate. Her pupils blow wide. I trail my slick fingertips between her folds, barely touching.

"First," I murmur, circling her clit without giving her the pressure she needs, "I want to play."

She shudders, hips jerking toward me. I press in just enough to pull a moan from her. That sound tears through me. I slide lower, testing, making sure she's ready.

"Yes," she gasps, head tipping back. "Fuck, Jacob."

A dark chuckle rumbles in my chest as I pop the lid of the lube bottle with my teeth. Her pupils blow wide with hunger at the sight, just like last night. "We'll get to that, Trouble."

I slick my fingers with lube and keep the rhythm, thumb circling her clit while my fingers press deeper, stretching her to take more. My free hand cups her breast, thumb rolling her nipple. She arches, greedy for everything I'll give.

She's perfect.

Her breathing stutters, her body writhing under my touch. Still working her with my fingers, I wrap my other hand around my cock, stroking in time with her movements, slicking myself with precum.

She props herself up, eyes locked on me, biting her lip as I work myself.

"You see what you do to me?" My voice is rough. "You see what kind of man I am when you beg me to make you come?"

She whimpers, gaze dropping to my fingers plunging into her. I speed up, adding a third. Releasing my cock, I spit into my hand, stroking it over her folds for more slickness, more heat.

"Jacob, please." Her voice trembles, muscles tensing. "I need you inside me."

Satisfaction rolls through me, but I press her flat, fingers unrelenting.

"Only good girls get fucked with my cock," I murmur, dragging my lips over her thigh. "And you—" I glance up, meeting her wild eyes as she bucks against me. "You've never been good."

I drive my fingers faster, each thrust slick, sinful. Her thighs quake, breasts bouncing with every movement. Her head tips back, mouth open on a strangled gasp.

I wrap my palm around her neck, light pressure as I slow my thumb over her clit, dragging a single torturous circle.

Her body locks, then bows, back arching as pleasure rips through her. Her cries fill the camper.

I don't stop until her shudders fade. Only then do I ease out, dragging my wet fingers up her stomach, watching her chest heave.

I climb over her and settle between her legs, my cock pressed to her soaked heat. I nuzzle her neck, drag my lips to her ear, nip before whispering, "You okay?"

A chuckle spills from her. "I'm more than okay, you devil."

I roll my hips, her gasp spilling against my lips—

BANG. BANG. BANG.

"Hey, lovebirds!" Trish's voice cuts through the walls, smug. "We need to head out soon, so finish up! You've got five minutes before I send Barbara in, and you know she'll kill the mood."

Lyla bursts into laughter. "She's got impeccable timing."

"Dammit," I groan, dropping my head to her shoulder, trying to will away the frustration, and the hard-on.

Lyla's fingers thread through my hair.

"Trish," I call, voice muffled against her skin, "you're officially my least favorite person."

"Yeah, yeah," she calls back. "You'll survive."

Lyla tilts her head, mischief gleaming in her eyes. "Five minutes, huh?"

I raise a brow. "What are you thinking?"

She doesn't answer at first. She pushes me onto my back, straddling my hips. Her hands glide down my chest, nails dragging enough to make my abs tighten. "I'm thinking that's plenty of time."

Fuck.

Before I can speak, she slides off the bed to her knees between my legs. My pulse spikes as she settles, eyes locked on mine—dark, dangerous, full of intent.

Then her tongue is on me.

A hiss escapes as she drags one slow lick up my length, stopping just over the tip. Her hand wraps around me, stroking, eyes never leaving mine. Her lips part, breath warm, tongue flicking until my hips twitch.

"Gorgeous," she whispers.

Then she takes me into her mouth in one smooth motion.

My head drops back, a growl tearing from my throat as the wet heat surrounds me. I fist her hair, guiding her as my hips roll up, pushing deeper.

"Just like that," I rasp. "Fuck, Lyla—just like that."

———

FOUR AND A HALF MINUTES LATER…

We peel ourselves apart, breathless and flushed. The camper, already too small, becomes a mess of tangled limbs, half-dressed bodies, and scattered clothes.

Lyla reaches for her dress, but I catch her wrist, bring her hand to my lips, press a kiss to her palm. Heat flashes in her eyes.

"You're distracting," she mutters.

"You're welcome." I grin, pulling my shirt over my head.

She huffs, rolls her eyes, but the smile curling at her mouth betrays her.

"I need to get to Lucy and change before we set off," she says, pulling her hair up. "Not walking around with my skin on display for the undead to chomp on."

She grabs my green Henley and tugs it over her head like it's hers. Maybe it is now. She lifts the collar to her nose—breathing me in.

My chest tightens. I want her in that shirt forever.

As I lace my boots, I catch her watching me, something sparking in her look.

"What?"

She hesitates, then shakes her head with a quiet laugh. "Nothing. It's been a while since I've felt this—" Her gaze flicks away.

"Normal?"

Her lips part, then she nods. "Yeah. Normal."

I press my palm to hers, calluses meeting calluses. "We'll hold on to it as long as we can."

She squeezes my fingers. "Good."

Before she can turn away, I pull her back into my chest, brush my lips over hers. "Thank you for a wonderful night."

A flush rises in her cheeks. "Anytime." She leans in, her lips finding mine again, slower, sweeter.

Something in my chest stumbles. The softness cuts through every rough edge I carry.

"Thank you for a lovely date," she whispers, voice warm enough to steal my words.

And then she looks at me—blue eyes bright, unguarded.

Damn.

I'm ruined for anyone else.

We step into the crisp morning air. Rain still clings to the earth, the camp buzzing with movement—gear packed, supplies loaded, weapons checked.

We don't make it three steps before Trish zeroes in on us, arms crossed, grin in place like a wolf catching prey.

"About time!" she calls, and heads turn.

One hell of a walk of shame.

Lyla groans. "Morning to you too, Trish."

Trish taps her bare wrist. "Morning? Feels like afternoon, considering how long you two were holed up."

Her gaze rakes Lyla—my shirt, messy hair, swollen lips—before landing on the hickey blooming on her neck. Bold as hell. I wonder how long before Lyla notices.

"Nice outfit." Trish grins.

Lyla flushes, tugs at my shirt hem like it'll help.

Leon leans on his truck, thermos in hand, watching with too much enjoyment. He takes a slow sip, signs, "*Good night?*"

I smirk. "Piss off."

His mouth twitches before he signs, *"She and I will need to talk. I want to know her intentions."*

A laugh escapes.

Lyla elbows me. "What'd he say?"

"He wants a chat. Wants to know your intentions with me. He's very protective."

She lifts a brow but pales slightly as we near Lucy. No one survives a Leon Q&A unscathed.

Lyla yanks the door open, dives for her clothes. I turn, shielding her from curious eyes. Denim rustles, a stomp or two, a muttered curse.

A tap on my shoulder. She's dressed—jeans, my Henley, hair pulled into a no-nonsense ponytail.

I pull her close, kiss her long and slow. She leans into it, reluctant to let go.

"Thank you for a wonderful evening again," I murmur.

She grins. "I'll gladly have date night in Ol' Bessy anytime."

"You did not just name my camper."

"Of course. She's family." Her gaze drops to my crotch. "And I've got dibs on naming something else now too."

Oh. Hell. No. "Leave my body parts out of your weird naming hobby."

She rolls her eyes. "Fine."

Why do I not believe her?

She hops into the driver's seat, slams the door. Engines idle in the background.

I lean into the open window, kiss her deep and lingering. Her fingers grip my collar, holding me there. When we break, her eyes are lazy, heavy-lidded, full of heat.

"So," she drawls, "when can we pick up where we left off?"

My pulse spikes with anticipation. "First chance we get."

She fires the engine, lips curling. "Good."

Joanie slides into the passenger seat with a CD in hand. My eyes snap to both of them. "No Spice Girls."

Lyla arches a brow, all mock innocence. "But they really set the tone for apocalypse road trips, don't you think?"

Joanie snorts. "You just don't know how to process the joy of nineties pop perfection."

I should be given an award for the effort it's taking me to not grin in this moment. "Just keep it down. Last time you two cranked it, we almost summoned an undead mosh pit," I say, pushing off the doorframe.

Lyla tosses me a salute as I head for the ER van.

I turn—then freeze. Jessica stands by her car across the clearing. Hurt, anger, betrayal—all written plain.

Shit.

Fuck.

Dammit.

I meant to talk to her, end things clean. I kept dodging it. Now I've blown any chance at calm conversation.

I've got to deal with it.

Just . . . not yet.

I'm not ready to pop the bubble still floating around me from last night. The guilt's already scratching at the edges, and I know it's going to get worse before it gets better.

Jessica slams her door, hard enough to rattle the frame.

"Are you getting in, or are you gonna stand there brooding all day?"

Trish sits in the passenger seat of the van, brow arched, fingers drumming her thigh.

"Just appreciating my morning," I say, tossing my bag in and sliding behind the wheel.

Trish snorts. "Yeah, I bet."

I grip the wheel as engines rumble around us. Earl's truck pulls alongside, his arm draped out the window.

"You want to bring up the rear today?"

"Yeah, no problem."

Before I can turn forward, Edith leans across him. "Jacob, sweetie?"

"Yeah, E?"

"Next time you and Lyla want a sex-filled night, maybe give us a heads-up? So we can unlatch the camper?"

I freeze.

"Oh, don't worry. I kept your mother distracted all night—which, let me tell you, was not easy. But I'd prefer not to hear your name screamed multiple times."

Dear Lord, please shoot me now.

Trish wheezes with laughter.

I scrub my hand over my face. "I— We— Just—"

"No need to explain," Edith says, breezy as ever, like she *isn't* actively destroying my will to live. "I love a good romance. From the sound of it, you two had a *wonderful* time. Makes me proud."

The air leaves my lungs.

Pretty sure Trish just ascended to another plane.

Earl, the smug bastard, just winks and tips an imaginary hat before rolling up his window and pulling ahead, leaving me alone with my suffering.

Trish finally calms down enough to breathe, still grinning like a damn hyena. "Damn. *Edith* is officially my favorite person."

I glare. "Say one word, and you're walking."

She leans back, lacing her fingers behind her head. "Whatever you say, *Gorgeous.*"

The convoy falls into line. Lyla's rig pulls close, "Wannabe" blasting like a battle cry. She swings in front of me, arm out the window, middle finger pumping to the beat.

My Grinch heart? Just grew a size.

TWENTY-NINE
OH, JOANIE

LYLA

WE'VE BEEN ROLLING for hours, Ohio's border somewhere ahead, and the convoy is quiet.

I should be tired too. Sleep hasn't exactly been plentiful.

In a good way.

A small smile creeps in as I grip the wheel. My body's sore in the best ways. Jacob's been a surprise. A very, very good surprise.

Every night for the past two weeks, we've parked the camper farther from the others. After that first night, and the talk that followed, I couldn't stomach the idea of anyone overhearing us again. Edith's comment still makes me shudder. Distance has been our friend.

But my eyes keep flicking to Joanie. She's been wound tighter than barbed wire this morning, staring out the window like the answers are hiding somewhere past the tree line. Not watching the road—watching *through* it.

The silence buzzes with something sharp and unfinished.

"Jo," I say, keeping my voice casual, like I'm not bracing. "You good?"

Her jaw flexes. "Fine."

"Bullshit. Spit it out."

She doesn't answer. Just reaches into her bag and yanks something out—a tattered notepad.

My stomach sinks.

"I found this under your seat last night," she says, voice low and shaking with fury. "Want to explain what the fuck it is?"

I glance down. The top page is covered in my handwriting—taunts, clues, locations. All meant for him. Every breadcrumb I planned to drop, bundled together in one neat, damning stack.

I knew I forgot about something.

Shitty shit shit.

"I—I was leaving notes for him," I admit, throat tight. "To lure him. To end it. I thought if he followed me, I could control the outcome. Keep everyone else safe."

Her laugh is hollow. Mean. "Control the outcome? Are you out of your damn mind? You handed him a road map straight to our doorstep."

"I stopped—"

"You shouldn't have even started!"

Her voice cracks on the edge of rage and betrayal.

I tighten my grip on the wheel. "I'm sorry, kiddo."

"Stop the car, Lyla."

"I'm not—"

"I said STOP the fucking car. Or I'm jumping."

"Joanie—"

She throws the door open.

"Shit—JOANIE!"

Before I can swerve to a full stop, she tucks her shoulder and rolls, still gripping her bag and the notebook.

My foot slams the brake. Tires scream. Dust erupts in a choking cloud. My hand braces against the dash as Lucy jerks to a violent stop.

I shove the door open, screaming, "Are you crazy!? You could have broken something!"

Joanie stands and immediately starts walking away, down the road toward the others' now stopped cars. Ignoring me.

"Joanie, stop! Please listen to me!" My voice cuts through the engine's ticking cooldown. Urgent. Pleading.

"I thought if I got you somewhere safe, with people, you'd stop chasing him," she blurts, the words tumbling over each other as she keeps walking away from me. "I thought if you believed it was over, you'd heal. But, no. You instead decide to keep your fucking obsession and lie to us, to me!" Then in a softer, hurt tone. "You were supposed to be better."

Gravel crunches behind us, low and sharp. Doors slam. Jacob. Trish. Leon. Edith. Earl. Clair. They're all there, all closing in. But their faces blur, their voices fade, because all I hear is the sound of Mark's last breath rattling out of him in my arms, the sobs of families I failed, and the low, amused laugh of the man who did it.

"Joanie, I joined this group because of him, but I'm staying because of you all. I knew he would follow all of you because he can't let anyone best him. I brought him here, on purpose, but I stopped leaving notes."

Joanie turns and laughs, but there's nothing warm in it. It's jagged. Bitter. "And you think that makes it okay?"

Her hand trembles as she digs into her bag, yanking something free, and throwing it into my hand. "It was in the warden's office. Sitting on the desk."

The paper feels rough under my fingertips, the edges frayed like they've been worried over a hundred times. I flip it open one-handed, and my eyes hit the jagged scrawl:

~~See you soon.~~

This isn't over.

I look up into her eyes as she guts me. "I guess you'll get your wish after all. I just hope it was worth it."

The others have finally joined us. Jacob's voice slices through the air. "What happened? Are you both okay?"

"Ask her." Joanie's breath comes fast. "She's the one who's fucked up." Her eyes lock with mine, her words a snarl. "She lied. Straight to my face." She holds out the notebook.

Jacob takes it from Joanie's hand. His body goes rigid as his eyes rake over the handwriting. The silence that follows is like a guillotine dropping.

His grip tightens on the sheets of paper. "What is this, Joanie?"

Tears spill over. "I saw Lyla sneaking into the woods at night. More than once. You told us not to go alone, so yeah, I thought it was weird. But then I followed her, over a week ago, and caught her carving marks into a tree. After that, I started checking her stuff. Easy enough, with you two shacked up together." Her voice cracks into a sob. "And last night? I find this notebook. Messages for that psychopath she's so fucking obsessed with."

I don't look away from him. I want him to see the horrible truth for what it is. "I brought him to us. To me. So when he came, I'd be here to protect everyone—and kill him for good."

Trish's voice cuts in. "Who the hell are you talking about?"

The air goes heavy. Still.

Jacob takes a step forward, closing the space like a predator locking on to prey. Fury ignites in his eyes, hot enough to burn. "You led him to us?" His voice rises, every word loaded and lethal. "You dragged every single one of us into his sights?"

"I wouldn't have let anything happen—"

"Just like nothing happened to Mark?"

The world stops.

The name slams into me like a blow to the ribs, knocking the air from my lungs. My head snaps toward him, heat and ice colliding in my veins. "You don't get to use him against me."

"Why not?" His voice is a blade, each word honed to wound.

"It's the truth. You couldn't save him, and now you've lined up the rest of us in his place."

My chest heaves, rage scraping against grief until I can barely tell them apart. "That's not what this is—"

"That's exactly what this is!" he roars, the sound tearing through the space between us. "You made a call for everyone here without a single damn word. You turned this group into bait because you couldn't let go of your grudge. You didn't just gamble with your life —you gambled with all of ours."

"It's not a grudge—it's justice!" My voice tears out of me, raw and scorching. "I was going to tell you, but I knew you'd do whatever it took to bury us so he'd never find me. And you don't get to make that decision for me any more than I get to make it for you. When I stayed, I realized you all deserved the choice. To fight or to run."

He laughs—short, sharp, and cruel enough to cut. "A choice? This isn't some noble stand, Lyla. It's about protecting the people I'm responsible for. About not tossing lives onto the table like poker chips in your personal war." His jaw tightens, his words landing like fists. "You were selfish. You risked every single one of us so you could take your shot."

"I was protecting you—"

"No." The word snaps out like a whip crack, slicing clean between us. "You were protecting your pride. That's all this ever was. And I'm done with it."

The ice in his voice is worse than any scream—it's final, unyielding.

"Leave."

I blink, stunned. "What?"

"Get in your car and go." His eyes don't waver, don't soften. "We'll take care of ourselves. We don't need your recklessness poisoning this group."

The air between us turns to ice. The group stands frozen, eyes flicking between us. Even Joanie looks like she's been punched in the gut, her lips parting like she might speak, then closing again. No one moves. No one dares to.

"You don't mean that," I manage, though my voice shakes, equal parts fury and something dangerously close to hurt.

Barbara steps forward. "Jacob—"

"I mean every damn word." His voice is a blade.

Something in my chest buckles, threatening to split wide open. "I stopped leaving clues the night we had our date. I chose you, all of you, over him. I could've kept the trail hot, but I didn't. I was going to tell you, Jacob, but every mile we traveled . . . every night I saw you safe . . . it got harder and harder to rip that apart. I figured if you didn't know and he never found us that it didn't need to be told."

His eyes lock on mine, and there's no warmth left—only hurt, sharp and unyielding. "I don't want to hear your excuses for what you did. You need to leave. Now."

I want to scream, to rage, to tell him he's wrong—that everything I did was for them. I want to grab him by the shirt and make him see it. But the set of his shoulders, the rigid line of his jaw, the way he doesn't so much as blink tells me it's pointless. The verdict's already been handed down.

Tears well hot and fast, threatening to spill, but I force my spine straight. If he's going to push me out, I won't give him the satisfaction of watching me crumble.

For a long, pulsing second, I just stand there, my fingers curled so tight around the note that the paper softens under the heat and sweat of my grip. Then I shove it into my jacket pocket, turn on my heel, and walk to Lucy—every step heavier than the last.

The driver's seat feels cold as I drop into it. My hands are steady, but only because I won't let them shake.

I start the engine and slam my foot on the gas.

In the mirror, Jacob stands with his arms crossed, shoulders squared like I'm just another problem he's solved by cutting loose. The others watch, silent and still, as the distance swallows me.

Thirty minutes blur—dark trees, cracked pavement. Just nothing.

The tears come hard and fast, relentless, hot streaks down my cheeks.

Lucy's headlights cut into the dark, and a small town rises ahead —quiet, half-ruined, waiting.

I don't know if I'm looking for answers, or a fight.

Only that I'm alone. And this time, I'm the one who made it that way.

THIRTY

MOM TO THE RESCUE

JACOB

IT'S BEEN one day since Lyla left, and I feel like shit.

Camp's quieter than usual.

Not in a peaceful way—more in a *don't poke the bear* kind of way.

Yeah, I guess I'm the bear.

Everyone's going through the motions tonight—stringing up cans, checking weapons, patrolling the perimeter, but they do it in silence. No jokes. No "you good?" Not even from Joanie. She's been avoiding my eyes since the moment Lyla drove off.

I don't blame her. Hell, I wouldn't look at me either.

I've been sitting on the edge of my bed in the camper, elbows braced on my knees, staring at a rust stain in the corner. It's been there since before the outbreak, water damage from a leak I didn't notice fast enough. I focus on it like maybe if I stare long enough, I can burn out the image in my head.

The image of her face when I told her to leave.

That flare of hurt she tried to swallow down.

The way her eyes shone, not because she was crying, but because she refused to.

I told myself I was protecting the group. And maybe that's still true. But the knot in my chest hasn't loosened once since her taillights vanished into the dark.

The door slams open so hard the hinges scream.

Mom barrels in like a storm front, shoulders squared, eyes locked. "All right, Jacob Anthony Armor, you're going to tell me what the hell is going on—*now*."

I don't even look up. "It's handled."

"Like hell it is." The door snaps shut behind her with a sharp crack, rattling the frame. She plants herself in the middle of the room, hands on her hips, shoulders squared like she's ready to go a round with me. "Half the camp is walking on eggshells, Joanie's in the van crying into Trish's shoulder, and I watched Lyla tear out of here like the devil himself was snapping at her heels. So you're going to start talking before I wring it out of you."

I drag a hand through my hair, the muscles in my jaw working overtime. "You wouldn't understand."

Her eyes narrow. "Try me."

That's the look. The one that says there's no dodging her, no ducking out. Chin tilted, eyes sharp enough to skin me alive. I blow out a slow breath and start from the beginning.

I tell her everything. Da Vinci. His sick, twisted history. Lyla's obsession with hunting him down. The "artists." Da Vinci's part in Sheila's death. Mark. Every bloody, gut-churning detail. I don't spare the ugly parts.

By the time I'm done, her arms are crossed, but her eyes are burning in a way that makes me uneasy.

"Let me get this straight," she says, her voice low but cutting. "Lyla's been tracking a man responsible for the deaths of God knows how many people, including her partner. She swore to their families she'd bring them justice. She finds him, tries to end him, fails, and then decides the only way to protect us and finish him at the same time is to join our group. To keep us close."

"She used us as bait, Mom." My voice spikes as I shake my head, the heat flaring again in my chest. "She admitted it. I even interrogated Joanie after she left to be sure. She deliberately put every single one of us in his sights. No discussion. No warning. Just her choice, and we get to live, or die, with it."

"I'm aware of that, and I'll deal with that when I see her again." Mom's eyes lock on mine, searching, sharp. Then she asks, "But wouldn't you do the same thing?"

My brow furrows. "Wouldn't I what?"

"Wouldn't you do anything for the ones you love?"

"That's not the same," I bite out, but even I hear the thinness in my voice.

She steps in, her tone dropping low but hitting harder with each word. "Isn't it? You've thrown yourself into danger more times than I can count for this group. For me. For people you barely knew at first. You'd rather take the hit than watch someone else bleed. That's exactly what she was doing, Jacob. She just didn't tell you because she knew you'd chain her to a tree before you'd let her go through with it."

A tight ache blooms in my chest, squeezing hard. "She lied to me. She put everyone in danger. I kicked Pete out for doing the same damn thing. Why should I allow her back in?" What I don't ask is why should I let her back into my heart?

"Oh please." Mom throws her hands in the air. "Pete did what he did because he was a selfish asshole and a coward. He tried to kill you all. Lyla may have led a dangerous man to us, but she did it chasing justice, for people she swore to protect. She didn't leave us to fend for ourselves against that maniac. She stayed with us and was willing to die for us. I bet everything I have in Earl's truck that she would have told us to go and save ourselves while she fought him alone. Died alone. That is not even in the same realm as what Pete did."

She takes a deep breath, hands on her hips, before continuing, "And you've never lied by omission? Never kept something to yourself because you thought it was the best way to protect someone?" Her brow arches, sharp as a blade, finger pointing in my face. "Don't you dare lie to me, Jacob."

I glance away, jaw locking until my teeth ache. Damn it, she's right. She's so damn right. I've always been reactive—jump first, think later. And when Lyla said she'd led him to us, I didn't stop to think at all. The anger came like a flood. The hurt? That came even faster.

A hard smack lands at the back of my head.

"Fuck, Mom!"

"And now I'm pissed that I had to knock sense into you!"

Beneath the anger, beneath the justifications I keep feeding myself, there's guilt. Heavy. Sour. It sits in my gut like rusted metal, corroding everything it touches. Because now she's out there alone, and I might've just made damn sure she stays that way.

"I don't even know where she's headed," I admit, my voice low, rough. "She's not going to make it easy for me to find her. And if he's still out there—"

Mom reaches into her jacket pocket without breaking eye contact and flicks something at me. Reflex kicks in—I catch it. Leon's truck keys.

I look up at her, confused, but she's already folding her arms, planting herself like a wall I'm not getting around. "Stop sitting here feeling sorry for yourself and go look. Bring her back. I have a feeling Lyla is closer than you think."

The keys are cold in my palm, the weight of them pulling at my chest. I stare at the jagged teeth, then lift my gaze to hers. "She might not want to come back."

She opened her wounds to me, told me about her partner, about the guilt eating her alive, and I threw it all back at her. Took her pain and weaponized it. Mark's death, her biggest regret, and I acted like it was her fault. Like *she* was the monster.

God, I want to punch myself in the dick.

Her mouth tightens into something unyielding. "Then make her want to. You're stubborn, Jacob—hell, it's your defining trait. Time to use it for something that matters instead of driving people away."

My throat feels tight, but I nod once. "All right."

I'm halfway to the door when she calls after me, her voice sharp enough to hook between my shoulder blades. "And when you do find her? Maybe lead with something other than 'get out.' "

A humorless huff escapes me—half laugh, half self-loathing. "Yeah. I'll work on that."

The door swings shut behind me. The keys clink in my grip like a promise. And for the first time since she drove off, I've got a direction.

And I'm not stopping until I find her.

THIRTY-ONE
DEAR MARK

LYLA

I'M PARKED in front of a small, crumbling church on the outskirts of Volant, PA, two towns ahead on the group's route. Its sagging roof and shattered stained-glass windows scatter moonlight across the interior in broken shards of color. Overgrown hedges and a rusting dumpster should hide Lucy from casual sight.

Even though I'm out, I can't just disappear and leave the group to fend for themselves. So a day ago I drove into the next town on their agenda, crashed in Lucy, scavenged all day, took out a few infected to bleed off some rage, and now I'm stuck here, missing them like hell.

I'll wait for them to come through town, likely tomorrow morning, then I'll follow them from a distance. I'll trail them all the way to Montana if that's what it takes to make sure they're safe.

I have to make sure they make it.

The heavy doors of the church groan as I push them open. The sound echoes deep, hollow, like the last breath of something sacred.

Inside, the air is still. Thick with dust and the faint scent of wax and old paper. I walk down the aisle slowly, each step loud in the silence, sending a shiver crawling up my spine. My fingers drift across the tops of the pews—smooth, worn, empty.

No prayers. No peace.

At the altar, I stop. The carvings are worn down, barely visible anymore, prayers etched by hands that once begged for mercy. My palms press against the wood, and I lean in, closing my eyes, picturing Mark.

His stupid half grin. The way his eyes crinkled when he laughed. That damn pen was always spinning between his fingers when he was thinking. He was calm when I wasn't. Solid when I fell apart. My partner. My safe place.

Then—

Blood on the floor.

His body broken.

The sound of him choking on his own breath while I screamed his name and tried to hold him together with shaking hands.

A sob rips out of me—raw, haunting. I clutch the altar until my fingers ache, my chest splintering under the weight of it all. The grief is jagged and endless, cutting deeper with every breath.

"What do I do, Mark?" I whisper.

No answer. No warmth. Just silence. Just the creak of old wood and the echo of everything I've lost.

I drag a shaking hand through my hair, vision blurring with tears I can't stop. Hot and bitter, they streak down my cheeks, cutting through the dust on my skin like they're trying to burn away everything I've been holding in. Every mask. Every lie. Every failure.

"I swore I'd get justice," I whisper, voice cracking on the words. "For you. For them. And now, it just feels like I failed all over again."

The past I tried to bury is clawing its way back up, dragging me with it. The blood, the screams, the moment Mark slipped through my fingers. I can't outrun any of it. It's in my chest, my throat, my bones.

My knees buckle and I stumble into the front pew, collapsing like the fight's been knocked out of me. My hands grip the edge of the bench, nails biting into the wood.

I sit there and weep for the people I've lost. For the justice I swore to give them. For the hurt I caused Jacob. For the weight I've been dragging behind me like a chain I never unhooked.

The sobs come hard, shaking my whole body. I can't stop them. I don't try.

Then a sound behind me. A faint rustle. I don't look. I don't need to.

His presence rolls in like warmth on skin chilled too long. He doesn't say a word. He just sits down beside me, close enough for me to feel the solid calm of him anchoring me to the now.

His hand finds mine.

Fingers thread through fingers like it's instinct. Like he's always known where he belongs.

The silence between us is full—not empty. Heavy with the things he doesn't ask and the things I can't say.

But his grip is steady.

And for now, that's enough.

When I finally turn, moonlight filters through the shattered stained glass, spilling across Jacob's face in streaks of blue and gold. The colors shift like something holy, something not meant for this broken place.

"You tell everyone about what I did?"

He watches me. "I told my mom, which means everyone will know within an hour."

I nod, but my throat is too tight for words.

"I'm so sorry, Lyla," he says softly.

My head snaps to him. "Why are you sorry? I'm the one who is sorry. You were right. I was selfish. I was using people to get what I wanted." I pause. Tears running down my cheeks. "I was just so tired. Tired of failing. I thought if I brought justice to those women, gave

Mark peace, that I would be whole again. That all the sacrifices I've made would be worth it."

My voice breaks. "But now? It feels like none of it mattered. He died because of me. His daughters lost their father. His wife lost her husband. Because I made the call. Because I thought I could fix it all. And then I did it all over again with you and your family."

Jacob shifts, his voice low but solid. "Look at me."

I do. Slowly. Like it hurts to meet his gaze.

"You're not a failure," he says, calm and sure, like it's not even up for debate. "You went into hell and came back swinging. You saved lives. You didn't just chase justice—you *delivered* it."

He leans in, ticking the names off like anchors to the truth. "Earl. Edith. Clair. Poppy. Jessica. My mom. You saved them, Lyla. That matters. *You* matter. Yes, you fucked up, but I understand why you made the choice to stay with us."

The tears fall harder—hot, endless. Jacob cups my face and presses a soft kiss to each cheek. His forehead rests against mine, and I let myself fall into the rhythm of his breath. Ours, together. Calmer.

"I'm sorry it took me a day, and my mom smacking me in the head, to finally realize it and come find you. I should've chased after you the second you started that engine."

The image of Barbara smacking him upside the head pulls a weak huff from my lips.

"I didn't know Mark," he says gently, "but if he loved you, and it sounds like he did, he wouldn't want this to be all that's left of you. He'd want more for you. *You* should want more for yourself."

"I do, thanks to you," I whisper.

"I know what guilt does," Jacob continues, voice rough with the weight of his own scars. "I carry it every damn day for Sheila. But you showed me it doesn't have to own me. And I'm not letting it own you."

His grip tightens around my hands, not letting me float away.

"If you need to go back," he says, quiet but certain, "if you need to finish this, I'll be there. We'll face it together. Because like it or not, you're mine. All of you. Even the parts you think are broken. I'll fight until you find peace. Just say the word, and we leave tonight."

A sob rips from my chest, jagged, but lighter, like the dam inside me is finally cracking. I suck in a breath, my whole body trembling as the war inside me hits its peak.

Can I let go?

Can I put down the hate that's been my fuel for so long?

Mark deserved justice. Every woman da Vinci hurt deserved justice. I wanted their names to mean something, to matter beyond the way they died. But justice isn't revenge. One heals. The other destroys. And if I keep chasing blood, I'll lose myself for good.

I close my eyes and breathe deep.

And when I open them, Jacob is still there. Still holding on. Still waiting—not pushing, just ready.

His thumbs brush away my tears as he whispers, "I go where you go."

His words unravel something deep inside me, tugging loose the knots I've tied tight around my heart for far too long. I grip his wrists, pulling him closer, and kiss him like it's the first breath after drowning.

I'm done giving da Vinci power over me. He's taken enough.

I am not just rage. Not just grief. There's still something in this world worth holding onto. Worth fighting for. Worth *living* for.

Mark. All the women we lost. I'll carry them with me, not as wounds, but as memory. As strength.

Jacob's forehead presses against mine. His hand stays at the back of my neck, centering me in the quiet. "Where do you want to go, Lyla?"

I speak it aloud, letting the truth rise from the ashes inside me. "Home."

Jacob blinks, and then a smile breaks over his face—real and unguarded, bright enough to push back the shadows. He leans in again, and this kiss is deeper, a promise sealed between us with no need for words.

The air in the church feels different now. Lighter. Like something long buried has finally been released.

He pulls back slowly, his hands still cradling my face, grounding me. The golden flecks in his eyes catch the light, warm and steady as he murmurs, "Then let's go home."

But before he can rise, I catch his wrist, my fingers wrapping around it, stopping him.

He looks down, confused, until he sees the grin tugging at my lips.

"There's something I need to do first," I say, my voice low and teasing, the smile turning wicked.

THIRTY-TWO
CHAOS FULLY IN SESSION

LYLA

JACOB'S BROW LIFTS. "What's that?"

I don't answer.

I slip out the side door and head for Lucy. Pop the back, pull out the boombox Joanie and I found scavenging a half-collapsed neighborhood, buried under a pile of junk in someone's garage, miraculously intact—and still loaded with working batteries.

Joanie lifted it over her head like Lloyd Dobler in *Say Anything*, beaming. "Pretty please, with a shitload of sugar on top, can we take this and jam out at night?" Her glee was contagious. We named it Gerald.

I cradle Gerald now and head back toward the church.

Jacob's eyes narrow as soon as he sees what I'm holding. "And how exactly are you planning to use that?"

A grin spreads across my face. I pat the top of the boombox. "By attracting every infected in the area and killing them. Violently."

His eyebrows shoot up. "You realize that's incredibly dangerous, right?"

I shrug. "Dangerous, therapeutic—tomato, tomahto."

He groans, dragging a hand down his face, but a smile tugs at his lips. "You've got a really weird idea of self-care."

I sling Gerald under my arm and head for the front doors, blood humming in my veins like I'm about to exhale for the first time in years. This isn't just about killing. It's about control. Taking something back.

I pause at the threshold. "You in or out?"

He folds his arms, pretending to think, but the answer's already there in the curl of his mouth. "Someone's got to make sure you don't get yourself killed."

"Glad to have you on board, Gorgeous."

The heavy front doors groan open, dragging against stone. The last of September's summer air hits my lungs. I breathe deep, catching the last of the season, thick with heat, but tinged with the whisper of colder nights to come. Fall is close. A faint moan echoes in the distance. Close enough to be a threat, far enough to make this fun.

I stride forward, place the boombox on the top step with reverence, like I'm offering it to the night. Dig into my bag, fingers brushing the scratched CD case Joanie and I swore we'd save for a moment like this.

Slide it in.

Press play.

Crank the volume.

The opening notes of Beethoven's Symphony No. 5 slice through the night—bold, ominous, fate knocking on the door of the damned. Strings swell, brass thunders across the broken streets. A funeral dirge disguised as a masterpiece.

Glorious.

Jacob cocks his head, arms crossed, watching the sound ripple out like an invitation to hell. "Classical music?"

I spin Sweetness between my fingers. "I'm an interesting woman."

The first infected shamble into view, pulled from the dark like moths to a flame. They stagger from alleys, out of buildings, rising from wherever they've been hiding. Hungry. Twitching. Groans rise, echoing off crumbled walls.

Jacob steps up beside me, shotgun resting easy in his hands. But I know the tension in his shoulders, the way his stance tightens. He's ready to move.

And so am I.

"Let's call this our second date," I say. "Fun activity, shared experience. Like bowling. Only bloodier."

He huffs a laugh. "Okay, psycho."

I tap my blade against my palm. "Most kills before the music ends wins?"

His grin turns sharp. "What does the winner get?"

I drag my gaze to his mouth, then back up. "The loser has to beg the winner in bed."

His pupils flare. "You're on," he says, voice dark.

The violins swell. The dead close in.

The first corpse lurches onto the church steps.

We move.

Sweetness sings through the air, cutting through decayed flesh. A body crumples, its eyeball dangling before hitting stone with a wet plop. Black, tar-thick blood sprays across my arms.

The next groans—joints snapping. I drive my blade up through its chin. Bone crunches. It drops.

Every kill wears his face. That smug, hollow-eyed stare. That crooked leer. I bury my knife in another skull, rip it free, kick the body into the next one.

They come faster. Gaping mouths. Snapping teeth. Skin like melted wax. One in workout gear reaches for me with fingers stripped to the bone. I grab its wrist, twist, slam my blade into its throat. Blood gurgles. It collapses midscream.

The rage pours through me—hot, endless, volcanic.

Jacob moves beside me—fluid, brutal. Shotgun blasts tear holes through undead flesh. When the shells run dry, he draws his machete, moonlight flashing on silver as he steps back into the fight.

The symphony climbs—violins frantic, drums pounding.

More pour in.

They sprint now, jaws snapping. One's missing its lower jaw, tongue flapping. I slash its throat, shove into the next, drive my blade through its eye socket.

Breathe. Strike. Move. Kill.

The dance continues—violent, precise, relentless. My blade sings with the orchestra's screech.

Jacob and I move back-to-back, seamless. His machete arcs wide as mine drives deep. We twist together, pivot, slice. Blood sprays. Bones crack. Flesh tears.

The music builds toward its crescendo. My pulse races to match. Every kill bleeds the rage from me. My muscles burn, but I don't stop.

The final note hits.

I drive my knife through the last skull. Twist. Rip free.

The hate, the vengeance, the grief—gone, leaving exhaustion in its place. My chest heaves, lungs wide and clear.

I press stop on the boombox.

Silence. Just our breathing—rough, human.

The world around us is painted in blood and ruin. And I feel better.

Jacob bolts for the church doors, grabs my hand, yanks me with him. We reach them just as fists slam into the other side. He throws them shut—BOOM—and we drag a pew across, bracing it with shaking arms.

We stand there, sweat-slicked, blood-soaked, hearts hammering.

Then he moves.

Three strides, and Jacob's on me—hands in my hair, lips crushing mine. Raw, desperate, and I match him. I fist his shirt, yanking him closer like I can fuse us into one body. His fingers dig into my scalp, his breath ragged.

He pulls back just enough to rasp, "Feel better?"

"Hell yeah."

He kisses me again, quick, bruising, then slides his machete home. "Good. You've got zombie goo on you."

I glance down. Dark blood splattered across my arms and stomach. "So do you."

"Guess that makes us a matching set."

"How romantic," I mutter. I scoop up Gerald, sling my bag over my shoulder. "So, how many did you get?"

Jacob wipes my blade and sheathes it on my thigh without a word.

"Dodging the question?"

He steps in, body heat brushing mine, smirk dangerous. "Maybe I lost count."

"How convenient."

"I guess that means I lose." His eyes glint. "How would you like me to beg?"

My mouth curves. "Oh, I have ideas."

A thunderous bang shakes the doors. The barricade groans. Moans rise—shrill, starving.

Jacob's grin vanishes. "We overstayed our welcome."

"Time to go."

We move through the sanctuary's hollow bones.

At the back exit, my fingers brush the frame. I pause. I glance toward the altar. The pounding is faint now, but still there—like a heartbeat.

"Goodbye, Mark," I whisper.

When I turn, Jacob's waiting.

I reach for him.

He meets me without hesitation, fingers sliding into mine.

Without a word, we slip into the night, leaving the blood and ghosts behind.

THIRTY-THREE
WAIT.

LYLA

I EASE Lucy into park as Jacob hops out of Leon's truck. That's when I see her near the tree line, worn Converse planted in the dirt.

She takes a few hesitant steps forward, shoulders hunched, arms wrapped tight around herself like a shield. The spark in her eyes is gone. What's left is hesitation, uncertainty, like she doesn't know if she's allowed to trust me anymore.

My chest tightens. I have a lot of work to do.

Her gaze flicks between me and Jacob as he rounds the hood.

Jacob's fingers give mine one last squeeze before letting go.

"Looks like someone wants to talk to you," he murmurs, voice low.

I nod, throat tight.

He kisses my temple and whispers, "I'll give you two some space."

He turns and disappears into the rhythm of camp, leaving me with a knot in my stomach and silence pressing in.

Joanie stops a few feet away. Her boots scuff the ground, hands stuffed in her jacket pockets.

"Hey," she says, chin up in that defiant teenager tilt.

I nod toward Lucy. "Want to talk?"

Another nod.

We walk side by side toward the car. The door creaks as I open it, hinges groaning. Inside, worn leather, old oil, and faint traces of campfire cling to everything. It wraps around us, oddly soothing, like Lucy knows we need the extra love for this.

Joanie slides into the passenger seat, stiff and uncertain. She picks at a loose thread on her sleeve, fingers twitching. Her foot bounces. Her mouth presses into a thin line.

The silence stretches—thick, loaded with everything unsaid.

This is Jo, my Jo. The same girl who followed a stranger when she was lost. The one who held my hand when I bared my soul at the edge of a prison compound.

Joanie's head snaps up. Her eyes are glassy, rimmed red, tears clinging to her lashes.

"I'm so mad at you, Lyla. You shouldn't have kept it from me," she says, voice low but firm. "But I get why you did."

I watch her, silent. Letting her get it all off her chest.

She exhales like she's been holding it this whole time, her whole body sagging. "You remember the first time we met?"

I watch her profile as her gaze locks on to the woods beyond the windshield.

"My dad lied to me that day." Her voice wavers. "He went to scavenge food at a neighbor's house. When he got back, he hid his bite."

She turns toward me, and the tears are already streaming, dripping off her chin, soaking into her shirt.

"We always checked each other after scavenging. But that time, he was off. Shifty. I asked if he was okay and he said he was fine. Told me to leave him alone." She lets out a bitter, hollow laugh. "You know what happened after that."

My mind flashes back to the moment I first saw her in that house. I'd crouched low in front of her, our faces close—sharing the same breath. Her hands hung limp around the revolver, knuckles torn and smeared with her parents' blood. I curled my fingers around the cold metal and tugged. She didn't fight me.

She trusted me even then.

She wipes her cheeks hard, furious with the tears. "I don't like being lied to. Especially not by someone I trust."

"I get that," I say. "And I'm sorry for not being honest with you." Fresh tears prick my eyes. "You have to understand how hard it is for me to let him go. It was wrong, even if I thought it was for the right reasons, but I'm sorry I forced this burden on you. You mean so much to me."

"I'm sorry I freaked out and basically threw you under the bus with the group." Her lips twitch. "Even though you deserved it."

I chuckle. "Fair."

"I don't want to lose you." Her voice breaks. "You're all I have left."

The words hit like a gut punch. Something cracks open in me.

I lean in. "Jo, you're not going to lose me. I'm sorry I hurt the trust you have in me, but there won't be any more secrets. We don't protect each other by hiding things."

Her chin trembles, but she nods. "You promise?"

"I promise." I squeeze her hand—tight, sure. "You're stuck with me, kid, for good."

Her breath catches, then a shaky laugh slips out. "Really?"

"Really." I squeeze her hand again. "You're mine, Jo. My family. End of story."

Her smile blooms. "Dynamic duo against the apocalypse," she murmurs.

"Exactly." I chuckle. "Hopeless, but unstoppable."

She leans back, steadier now. "I really do love you. You're like the big sister I never had."

Warmth unfurls in my chest. I nudge her shoulder. "Love you too, Jo-Jo."

She glares. "I fuckin' hate being called Jo-Jo."

The laughter bursts out of me—loud, raw. Joanie lasts two seconds before cracking, and then we're both doubled over, snorting and giggling. The tension snaps, gone in an instant.

By the time I wipe my face, my cheeks are damp. "Feeling better?"

"Much," she says, grinning. "You?"

I lean back, head against the seat. "Getting there."

Joanie's gaze drifts out the window. "Looks like Jacob's having a serious talk too."

I follow her line of sight. Jacob stands near the edge of camp with Jessica. Her lantern flickers low, casting long shadows. The knot in my gut tightens.

"Yeah," I murmur. "Guess they needed to talk too."

Hopefully he's shutting that down. I meant to tell him how Jessica's been avoiding me. Watching. Listening. Always . . . off.

Joanie tilts her head, whispering, "She creeps me out. With her dead eyes? She ticks some of those boxes you taught me. The killer signs."

A startled laugh escapes me, but it fades fast. The comment lands too true.

The hairs on my neck rise. The feeling I've been ignoring roars back. Tight. Crawling.

"Say that again."

Joanie blinks. "I said she displays those killer signs."

My breath stalls.

Flashes fire through my head.

"She was a surprise."

"They thought it might be the work of a known serial killer by how she was displayed."

"They kept the details out of the papers."

One line crashes into the next, speeding too fast to keep up. But something's wrong. Something's not lining up.

I shove Lucy's door open.

Joanie startles. "Everything okay?"

"Not sure." I scan the camp. "I'll catch up with you later."

She sighs. "Just don't get into too much trouble."

"No promises."

My eyes land on Trish, perched in the med van's open hatch, legs swinging, nose buried in a vampire romance.

"Trish," I call, urgency bleeding through.

She looks up, surprised, marking her place with a spare bandage. "Lyla? Shit, you're back!" Her expression shifts to concern. "What's wrong?"

"I need to ask you something about Sheila's death."

She straightens. "What about it?"

"Were there any details in the papers? Anything about the crime scene?"

She frowns, shaking her head. "No. The cops kept it locked down. Just the basics made it out."

"You're sure?"

"Pretty sure. They said she was found in an alley downtown. No suspects. No real info."

"What details did get released?"

"Her name, time of death, that she was a teacher and engaged to Jacob. That's it. Jacob never talks about the details, just that she was found behind the grocery store. Murdered. The world was already falling apart so the news moved on fast."

"Did Jessica ever talk about it? Any details?"

Trish stills. "No. Why are you asking about Jessica?"

Chills wash through me.

"It was hard for him to see her displayed like that."

Jessica's words hit like a sledgehammer. I'd brushed them off. Now?

I glance toward the tree line where she and Jacob disappeared, dread curling in my gut. I have some questions for Miss Jessica, and I'll do whatever it takes to get the truth.

Trish grabs my arm. "Lyla, you're freaking me out. What are you saying?"

"Jessica knows things she shouldn't."

Realization flashes in her eyes. "Wait—"

Leon strides up, calm but alert, eyes scanning our faces. His gaze locks on mine. His jaw tightens instantly.

I grab his arm. "I think I know who killed Sheila."

He freezes, then pulls a small notebook from his pocket. One practiced flick, one word scribbled.

Explain.

"I will on the way. I don't have much, but I think you'll agree Jessica is hiding something."

The night hums with crickets and camp murmurs, but no sign of that lantern's glow.

I turn, heart thundering.

"We need to find Jacob. Now."

THIRTY-FOUR
COLD AS ICE

JACOB

THE FOREST CLOSES IN, thick with shadows and silence. Behind me, the campfire's glow is barely visible, a smear of warmth in the distance. Out here, with only Jessica's lantern and the hot breath of night, I feel exposed. Vulnerable.

Jessica walks ahead, shoulders tight, leading us into a narrow clearing where the air runs cooler. My fingers twitch, instincts humming.

"All right," I say, folding my arms. "We're far enough. What did you want to talk about?"

"Why did you bring *her* back, Jacob?" she asks, voice low. "You said it yourself, she put us all at risk. She's not worth having around."

She dims the lantern, letting the darkness creep in. My jaw tightens.

"I was angry," I admit. "But I didn't stop to think about *why* she did it. She made a mistake, but she's trying to make it right. That deserves a second chance."

She steps closer, her silhouette now just a shadow.

"I don't think she deserves one," she presses. "She should leave. Now. I don't trust her—and neither should you."

The words hang there—heavy, final. My gut twists.

I shift, inching back, putting space between us. "As my friend, I need you with me on this."

The concern in her eyes vanishes. What's left is something harder. Sharper. Icy enough to freeze blood.

"A friend?" She repeats, like the word's foreign. Then she blinks, resets, tone shifting to hope. "I thought we were ready to take things to the next level."

Shit.

I guess we're going to have this discussion now. I keep my face neutral, voice even. "Jessica, you've been there for me, especially after Sheila. I'll always be grateful for that. I know losing your best friend was devastating."

I pause.

"But we've only ever been friends."

She laughs, sharp and broken, like glass under a boot. "Friendship," she spits. "That's what you call it?"

She steps toward me.

"I've given you time. I've waited. I've been everything you needed after Sheila, and you still can't see what's right in front of you?"

What the fuck? "Jessica, this isn't—"

"No!" she snaps, cutting me off. "You don't get to dismiss me. I stood by your side while you mourned Sheila. I went back into that prison to save your mom, and for what? So you could shack up with another woman who ended up lying to you?"

Who the hell is this woman?

"And now," she sneers, "you bring her back? That little smart-mouthed bitch doesn't deserve your attention. I do!"

Fury slices through me. The venom in her voice when she talks about Lyla makes my blood run ice cold.

I straighten, letting rage settle deep, sharp.

"Watch it, Jessica."

She freezes.

"You say one more thing about her," I say, tone razor sharp, "and I'll introduce you to the side of me I've worked hard to keep locked away. And it's itching to come out."

"You don't get it," she breathes, wild now. "You have no idea what I'd do for you."

Her gaze drifts over my face. Hungry. My skin crawls.

"You don't have to keep punishing yourself," she murmurs, soft as poisoned sugar. "I could make it better. You deserve to be happy, Jacob, with someone who has only been faithful to you. Don't you think Sheila would want that?"

Her hand lifts toward my chest.

"Don't you think it's time to let me in?"

I step back.

"Jessica," I say, voice final. "I've found someone. It's not you. It was never you. I've never done anything to make you believe this, us, was going to happen. I'm sorry you felt differently, but you need to accept the truth. I've only ever seen you as a friend."

The truth hits like a hammer. Jessica pales. Her head shakes slowly, eyes wide, rejecting it.

"Lyla sees my scars," I add. "Yeah she fucked up, but she's heard and seen the worst parts of me. She didn't run. She understands. She let me see her pain too. She's the one I want. She's the one I choose."

Jessica's expression fractures, rage warring with disbelief. Something breaks. Her hands ball into fists. Her shoulders coil tight. "After everything I've done for you," she hisses, "everything I've given you, and you're just going to throw me away? For her?"

"This isn't about Lyla. It's about you. About your refusal to accept reality."

Jessica's breath turns jagged. Her hands tremble, nails digging into her palms.

The air thickens, the forest holding its breath.

"I'm sorry that's how you feel," she says, voice wobbling but threaded with steel. "But I'm not something you can just throw away."

Her hand moves toward her back, disappearing under her shirt. The tears on her face shine like a mask, but her eyes have shifted.

It's not heartbreak anymore. It's intent.

My pulse spikes. Muscles tense. The world narrows.

My gaze locks on her hand.

The lantern's glow casts her in haunting light, shadow stretching behind her like a specter. She looks like death.

I reach over my shoulder, fingers closing on my machete. "Jessica, what are you—"

A voice cuts through the dark, calm and deadly. "How did you know she was displayed, Jessica?"

Jessica's head snaps toward the sound, gold hoops flashing. Her breath hitches. She locks up. Her hand freezes under her shirt.

Lyla, Leon, and Trish step from the darkness like wraiths. Weapons drawn, eyes sharp, focus locked on Jessica. The clearing shifts. The air turns against her.

Lyla's pistol is aimed between Jessica's eyes.

Jessica's breath stutters. "E-excuse me?"

A dark smile curls Lyla's lips as her finger flicks off the safety. "You heard me, sweetie. Answer the damn question."

What the hell is going on?

THIRTY-FIVE
PSYCHO KILLER

JACOB

I GLANCE AT LYLA, eyes frosty, unwavering, and something clicks into place. Just seeing her there, fierce and unshaken, grounds me. My pulse slows enough to breathe.

"What are you saying?" My voice is lower now, tighter.

Lyla doesn't look away from Jessica, but there's a flash—guilt, frustration, like she wishes she'd figured this out sooner.

"Jessica knows something she shouldn't about Sheila's death." Lyla finally looks at me. "It clicked when I saw her lead you into the woods. She said something to me after the bonfire, right after Pete got kicked out."

"What did she say?"

Lyla scoffs, humorless. "The usual stalker anthem. 'Stay away from him. You'll never understand him like I do.' But then she said something about Sheila. Something that didn't sit right."

She watches it land.

"She said it must've been hard for you to see Sheila displayed like that."

My blood drags, heavy, while a low buzz hums at the edges of my skull.

"There were no details in the paper," Lyla continues, voice almost a growl. "Nobody outside of law enforcement knew how Sheila was found. Not even most of the task force. You said yourself, you didn't talk about it."

Bile rises in my throat. My grip tightens on the machete. I try to tell myself it's a coincidence. That it doesn't mean what it sounds like.

Lyla turns back to Jessica, voice going soft. "So, what do you have to say, Jess?" She draws out the S like a hiss.

Jessica scoffs. "I don't have to answer to you, bitch."

Lyla laughs, the sound echoing through the clearing like she owns the night. And somehow, in this twisted moment, I fall hard for her.

She tilts her head, voice dripping mock sweetness. "You kind of do, sugarplum, seeing as I have a gun pointed at your head."

Jessica's chest rises too fast. Her gaze burns, but beneath the rage she's unraveling.

A low growl builds in my throat. My voice comes out calm, deadly. "How. Did. You. Know."

Silence swallows the clearing.

Jessica freezes. Her hands clench. Her eyes dart—Lyla, Leon, Trish, back to me. No exits.

"It was in the news," she blurts, too fast, too flat.

"Liar."

She flinches.

I step closer, until there's barely space between us.

"They never released details about Sheila's death. Not how she was found. Not what he did to her. That was for investigators. For me."

Her lips part. Nothing comes out.

"I didn't tell anyone. Not one damn soul." My voice drops to a whisper that tastes like blood. "So tell me, how the hell did you know she was displayed?"

She stares, shivering, breath shaking. Begging for something—redemption, rescue, a way out.

I give her none.

Lyla steps beside me, voice sharp as a gunshot. "You know how, Jacob."

Her words detonate inside me.

My chest caves. The world tilts. My stomach lurches like I've been punched.

I don't want to believe it, but the truth is already screaming in my bones.

The woman I trusted, the one who stayed, who held my hand, who said she understood—she's the one who took Sheila from me.

"How could you?" My voice scrapes from a hollow place. "How could you?"

Jessica says nothing. No denial. No defense. Just silence.

Trish stumbles back like she's been hit, hand over her mouth. "I think I'm gonna be sick."

Leon steps forward, grip white-knuckle tight around his hatchet. His jaw is locked so hard I hear the grind. The blade catches lantern light and gleams—cold, ready.

Jessica's face twists with desperation. Her voice bursts out, unhinged. "Jacob was supposed to fall in love with me!"

The words land like a blow. She says it like it was inevitable.

"From the moment you stepped into that school," she pants, "I knew we were meant to be."

She laughs—jagged, bitter, unhinged.

"But no," she spits. "You had eyes for Sheila."

My stomach turns.

"Sheila," she mocks, venom shaking her voice. "The golden girl. Perfect job. Perfect reputation. Worshipped. And me? Nothing."

Her eyes are wild, unfocused.

"We grew up together. Same classes. Same town. She had better parents, better things, a better life. And still, she took everything. Even you."

The air feels toxic.

Trish steps forward, voice sharp. "Sheila always stood up for you. She defended you when others dragged your name through the dirt. She believed in you. That's why I gave you a chance."

Jessica snarls. "She really did right by me. So selfless, wasn't she? So perfect."

Trish's fists clench. "Having a shitty life doesn't give you the right to be an asshole—and it sure as hell doesn't give you permission to murder."

Jessica flinches but doesn't argue.

"She didn't deserve to die because you felt entitled," Trish spits. "How dare you try to justify what you did to her?"

Jessica shrinks, gaze dropping.

"Why kill her like that?" My voice cuts cold. "Why mutilate her?"

She doesn't answer.

Lyla steps in. "My guess? Jessica spent months reading up on a certain prolific serial killer. Memorized every article. Studied his patterns. And when the opportunity came, she copied his work."

She takes a step forward. Jessica doesn't move.

"Da Vinci's murders were everywhere. The media turned him into a sick celebrity. Some people got obsessed. Some wanted to be him."

Lyla's gaze sharpens. "Stage Sheila's death to match his. Let the cops do the rest. Then the world ends, everything's buried. No justice. No follow-up."

She looks at me. "If I'd had time to dig into the case, I'd have seen through the bullshit."

It was all there. The signs. The obsession. The lies. And I never saw it.

All this time her killer was beside me. Laughing. Waiting.

I look at Jessica—really look. How did I not see her for what she was?

"So," Lyla says, casual as dinner plans, "what should we do with her?"

Leon watches Jessica, hatchet in hand. Eyes penetrating.

"What do you say?" I ask him, voice flat.

He signs without hesitation.

I translate. "Leave her to fend for herself."

Trish folds her arms. "I say we put a bullet in her skull. Quick. Clean."

"I second that," Lyla says.

Leon signs again, sharper.

"He says we didn't let him finish," I translate.

Leon's eyes don't leave Jessica.

"He says we should let her fend for herself," I pause, grin sharp, "in the middle of a horde of flesh-eaters."

Lyla whistles. "Brutal. I like it."

Jessica's bravado cracks. "Jacob, *please*. Don't let them do this. I messed up. But you know me."

No. I thought I did.

Lyla steps close, her hand cupping my cheek. Warmth in the storm. "It's up to you. I'm sorry I didn't figure it out sooner."

I kiss her forehead, take the gun from her hand. "Don't be sorry. I should've seen her for what she was."

"Okay," Trish snaps. "You two can be sorry after we handle the psychopath." She flips off her safety. "Let's agree we all missed it and move on."

Leon signs. "*Works for me.*"

I turn to Jessica. She's small now. Frail. All that's left is the panic of someone who knows the end is near.

"I say we go with Trish's idea." I raise the gun. "I don't have the patience to find a horde. Not tonight."

Trish grins. "Hell yes."

My finger curls on the trigger. This is personal. Justice. Revenge. Closure. It's hard to tell the difference anymore.

Jessica's eyes widen, childlike. "Jacob, please—"

I aim at her head. All she finds are eyes that see her for what she is. Murderer. Monster.

My finger finds the trigger—

The world explodes.

A roar tears through the night.

Music crashes through the trees, loud, distorted. Headlights slice the dark, swerving through the forest. Behind them—

A swarm.

The dead pour from the shadows. Endless. Groaning with hunger.

Everything slows. The engine. The music. The sound of hell coming to our doorstep.

Lyla's breath hitches.

Trish curses.

Leon readies his bow.

My grip tightens on the gun.

The music gets louder. Closer to camp.

And then—*impact.*

THIRTY-SIX
OF ALL THE GIN JOINTS

LYLA

FLAMES tear into the sky through gaps in the trees, orange and alive. Groans rise—low, guttural, broken by sudden shrieks. Dozens of undead flail, stumbling over roots and splintered logs but never stopping. They charge toward the noise, jaws snapping at the air.

Gunfire cracks in sharp bursts. Screams follow.

"Shit!"

Jacob's voice rips me around—Jessica's gone. Vanished into the woods like smoke. No sign of her.

Lucky bitch.

"Let's go!" Trish bolts, Leon and Jacob close behind.

I'm right after her, limbs pumping to my erratic heartbeat. Branches whip my arms. Bark scrapes my knuckles. Every step slams into the earth. My lungs tear, but I don't stop.

We break through the trees—

Camp is hell.

The red truck explodes, metal shrieking as fire blasts through the hood. The ground bucks. Heat punches my face. Smoke curls thick and choking. I gag on the sharp bite of burning gas, rubber, and worse, flesh. The air tastes like death.

Screams carry across the wind. Storm clouds slide over the moon, rumbling low.

Joanie's at the truck, blood streaking her arms as she claws at twisted metal. Her hands are raw, but she keeps ripping, trying to wrench the doors open. Inside, Edith and Earl slump still. Shadows behind cracked glass.

The swarm closes in. Some are impaled on the wall of stakes, others tangled in the stringed cans, pulling so hard the cords cut through their flesh. A few drag themselves forward, ankles left behind in the bear traps.

Holy mother of fudge, cracker, nickels, Batman!

Clair and Barbara hold the line near the vehicles, rifles barking fire. Each shot punches through rotting flesh, forcing space in the crush of bodies. Muzzle flashes light snarling faces, gaping mouths, clawed fingers. The horde doesn't slow, gazes fogged with desperation and hunger.

"Stay in the van, Poppy!" Clair's voice cuts through the chaos. The girl's pale face presses to the glass, eyes wide.

Music still blares from the smashed car—a distorted rock–hip hop mix warped into something cruel. It needles through the gunfire and screams, a sick soundtrack to the end.

Three figures step through the smoke ahead. Not stumbling. Not lost.

The lead limps, blood streaking his chest, searching until his gaze finds mine. Black pupils dig into me like claws.

The fire roars. The undead shriek. But all I hear is the silence between us.

"Trish, help Joanie! Leon, cover us!" Jacob's voice yanks me back.

Trish is already beside Joanie, both straining at the door. Joanie's arms shake, fingers bleeding, profanity spilling out like it'll give her strength.

Jacob tosses my gun to Leon. "Shut off that damn music!" He

swings his machete into the head of a nearby infected. Leon melts into the shifting dead, gun popping with every step.

Fire glints across Franklin's face—fresh cuts, someone else's blood smeared on his skin. His knife hangs loose in his hand, dripping red. He raises it in a mocking salute.

"You didn't think you could hide from me, did you, Lyla?" His voice is smooth and cruel. His smirk's all show, but his eyes are empty. "Thanks for the music idea."

Lars and Pete emerge from the smoke. Lars smiles wide, swollen tongue flicking out like a snake. Pete hangs back, eyes darting to the flames, the swarm, then me.

Jacob steps in front of me, sure and quiet. His stance is loose, but the tightness in his shoulders, the flex in his arms—he's ready.

I lift my chin, eyes locked on the bane of my existence. "Jacob, meet da Vinci, real name Franklin, and Lars, the face licker. Old acquaintances."

Jacob's jaw tics. His eyes cut to Lars. "He licked you?"

"Yup." I pop the *p*, sweet and sharp. Rage coils inside me, ready to strike. I want him dead.

Jacob doesn't speak. He goes still. The dangerous kind. Quiet. Focused. Like a bomb seconds from going off.

I *love* it.

Pete twitches. Nervous.

Jacob turns to him. "I'll take Pete and tongue boy. You handle that piece of shit."

The music cuts. Leon's knife severs the last cord, and the speakers die with a sharp pop.

No more distortion. Just undead moans, low and wet, sliding under my skin. The crackle of burning metal. The ragged breaths of the living.

"Leon! Keep the infected off Lyla!" Jacob calls.

Leon nods, gun firing—punching through skulls.

Jacob turns to Pete and Lars. "All right, boys. Shall we?"

He jerks his chin toward the clearing, drawing them away like it's a dinner invite.

"Will do." I don't look away, even as he vanishes into smoke and flame. Two on one isn't fair, but Jacob doesn't play fair.

The undead are distracted by the fires and screams ahead. They haven't noticed us. Yet.

My focus locks on the bastard in front of me.

"You're all going to die," Franklin says, smug.

"You know I'm actually happy to see you?" I mean it. I hate what he's done, how he came for my people, how he ripped open the peace I had. I wish I'd stopped sooner. The clues, the marks, the notes—I left too many.

I glance at Pete's retreating back. Yep. Should've killed him too.

But right now? Just me and Franklin, blades in hand?

That's a gift.

I could've lived the rest of this broken life with Jacob, Joanie, and the others. We would've scraped together something real. But the opportunity to finish what should've ended long ago?

That's not fate handing me a chance. That's fate handing me a *knife*.

I smile slowly, draw Sweetness from my thigh, spin her once in the firelight, catch her by the handle.

Let's kill this bastard, girl.

His grin falters—a flicker of doubt.

I advance.

"Welcome to the end of the game, Franklin."

His eyes flare red—the monster beneath the man.

I raise the blade.

"You're not the nightmare anymore. *I am.*"

THIRTY-SEVEN
BATTER UP!

JACOB

THE DEAD SURGE from all sides.

Moans tangle with the crackle of fire, the screams of the dying, the shouts of the fighting. I don't hear any of it.

I see them.

Lars—grinning like a devil in a blood-soaked carnival. Knife loose in his hand, like this is just another round in a game he's sure he'll win.

Pete beside him, white-knuckled on a bat, nerves leaking from every stiff movement.

I crack my neck and knuckles, rolling my shoulders loose. The machete's grip fits my palm like it grew there.

No nerves. No hesitation.

The second they stepped from the smoke, everything inside me slid into place. The part I've buried broke free. Not rage. Not fear. Clarity.

There's no mercy here.

I step forward, locking eyes with Lars. "Come on, then."

They charge.

Lars swings wild, blade slicing for my throat. I drop low. Steel whistles past my ear.

Pete comes from the side, bat arcing for my ribs. I pivot, take the blow on my arm. Pain flashes white-hot.

My fist smashes into Lars's jaw. His head jerks, teeth red.

I spin, boot slamming into Pete's knee. He buckles with a scream. My elbow caves his nose with a wet crunch. Blood sprays. He drops.

The dead close in at the sound of our fight. Groaning. Clawing. One lunges—jaw unhinged, eyes rotted. I seize the back of its tattered shirt. The name stitched into the bloodstained tag: *Chad*.

The machete comes down. The head severs clean, thudding to the ground.

Peace.

Rotting fingers claw through smoke and flame. My blade drops, splitting the skull of a woman in a scorched sweatshirt reading *#blessed*. I pivot, slice the neck of a cheerleader—one pom-pom tangled in her sneaker, the other clenched in her fist.

Pete and Lars fight off their own infected. I glance toward Lyla.

Her blade flashes, silver arcs in the dark. She's locked in with da Vinci, moving like death—every strike deliberate.

Leon's behind her, arrows flying with sniper precision. Running low.

"Hold on!"

Joanie's scream cuts through the chaos.

My machete arcs down, severing the leg of a teenager in a soot-streaked shirt. I look back long enough to see Joanie and Trish dragging Edith and Earl from the wreckage. Earl's limping but breathing.

Edith, burns down her arm and leg, still shoves Earl toward safety.

"Go help Jacob!" she yells.

Trish hauls her into the van, slamming the door as an infected smashes into it. Bone cracks. Black blood paints the side.

Another corpse latches on to my arm, gold teeth snapping. I rip its hand free, kick it down, and drive the machete through its skull. Bone crunches.

Earl's beside me a second later, pipe smashing into the head of a backward-capped corpse with *Eat Me* across the brim.

We fall in back-to-back, swinging fast. Skulls cave. Bones shatter.

Pete's bat slams into my machete, the jolt rattling my arms.

"Can you hold off the other guy while I deal with Pete?" I mutter, twisting from the next blow.

"Sure, I'll just take care of the infected too. Anything else, Your Highness?" Earl grins through the blood.

He brings the pipe down like thunder. Another cheerleader crumples. Then he kicks Lars in the chest, knocking him back a few feet.

Pete keeps swinging wildly—desperate to land just one hit.

The air chokes with smoke, blood, and death. Gunfire cracks. Flesh tears. Bones snap.

I'm right at home.

Pete's slowing—stance sloppy, chest heaving, hands trembling.

I smirk, blood running down my face. "Hey, bud."

His eyes dart across the battlefield, frantic. His next swing goes wide. "They made me—"

Wrong move.

I feint left. He jerks.

I lunge.

The machete drops midmotion. I don't need it. My hand snaps his wrist, twisting.

CRACK.

The bat clatters to the dirt. His arm hangs wrong.

He opens his mouth to scream—my fist shuts it. A brutal cross to the jaw sends him spinning to the ground.

Boot meets ankle—*SNAP.* His scream tears the night.

Behind me, Earl grunts, pipe and bat swinging in relentless

rhythm. He circles Lars, keeping his distance, baiting him while the infected start to close in.

"Make it quick, son," he growls.

"Almost done."

I stomp his other ankle—*CRUNCH*. He howls, writhing in the dirt.

Cold peace settles in my chest.

I grip the machete from the blood-soaked grass. Pete's crawling, dragging twisted ankles through leaves. I grab one and yank him back.

He yells, clawing at the ground, nails digging furrows.

I flip him over. Blood and dirt cover his face. His eyes are wide, pleading.

"Jacob, please—"

I shake my head. "I told you, if I ever saw you again, I'd kill you."

I drive the machete into his chest with a wet squelch, right under the ribs. He chokes on the scream. I clamp a hand over his mouth.

"This is me making good on that promise."

I twist. Blood pours hot and thick. His hands clutch his belly, trying to hold in what's spilling out, but I keep twisting until entrails burst free, sliding down his sides into the dirt.

I don't blink. I hold his gaze until everything in him dies.

Then I rip the blade free.

Hot blood coats my arm.

With one shove, I kick his body into the hungry hands behind me.

They descend—tearing, cracking, feasting.

Bye-bye, Petey.

THIRTY-EIGHT
TROUBLE IS IN TROUBLE

LYLA

HEAT LASHES MY SKIN, sweat running into the burning cuts striping my arms. Each movement pulls at them, skin splitting, fire under my flesh. Smoke clogs the air, acrid and heavy, coating my tongue with ash. Breathing's a luxury I don't have time for.

My focus is a blade—razor sharp.

The last ghost of my past still walking.

Franklin's face twists with rage, his mouth curled in a snarl that pulls tight over his teeth. It's almost funny—if I didn't know exactly how many people those teeth have smiled at before he gutted them. If I hadn't been one breath away from being one of them.

His blade flashes in the firelight—quick, deliberate, a predator's promise.

Blood runs hot and sticky down my arms, each slice a screaming reminder of the price I'm paying for this. My chest saws for air.

Something whistles past my head—

THUNK.

An undead old woman in a cat sweater drops behind me, Leon's arrow buried deep in her eye socket. She folds in on herself, jaw snapping once before going slack. One step closer and she'd have had my throat.

I flip Sweetness in my hand, feeling the weight settle into my grip. Dangerous. Ready.

"What's the matter, Frankie?" My tone drips mockery. "Feeling a little off your game?"

His eyes spark with fury, teeth bared. "I'm going to shut that mouth of yours for good," he spits. Hate radiates off him like heat. "You'll be the final piece in my collection."

Try it, asshole.

He lunges.

I meet him head-on.

Steel smashes steel, the ring of our blades cutting through the chaos. The vibration stings my palms, jolting up my forearms. We move fast, too fast for fear to keep up.

He slashes high—I duck under the arc, the wind of it grazing my scalp. He twists low, trying to take my legs, but I pivot, the tip of his blade skimming the fabric at my thigh.

A sudden sting at my ribs—warmth spills fast under my shirt.

I grit my teeth, take the pain, and sharpen it into something lethal.

Sweetness flashes upward, catching him across the chest. The blade bites deep, parting fabric and flesh. His hiss is drowned by my boot slamming into his gut. He staggers, heels skidding on the dirt before tumbling backward into three undead cheerleaders. Their chipped sparkly nails claw for his flesh, teeth snapping inches from his face.

I take the opening. Step in. Drive Sweetness into the skull of a woman with smeared black eyeliner, her jaw dropping with a wet crunch before she slides to the ground.

Every muscle screams, but stopping isn't an option.

The world is a blur—blood misting the air, shadows lurching in and out of firelight. Franklin's blade carves brutal arcs, slicing through the arms of anything that gets close.

Leon's still firing until his last arrow punches into the throat of a mullet-wearing corpse. The body collapses in a gurgle of black blood.

Shit.

Leon draws his hatchet as the dead surge toward him.

Franklin bursts from the tangle of cheerleaders, face twisted, chest heaving. He's not looking at the horde—he's looking at me.

He barrels into me like a freight train. Sweetness rakes his right leg as we slam into the dirt, the blade sinking in enough to draw a snarl.

He lands on top, his own knife raised high, eyes wide and shining with mania.

I catch his wrists. Our muscles lock in a vicious stalemate, tendons straining, skin slick with sweat and blood. The knife hovers inches from my throat, vibrating with the force between us.

His breath is hot and sour in my face, his weight crushing the air from my lungs.

My arms shake, every tendon screaming, strength bleeding out fast.

He drives harder, the point edging closer, cool steel brushing the hollow of my throat.

I grit my teeth, lock eyes with him—

And feel my arms start to give.

THIRTY-NINE
MINE

JACOB

LARS ROARS as he rips free from the horde, fury wild and blinding. He lunges, knife flashing, but it's rage, not skill, driving him. He swings wide.

Mistake number one.

I sidestep. Effortless.

He stumbles past, thrown off by his own momentum.

Mistake number two.

My hand snaps out, wrenching the machete from his grip before he can blink. His eyes widen, but too late—my fist slams into his gut, deep and hard.

He folds with a sharp wheeze.

My knee crashes into his face, snapping his head back. His body smashes against a thick tree trunk with a dull, solid thud.

Before he can slide down, I drive the machete straight through his gut, pinning him to the bark.

He screams—raw, primal, torn from somewhere rotten.

He thrashes, claws at the handle, but the blade's buried deep. Blood pours from the wound, thick and relentless, draining him with every drop.

I let him feel it. Every second.

I kneel, pick up his knife, and grab his jaw, forcing him to meet my eyes. His breath rasps, uneven. Rage still burns in his stare, but it's fading.

"Look at me," I growl.

His gaze locks on mine.

"So," I murmur, pressing the knife to his cheek, "you're the one that licked my woman?"

His lips curl in a blood-slick sneer. He spits, the red smear sliding down his chin.

I press harder, steel biting skin.

"I don't like when people touch what's mine."

I tilt his head toward the fight.

Leon boots an undead into da Vinci, knocking him off Lyla. She yanks her blade from his leg, breath sharp, and moves to Leon's side —hacking, slashing.

Da Vinci wrestles under the weight of a massive, bear-like corpse, its death grip locked tight.

Lyla moves through the chaos like she owns it—blade flashing, firelight turning her into something untouchable. Dangerous. Divine.

"And she is mine."

I force his jaw open, fingers gripping his tongue, yanking it past his teeth. He convulses, choking on the sound.

Steel touches the back of his tongue.

Earl holds the line behind me, buying me this moment.

"And since this," I grit, voice like a blade, "touched what's mine . . ."

His pupils blow wide. Panic floods his face. A gurgled plea dies in his throat.

"I get to take it."

My hand saws slow, deliberate, dragging out every shred of agony. His scream is wet and broken, drowned in his own blood.

He spasms like a dying insect.

The severed tongue hits my palm—twitching, slick.

I look at it once, then hurl it into the horde still feeding on Pete's corpse.

"Jesus," Earl mutters.

Lars's shrieks collapse into gurgled whimpers, then just air. Blood runs down his chin to his shirt.

The smell hits the horde like a flare. Vacant eyes turn toward their next meal.

I wipe the blade on my thigh and move toward the only thing here worth running to. The sounds of jaws tearing through flesh and Lars's quiet cries of terror are behind me as Earl hands me back my machete.

"Now," I say, "let's go support my girl."

FORTY
FINAL BOSS

LYLA

FRANKLIN ROARS BEHIND ME, driving his blade into the lumberjack Leon hurled his way.

I bury Sweetness into the soft skull of a soccer mom as Leon grabs my collar and shoves me backward, right toward my nemesis. Like he's annoyed I dared to help.

"Thanks for the encouragement, asshole," I snap.

Leon's hatchet splits the neck of a teen girl in a shredded *I Woke Up Like This* tee. He throws me a sarcastic salute.

My eyes lock with Franklin's—just as Jacob's voice cuts through the chaos. He and Earl push forward, carving a path toward Leon to hold the line.

Relief slams into me.

He's alive.

I exhale.

I love this man.

My gaze flicks toward him just for a second. Whole. Focused. Covered in blood, but alive.

Thank all that is holy.

I turn back to Franklin, blade ready, but call over to Jacob. "So, I'm guessing you were successful?"

Out of the corner of my eye, Jacob cleaves the head off an infected cheerleader with pigtails. Blood arcs like a geyser. He grins at me, "Were you worried about me, Trouble?"

Before I can react, Franklin charges.

"Enough!"

I drop low, feint left. He takes the bait, and I slash across his thigh.

A grunt rips from his throat as he stumbles, blood pouring down his leg. Hatred burns in his eyes.

"You should've stayed dead," I singsong, rolling my shoulders loose.

Jacob's voice cuts through the storm. "You done playing?"

Eyes locked on Franklin, I reply, "Almost."

"Well," Jacob grunts, driving his blade into another skull with a wet crunch, "if you could speed it up, that'd be great."

A laugh slips out. "I always aim to please."

That earns me a huffed chuckle from him.

Franklin straightens, blood dripping, knife glinting in the firelight—feral, gleaming, hungry. Still smiling.

What a demented, sick platypus.

I step forward, matching him.

"What kind of woman would you be without me, Lyla?" he sneers, circling. He buries his knife in the skull of an infected midstep, then turns back to me. "Don't you remember? You had nothing before me. No purpose. I gave you something to live for. Something to be."

My grip on Sweetness tightens, rage curling in my chest.

"I remember *everything*," I growl.

He steps closer, smile twisting into something smug and delusional. "I made you. Without me, you're—"

I strike. Fast. Hard.

He's faster.

Pain rips through my shoulder, his knife cutting deep. Blood spills hot down my arm. I stagger, biting back a scream.

"You're a shell," he hisses, licking my blood from the blade. "Empty without me."

Disgust flares. *That can't be sanitary.*

"Lyla!" Earl's voice snaps, sharp and protective.

Jacob stops him. "She's got it."

No hesitation. No panic. Just belief.

Earl growls but turns back to the fight. Leon moves through the undead—silent, efficient, heading for Clair.

Franklin lunges for my throat.

I dodge—barely. His blade whistles past my skin, but his fist smashes into my jaw, dropping me hard. Pain explodes across my face, vision blurring. His breath rasps as he closes in.

"You and I—we go down together. Always meant to."

I cough blood.

"I'll make it quick," he whispers, fingers sliding through my hair. "I'll follow right after. Then you'll be whole again."

Jacob shouts from the distance, "Quit milking it and finish him!"

I smirk. "Fine."

I always was a good actress.

In a flash, I twist, drive both feet into Franklin's chest, knocking him back and stealing the breath from his lungs.

Fuck. This. Shit.

With a roar, I surge forward—low, fast. His blade slices air as I slam into his chest. We crash to the blood-soaked ground.

He wheezes, scrambling for his knife. I'm already on top of him, straddling his chest, knees crushing his arms into the gore-matted dirt.

He can't move.

His dead eyes stare up at me—still defiant.

Then I see them.

They're with me now. Hovering behind me. Watching. Waiting for me to finish it so they can finally rest.

And through the screams, through the groans of the undead closing in, I hear Mark's voice, steady and calm in my mind.

"Let it all go, Lyla."

I raise my knife, rage and grief bleeding into the moment. Rain starts to fall, lightning cracking overhead.

"Without you," I whisper, voice shaking, but true, "*I am* everything."

Then I drive the blade straight into his heart.

Flesh tears. Bone gives. His body jerks, a last, desperate twitch. His eyes go wide—shock, pain, then nothing.

I twist the blade.

Deep.

Slow.

His chest rises once. Shudders. Then falls still.

A breathless exhale slips from his lips, the last of him leaving as his fingers twitch once, then go limp.

Blood spills thick and dark, pooling beneath his body, soaking into my jeans, my skin. The snarl of the undead, the shouts from the group, the roar of flames devouring our camp—they all fade.

The weight I've carried for years starts to peel away, like chains falling off bone.

Freedom.

I rip the blade free and bring it down again.

Once—for the woman he left tied to a tree.

Again—for the girl he carved in her own home.

A third time—for the brother who cried in my arms.

Again. Again. Each strike a sentence.

He will never hurt anyone again.

I drop back on my heels, dragging in a breath thick with the stench of death. The knot in my shoulders unravels. Exhaustion slams into me.

Rain drips down my face.

"Ammo's almost gone!"

Barbara's voice cuts through the snarls of the undead.

Across the clearing, the fight rages. Joanie works Jacob's shotgun like a machine, Clair beside her, Barbara counting shots.

"Make every shot count!" Jacob's voice booms. He and Earl move fast, blades flashing.

Trish bursts from the van, blood on her scrubs. "Edith's stable for now, but we need to move! Now!"

Jacob calls over his shoulder, "You coming, or you gonna piss on his corpse?"

Tempting.

I look at Franklin's ruined body. Part of me wants to burn it, salt the ground, make sure nothing of him ever rises again. But there's no time.

The herd's thinning. We have a chance.

I push to my feet—

BAM!

I hit the ground hard, breath ripped from my lungs as a body crashes on top of me. Pain bursts in my shoulder as Sweetness skitters out of reach.

My ears ring. Vision swims. Limbs feel like cement.

Hot, foul breath ghosts across my skin.

Well, shitsticks.

FORTY-ONE
LOOSE ENDS

JAGGED ROCKS TEAR at my already shredded skin as I twist, gasping, trying to see who tackled me—

And my stomach plummets.

Pale, lifeless eyes.

A face I once knew, now twisted, slack-jawed, and ravenous.

"You've got to be fucking kidding me," I hiss.

Her once-perfect hair hangs in filthy clumps, matted with blood. Skin waxy gray, gold hoops still swinging in her ears—bright, mocking.

Even in death, she's a pain in the ass.

"Wow, Jessica," I grunt, struggling beneath her, "you look refreshed."

She snarls, jaws snapping inches from my face. Raw, animal hunger.

Her grip is iron. Still fresh—no rot, no sluggish decay.

I shove hard. She barely moves.

"Easy there, sweetheart," I pant, "I don't bite on the first date."

My arms tremble, muscles screaming. Franklin, the church fight, the swarm—it's all caught up to me.

She presses closer.

Rotted, wet breath ghosts my cheek.

Panic cuts sharp.

"Jacob!" My voice cracks.

Too far.

Jessica lunges, jaws open for my throat.

I catch her face, shove her head aside, barely keeping teeth from flesh. She straddles me, pinning me down, fingers clawing at my jacket.

I buck, twist, kick—nothing.

She doesn't move.

Her head snaps up. Dead eyes lock on mine. Lips twitch. Almost a smirk.

My arms shake, tingling from strain. I can't hold her much longer.

She dives again.

Mouth open. Teeth ready. Saliva pooling in her gums.

Shit—

BANG.

Her skull jerks back. A perfect hole between her eyes. The light, dim and hollow, snuffs out instantly.

Her body slumps onto me, heavy and still.

I shove her off, her corpse thudding into the dirt.

"And here I thought we were bonding," I mutter.

Trish stands a few feet away, pistol raised, smoke curling from the barrel. Her gaze flicks from me to Jessica's body.

I push up, breath ragged, every muscle burning. My ribs ache, legs heavy. I wipe blood from my arm and flick it away. It doesn't help.

Jacob rushes in, scanning me before his eyes drop to Jessica's ruined corpse. His jaw tics. Fingers twitch.

"You okay? Did you get bit?" He steps close and runs his hands over me, checking for damage. His fingers linger at my waist, then my ribs, then maybe somewhere that doesn't *need* checking, but I don't stop him.

I pat myself down along with him. "No, but give me a few more seconds to be sure."

Jacob grabs ahold of my face and watches my eyes. I grin, but wince at the throbbing pain in my shoulder. A few seconds tick by and I'm still me.

Phew.

Jacob glances at the body. Jessica's limbs are twisted, mouth still half-open like she never got the last word. "Guess she couldn't take a hint," he mutters.

"She was always persistent," I say, but the words fall flat in my throat.

Jacob exhales, lifts his shotgun.

One breath.

BOOM.

Her head vanishes into pulp and bone. Blood pours from the torn neck, seeping into the dirt.

I whistle low. "Well, that's one way to get closure."

Jacob gives me a sly wink, steps in close, tilts my chin. His thumb smears away blood on my cheek. "You sure you're okay?" he murmurs.

I let his touch anchor me. "Better now. Though I could do without the surprise tackles."

Jacob chuckles. "Adds a little excitement to the night."

I smile. "As if we needed more."

"Hey, lovers!"

Joanie's voice kills the mood instantly.

Joanie jogs over, shotgun slung over one shoulder, face smeared with gore and sweat. Her eyes are wide, locked past us.

"Hate to interrupt your little *moment,* but we've got a big fucking problem."

We spin.

Shadows move. Groans rise.

A fresh wave of undead shuffles toward us drawn by the noise, the blood, the bodies. Their empty eyes locked on us.

"Can't they take a damn hint?" I mutter, dragging a hand down my face, smearing blood across my cheek.

"Apparently not," Trish snaps, reloading smooth and fast. She claps a hand on Joanie's shoulder. "Let's go."

Jacob grabs my wrist, pulling me toward the wreckage.

The red truck burns hot, flames devouring it from the inside. Smoke pours upward, a beacon for the dead.

"Get the gas canisters," Jacob says, already sprinting.

"Shit." I run beside him.

Joanie and Earl flank us, weapons swinging—Earl's bat crunching skulls, Joanie carving flesh with Jacob's machete.

Trish guards the van with Poppy and Edith. Leon and Clair haul crates—medicine, food, ammo.

"Watch out!" Clair yells as the truck frame groans and then explodes. Leon throws himself over her, shielding her from the blast.

Jacob and I grab the last jug, fingers brushing as we haul it toward the camper.

The moans grow louder. Closer.

Clair fires her last round before switching to a knife. Leon's hatchet clears a path. Jacob and I slam the truck and camper doors shut, locking them down.

"We're running out of time!" Joanie calls.

Jacob looks at me, then at the bodies piling around us. His jaw hardens. "Split up. Get the vehicles moving."

Leon takes the wheel of his truck. Clair heads for her car.

I toss Joanie and Earl Lucy's keys. They sprint off, doing rock, paper, scissors midrun. Classic.

Engines roar. Headlights cut through the smoke.

I dive into the back of the med van. Barbara's at the wheel, Poppy beside her. Trish and Jacob pile in. Joanie peels out ahead of us, tires screeching over blood-slick dirt. Guess Earl lost.

Trish shoves me back on the bench, grabbing bandages. "Let me guess. You were too busy playing badass to notice you're bleeding everywhere?"

I glance down. My arms and shoulder are shredded, smeared with blood. Most of it mine. All of it ignored until now.

Jacob grins. "She *was* a badass."

Trish rolls her eyes and presses disinfectant to my shoulder.

I flinch. "Shit, Trish, buy me dinner first."

"Psh, I'm way out of your league," she says dryly.

I glance at Jacob—face streaked with blood and dirt, knuckles split, hands coated in dried gore. Worn down but unshakable.

The van jolts over rough ground, fire shrinking in the mirror.

Jacob takes Edith's hand.

Her arm and leg are scorched, burns blistered across skin. One arm broken, splinted with duct tape and sticks. She's breathing, barely.

Her eyes are glazed, pupils dulled by painkillers Trish must've pumped into her to keep her from screaming.

"Hey, E." Jacob's voice softens as he strokes her hand, careful to avoid the burns. "How you feeling?"

She smiles, slow and sleepy. "I'm okay, sweetie. You know it'll take more than a few burns to send me packing."

Jacob huffs out a laugh, blood trickling down from a cut on his forehead. "Yeah, that sounds about right."

She lets out a breathy chuckle, then drifts, her eyelids fluttering closed.

Jacob's gaze slides to me, warmth spreading in my veins.

"You good?" he asks, voice low, just for me.

I take a breath. My chest still feels tight, like the fight is sitting on top of it. But I nod. "Yeah. You?"

He reaches up to push a blood-crusted strand of hair from my face. His touch lingers, his thumb brushing my bottom lip. "I'd be better if I got my reward."

I blink. "Reward?"

His grin widens. "I lost the bet, remember?"

Heat rises in my cheeks, but I play innocent. "Doesn't count as a reward when you lost."

His hand slides down to my waist, fingers dipping in and out of the back of my jeans just enough to make me forget I'm covered in blood. "Depends on how you look at it."

My breath hitches. His lips brush mine—barely there.

I fist his shirt and pull him in.

His mouth is sure and warm, his hand tangled in my hair. It steadies me in a way nothing else can.

"Aww," Edith mumbles sleepily from the gurney.

Trish groans in front of us, still stitching up my shoulder. "Christ, I'm working here. Can we not?"

We break apart, grinning.

"Sorry, Trish," I say.

Jacob wipes my lip with his thumb, eyes still on me. "Definitely not sorry."

I lace my fingers with his as the fire fades in the distance.

He and Trish are still bickering, voices low and sharp, but it all fades to background noise as I stare out the rear window.

Smoke curls into the night sky, the last shadows of dark bodies swallowed by distance.

The world is still broken. The road ahead unknown.

But with his hand in mine, it doesn't feel so terrifying anymore.

EPILOGUE - FINDING A POINT

LYLA

THREE WEEKS LATER…

I wake to the weight and warmth of Jacob's arm draped over my waist. His breathing is deep, his face unguarded in sleep. No furrow in his brow, no tension in his jaw. Just peace. Rare. I sink into the moment, the quiet of existing together without a fight waiting outside.

Sunlight slips through the curtain. Time to move.

I nudge Jacob. He grumbles, grip tightening. Dark eyes blink open, still heavy with sleep, lips curling into that crooked grin.

"Mornin', Trouble," he murmurs, voice gravelly. He brushes a kiss to my forehead, lips warm against my skin.

I smile, even with the weight of our situation pressing in. Fuel's low. We need to reach the next town, but what's waiting there, or if we'll make it, is a question I can't shake.

Jacob props himself on one elbow, watching me like he knows what's in my head. His fingers run through my tangled hair. "Next stop's gotta be a truck stop, gas station. Maybe a farm with a generator. We'll figure it out."

I press my face to his shoulder, stealing one more second of warmth before the day takes it.

His arm tightens. His voice stays low, teasing. "You only wake me so you can crawl all over me."

I snort. "You're the cuddler here."

He smirks, and in one smooth motion, I'm beneath him, pinned. His weight settles over me, hands braced on either side of my head.

"I can't help you're so damn comfy to squeeze."

I arch a brow. "Which parts are your favorite?"

His mouth hovers over mine—

KNOCK. KNOCK. KNOCK.

"Wakey, wakey, assholes," Joanie calls from outside, smug. "Time to move before we're brunch for the flesh-eating trolls."

"Language, smart-ass!" I yell, voice muffled by Jacob's chest.

He groans, forehead dropping to mine. "Next date night, I'm parking us so far off-grid they'll need smoke signals to find us."

I laugh against his lips. "And waste gas? No chance." One last kiss before I shove at his chest. "Come on. Time to drive and kill some undead."

We dress quickly, moving around each other in practiced rhythm. Boots hit the floor. Zippers zip. Fingers brush, shoulders bump.

Outside, the air bites with late fall. A constant reminder that we're running out of time. The sun spills gold across camp. Shadows stretch long—proof we survived another night.

The others are already up. Weapons checked. Supplies packed. Tension threads through it—tight, silent. Fuel's low, and we can't stay still.

Edith sits near the fire pit, right arm and leg propped in scavenged casts. Bruises fade, but burns still stand out against pale skin. She still smiles.

"Look at you two. Always late."

Jacob frowns dramatically. "Scold her. She can't keep her hands off me."

I elbow him.

Edith chuckles, shifting with a wince. Pain dances across her face, but she nods through it, determined to hide it from us.

"How are you feeling?" I ask, keeping my voice soft.

"Better than last week. Casts still itch like the devil though."

I give her shoulder a light pat, careful of the bruises beneath the bandages. "Hang in there, E."

She nods, that same unshakable grit in her eyes, tired but burning. Even now, wrapped in casts and painkillers, she's tougher than half the people I knew before the world fell apart.

We've slowed our pace for her, and for us. Time to breathe. To recover. The physical stuff heals. The rest, we just carry.

Now it's time to push for Montana, if we can find fuel.

A few yards away, Jacob, Leon, Trish, and Earl huddle around Earl's new truck—a beat-up green monster Joanie and I named Jude. Leon's ride finally got a name too: Prudence. He doesn't know it yet, but we're pretty proud of ourselves.

They lean over Earl's map, marked with circles, notes, and guesses. Jacob's hand covers one corner, hiding something.

Weird.

I step up beside him. "Morning."

His arm slides around my waist. Leon signs, Trish translates. Earl taps a spot on the map. "Head north, skirt the edge of this town, maybe hit a salvage yard or truck stop. If roads are clear, we could be near Chicago in two days."

Leon taps a red circle. Jacob translates. "More options in Chicago. Risky, but our best shot at fuel."

Trish crosses her arms. "You want to go into a city? Are you insane? More undead. More people ready to shoot. More chances for us to die."

"We've already lost too much time," Jacob says, fingers drumming against the hood. "If we don't make a big haul soon, we'll be crawling through snowdrifts before we even hit the Montana border. This could be our only shot to make it out before winter traps us."

No one speaks. The weight of the choice presses down like the cold already settling in the air.

Chicago isn't just another stop.

It could be the last.

Before Trish can argue, Leon's posture shifts—alert.

Clair approaches with Poppy at her side, walking taller than before. Clair meets my eyes. "Lyla, will you teach me to defend myself? Maybe Poppy too?"

Joanie lifts a hand. "Hell yes. I'm in."

Leon signs. Jacob nods. "He can teach survival skills too."

I ask, "Why now?"

Clair glances at Poppy. "We waited for everyone to heal. Poppy asked. She hated feeling useless last time."

I nod. "I'll tailor lessons for size and strength. Enough to hold your own."

Relief blooms across her face.

Joanie pumps a fist. "Let's get dangerous."

Trish mutters, "You just want to stab stuff."

"Everyone needs a hobby," Joanie says.

I watch as Clair and Poppy head off toward their car. Pride sparkles in my chest.

When I look up, Leon's watching Clair. Expression soft. The rest of us catch it instantly.

Earl grins. "Well, I'll be damned. Leon's got a crush."

Leon snaps his head up, caught.

Jacob laughs. "Oh, Earl. You have no idea."

A flush creeps up Leon's neck.

I press a hand to my chest, feigning a swoon. "A man who blushes? Be still my heart."

Joanie elbows him. "Hey, no judgment, big guy. Clair's cute. Are you thinking of making a move? If so, I got some killer one-liners you could use."

Leon signs fast like he's trying to put out a fire. His expression is caught somewhere between *leave me alone* and *oh God, abort mission.*

Jacob snorts, barely holding in a laugh as he translates, "He says no. Also, we should all shut up."

Earl claps a hand on Leon's shoulder with a grin that could only mean trouble. "Don't worry, son. You just let us know when you're ready for dating advice."

Leon yanks his cap lower over his face, and I swear for a second he actually considers walking into the woods and letting the nearest undead finish him off.

Trish snickers. Jacob smirks. Even Earl's looking proud of himself.

Leon throws up his hands in a halfhearted protest before turning on his heel and stalking toward the camper. He moves with dramatic purpose, suddenly *very* invested in checking supplies. He's all business now—except for the red creeping up his neck.

Jacob leans in. "We're gonna tease him, right?"

Trish crosses her arms, grinning like she's already drafting the first ten jokes. "Mercilessly."

Joanie pumps her fists. "*Fuck yes.* New group activity."

Without missing a beat, we deadpan, "Language."

Joanie scoffs, rolling her eyes so hard I'm surprised they don't pop right out of her skull. "You people and your double standards," she mutters, stomping off toward Lucy, still grumbling. "I hear Jacob swearing all the damn time, but *noooo*, when I do it, it's all 'Joanie, watch your language.' Hypocrites."

I yell to her, "Love you!"

She flips me the bird. "Fuck off!"

Yeah, she loves me.

The group scatters, drifting toward their vehicles. Everyone falls into the rhythm—checking, rechecking, securing supplies. The hum of pressure lingers.

As I head toward the camper, I hear Earl behind me. "Jacob, what *is* that?"

Jacob plays innocent. "What's what?"

"That! That coffee ring under your hand. Did you do that?"

I keep walking, letting Earl unleash whatever wrath he's about to dish out. Serves Jacob right for that handsy comment to Edith earlier. Karma, hot and immediate.

I haul a crate of canned goods into the camper and start securing it, probably with more force than necessary. The straps bite into my palms as I tighten them, but it helps. Kind of.

The closer we get to empty, the more real the city idea becomes and I hate that.

Cities are death traps—*outbreak survival 101*, according to Earl. Populated areas mean more of everything: barricades, wrecked cars, desperate people, and too many of the infected.

But Leon might be right. It could be our best shot at finding what we need to get to Montana before we are stranded for the whole winter season.

I tug the strap tighter. Too tight.

The crate creaks in protest.

Jacob steps up behind me, solid and steady. His hand settles on my shoulder, then pulls me into his arms. He smells like pine, smoke, and the road.

"So," I murmur as his lips brush my temple, "how much trouble are you in?"

"He says I'm not allowed to look, borrow, or even *breathe* on his precious maps," he pouts.

"Aww, poor baby."

Jacob scoffs, but he lifts his hand and smooths the line between my brows with his thumb, his favorite thing to do when I'm stressed.

His eyes lock on mine, unworried. "We'll find gas," he says quietly. "We'll make it work, Lyla."

I breathe out slowly, the pressure inside me easing by degrees. "One day at a time, right?"

He nods, arms tightening around me like he could hold the world back if I asked.

The morning light spills golden across his face, catching in the messy short strands of his hair. For a man usually covered in dirt, blood, and sweat, he looks almost angelic. But it's more than that. It's the way he's looking at me—like there's no version of this story where we don't make it.

Around us, camp life stirs—boots thudding, gear shifting, engines coughing awake—but it all fades. Right now, it's just us.

Jacob reaches up, brushing a loose strand of hair behind my ear. His hand nestles at the base of my neck, his thumb caressing my jaw, causing something soft to bloom in my chest.

His voice drops, barely a whisper. "I promise, once we reach Montana, we'll make a real home."

A real home.

It still feels impossibly far off, but when Jacob says it, I believe him. I believe in us.

My fingers tighten in the fabric of his shirt as I rise onto my toes, closing the space between us.

"I believe you, Gorgeous."

His lips meet mine—warm, steady, familiar in all the ways that matter. There's nothing rushed, nothing desperate. And for one perfect beat, the rest of it disappears.

No undead. No fuel shortages. No impending snow doom. No what-ifs.

Just this.

His arms around me. His mouth on mine, exploring every delicious space, marking me as his.

Like I'm something worth fighting for.
Whatever's out there, we'll face it together.
"Quit making out and help us pack, dipshits."
Together with Joanie, of course.

Go ahead, catch your breath.

You'll need it.

The chaos, gore, romance, and undead madness are only just getting started.

Clair and Leon are up next.

ACKNOWLEDGMENTS

I can't believe I'm writing this part. To see this dream come to life is overwhelming, and there are so many people I want to thank for helping me get here.

To my brother and sister—thank you for always letting your little sister tag along. The movie marathons, video game nights, and music-filled hangouts shaped who I am and fueled my spooky soul and dark sense of humor. I love you both more than I can ever say.

To my parents—thank you for giving me the space to find myself. Your trust and freedom allowed me to grow into the independent woman I am today. By letting me make my own mistakes, you taught me strength and resilience.

To my in-laws—thank you for embracing me with love and support from the very beginning. I'm so grateful to be part of your family and to be able to lean on you when I need it. A special thank you to my mother-in-law, who has lived with us this past year and helped care for our daughter. Your kindness and generosity know no bounds, and I'll never be able to thank you enough.

To my alpha readers—Elizabeth, Jennifer, Jessie, and Patrick— you read my story in its rawest, messiest form, and instead of letting me drown in doubt, you lifted me up. Your encouragement gave me the courage to keep going when it would have been so easy to stop.

To my editor, Elizabeth—you are an absolute rockstar! Your feedback and insight pushed me to be a stronger writer and storyteller, and this book is better because of you. I hope this is just the first of many projects we'll share.

To my friends—thank you for loving me as I am and for always being there to cheer me on. It's rare to find such genuine, supportive people, and I'm so lucky to have you in my life.

To Jessie—one of my dearest, spookiest kindred spirits. I'm so grateful I found you. And yes—you got your wish: you're a villain and a zombie all rolled into one. Love you endlessly.

To my bookstagram family—you were the spark. In 2023, when I started sharing my love for books online, I found encouragement, inspiration, and the courage to finally chase this dream. Thank you for your creativity, your passion, and for making this community such a beautiful place to belong.

I also want to thank you, the reader. Thank you for taking a chance on an unknown author and giving my very first story a place in your hands. I hope you had a blast in this chaotic, zombie-fueled world. The fact that you chose to spend time with this story means everything to me.

And finally, to my husband and daughter—you are my heart. You teach me every day what it means to be strong, brave, and unshakably resilient. You're my why. I fight for you both. Always.

ABOUT THE AUTHOR

Meet Lindsey—a self-proclaimed goofball with a love for the weird, the witty, and the wonderfully spooky, she thrives on corny jokes, jump scares, and *way* too much coffee. Lindsey's world is a swirl of bright colors, big imagination, and stories that bite—with love, of course.

By day, she's a marketing manager, crafting stories that sell. By night, she trades email campaigns for creativity, bringing her own worlds to life. The result? A genre-blending mix of romance, humor, action, and just the right amount of creepy—because why settle for one flavor when you can have them all?

When she's not writing, Lindsey is a proud mama soaking up outdoor adventures with her family. You can also find her lost in a book, enjoying a cozy video game, grooving to nineties music, cracking up at the latest pun, or indulging in her favorite pastime: watching scary movies with the lights off. (Obviously.)

You can follow her on Instagram, Facebook, and Threads (@authorlindseymontgomery) or keep up to date with upcoming releases and more on her website (authorlindseymontgomery.com) and newsletter.

www.ingramcontent.com/pod-product-compliance
Lightning Source LLC
Chambersburg PA
CBHW071752110726
47908CB00006B/1776